ALFRED HITCHCOCK'S

A BRIEF
DARKNESS

ALFRED HITCHCOCK'S
A BRIEF DARKNESS

CASTLE

Grateful acknowledgment is hereby made for permission to reprint the following: *You Can Die Laughing* by Robert Arthur, copyright © 1958 by H.S.D. Publications, Inc., reprinted by permission of Larry Sternig Literary Agency; *Parlor Game* by Gary Brandner, copyright © 1976 by Davis Publications, Inc., reprinted by permission of the author; *A Woman's Work is Never Done* by Helen Fislar Brooks, copyright © 1961 by H.S.D. Publications, Inc., reprinted by permission of Evelyn Singer Angency, Inc.; *Last of the Big-Time Spenders* by Duffy Carpenter, copyright © 1976 by Davis Publications, Inc., reprinted by permission of the author; *Make My Death Bed* by Babs H. Deal, copyright © 1960 by H.S.D. Publications, Inc., reprinted by permission of the author; *Murder on the Edinburgh-London Express* by John H. Dirckx, copyright © 1980 by Davis Publications, Inc., reprinted by permission of the author; *A Grave on the Indragiri* by Alvin S Fick, copyright © 1978 by Davis Publications, Inc., reprinted by permission of the author; *Beware: Dangerous Man* by C.B. Gilford, copyright © 1958 by H.S.D. Publications, Inc., reprinted by permission of Scott Meredity Literary Agency, Inc.; *The Letter Carrier* by Kathryn Gottlieb, copyright © 1979 by Davis Publications, Inc., reprinted by permission of the author; *Albert and the Amateurs* by Len Gray, copyright © 1973 by H.S.D. Publications, Inc., reprinted by permission of Scott Meredity Literary Agency Inc.; *The Unstained Code* by George Grover Kipp, copyright © 1973 by H.S.D. Publications, Inc., reprinted by permission of the author; *It Started Most Innocently* by O.H. Leslie, copyright © 1959 by H.S.D. Publications, Inc., reprinted by permission of the author; *Understanding Electricity* by John Lutz, copyright © 1975 by H.S.D. Publications, Inc., reprinted by permission of the author; *Meditations Upon a Murder* by Donald Martin, copyright © 1959 by Donald Honig, reprinted by permission of the author; *Martha Myers, Movie Star* by Raymond Mason, copyright © 1956 by H.S.D. Publications Inc., reprinted by permission of Donald MacCampbell, Inc.; *False Alarm* by Anne Morice, copyright © 1979 by Davis Publications, Inc., reprinted by permission of the author; *Home Ground* by A.F. Oreshnik, copyright © by H.S.D. Publications, Inc., reprinted by permission of the author; *The Fanatical Ford* by Arthur Porges, copyright © 1959 by H.S.D. Publications, Inc., reprinted by permission of the author; *Drawer 14* by Talmage Powell, copyright © 1965 by H.S.D. Publications, Inc., reprinted by permission of the author; *Thin Air* by Bill Pronzini, copyright © 1979 by Davis Publications, Inc., reprinted by permission of the author; *Next in Line* by Jack Ritchie, copyright © 1976 by Davis Publications, Inc., reprinted by permission of Larry Sternig Literary Agency; *The Small Hours* by Ernest Savage, copyright © 1976 by Davis Publications, Inc., reprinted by permission of the author; *Stately Ruins* by Frank Sisk, copyright © 1978 by Davis Publications, Inc., reprinted by permission of Scott Meredith Literary Agency, Inc.; *Happy As a Harp Song* by Pauline C. Smith, copyright © 1975 by H.S.D. PUblications, Inc., reprinted by permission of the

Contents

Introduction

In the files of Alfred Hitchcock we often encounter, as we should, the stuff of which nightmare is made. Sometimes subtly clad, so that its implications don't sink in all at once.

But might not such things happen to us...?

Take Talmage Powell's story in the present volume, for instance—"Bertillon's Odds." The point is onw we've probably all been brought up not to believe, find it hard to believe. Because we'd much rather not.

There are other nightmare situations. A man goes fishing, comfortable with a homely and reassuring little improvisation he has absolutely no reason to distrust. He should. A husband wakes up after a quarrel with his wife, goes to work, and finds the cops waiting for him at the end of a long day. A dream intrudes and intrudes and intrudes until the dreamer's mind is deranged. The very birds of the fields come forward with evidence against one.

Hitchcock's stories have always, however, also been filled with humor. Some people hold that humor and crime don't mix; they evidently haven't been reading our magazine (or a lot of other crime fictions). Jack Ritchie frequently sprang it on us in a gnelt way; here his story of a young thief helping out his uncle ("A Piece of the World") is an appealing one. Michael Zuroy's "Diminishing Wife" sheds new light on the problem of the spouse murder. And blackmailers and doers-in of aging, wealthy gentlemen are cheerfully nailed themselves by Larry Niven and Gary Brandner.

On the whole, of course, myster stories do often—perhaps nearly always—have to do with murder, and murder is a Bad Thing. (Along with blackmail, theft, fraud, treachery, and other infelicities.) And in crime tales, whether they are humorous or nightmarish or neither, what tends to predominate is Suspence or The Puzzle. What will happen in the end? Or, who did it, and how? The unexpected is the chief feature we look for, of the one sort or the other. The unexpected is the chief feature tinged with a certain threat, a certain chill—most often of the grave. Leaping the long shadow is involved, for those who have survived or those who might not.

We hope you find that mixture of qualitied here—of the unexpected, of clever solutions, of humor, of the unnerving. Find, at least, the peculiar fun of reading the crime story, knowing that it is, after all, just a story. (Almost.)

If you will, a brief darkness.

Brad Williams

Ley de Fuga

The jail was made out of a combination adobe brick and concrete block, typically Mexican with the merging of the old and the new. The cell in which he was locked was made of the concrete block. At one end was an open barred window through which he could see the beach and the motel. The other end was a barred door which swung on hinges out into the cool adobe brick office. The door to the outer office, which was always open, was in the wall to the left of the cell and during the day Raymond Packard could look through it and see the occasional car that traveled along the dusty road between Pornada and Ensenada, some twenty miles to the north.

Raymond Packard was the first guest to remain more than one night in the jail since the jail had been added to the building almost two years ago. Fat José Carrillo mentioned this at least twice a day, every time he brought in the tin plate with the tortillas, frijoles, and pan; or when he strapped his huge revolver around his huge belly to accompany his prisoner to the outdoor *excusado*. Carrillo was the chief of police of Pornada. He was also the chief jailer and sole guardian of the peace in the small oceanside town on the Baja peninsula. But Carrillo was friendly and seemed sincere in his regrets that he was forced to hold Packard a prisoner.

"It is only because you are a gringo and have killed a man," he apologized several times and in that order. "Never before in Pornada has a gringo killed a man and so I must wait for my orders from Mexicali and they must wait for instructions from Mexico."

Raymond Packard was thirty years old. His last birthday had been a double anniversary of sorts, as it had arrived on the start of his second week in the Pornada jail. Physically, he fell into the average statistical column of the tables published by the insurance companies, a little less than six feet tall, about one hundred and sixty pounds in weight. When dressed conventionally, if he held his head erect the end of his full beard extended just below the knot of his tie. To the uninitiated around Los Angeles, where he lived, he fell into the loosely defined category of beatnik. However, despite his beard and a somewhat parallel attitude toward society, he did not consider himself as such. He was an artist. The insomniac had sold some of his canvases for as much as one thousand dollars, but proceeds from such sales were not his only income. He was retained by three advertising agencies in Los Angeles as a commercial illustrator and thus, he reasoned, he could not be classified as a beatnik. But of course this could change. These accounts probably would be lost long before he ever got out of Mexico.

Shortly before noon on the tenth day of his imprisonment, a police car drove into Pornada from the north, its wand of authority jutting out of the rear fender and whipping the air as the machine swayed on the rough road. Nervously, he watched the vehicle until it disappeared around the curve of the hill, then slowly he walked over to the cell window. The car took a long time to complete the circle and when it finally did appear, it did not immediately turn up the rutted path to the jail. Instead, it slid into a parking stall in front of the motel, stopping next to Ray's dusty convertible. Carrillo stepped out of one door. The driver, a giant of a man, rose up from the other side, his shoulders towering above the roof of the car. Both men casually looked over the convertible, then strolled into the motel. They wouldn't see much after ten days, Ray thought dourly; blood on the cotton rug, broken shards from a tequila bottle. He watched and waited.

A quarter hour passed. The two men came out of the motel, slipped into the police car, and presently the vehicle began to bounce up the road toward the jail. With an apprehensive sigh, Ray turned away from the window, pulled a comb from his pocket, and ran it through his hair and beard. Then he sat down on the edge of his cot.

The two men came into the building like old buddies entering a bar, laughing at some joke told just out of earshot.

"Señor Packard," Fat Carrillo said proudly. "This is Capitan Eduardo Campeche." He turned the key in the cell door as he spoke, then pulled the barrier wide and with a flourish of his hand, ushered the giant inside.

Capitan Campeche smiled, as if the meeting was an honor, then leaned against the wall. "I am with the secret police in Mexico City," he said in flawless English, his voice a deep rumble.

"It hardly seems worth the trouble," Ray replied flatly.

The big detective shrugged slightly. "It is only because everyone involved is an alien, Señor Packard. Sometimes there are inquiries on a diplomatic level."

"I don't think there will be in this instance."

"The girl is back in Los Angeles." Campeche stated fact rather than implied a question, and from his inside jacket pocket, he pulled out some flimsy papers on which there was typewriting.

"I do not know, Capitan Campeche," Ray answered carefully.

"She drove back to San Diego in the car of the decedent, one William Funk, abandoned it at Lindbergh Field there, and flew to Los Angeles, traveling under her own name, Lois Stuart."

"I have heard the Mexican police are extremely efficient." Ray took an Elegante from the pack in his shirt pocket and lit it. "I gave her the keys to Funk's car by mistake. I guess she was too frightened to come back to the room."

"She is not your wife?"

"No, señor. Nor is she anyone else's . . . so she did nothing wrong."

The giant shrugged again. "Run through the action once for me."

This would be easy. It had been running through his mind for ten days and as many nights. A man had been killed and he had been the killer. "Lois is a model who works for me often," he said aloud and slowly, speaking as if he had memorized the sequence of his story. "We finished working early Friday afternoon and decided to spend the weekend at the Papagayo, but because it was a holiday, there wasn't any room. We went on into Ensenada and there still wasn't any room."

"You and Funk and the girl?"

"No, señor. We met Funk in the bar at Del Pacifico. It was he who told us about Pornada so we drove down here, each in our own cars."

"You knew him before?"

Ray shook his head. "But he was all alone. And he seemed okay, a little square maybe, but harmless."

"But that isn't why you killed him?"

A wit, Ray thought. There was nothing duller than a cop who thought he was a comic. He flicked the ashes from his cigarette into the cuff of his pants. "We went to the cantina in the middle of town after we checked in the motel," he continued aloud. "I was going to buy a bottle of tequila and then we were coming back to the room and have a nightcap and go to bed. But the cantina was a pretty live spot, so we had a few drinks there, danced, listened to the mariachis. When we got back to the motel, Funk went to his cabin; we went to ours. Lois had left her sweater in the cantina, so I said I'd go back and get it. When I got out to my car, Funk was taking his suitcase out of his. When I got back, maybe fifteen minutes later, I noticed the keys were still in his trunk lock. I took them out, went to my cabin." He paused and inhaled deeply.

"Don't quit now." Campeche said, his lips pulled back into a faint smile. Like a feline, a cat playing with a mouse.

"It happened very quick. The door was unlocked. The lights were on. The nightstand was tipped over. Funk had Lois backed into a corner. Her blouse was ripped and she was struggling with him. I picked up the tequila bottle and hit him and he fell down. I didn't aim or anything, but I think the bottle hit him on the back of his neck and broke it."

The smile faded from Campeche's face. "You did, Mr. Packard," he said with a shrug. "How come she didn't scream when he first grabbed her?"

"I don't know. None of us made any noise. I know I didn't say anything."

"She just let him come?"

"She told me Funk came in a couple of minutes after I left. For a while he just talked and then just before I got back, he went after her." Again he pulled deeply on his cigarette. "For a little while we thought he was just knocked out. Then we found out he was dead."

"Why didn't you go back with the dame?"

"Well . . . I was the guy who killed him. She hadn't done anything."

Campeche nodded and blew smoke from his cigar toward the ceiling.

"And maybe you figured it was only second degree at the most ... maybe justifiable homicide ... so you would just get off anyway?"

"I'm not a lawyer. I didn't figure anything."

"You'll have to stand trial in Mexicali." Campeche looked at the red end of his cigar thoughtfully. "The calendar's pretty crowded up there. It'll be a couple of years before the case will come up."

"Two years!"

"Maybe more."

Ray dropped his cigarette on the stone floor. His leg shook as he ground the butt with the sole of his huarache and he sensed a flush starting on his face. A jail term was expected ... but to serve two years before he was sentenced was ridiculous. "Will I be able to get bail?"

Campeche slowly shook his head. "We wouldn't be able to extradite you from California, maybe. We can't take that chance."

"A real great system," Ray said bitterly. "That's just a real great system."

"You should have thought of that before you clobbered a gringo in Baja. Don't forget, it costs us money to feed you ... and you'll probably get sick on the food, so we'll have to treat you."

"For God's sake ... this guy was molesting her!"

"It would have been better all around if you had let him," Fat Carrillo said and laughed.

Ray stared at the two men incredulously, not believing he had heard correctly. The Latins were supposed to be reasonable ... more understanding than the Saxons for crimes of passion. "You don't understand," he protested, struggling to control his temper. "She isn't that kind of a girl."

Campeche shrugged indifferently, dropped his arm around Fat Carrillo's shoulders and guided him out into the office. "We're having a little trouble with the body," the detective said casually to the police chief. "It's still in Tijuana. Apparently this Funk had no relatives."

"There are no facilities here, *capitan*."

"I understand." Campeche studied the papers in his hand for a moment, then stuffed them back in his jacket pocket. "Let's go," he said. "We'll get the statements from the other witnesses before I take the gringo back."

Fat Carrillo nodded, hastily banged the steel door shut, pulled out the key, then scurried after the hardboiled detective from Mexico City.

For a long time after the police car pulled away, Ray lay quietly on his bunk. He was stunned, more shocked, he thought, than he had been when he first realized that he had killed the greasy little Funk. Terrible as the taking of a life was, it had been both unintentional and justifiable. But this stupid gorilla Campeche obviously did not believe him. The puerile mind inside the big hulk had decided long ago that the killing was the outgrowth of some cheap shackup. Angrily, Ray smashed his fist into his palm and stood up.

He went to the window and looked out. A couple of cars, in addition to his own, were parked in front of the motel. From one of the cabins, a *criada* waved a shag rug as if it was a signal. Behind the cabins on the beach, a couple sunned, bodies close to each other. It would be a long time before he was that close to a female again, he thought bitterly.

Turning, he went across the cell to the gate and leaned against the bars. The gate moved slightly and he leaped back, startled. It was open!

Ley de fuga! The Latin answer to capital punishment when there was no legal execution. "The prisoner was shot while trying to escape."

Skin prickling in sudden fear, he backed away from the door, moving toward the cot. Two years or maybe more before he was brought to trial . . . and what a mockery the trial would be. With his limited Spanish he would understand none of it. Pausing, he stared at the gate, now slightly ajar. Fat Carrillo was a lackey to the giant from the capital. His whole manner showed this . . . fawning . . . laughing obeisantly . . . so anxious to hurry after the captain that he had pulled the key out of the lock before he turned it.

Slowly, Ray shuffled toward the gate again and pushed it with his foot. The heavy gate squeaked as it moved outward under the steady pressure. Odd he had not noticed the squeak before. Nothing happened. But nothing could happen yet. Both Fat Carrillo and Campeche had climbed into the police car and it had driven away. There had been no break in the even purr of the engine, as there would have been had it stopped to let Fat Carrillo out.

Tentatively, he stepped into the opening and leaned against the jamb. It was about seventy miles and three cities to the border . . . and only one road between here and there; one road with nothing but a few dead-end and dirt paths intercepting. *Ley de fuga* . . . But there was no one in the jail. Cautiously, his heart thudding against his chest, he moved out into the office toward a war surplus type desk in the corner. Gently he pulled open the center drawer. Familiar car keys, attached to the equally familiar fish head clip, lay on top of his wallet. Even the money was intact . . . little more than one hundred dollars.

Nervously, he wiped the corners of his mouth and his mustache with the back of his hand and moved toward the outer door. His huaraches squeaked loudly and he cursed the sudden impulse that had made him buy them in Tijuana on the way down. His clothes in the motel would have to be left behind, but they were a cheap price to pay for two years . . . two years in a stinking Mexicali jail before they would even bring him to trial. He stepped into the outdoors and slid along the adobe to the corner.

Pressing against the wall, he peered down into the town. The police car was parked directly in front of the cantina. Down the center of the main street, an Indian with a serape and sombrero bounced along on the high rump of a burro. A couple of other Indians lounged against an adobe wall, wide brimmed hats tipped low on their faces as if posing for a tourist's camera.

Quite possibly he could reach his car without being seen. No, he would be seen of course, but only by Indians and they would stare blankly at anyone who interrogated them ... or would they? But what difference did it make? Assume he could get the car out of the motel lot without the owner, Señora Hernandez, raising the alarm; he would still have to drive it directly past the cantina to reach the highway. And there was only one highway between here and the border. There were no telephones in Pornada, but there was an aerial projecting from the rear fender of Campeche's prowl car.

Gripping his car keys tightly in his palm, he pushed away from the wall. The heat from the sun struck him like a hot Santa Ana wind and the glare turned his eyes into mere slits. Defiantly he stopped and turned toward the town, daring the *ley de fuga*. The sounds carried clearly. A seagull cried raucously, as if sounding the alarm. Surf crashed on the sandy shore and from the town, the clop of the burros' hooves on the hard packed earth of the street drifted toward him like an erratic slow beat of a finger on a bongo drum.

With a deep breath, he moved toward the motel, carefully placing one foot in front of the other. The couple on the beach parted. The man rose, then helped the girl to her feet and waited as she tugged at her bathing suit. They strolled toward the motel. A cabin door opened and again a white shag throw rug was shaken vigorously ... a signal? Ray paused, glancing around him desperately. No one seemed to notice him.

Suddenly an engine roared alive and he wheeled toward the town. A combined cloud of dust and burning oil boiled into the air from the exhaust of an ancient bus parked in front of the post office, one cloud bursting below another as the unseen driver rhythmically pressed down on the accelerator. The unmuffled engine sputtered loudly like a string of firecrackers every time he released the pressure on the throttle.

Abruptly, Ray wheeled again and ran back toward the small jail. He veered around it like a deer in flight, then slid down the hill. He ran across the small mesa to the dirt highway and then, panting, slowly began to walk toward the north. Before he had completely caught his breath, the bus sputtered around the hill which hid the town.

Ray turned, stepped out into the road, and help up his hand. The bus slowed and stopped. A rooster in a crate on top of the vehicle crowed feebly in protest.

"*Donde vas*, señor." The driver grinned. "Where are you going?"

"Ensenada."

"Two dollars, señor." The youthful pilot goosed the engine again as Ray stepped into the vehicle.

"It is very expensive," Ray said, remembering that he should bargain to allay suspicion.

"One fifty," the driver agreed. He pocketed the money, then shifted gears as Ray slowly lurched his way back into the machine.

A dozen people on the bus stared at him with flat, expressionless faces; all Indians with black button eyes. The females wore rebozos around their shoulders despite the heat. The men sat stiffly in the hard seats, their backs to the windows. Only the seat across the rear of the bus faced toward the front. There was a space in the middle.

Dust swirled from under the double rear wheels, skidded around the square stern of the bus, then hung over the road like heavy fog. It completely obliterated the highway, its sides and everything behind it. But it was ostrich security. Ray could not see back beyond the dust, but the dust could be spotted for miles.

Two years . . . or maybe more. How long did he have? Usually during the daytime, Fat Carrillo dropped by the jail about every three hours. With Campeche in town, he might check more often, to boast of his efficiency. Campeche had said they were going to check witnesses. There were only two . . . the young Mexican bartender in the cantina and Señora Hernandez, whom he had asked to call the police. How long would it take to interview two witnesses? . . . a half hour? He glanced at his watch, then smiled wryly. He didn't know how long he had been gone because he had forgotten to look at it when he started. The bus roared on, not moving very fast despite the noise and illusion of speed.

Approximately a half hour later, the dust cloud disappeared and the ride became smoother as the wheels struck asphalt. The pavement had ended about seven miles from Ensenada, he recalled. It was almost too easy. As the thought occurred, Ray turned and looked out of the dusty rear window. Far down the road, another cloud of dust boiled up behind a small dot, moving up fast.

He slouched down in his seat, head even with the grimy plastic upholstery. The bus slowed and Ray, looking ahead, watched the driver staring through the rear view mirror. His eyes dropped down toward Ray, speculatively, then back up to the mirror, and then the bus veered over to the right slightly as a car whooshed past on the left. But no siren sounded. The bus driver did not brake his vehicle. Instead, he slowly resumed his speed.

With a partially concealed sigh, Ray straightened and tipped his head slightly, trying to see through the forward windshield. The car was out of sight. A young Indian at his side turned and stared intently toward him.

"*Por Castro?*" the Indian asked presently in little more than a whisper, his face expressionless.

Ray smiled and stroked his beard, then slowly shook his head. The Indian looked away.

The bus puffed into the outskirts of the city. Traffic increased. A blue and white patrol car slid past the window. Cops, in khaki uniforms, waved them through the intersections. The bus turned a corner and jerked to a stop in front of a depot. It was precisely three o'clock.

Everything seemed normal. Tourists and Indians drifted past on the street. Ray paused beside the driver. "Do you go to Tijuana?"

"In maybe two hours, señor, there is another bus that goes to Tijuana."

Two hours . . . two years or maybe more. Time was twos plus maybe. He swung down onto the sidewalk. In two hours the alarm surely would be out. Carrillo would remember the bus that had left Pornada and the bus driver would remember the man with the beard he had picked up on the highway near the jail. And there still was only one road north. At any one of a hundred places along the fifty mile stretch a roadblock could be set up, with no way to bypass it.

An older woman, shaped like a squashed S and wearing a woolen dress over a plethora of undergarments, stopped and peered at him as if he was a sidewalk canvas. He scratched himself as he brushed past and then laughed at her sudden gasp. Now that he was an outlaw he could afford to be completely antisocial.

He walked diagonally across the street, paused in front of a small bar, then entered. The signs were all in English. A bartender briskly polished a mahogany counter in front of him. "Yes, sir?"

"A beer and a hamburger."

"Sure."

It was like a Hollywood drive-in. The hamburger, almost instantly placed in front of him, was soggy and cold. The beer was excellent, however. "Where can I rent a car around here?"

The bartender shrugged. "There are many taxis, sir."

"I want at U-Drive-It. Like I could leave in Tijuana."

The bartender shook his head. "There's a bus that leaves around five. Tomorrow morning there's a plane."

"I don't want to wait."

"A cab would take you up, sir. Probably would want about twenty-five or thirty bucks. It's fifty miles up there."

"I know, and well worth it."

A cab might be the answer at that. He glanced at his watch. It was only an hour's ride to the border and if he continued lucky he might get across the border before Fat Carrillo got back to the jail. Finishing his beer, he dropped a dollar bill on the bar and went back to the street. He started to cross, then jumped back on the sidewalk with a sudden catch of breath. His heart pounded furiously as he slid behind a parked car for cover.

Leaning against the wall of the bus station was the giant Campeche, rolling a fresh cigar between his thumb and forefinger.

From any other angle, Ray thought wildly, he would not have seen the detective. The giant was leaning against the far wall and in such a manner that he could look through two windows to the main entrance of the depot. There was no sign of Carrillo. Nor was there any sign of the police car. Swearing softly, Ray backed away, keeping the parked car between him and Campeche's line of vision.

Something moved in back of him and he wheeled around. A young girl, tourist type, sidestepped, then tipped her head, looking at him curiously.

"Excuse me," he muttered. He moved past her and strode rapidly to the end of the block. As he turned the corner, he broke into a half run, heading toward the ocean, only half aware that he again was swearing softly, monotonously under his breath.

Ensenada was a small town. There was no place to hide for long. If Campeche was looking, so were all the other police. They knew their quarry was in Ensenada ... the bus driver would have told them this.

He ran across the street toward the Hotel Bahia, then abruptly slowed to a walk when he noticed a barber in an open doorway watching curiously. There was no way out. The highway would be watched. The airport would be guarded ... the bus station sealed. But there was no place to stay. As soon as the exits were bottled, then the canvass of the town would start. And he knew nobody in Ensenada.

Far ahead of him, a police car turned into the waterfront street. He veered between two buildings and down a flight of steps leading to the beach.

"You wanta see a good show, mister?" An urchin on the bottom step jumped up, leered, then shrugged and sat down as Ray silently passed.

Fifty miles to the border. But who in hell could walk fifty miles? He paused and glanced over his shoulder. Apparently no one saw him as a fugitive ... yet. At least, there was no sign of pursuit here. If he followed the coast north, it would be at least sixty miles to the border. At five miles an hour, it would take twelve hours. How fast did a man walk on sand? Behind him, a siren wailed and again he glanced back. The urchin jumped to his feet and scrambled up the stairs.

He mastered an impulse to run. A running man attracted attention. Sand spilled into his huaraches and he took them off, carrying them in his hand. This would appear normal; a tourist out for a walk along the shore. But sixty miles barefoot was impossible. The siren wailed louder and again he looked back. A fire truck raced through an intersection, then turned up the winding road which led to the high hilled residential section overlooking the community.

To his left, a large sloop skillfully glided into the harbor, tacking between the breakwaters. Another half dozen yachts lay at anchor in the sheltered water and from one, hi-fi music drifted into shore. He could sail. He could steal a boat and sail it to San Diego. But they would capture him before he passed the jetty. He walked on.

Within an hour he was tired. No one walked any more. The sand gradually disappeared, turning into slippery pebbles covered with moss and seaweed. Pausing, he put on his huaraches, conscious that he could still hear the sounds of Ensenada behind him, a distant auto horn, a faint cry. He could not stop.

About now, possibly, a policeman was entering a small bar. "Yeah, he was in here a while back ... guy with a beard, yeah. He had a hamburger and a beer."

Or the huge Campeche bent over to talk to a small urchin. "*Si*, señor. He went over there," pointing north along the shoreline.

He jumped up onto a large, wet piece of driftwood. His foot slipped, throwing him from the log to the wet stones. He lay quietly, panting, looking out to sea. The sun, a huge red ball, was flattened on the bottom where it struck the ocean. Rolling on his elbow, he looked back toward the land. Dusk was very near. High overhead, an invisible jet plane moved slowly through the sky, its vapor trail a fire streamer, reflecting the red from the sun. The sun gathered speed in its plunge and now he could actually see the curvature of the earth in it. An orange dwarf . . . a very small, unstable star which could explode at any second. It looked now as if it was slowly being extinguished as it dipped into the ocean. What had happened and what would happen was unimportant. He started to rise, then froze as a light flashed on the bluff behind him. It was a car reflecting the dying glare of the sun in its windshield.

Instinctively, he threw himself on the pebbles, pressing close to the large piece of driftwood that had toppled him. Then, wriggling like a worm, he pulled himself up to the end of the log to peer around it. The car was a silhouette with a long wand riding up in back of it, swaying back and forth lazily on its powerful spring. The door opened and another shadow stepped out . . . a giant shadow that moved to the edge of the bluff. Both hands raised to its eyes and the shadow pivoted. Binoculars, sweeping the beach! Frantically Ray burrowed back in the pebbles. Then he stopped, fearful that the breeze would carry the sound of his movement up the slope.

Presently the sun disappeared. For a brief moment, the horizon glowed. Then this light slowly faded away and as if this was a signal the offshore breeze freshened. For a long time, he lay motionless, straining for some sound . . . a step crunching on the gravel to foretell his discovery . . . the sound of a car starting to signal that he had not been seen. But the surf was too loud. After a while he could no longer stand the suspense and he sat up abruptly. The police car was gone.

But behind the spot where it had been parked was a faint red glow, flashing like a rotary emergency light on a police car. He jumped to his feet and ran along the shore. The pebbles turned back into sand as he rounded a small point. He halted. Here the shoreline curved in a small crescent and scattered along the beach were a dozen gaily striped cabanas, the bright reds and whites bright even in the dusk. The Papagayo. Red light from a huge neon sign at the resort flickered over the canvas beach shelters at the bottom of the hill. For a long moment he stared incredulously, first at the cabanas, then up the winding steps to the hotel, and finally on the dial of his watch. Four hours had passed since he left Ensenada and he had traveled less than seven miles . . . an average of two miles an hour. At this speed, Tijuana was thirty hours distant. A jet plane could make three round trips between Los Angeles and New York in the same length of time. This was ridiculous. The road would be safe at night. There was little traffic and when a car came, he could see it in plenty of time to leave the road. He decided to take a chance.

Boldly he walked up the stairs. Only a half dozen cars were parked outside the resort. Up here, sounds carried clearly. A girl, out of sight, giggled. Glasses tinkled on the patio to a soft mariachi background. Glare from the sign and floodlights extended from the top of the stairs, across the parking lot to the wall of the hotel.

"Señor."

He jumped, spinning in the direction of the voice. It belonged to an older man in a dirty khaki uniform, a guard for the parking lot.

"*Andele,*" the watchman said, flipping the back of his hand contemptuously. "Move on."

Grimy pants and shirt, slept in for ten days; huaraches over dirt-encrusted feet. Small wonder, Ray thought bitterly, that the guard saw only a tramp in front of him. "*Ya mi voy,*" Ray said sullenly, shuffling toward the exit. "I'm going." At the gate he paused and looked back. The guard had followed him and now he, in turn, stopped, staring speculatively. "Go shine your cars," Ray said angrily.

Again the guard flicked his hand as if brushing away a troublesome insect. Eleven days ago it had probably been the same flunky who bowed and scraped when they drove into the place. Ray spat on the ground, then stepped out onto the road leading to the main highway.

It was easy to move along the highway at night. There was little traffic and few sounds. The few cars there were, hurtled by. At first, when the road was straight, he heard the distant scream of the approaching engine about the same moment he saw the headlights as a single white pinpoint on the highway. There was more than enough time to leave the road and hide in a *barranca*. Later on in the night, the highway began to curve lazily through the hills and then he heard the engines long before he saw the lights. Finally he did not bother to leave the pavement, staggering on and on, his mind dull, projecting no thought other than the placing of one foot in front of another.

Eventually he became aware that he was thirsty and when this thought penetrated his conscious mind, the thirst became overbearing. After a while he saw a faint flickering yellow light far off the road and he turned into the field, heading toward it. A wire fence struck him across the chest. A horse neighed and galloped away with a quick pounding of hooves. Bending over slowly, he eased through the strands and stepped in mud. He wouldn't have to go to the house. Almost at his side was a livestock watering trough. He dropped to his knees and dipped his mouth to the water like an animal and, when slaked, crawled a few feet away on his knees, then stretched out on the soft ground.

Somewhere nearby a dog barked loudly and then the outcry was joined by another. He was wet and the sun was red through his closed eyelids. His neck was stiff and his body ached in a hundred muscles.

Rolling over on his stomach, he opened his eyes. Two curs bolted backwards and their barking became more frenzied. A short distance in back of the dogs, a teenage boy stood silently, staring, his face a blank. Then, as Ray struggled to his feet, the boy turned and started to run.

"*Alto!*" Ray cried, his voice a harsh rasp. "Stop!"

The youth obeyed, turning around.

"It's all right, friend," Ray said, rubbing the back of his neck. "I was drunk."

"*Borracho?*" The youth tipped his head curiously, like a puppy.

"That's right ... one great big *borracho* last night."

The boy shrugged slightly and hissed to the dogs, who immediately fell silent.

"Do you have coffee?" Ray nodded toward the small house in the distance. "I'll pay you."

Slowly the youth raised his hand and held his thumb and forefinger about a quarter inch apart. Sign language ... Wait for a minute. Then abruptly he turned and ran toward the house, the dogs loping at his heels.

It had been a mistake, Ray thought suddenly with a nervous glance toward the highway. The parents would ask questions. They might have a radio and surely the news had been broadcast that a gringo murderer had escaped from Pornada and was believed heading toward the border ... a killer with a long beard.

Turning, he sloughed his way through the mud to the fence and then across the marshy grass to the highway. Either the huaraches had shrunk during the night or his feet had swollen, for the leather bindings cut painfully into the back of his feet and beneath his ankles. He sat down and tried to pull them off. They wouldn't move. Angry red skin bulged painfully both above and below the bindings. He fumbled in his pocket for his penknife. It was gone. So was his loose change. But his wallet was still in his hip pocket.

An engine started ... an old one with no exhaust muffler and he traced the sound to a Model A Ford pickup truck at the house of the young boy and his dogs. It bounced along a dusty side road to the highway, two persons in the front seat, and when it reached the asphalt, it turned north in his direction. Wincing with pain from his bound feet, Ray hobbled erect as the truck drew abreast and stopped.

It was the same boy, but the driver was very old, probably his grandfather. Neither said a word; they made no gesture.

Ray pointed to his feet, held one foot up, then made a scissoring motion with two fingers. The boy nodded gravely, pulled a switchblade knife from his pocket and passed it down, handle extended.

Trusting souls, Ray thought wryly as he slid the razor sharp blade under the leather binding. No pressure was needed. The leather strap parted as if it was paper. "Your truck was made the year I was born," he said aloud.

"*Mandel,*" the old man said.

"Never mind." His feet free from the Indian shoes began to tingle and itch, the way a limb tingled after it had fallen asleep. Slowly Ray folded the knife and passed it back. Roadblocks or not he could walk no farther. Pulling out his wallet, he extracted a twenty dollar bill and held it up. "Tijuana?"

The boy nodded and plucked the bill from his hands as if it was a ripe cherry on a tree. He looked at it carefully on both sides, then slid across the seat and motioned for Ray to climb in. The seat seemed incredibly soft. The pickup lurched forward.

Ahead of them, a small black sedan swung wide on a curve. It had the appearance of a police car and Ray tensed, glancing toward his companions with quick suspicion. The car whooshed past. Two fishing poles pushed out of a rear window. He sighed and wiped his forehead with the back of his hand. It was caked. Bending forward, he tipped the rear view mirror in his direction. At first he stared in disbelief. Then he shook his head and laughed. His hair, his beard, his face were plastered with mud. Shirt and pants were the same. He looked like a ghoul in a Grade B horror picture. The old man smiled politely and turned the mirror back.

Shrugging, Ray rubbed dried mud from the crystal of his watch . . . a little after nine. If his luck held, he should be at the San Ysidro border station in an hour. It was only an hour's drive from Ensenada in the ordinary car. The distance he had walked should make up the difference for the slower speed in the clunker. As soon as he crossed the border, he could shower . . . call Lois collect. She would come down and get him. His head dropped forward and he fell asleep.

A horn blared almost in his ear, jolting him upright, instantly alert. He was on the outskirts of Tijuana. He was almost safe. The boy smiled and nodded politely. The Mexicans were always very polite, like the Japanese, he thought, looking at his watch. Quarter past ten. And like the Japanese, one never knew what they were thinking. There had been no roadblock. But this was logical. Police rarely kept roadblocks up for more than a few hours. The quarry had either got through by this time or was not going to try.

The old man shifted to a lower gear to climb a small hill. A convertible of the same brand, but thirty years newer, paused at the exit of the Sierra Motel as they approached. A Hollywood type blonde looked at him as they passed. Her mouth fell open and red fingernails flashed up to a heavily rouged mouth.

"And you too," Ray said aloud, then turned to the boy and gestured for a cigarette. The boy shook his head and shrugged.

The truck caught the green light on the main street and turned left toward the center of the city. A neat, young Mexican girl on the sidewalk turned to stare at him and with a nervous sigh, Ray slid down in the seat to avoid such attention. The truck sputtered past the Fronton

Palace, down past the cellar nightclubs and the honkytonks and the markets that stretched for blocks under arcades. The streets became more crowded and a few stared at him curiously, but not with alarm. Then the old man made an abrupt U turn and stopped directly in front of the Ceasar Hotel.

"Tijuana," he said quietly.

"No, no," Ray replied quickly, sitting up. "United States ... Los Estados Unidos."

"*No tengo papeles*," the old man replied firmly.

"*A la linea*," Ray protested, trying to control his rising temper. "To the line."

"Tijuana," the boy echoed. Ominously his hand slipped into his pocket ... the pocket with the switchblade knife.

Two Mexican pitchmen on the street moved toward the curb in front of the truck. A police whistle trilled shrilly, jerking Ray's attention to the corner. A traffic cop gestured irritably for the old man to get out of the no parking zone.

"*Andele*," the old man said softly and revved the noisy engine. It backfired as he eased the pressure on the gas pedal and the explosion turned a dozen heads in their direction.

The whistle shrilled again angrily and the cop started to walk toward them.

"Okay, okay," Ray muttered, then pressing his lips to muzzle his temper, he stepped down on the hot pavement.

The truck lurched into the traffic before Ray stepped up on the curb, racing away as if seeking escape ... escape from what? One of the pitch artists began to laugh and then was joined by his companion. A middle-aged couple with a pinched expression of distaste paused and stared at him. A street photographer leaned against his gaily caparisoned burro and began to giggle. The traffic cop pushed back his duck-billed cap and looked over curiously.

Two cabs were parked diagonally at the corner. Lips still compressed tightly, Ray strode to the nearest one, soles of his feet burning on the hot pavement, pulled open the rear door, and jumped in.

The driver, a tough *pachuco* type, leaned over the back of the front seat. "Where to, buddy?"

"The border."

"Five bucks, buddy."

It was no more than a mile to the border. In Tijuana, the fare should be no more than fifty cents. "Let's go."

"I don't think you got a fin, buddy."

Contemptuously, Ray pulled out his wallet and removed a ten dollar bill. He snapped it in front of the driver. "You get me there in five minutes and I'll double your fin."

The cab hurtled back in the street, then U-turned and raced down the thoroughfare.

"But don't get us pinched," Ray said sourly, looking back through the rear window. "Either way you get the sawbuck."

The driver nodded, but didn't slow. Tires screamed in protest as the taxi skidded onto the old bridge over the dry Tijuana River, then sped toward the border. Ahead of them, just beyond the other end of the bridge, was the high arch that marked the Mexico-United States boundary line. On the right side of the arch, a half dozen lanes moved through stalls operated by the U.S. Border Patrol. On the left was the Mexican port of entry.

"Way over to the right, friend," Ray ordered, again glancing back. There were no signs of pursuit." And as close to the line as you can get."

"I can't go beyond the turnaround, buddy. That's about fifty yards." The cabby pulled sharply to the right as he swung off the bridge, then braked dramatically along the curb. "Four minutes flat," he announced happily.

About a dozen cars were in the two open lanes leading into the United States. Two border patrolmen leaned in windows of the forward vehicles. Another stood on the steps of the Customs Building. Taking a deep breath, Ray nodded, opened the door, then passed the ten dollars to the grinning driver.

He stepped out on the sidewalk and glanced across the small square toward the Mexican port of entry. Two khaki clad guards leaned casually against a pillar. Another waved a tourist through. It was normal. He glanced over his shoulder and froze motionless.

Strolling toward him with a sadistic grin on his face was Campeche. He was only twenty yards distant, his huge body moving with a dreadful feline grace . . . a big cat stalking the immobile lamb. His slow walk was almost hypnotic. So supremely confident he was that he even slowed his pace as he narrowed the distance between them. Ray thought of a wild rabbit, held motionless by the glare of onrushing headlights on a highway.

Then someone began to giggle, and the giggle broke the spell. He caught a brief impression of a laughing peddler, holding two clay souvenir bulls in his hand as he wheeled around and ran.

His feet slapped the pavement hard, but the pain came in his chest from his tortured breathing. *Ley de fuga.* At this instant, the pistol was being aimed at his back. Ray dodged, jerking first one way and then the other. Campeche wouldn't dare shoot this close to the border, unless he was sure of hitting his target.

Then incredibly the shadow of the arch fell across him. Arms went around him, wrenching him around in a complete circle, then pushing him hard against a wall. Gasping for breath, he followed the arm on his chest up to a shoulder, down to a badge . . . The U.S. Border Patrol! He was in the United States.

His feet began to burn. A sharp pain lanced his side and his head began to pound unmercifully.

The cop slowly released his grip and backed away, saying nothing, looking at him curiously. Gradually he became aware that everyone was staring at him now. No one laughed. They all stared, as people will stare at the scene of a fatal auto accident.

Only one person moved ... Campeche. The big detective, still grinning, walked slowly right up to the arch, then stopped and leaned against one of the stanchions.

"I'm not in Mexico any more," Ray screamed the words involuntarily.

The big detective nodded slowly, then began to chuckle softly. "Tell me, Mr. Packard," he said presently. "Tell me just one thing."

"What?" Ray's body began to tense. The giant was clever, as well as sadistic. He would pull some trick. Ray glanced around quickly for the border patrolman, then frowned suddenly. His own convertible was parked just beyond one of the stalls. His suitcases showed plainly in the rear seat.

"Why in hell didn't you drive up?" Campeche asked.

Ray looked again at his car, then back to the giant. Then, slumping down on the sidewalk he sobbed uncontrollably.

Jack Ritchie

A Piece of the World

Unfortunately the elastic band broke. It was an ordinary black mask which is slipped over the upper part of the face. I had purchased it at a novelty store the day before, but evidently it had been on the shelves for a long time. I sighed as it fluttered to the floor, but I kept the gun steady.

The bartender and the four patrons stared at me. My Uncle Eldridge did not stare. He closed his eyes.

Well, I thought wearily, I might just as well go through with it. I spoke to the bartender. "Empty the till into this paper bag. And do not attempt anything rash. I will kill you if you do."

He rang up a NO SALE and did as he was told. My uncle and the other patrons had their hands in the air. Two of them wore sport shirts. The other two were in suitcoats and hats, and their eyes were narrow as they watched me. I had the feeling they were just waiting for the slightest lack of attention on my part.

I moved the gun in their direction. "Take your wallets out of your pockets and put them on the bar. But be careful. Very careful."

They did as I directed, including my uncle. I dropped the wallets into the paper bag. "Now all of you stand with your faces against the wall. And keep your hands up."

The bartender came from around the bar and joined the others.

I took the paper bag and backed toward the rear door. On the way I picked up the briefcase my uncle had left on a stool. It contained thousands of dollars.

Outside, I quickly closed the door and began running. It was my intention to travel through a few alleys and then merge into the night street crowds. By the time I reached the first street, I was already puffing. I wasn't used to quite so much exercise.

A squad car was parked at the curb.

I stopped in my tracks.

The two officers appeared to be having cigarettes and idle conversation. Apparently they hadn't noticed me.

I had just about made up my mind to stroll as casually as possible past them when behind me came the sound of running feet and police whistles. The two policemen looked up and saw me.

I'm afraid I panicked. I dashed across the street and into the next alley. I don't know how many fences I climbed or how many dark passageways I stumbled through in the next ten minutes. Eventually I threw away the paper bag, but I still clung to the briefcase. From the converging sounds of the police whistles and the whines of the sirens, it appeared to me that the entire police department must have been alerted.

Finally I found myself huddled in the dark corner of an alley, completely out of breath and utterly at a loss about what to do next.

Seventy-five feet ahead, a huge semi-trailer stood parked against the unloading platform at the rear of a supermarket. The driver and two men in white aprons came out of the exit. They appeared to listen to the sirens and then evidently made up their minds to investigate. They trotted down to the farther end of the alley and stood there looking to the right and the left, trying to pinpoint the excitement.

The lighted doorway seemed to beckon like a sanctuary. I took a deep breath, dashed past the semi, up the stairs of the unloading platform, and into the rear of the store.

The area I entered was evidently used for storage, for a wall separated it from the store proper and hundreds of cases of goods were stacked about.

I glanced into the store itself. It was lighted, though it was at least an hour after closing. Evidently the men I had seen were the employees who restocked the shelves during the night hours.

Where could I hide? Certainly not in the store. My eyes fell on the stack of one-hundred-pound sugar bags that reached almost to the ceiling. There appeared to be some kind of a trap door up there. I scrambled up the bags until I reached it. Apparently it hadn't been opened in years, for it took considerable effort before it yielded and moved up. I pulled myself quickly into the darkness and lay there trying to regain my breath.

After a while I noticed a small shaft of light from a slight crack beside the trap door. I put my eye to it and peered down.

The truck driver and the two stockboys returned. Someone called up from the basement. "What was all that noise about?"

The truck driver shrugged. "I don't know. We'll probably read about it in the papers tomorrow."

The men finished unloading the truck by eleven and it was driven away. I crawled to another shaft of light a dozen feet or so farther on and watched as the stockboys wheeled the stacks of cartons to appropriate positions in the aisles. There they cut open the cases, stamped the prices on the individual cans and boxes, and stacked them on the shelves.

By four o'clock in the morning they had finished. They removed the empty cartons from the aisles and swept up. Before they left the store, they turned out all but a few strategic lights here and there.

I waited another half an hour before I opened the trap door and let myself down. One light had been left on in the rear storeroom and I could see a telephone on the wall. I went to it and dialed.

My uncle recognized my voice immediately. "You fool!"

"I'm sorry," I said. "The elastic band broke. But don't worry. I read somewhere that witnesses are very unreliable, and probably the people in the bar gave five different descriptions of me. And with yours, that would be six."

"You idiot," Uncle Eldridge said. "I had to *identify* you."

"Identify me? I don't understand."

"Look," he said, "it just so happened that two of the people in the bar were off-duty detectives. The second your mask fell, they had your face fixed solid in their minds. So what could I do? From the size of the army chasing you, I thought they'd get you for sure. And then what could I say? That I hadn't been able to recognize my own nephew? I had to protect myself and think about you later."

I felt exceedingly disappointed. "What will I do now?"

"Where are you?"

"In a supermarket."

He swore.

"It's all right," I said. "The place is closed and nobody knows I'm here. I could probably hide here for days."

"Have you got the briefcase?"

"Yes."

"Then stay put. I'll think of something. I'll have to get you out of town tomorrow. Out of the state, maybe the country."

"But, Uncle," I said. "I don't like traveling. As a matter of fact, I detest it."

"I don't care what you detest." He was quiet for a few seconds. "What really worries me is what I will tell Big Mac now."

Over the phone, I thought I heard the buzzer of Uncle Eldridge's apartment and I wondered who would be calling on him at that hour of the morning. His voice became tense. "Look, stay put, Don't call me for a couple of days." He hung up.

I put the receiver back on the hook and went to the employees' lavatory where I washed the dust and grime from my face.

I would have to stay here at least forty-eight hours and that meant I ought to provide myself with some food. I put on one of the white aprons hanging on a peg and picked up an empty carton. If some early morning passerby happened to see me in the store, he would probably think I was one of the stockboys.

A supermarket these days seems to be a combination grocery store, meat market, drugstore, variety shop, and considerably more. I wandered through the aisles feeling almost like a small boy released in a candy shop. I supplied myself with the essentials—milk, bread, and cold cuts and a few other items, including an imported Edam.

I also picked up a flashlight and batteries. By the time I ascended the stack of sugar bags, my box was rather heavy. I closed the trap door behind me and turned on the flashlight.

The area I stood in appeared to be approximately nine feet high, twenty feet in depth, and stretched across the entire width of the store. Apparently another establishment had preceded the supermarket in this building, and this space had been used for storage. But now it was empty and thick with dust.

The beam of my flashlight located a number of empty light sockets on the ceiling. I decided I might as well get some light bulbs, too. I was about to lift the trap door when I heard a noise down below. I turned off my flashlight and put my eye to the crack.

The rear door opened slowly and a rather thin man cautiously peered in. Then he pocketed his keys, entered, and closed the door behind him. He took the precaution of making certain that he was the only person in the building. Then he emptied several large trash boxes against one wall. He removed a candle from his pocket, lit it, and set it among the scrap paper at the base of the pile. He stepped back, viewed the arrangement, and smiled.

My eyes widened. A firebug! The candle would burn down to the trash in half an hour or so and the store would soon be ablaze.

He regarded his handiwork once again and then quietly let himself out the back door.

I waited five minutes and then descended. I extinguished the candle and threw it aside. Really, I thought, the incredibly strange people who inhabit this earth!

I went into the store and got some light bulbs and a broom. After eating, I swept my loft a bit. Then I extinguished the lights and lay down on the floor, using the briefcase as a pillow. I closed my eyes and attempted to sleep.

Uncle Eldridge is a collector and he works for Big Mac. I don't know exactly what it's all about, but he goes to different places in the city at night and each one of them gives him money.

Why had he chosen me for this particular scheme? I would have considered myself a most unlikely candidate. I suppose it was because we are related and he thought he could turn to me in time of trouble.

"There'll be at least thirty thousand in the briefcase," Uncle Eldridge had said. "And five of that is yours. You could use five thousand, couldn't you? Maybe travel a little?"

But I didn't care for travel. On my yearly vacation I go nowhere except to the library and back to my one room apartment.

"No, Uncle," I said. "I wouldn't want any of the money."

His eyes flickered. "Well, thanks, Fred. As a matter of fact, I owe the syndicate thirty thousand, not twenty-five. The extra five will square things right up to the zero mark."

"How could you possibly owe that much money?"

He shrugged. "Just one of those things that happen, Fred. The horses all run against me. So now I got to cover or be covered, if you know what I mean."

"But I'd think that surely Big Mac would give one of his own employees more time to pay the money back? Did you ask him?"

Uncle Eldridge cleared his throat. "It's like this, Fred. I didn't do the betting with Big Mac. I went down to St. Louis weekends and that's where I owe it." He patted me on the shoulder. "You and I have nobody else in this world but ourselves. You can't let me down, Fred. It means my life, and I'm not kidding."

I sighed. "All right. But frankly I dread the entire thing."

And now I lay here in the darkness. I am a bookkeeper. I rise at seven. I shower, I shave, I dress, I prepare my own breakfast. At eight I leave for work. It is a journey which requires almost an hour and four transfers. At six I am back in my apartment. There follows another hour for making and eating the evening meal.

And then, seven to eleven, I read, I listen to music, and I think. Four hours out of every twenty-four, I live.

"It'll be easy," Uncle Eldridge had said. "You just walk in, point the gun, and take everybody's wallet. And my briefcase."

"But you don't intend to tell the police there was nearly thirty thousand dollars in the briefcase?"

"Certainly not. They'll start asking questions about how I happened to be carrying all that kind of money and that could lead to trouble. All they got to know is that it was a simple bar holdup and the briefcase went with my wallet."

"What will you tell Big Mac?"

"The same thing. It was an ordinary heist and I was unlucky enough to be there. And if he don't swallow that, I'll remind him that a lot of punks know I'm a collector and it could be one of them decided to make a strike."

"And you think he'll believe that?"

"Look," Uncle Eldridge said. "In his business you got to think suspicious and I expect him to. So he'll brood over three things. One: Was it just a holdup? Two: Or was it really a hijack job by some punk who knew the score? And three: Is the collector trying to pull something?"

"And when he gets to number three?"

"He might even get a little physical. But I can take a few bumps for thirty grand, and I'll keep blinking innocent like he never saw before. So he'll remember that I been working for him three years and I been clean. Finally he'll say to himself, 'All right. I'll let it go this time. But if anything like this happens again, the blood's going to flow.'"

"He'll do that after losing thirty thousand dollars?"

Uncle Eldridge snorted. "To him thirty grand is toothpick money. The only thing that might really bother him is the principle of the thing—like somebody in the organization having the nerve to rob him."

I became aware of the sound of voices below and went to the peephole which gave me a panoramic view of the entire store. It was almost eight and various clerks were arriving to start the day.

The hours which followed were long, though I did catnap often. At nine in the evening the supermarket closed and, as in the previous night, the stockboys took over and worked until four in the morning.

After they left, I went downstairs. I washed up and donned the white apron. I made several trips from the store to my sanctuary, during which I transferred more food, an extension cord, a small table lamp, a bridge table, and a folding chair. I browsed a bit at the magazine and bookstand and selected half a dozen pocket books. My eyes turned to the newspaper stacks and I saw my picture on the front page of one of them.

The article consisted of two columns down at the bottom of the page. NEPHEW ROBS UNCLE, TWO DETECTIVES. It told about what had happened and how the two detectives were now suspended pending an investigation.

There was a quote by Uncle Eldridge. "I don't know what got into the boy. He's been trying to borrow a couple of hundred from me for the last month, but I had to turn him down. He got pretty mad about it and maybe he thought he'd get the money this way. All I had was about twenty bucks but he could have had that if I'd known he was so desperate."

I was upstairs arranging the extension cord and the lamp when I heard the noise below. I switched off the lights and crept quietly to the trap door.

It was that man again. He glared about, then once again, he emptied the trash containers against the wall. This time he lit two candles and placed them in the midst of the paper. He moved about, apparently testing for drafts, and then, satisfied, he left.

I sighed, went down, and snuffed out the two candles. I searched through the manager's desk until I found his name, address, and phone number, and then I dialed. "Mr. Nelson?"

From the muddle of his voice, it was obvious he had been awakened. "Yeah?"

"Sir," I said. "I'm afraid someone is attempting to burn down your store. You better investigate."

He growled. "Is this some kind of practical joke? You have any idea what time this is?"

"I'm sorry, sir," I said. "But this is almost the only time of day I can call. And it isn't a practical joke."

He seemed to wake up. "Who is this?"

"Just say I am a friend of the supermarket. This individual has already made two attempts to burn down your store. Somehow they failed. But I have the suspicion he will try again tomorrow. Somewhere around five o'clock in the morning, I believe." I hung up and went back upstairs.

During the day and evening, I read two books. I lay down to sleep at ten and woke about three in the morning, a bit stiff. The floor is not exactly the most comfortable place to sleep. I went to the trap door, removed the plug, and looked down.

The stockboys moved about quite industriously, because the manager was present, I imagine. In a corner, he conferred with two uniformed policemen and two other men, possibly detectives.

At four o'clock the stockboys had finished and they left. The manager and the policemen began arranging places of concealment for themselves.

One of the detectives clambered up the sugar stack. For a moment I thought we looked eye to eye, and that all was lost. But he turned his back to the trap door, arranged several of the sacks in the form of a barricade, and crouched behind them.

All of us waited. By my watch, it was five after five when the rear door was unlocked and opened.

It was the punctual firebug, and this time he had apparently lost faith in candles. He carried a gasoline can, and he appeared to be exceedingly vexed. Once again he piled trash against the wall. He poured gasoline on the accumulation and reached into his pocket. He brought out a book of matches.

Directly below me the detective rose to his feet. "Hold it! This is the police! You're under arrest!"

The police converged upon the unfortunate individual, and within a matter of seconds the bewildered man was handcuffed. One of the officers observed the manager's astonishment. "You know him?"

The manager nodded. "I fired him for loafing on the job."

By the time the excitement had gone, it was almost daylight. I went down and dialed Uncle Eldridge.

"Why didn't you call?" he demanded.

"You told me not to."

"Well, never mind that now. Where are you?"

"Still in the supermarket."

"I mean which one? What's the address?"

I scratched my head. "I don't know the address, and there don't seem to be any numbers on the show windows."

"You can't be too far from Eighth and Hadley. That's where the bar was. So listen. I want you to go over to Ninth, between Hadley and Atkinson. Wait in the alley on the even numbered side of the street. And don't forget the briefcase."

I thought I heard someone coughing while Uncle Eldridge was speaking. "Are you alone? I heard somebody cough."

"It's the TV," he said. "One of them early morning programs."

I looked up at the window high in the storeroom. "It's just about daylight, Uncle. Don't you think there's a good chance the police might pick me up if I went out now? Ninth and Hadley could be a dozen blocks from here."

He didn't answer for a second and I thought I heard the TV in the background again. Then he said, "All right, we'll play it safe and certain. You be there tomorrow when it's still dark. What time can you make it?"

"I think five o'clock would be about the right time," I said. "The stockboys don't quit until four or a little after."

"Be there," Uncle Eldridge said, and he hung up.

The next morning the stockboys quit at their usual time. I waited ten minutes and then picked up the briefcase.

The phone downstairs rang. I glanced about to see if I'd left anything, then turned off the lights, and opened the trap door. I went down the sugar bags and to the door.

The phone was still ringing. I was about to leave anyway, so why not? I picked up the receiver. "Hello?"

There was a slight delay, then, "Is that you, Fred?"

"Yes," I said "How did you know I was here?"

"I didn't. I just looked in the phone book and called every super-market around Hadley. But luckily I got to you in time."

"I'm just about to leave, Uncle."

"Forget that. Some of Big Mac's boys would be waiting to pick you up and what they got in mind for you is fatal."

"But, Uncle, you were the one who told me to ..."

"Look, Fred, when you got a couple of guys lighting matches and not for cigarettes, you get to telling them the truth eventually."

"You told them about us?"

"Not exactly. I said I didn't know you were going to pull the heist, and that I was going to talk you into bringing back the money."

"And Big Mac believed you?"

"I wouldn't bet a dime on it. But, at least, he put me on the shelf until he could get his hands on you." Uncle Eldridge was talking fast. "They left Red Bronson to see that I stayed put, but Red's attention wandered. Right now he's on the floor of my apartment wrapped up with all the clothesline I could steal from my landlady. Now that I know where you are, I'll pick you up in five minutes. I'm only a few blocks from there. Meet me at the rear of the store."

I sat down on some cartons and waited. I heard the car pull into the alley and stop, the motor idling. I pressed the bar that unlocked the rear door from the inside. It swung open and the stop at its base lowered and held it ajar.

Uncle Eldridge had his car parked at the loading platform and he was alone.

I stooped down and handed him the briefcase through the open window. "Where will we go?"

He shrugged. "How do I know? The world's a big place."

I stared out into the darkness.

"Hurry it up," Uncle Eldridge snapped. "We haven't got all day."

I wondered what would happen now. A thousand miles away, would I get another bookkeeping job and live four hours a day? And then I shook my head. "No. You go on."

He frowned. "Are you crazy?"

"Maybe," I said. "But I'm not going with you."

He regarded me for a few seconds. "All right. Have it your way. I haven't got time to argue. But I always did think you were a little nuts." He put the car into gear and it roared down the alley.

I went back into the store and closed and locked the rear door. Upstairs, I turned on the lamp and picked up a book.

Yes, the world was a big place, much too big for me. But here it was warm and just my size.

Marguerite Dickinson

A Murderous Slice

The summer Dolly Tyler was killed, my parents were in Argentina on a combination pleasure and business trip. Dad had given me a T-Bird when I graduated from State. "Don't worry about getting a teaching job right away, Annie," he said. "Have fun."

An obedient daughter, I got a reservation at the Potowatomi Inn in Northern Michigan where we'd spent our summers for years. My days were a round of sunbathing, swimming, reading, and golfing. To complete this euphoric pattern, I fell in love.

Dan and I played golf this capricious August morning, sparkling sunshine one minute, dripping mystic drizzle the next, but who cared? Dan had carded a lean thirty-four on the first nine and I wasn't displeased with my forty-two. We were about to start on number ten when she came out of the clubhouse, swinging pertly.

"Here comes the Bad Witch," I murmured. Dolly had been pestering him all summer.

Barely nodding to me, she grabbed Dan's arm and pulled him aside. She forced a pink slip of paper into his hand, which he crumpled and shoved into his pocket. You knew if there'd been a trash barrel handy, it would have gone there instead.

Dolly Tyler was a pastel blonde with milky-white skin, and that day her eyes were lavender. She changed the color of her contact lenses to match her cashmere sweaters. She was such a lousy golfer you might wonder why she bothered to play, except that's where the men were. She was married.

I hit my tee shot on number ten (a par three, and I'm usually on the green with my four wood) into the trap. It was a fried egg and took two blows with my wedge to blast out. I was chewing sand, literally.

"You're not going to let a big nothing like her spoil your game, are you?" Dan asked.

"If we got married right now," I answered, "these predatory females would have to leave you alone." He made no comment. I leaned over to line up my putt on the rain-drenched green.

"You sink that," he commanded, "or I'll belt you one."

Dan Preston was a pre-med student who worked summers as recreation director at the inn. He was big and gruff, with a craggy sunburned face, and eyes the color of Danish porcelain. It hadn't take me long to discover that his brusqueness was coverup for an understanding and tender nature.

My putt was a thirty footer. It rolled boldly toward the cup, setting off a miniature sprinkler system that dwindled as the ball slowed. Slower, slower, then the satisfying "ponk" as it dropped.

Dan put his arm around my shoulder and we took the mold-leaf path through shadowy woods to the next tee. Our Indian caddie jogged on ahead with our bags. Suddenly Dan stopped and pulled me around to face him. I'm five foot six but even in high heels have to look up to him. "I'd be mad as hell," he said, "if my only child, a blue-eyed, black-haired beauty, ran off with some character who couldn't support her, and whom I'd never met."

"We could at least announce our engagement."

"Not until you get an answer from your cable." Then he bent to kiss me and the evil witch's spell was broken. It was, that is, until we were coming in on number eighteen and I saw her standing there under that big sun hat she always wore, waiting . . .

It had started to rain heavily as we left the club, but by the time we'd had lunch in town, done a long list of errands for the inn's manager, and driven back there, it had cleared again. Careful to sneak up the back stairs (bridge-minded guests had an airy way of disregarding Dan's day off) we changed into bathing suits and met on the beach.

There is something calming about floating in warm water, an occasional raindrop plopping on your nose. I was feeling better by the time we walked hand in hand up the deserted beach. Dark pines ringed the slope above us, hiding the inn and most of the cottages, but the Tylers' lavish chalet stood out in isolated splendor. I thought of eccentric old Mr. Tyler and the anemic doll he was married to, and let go of Dan's hand. "Her husband should lock Dolly up in that eagle's nest and throw away the key."

"He practically does. That's why she's been bugging me to help her."

"Help," I sniffed.

"She caught him taping her telephone conversations."

"A likely story."

"Race you back to the inn," he said.

We arrived, breathless and laughing, to find Paul Whipple, the manager, pacing up and down on the sprawling verandah of the old fashioned brown building. He tripped on a wooden rocker, and nearly fell into a tub of white petunias when he saw us. "Where have you kids been?" he called out, his mustache wiggling with agitation, "Chief Amory wants to talk to you."

"Whatever for?" Mounting the steps, my hand reached instinctively for Dan's solid arm.

"Dolly Tyler's body was found two hours ago in that wooded area behind the caddie shack. Amory has been questioning the club personnel, and everyone who played the course today."

I grew rigid. There was a queer crawling up the back of my head, as though someone had injected a massive shot of Novocain directly into my brain. But it didn't numb memory, didn't blur the picture of Dolly standing there waiting, nor of Dan's second shot slicing toward the woods—

I felt the muscle in Dan's arm tighten as we reached Mr. Whipple. Dan pulled his elbow in, pressing my hand warningly against his tanned ribs. His grey-blue eyes, darker than usual, were seeking mine. "Say nothing," they warned.

Paul Whipple, a bachelor in his fifties, had a suite at the rear of the hotel which he laughingly called The Casbah. There was a rakish striped awning over its private entrance. A fan on a standard moved lazily back and forth in the hot room where Potowatomi Point's chief of police waited for us.

Jeff Amory, in his business suit, looked small for a policeman, but he was big on aggressiveness and gristle. Not rising from the yellow chair, his eyes traveled my body. "You've changed some from the determined slugger who beat me at golf six years ago."

The fact that a sixteen-year-old could outplay him had rankled deeply. I saw that it still did.

He asked after my parents and, when I said they were in Argentina, he said he'd read about my father being made director of Amalgamated Motors International Staff, adding, "Kind of an invasion of privacy the way they publish those hundred-thousand-dollar bonuses." He was watching Dan.

"You wanted to question us?" Dan asked.

"Right. Sit down, please."

After Paul Whipple had assured us our damp suits wouldn't harm Naugahide, we seated ourselves on the sofa. The manager went to a portable bar and mixed himself a scotch and soda. The rest of us declined.

Amory said, "Dan, I understand you saw a lot of Mrs. Tyler earlier this summer. In fact, right up until Miss Blackstone arrived—"

"My arrival," I broke in, "had nothing to do—"

Amory turned that muscular face my way. "Perhaps you'd like to change from your bathing suit. I can question you later."

I pressed my lips shut and stayed where I was.

Dan admitted that he *had* seen a good deal of Dolly Tyler, not by choice, but because her husband asked him to take her golfing, water skiing, even dancing over at the Par Four where the local young set hung out. "It was embarrassing," Dan said, "but since Mr. Tyler is head of the association that runs the inn, and since I'm recreation director, I couldn't refuse."

"Seems like you started refusing regularly, soon as Miss Blackstone entered the picture."

Dan frowned. "That was because Dolly told me her husband had changed. That all at once he was acting so jealous she was afraid of him. I was glad to get off the hook."

The room was hot and stuffy. I felt hemmed in and found it hard to breathe. "Sounds like someone wanted Dan for a patsy," I said. "Have you questioned Mr. Tyler?"

Amory gave a tired snort. "Of course! He and Paul Whipple were having lunch at the Algonquin Bar and Grill at the time of the murder. Tyler got there at twelve-oh-five, isn't that what you said, Paul?"

The manager, adding another jigger of scotch to his drink, did not turn around. "On the dot."

"The Indian caddie who carried double for you kids," Amory continued, "said the last time he saw Mrs. Tyler alive, she was heading for the woods where Dan had gone to look for his ball. The caddie said he couldn't help because you, Miss Blackstone, were having problems in the rough on the other side of the fairway. He said it was odd, Mr. Preston's ball going over in those woods like that. He said it was the first time he'd ever seen Mr. Preston slice. Hook, yes, but never slice."

The fan whirred and turned from side to side, a giant face studying us. My stomach churned.

"These Indian boys make good caddies," Amory said, "quiet, observant—" He paused, then, "Dan, what was it Mrs. Tyler handed you when you were waiting to tee off on number ten? What was it?"

"We don't have to answer these questions," I heard myself saying in a tremulous voice.

"Let me handle this." Dan sounded angry. "You won't believe me, sir, but I forgot all about that note. It's still crumpled up in my pocket."

"You're only thirty percent right, son." Amory pulled a crushed pink wad from his pocket. Smoothing it out, he leaned across the coffee table and handed it to me.

A cluster of maroon tulips dominated the pink notepaper. Judging from its ragged top edge, it had been torn from a gummed pad. "Dear Dan: I can't stand it another day. I want to go to California like you said. I'll meet you behind the caddie shack when you finish playing. *You'd better be there.* I mean it. Dolly."

Dan read it over my shoulder, then got up, bare feet planted, the white towel draping his chest like a martyr's toga. "I made the mistake of telling her," he said, "about my uncle in Beverly Hills. He gets fabulous settlements for some of his movie clients. Dolly asked me to get in touch with him. She said Tyler would divorce her in a minute if she'd sign off for a paltry ten or fifteen thousand, but after spending five years with the old goat she wasn't about to let—"

"So," Amory cut in, "you agreed to arrange it with your uncle. Later you two would get together and she'd get you up in practice—"

"Pardon me, sir, but you've got to be kidding!"

"Then all at once you found yourself with another deal. You realized a loaded father-in-law was better security than a kooky dame. But Dolly wouldn't get off your back. She's been pestering you all summer. And when she followed you into the woods this noon (where you'd deliberately sliced your ball so you *could* meet her and tell her once and for all that you'd had it) she wouldn't listen. You knew she meant trouble, big trouble, and you lost that famous temper of yours. Everyone

I've talked to says you're not a guy to push around. You lost your temper *and* your head. You strangled her. Then to make sure, you clobbered her skull in with her own nine iron."

Dan looked dazed. "No! That's not true."

"But you did see her, talk to her, back there in the woods?"

Gasping like a beached fish, I came to my feet. "Wait a minute!"

"Sure I talked to her," Dan answered Amory, "but when she started telling me a lot of weird things she 'had' on her husband, and said the last maid he'd fired was willing to testify in court—"

"Will you shut up!" I cried out. "Unless Chief Amory takes you down to headquarters for formal questioning he has no legal right to—"

Amory stared at me, the muscles in his jaw working. "You've got something there, miss. Better get your clothes on, son."

Dan didn't even glance my way as he walked out. Thunderstruck, I ran after him. Outside a trooper lounged against the brown frame building, smoking a cigarette.

Dan swung around as I ran up behind him. "I want you," he said in a low, tense voice, "to pretend we're good friends, nothing more."

"But I—"

"Do as I ask. Think what the publicity—"

"I don't give a damn about the publicity. I'm coming with you."

He grabbed my arms and shook me, the force of his fingers painfully sharp. "No!" The trooper dropped his cigarette and started toward us, hand on holster. Dan's whisper was urgent. "You're not playing with kids. Stay out of this or you'll get hurt."

It soon became obvious that Amory didn't want me down at head-qarters, either. When I returned to The Casbah he asked a few routine questions, then told me that since the time of Dolly's murder had been pinpointed by that sudden outburst of heavy rain, statements from the caddie and a women's locker room attendant had automatically alibied me.

After he'd gone, I sank back on the couch and began to cry, tears dribbling down my cheeks.

Paul Whipple gave me a box of facial tissues. "Nice going, Anne. You've handed your boy to Chief Amory on a silver platter, complete with motivation."

"Motivation?"

"You heard what he said about a rich father-in-law. If you'd under-play your feelings it would do more for Dan than all these dramatics. Every time you opened your mouth you gave Amory additional ammunition."

I sat there feeling like a moron. So that's what Dan had meant . . .

"I'll have our dinner served here, Anne."

"No thank you, Paul. I don't intend to skulk around as though I had something to be ashamed of."

But after showering and changing into a blue linen dress, I was reluctant to leave my room. Peeking through chintz curtains, I watched late cocktailers strolling down the cement walk from their cottages toward the inn and dinner. The excited chatter of voices from the verandah below my window meant, I knew, that everyone was discussing the murder.

When I finally walked into the pine-paneled dining room it was almost deserted. But not quite. Mr. Tyler, a massive hulk in his white suit, sat dwarfing the table for two he'd shared with his wife. He stood up and begged me to join him. I was too astounded to think of an excuse.

"I've had dinner," he said, "but if you don't object to my cigar—?" Not waiting for an answer, he proceeded to light one. His sandy hair was turning white, and the small eyes made me think of a polar bear. "You must be pretty upset about Dan?"

I nodded.

"I don't think he did it," Mr. Tyler said.

My mouth fell open.

"I've known that boy for some time. I admire his guts. That's why I got him a part-time job back home, as well as his summer job here. That's why I helped him get a scholarship at medical school. It wasn't his fault Dolly thought—" He picked up the pencil on the table beside his check. "The killer could have been a workman—a wino—or one of those caddies. Dolly didn't realize how provocative she was in those pretty clothes of hers." The small eyes reddened. "She spent a lot on clothes." He was studying the bill.

Cottagers signed for any meals they had at the inn. If they didn't stipulate differently, they were charged a twenty percent gratuity for the waitress. Mr. Tyler stipulated differently. He put down ten cents.

I looked hastily away as he leaned toward me. I got a whiff of cigar breath, then felt his moist hand cover mine. Grizzled hairs sprouted from under the white coat sleeve. "As an old golfing friend of your father's, let me advise you to stay out of this. The publicity would hurt him and won't help Dan. I'll handle Jeff Amory. He owes me a favor or two. I'm sure I can convince him of your sweetheart's innocence."

I reached for a glass of water with my free hand. My skin was crawling. "He's not my sweetheart," I managed. My cold roast beef and potato salad came then. Mr. Tyler patted my hand and got up. Watching the bulky white back as he lumbered off, I wondered just how indebted Jeff Amory was to this rich and influential man.

Pushing my plate aside, I drank my iced tea, then went to the lobby, glad to find it deserted except for the desk clerk. I headed for the wing at the back of the hotel where the help lived in the season.

Two college kids Dan and I had often double-dated with were playing ping-pong in the recreation room. I asked for news of Dan.

"They haven't booked him yet," Bruce answered, ball poised to serve, "but I understand he's being held on an open charge for twenty-four hours."

My stomach felt queasy and I had to swallow as I turned to Nan. "We've got to help him. Do you know of anyone who might have been having an affair with Dolly?"

She gave a short nervous laugh. "Last summer she was sneaking into The Casbah almost every—" the celluloid ball came slamming onto her side of the table and she had to duck out of its way.

"If you have a statement to make," Bruce advised her, "better make it to Chief Amory."

Though it was only a little after eight when I got back to my room, I undressed and put on pajamas, then pulled back the spread and crawled into bed. Snapping off the light, I lay there listening to the distant broom-swish sound of waves fondling sandy beach. From the verandah below, voices mingled with the creak of the old fashioned chain swing. Was the killer down there smiling to himself in the dark? Was it true that my interference was doing more harm than good? I thought of Dan pacing behind bars, and knew I wasn't going to stop interfering until I found the discrepancy behind one of the alibis everyone except Dan seemed to have.

By seven the next morning I was parking my car in the empty lot at the golf club. My sneakers left a dark green trail in dew-sparkled grass. I could literally see moisture being sucked into the air by a vigorous morning sun. In spite of the tropical atmosphere, I shivered and wished I'd worn something warmer than shorts and a matching print blouse. I started toward the spot where Dolly's body had been found.

The caddie shack was locked, but the door of the nearby maintenance shed was ajar. I peeked cautiously inside. Two tractors loomed in the dimness, their cumbersome attachments uncoupled and lying nearby. The pegboard above a workbench was neatly hung with tools.

I went back to the path between the low green buildings and began an inch-by-inch survey of the soggy ground across which Amory had said Dolly's body was dragged. He was able to pinpoint the time of murder because she had been pushed under the low branches of a Norway spruce before rain heavy enough to drench this protected area had begun.

Dan and I had pulled out of the club parking lot yesterday just as it began to pour.

Kneeling by the massive tree, I spread the low branches and began to sift rusty-brown needles through my fingers. I found nothing. I heard a car and ran to the maintenance shed. It was dark and humid inside, a smell of oil and damp earth filling my nostrils. Shuddering, I realized the murderer could have stood right where I was, door ajar, and heard everything Dan and Dolly might have said.

My back tensed as a car door slammed. Seconds later the fat greens-keeper walked into the shed, carrying a can of oil and wearing his habitual harassed expression. It changed to fear as I stepped forward. "I'm sorry to startle you," I said, "but I'd like to know if you saw Mr. Tyler around here yester—"

"Miss Blackstone!" His eyes were accusing, his mouth petulant. "I've been ordered to keep people out of this area until they get a man over here." He put the oilcan down on the workbench and started out the door. I followed.

"Just a couple of questions."

"You'll have to ask them of the police." He was hurrying as fast as his short legs would carry him. He went to an old blue car parked at the end of the service entrance road and began unlocking its trunk. "I'm not supposed to discuss the murder with *anyone*. You should have seen the people flocking around here late yesterday! Honestly, it isn't enough I can't get decent help. Every time I turn around somebody is complaining."

"You've known me a long time," I said. "Surely you can trust—" I broke off, frowning, as I saw what he had in the trunk. "Isn't that the golf scooter Mr. Tyler was trying to sell?"

The greenskeeper's full lips pouted. "It is not! This one I picked up for half the price he wanted for his. Now he's trying to convince the board I didn't need one. But it'll soon pay for itself in time saved."

Puffing, he pulled the scooter from the trunk and I helped him lower it to the ground. "I can contact my boys anyplace on the course in seconds," he said. "Just had it over to Shortie's for a checkup. I can get there faster in this thing than in my car—one minute flat."

"All the way to Shortie's?"

He pointed to a narrow opening through trees. "Last week we cleared a path leading right to his place. Taking the highway, you got two stops at those junctions, you got to go around Middlebury Orchards. Takes you four and a half minutes. Like I told the Board, three and a half minutes may not sound like much, but when you're running over for supplies four and five times—"

I wasn't listening to him. I was listening to the computer clicking in my brain. "Does Mr. Tyler still have his scooter?"

"I wouldn't know," the greenskeeper said shortly. "Now if you'll excuse—"

The alibi covering both Whipple and Tyler hinged on a delicate matter of timing, I thought as I walked back to my car.

Shortie's place is almost back to the inn. It's located at the junction where you take the highway to the right, if you're going into Potowatomi Point, or veer left to go to the inn. He has a garage-gas station, and cottages he rents by the week. I spent a half hour there, then headed for town.

As I entered the municipal building Chief Amory saw me. He beckoned to me, offered me a chair next to his desk, and said that Dan and his attorney were in the magistrate's office trying to set bail.

"I didn't come to see Dan. Mr. Tyler killed his wife, and I can prove it."

He sank into his chair with the smile of one who has bitten into a rotten olive. But he pulled a notebook from his drawer and said, "Okay, give me the facts."

"You say it was impossible for Mr. Tyler to be at the golf club at the time of the murder and still meet Paul Whipple at the Algonquin Bar and Grill when he did. But what if Tyler parked in a clearing by one of Shortie's vacant cottages and cut through?"

"I've played the course a few times," Amory's tone was nasty, "and believe me, there isn't a spot where Tyler could have cut through without being seen. There were players on every hole before heavy rain started. A track star, let alone a two hundred pound man, could never get to the murder spot and back in time."

"He could if he used a motor scooter," I said. "Mr. Tyler has one. It's the kind that you dismantle the steering stick and it'll fit into your car trunk. If he used that, and took the new path catty-corner to Shortie's—you knew about the new path the greenskeeper cleared?" The flicker in his eyes told me he did not. "One minute to the shack—he could run his scooter right in—"

"Of course," sarcasm underscored the words, "there wouldn't be any workmen about!"

"It was noon. Those boys stop right at the stroke of twelve, and take their lunches over to the picnic tables. One minute for Tyler to get from the spot where he'd concealed his car behind one of Shortie's cabins, say four, even five minutes waiting and eavesdropping on Dolly and Dan. Then when Dan left, Tyler jumped out, killed her, dragged the body—you said yourself this could be done in two or three minutes when I argued about the short time Dan was back there with her——dragged the body under that Norway spruce, jumped on his scooter, and in one minute was back to his car and off for the meeting with Whipple."

Amory was writing rapidly in the black notebook. He stopped, studied his notes, then looked across the desk at me. "Even so—"

But I was ready. "You're going to say he'd have to pick up nine or ten minutes someplace."

"Right, and I've got three people who agree on the exact time Mr. Tyler left his place to go meet Whipple at the Algonquin."

"But you've only got Paul Whipple testifying to the exact time Tyler got there."

Amory's eyes narrowed. "You're accusing him of being in on this, too?"

"No, but if Tyler made a flat statement that they met at a certain time and Paul wasn't sure, he'd back Tyler up. Especially since he didn't want his last summer's affair with Mrs. Tyler uncovered by an investigation." I saw by his expression that Amory knew all about that. He stared down at his notes, then up at me again, his smile bleak. "So Tyler could have picked up nine or ten minutes, the way you see it. You wouldn't like to push your luck and try for twenty or thirty?"

"What do you mean?"

"Your theory sounds great, but how in the devil could Mr. Tyler figure it to the split second? Know the *exact* time and place your boyfriend and his wife were to meet?"

The impact of his question forced my sweaty hands against the blunt edge of the desk. I clung there, unable to speak, then, "He could have called the pro shop and found out when we were coming in on eighteen. He knew Mrs. Tyler had a golf lesson."

"No, ma'am! That lesson was spur of the moment. She was supposed to be having her hair done. Tyler spent the morning with a farmer whose property the association plans to buy. He and Paul were going to check the title after their lunch in town. Mr. Tyler did *not* call the club, he did *not* call the beauty parlor. He couldn't possibly have known about her change in plans."

Pushing myself up, I fought back tears. "Sorry I wasted your time."

"Not at all. I'll check out that motor scooter. Not that it has any bearing—" He tapped his desk impatiently with the black notebook.

"When?"

His face seemed to flatten like a mean horse with its ears laid back. "Maybe I should take you into protective custody. Don't look shocked. On the thousand to one chance you're right and we have the wrong man, I don't want your so-called murderer presenting me with another battered female corpse."

I went back to the inn, tried to eat lunch, answered politely that I knew nothing when people asked about Dan, then changed into my bathing suit and headed for the beach.

At the top of the wooden steps leading down to the shore, I had to fight a strong compulsion to turn off onto the cement walk that meandered from one private cottage to another, ending at the snobbishly aloof Tyler place.

Picking a spot on the sand away from other bathers, I lay down on my towel. Bright sunlight painted orangy-red abstracts against my closed lids. I felt the emptiness of complete helplessness. Nothing to do but wait. I was itching to get into the Tyler garage and see if the scooter was there. Dying to get into that house and see if it contained bloodstained clothing, letters; *anything* that might help me free Dan.

Movement caught the corner of my eye and I turned my head. *Impossible!* I stared at the top-heavy figure in flapping tan swim trunks. I couldn't remember when I'd last seen Mr. Tyler go swimming, and *never* before sundown. He was carrying an army surplus raft. He walked, looking neither right nor left, until the water was breast-high, then scrambled onto the raft and began paddling out to deeper water.

I heard a sigh and realized I'd been holding my breath. Picking up my towel, I walked back to the steps leading to the inn. "You're out of your mind," I told myself. But when I got to the cement walk, I turned right, forcing myself to stroll as I passed one cottage after another. I saw no one. When I came to the steps leading on up to the big-windowed Tyler place, I was bent double, like a thief. Through the trees I could see the raft bobbing far out in the bay with the vague blob on top of it.

I began to run. The garage was back of the house at the end of a road cut into the hillside. Two cars were there, both trunks locked, and, of course, no keys. I walked back up the winding path to the rear of the house. There was a Dutch door leading into the kitchen. The upper half was open. An empty house has the same unaware vulnerability as a person you are observing when he doesn't know you are there. I turned the knob and went in, hurrying through the kitchen and into the living room with its dining ell. The view from the window was magnificent. Far below stretched the bay. Empty.

Criminologists claim a certain amount of lawbreaking is done for kicks. If my dry mouth, pounding heart, and sweaty hands were what they meant by kicks, they could have it. Then the raft bobbed into sight, a tiny speck on blue-green water.

I surveyed the room I was in. I searched every surface for a set of car keys, opened every drawer. No luck.

Tyler's bedroom was done in sombre tones of brown and black. The smell of dead cigars in a copper ashtray caused me to swallow stickily. The drawer in his desk was full of balls of string, folded paper bags, bits of partly used paper—even some odd-sized used carbon sheets—but no letters, no notes, no keys. Nor did I find anything in the clothes hanging in the louvered closet.

I ran out to the big window again. The raft was still bouncing away in the distance. I convinced myself (it was hard, but I did it) that Tyler was too miserly, and too afraid of being noticed, to leave the raft there and swim back.

Next I tackled Dolly's room, all pink, with a dressing table glittering with cut crystal. A small desk had nothing on it but a telephone (pink, of course) and the tulip-bordered pink pad from which Dan's note had been torn. I snatched it up eagerly, but if there had been indentations Mr. Tyler might have deciphered, they weren't there now. I was so frustrated, I flung the pad down with a sob. It slithered off the desk and to the floor. When I picked it up, something dark protruded from one corner. It was a small square of fresh carbon stuck under the third sheet down, and obviously cut to a size that it wouldn't be noticed.

Trying to hold back mounting jubilance, I ran back to Mr. Tyler's sombre room. The piece of carbon in my hand matched the used one in his drawer. I should have got out of that house right then. But I remembered the cloisonné hand mirror on Dolly's dressing table. Sitting down on a tufted velvet stool, I found that by slanting the piece of carbon so light from the window behind me reflected on it, I could look into the small mirror and read the words easily. There were Dear Pauls, Dear Bruces, and finally, "Dear Dan: I can't stand it another—" Something cut off the reflection. I raised my eyes from the hand mirror to the large one over Dolly's dressing table.

How could a creature so huge move with such silence? He looked more like a polar bear than ever. Grizzled whitish hairs sprang from his chest, even from the massive shoulders. The white-lashed eyes were staring down at the carbon in my hand. Then he looked up, his knowing gaze meeting my eyes in the mirror.

The stool fell as I got to my feet. He kicked it aside, he hard stomach pressing into my back as one of his arms slid around my waist. I started to scream but his other hand came swiftly over my mouth, thumb and forefinger clamping my nostrils shut. "Now, now," the said, as I tried to claw him away. "We don't want any marks on you, and we don't want any on me."

I jerked my head back and forth, fighting for air. "Take a big breath," he said surprisingly, and removed his hand from my mouth. As I gulped in, I felt him lean back, felt my bare feet leave the carpet. I started to scream. He gave an abrupt, crushing bearhug. I felt as though my ribs met my backbone. The scream swooshed to nothing as air jetted from my lungs.

There followed a nightmare of blackout and movement; of nausea, of fighting the slithering silk binding me in total cocoon. The scent of Dolly's perfume clung to the pillow, sucked against my face, and I strained and twisted for air. Falling darkness, bumping movement, then the feel of a running engine vibrating through my body. I was in some sort of cramped space, still mummy-trussed, but the pillow, thank God, had been removed. I sucked in great gulps of polluted air before I realized its significance.

"Her color is good," I heard Dan saying. "No bones broken."

There was a sound of pines murmuring in a soft breeze, then footsteps on gravel. I concentrated on the wonderful business of breathing before slowly opening my eyes. Dan's face hung over mine, and I realized I was lying on grass, my head in his lap.

"Mr. Tyler—" I began, my voice edging toward hysteria.

"It's all right, sweetheart," Dan said gently. "He has already been taken to the police station."

"But the carbon—"

"You only got a whiff or two of carbon monoxide gas," said another voice. A pair of grey pantlegs came into view. "Lucky thing," Chief Amory continued, "you kept bugging me about the motor scooter or I might not have decided to come looking for it this afternoon, nor insisted that Tyler open his trunk when I found him here backing out of his garage."

"The carbon sheets!" I struggled to a sitting position. When I'd explained, Amory said, "Even if we don't find them, Tyler will have a tough time trying to tell a jury why he had you stuffed in the trunk of his car, a hose from the exhaust aimed at your nose."

"My patient needs rest," said Dan firmly.

"How did *you* get here?" I asked.

"As soon as my lawyer bailed me out, I came to the inn looking for you. One of the cottagers said she saw you heading for the Tyler place."

Chief Amory was still staring down at me. "You get an idea you really ride it. Good quality for a policewoman. If you need a job, let me know."

"Then my theory about Dan being set up for patsy was right?"

"Don't rub it in!" Chief Amory strode off.

"Persistence is a dandy quality for a doctor's wife, too," said Dan, helping me to my feet. "That is, if you don't get yourself killed first. Maybe I'd better take immediate steps to prevent that."

The soreness in my ribs and throat seemed to fade away. "We'll cable my parents again and if we don't hear right back, it's their own darned fault. I can get a teaching job in Ann Arbor. We'll find an apartment on campus—"

"You're talking too much!" Dan bent toward me, his voice filled with tender laughter. "I can do something about that, too."

He was so right.

Richard Hardwick
High Tide

Gradually the outward flow slowed, until imperceptibly all movement of the water had ceased. Almost at once the tide would start to move in again from the sea in its endless cycle, rising in the sound, then in the river, and finally in the creek that cut in against the low bluff before Ray Garvin's nearly completed house.

Across the creek from the unpainted dock a brisk northeast wind made waves in the tall marshgrass that stretched like a bright green meadow all the way to the river, a quarter of a mile away.

His arms resting on the rail, Lloyd Reed stood near the end of the dock and looked down at the man in the skiff.

"What kind of shape is it in, Ray?"

Ray Garvin poled the heavy skiff to shore and climbed out onto the mucky creekbank, tossing the line up to Reed.

"It'll take some work if this thing's going to hold the monorail."

He took a jackknife from his pocket, unclasped it, and dug the long blade at a piling, testing the soundness of the wood.

"How old would you say this dock is, Lloyd? Ten, twenty years?"

"I don't know if it's the same one, but there was a dock here when I was a kid. I remember coming out here with my old man, and that's been better than twenty-five years ago," Reed said.

Garvin folded the knife and dropped it back into the pocket. "It would have been a good thing if it had burned along with the old house." He moved beneath the dock and took hold of a crossbrace. "I suppose I ought to take it down and start from scratch." He shook the timber, holding it with both hands and putting his weight into it.

"*Hey!*" Reed yelled. "Don't *shake* it down!"

Garvin thought of the three steel beams piled on the dock above him, and he made a mental note to have the workmen take them off Monday and stack them ashore on the bluff. Might as well be on the safe side.

He shook the brace a final time and turned it loose.

"I'd take it easy down there, Ray," Reed said. "These beams aren't stacked too well—"

His words were cut off suddenly by an abrupt sound, like the crack of a heavy rifle. It came from directly above Garvin, sending a shower of splinters and powdery rotted wood after it.

Garvin's reaction was instinctive, even before Reed's shouted, unintelligible warning. The thought was instantaneous, to get out from under the dock. He threw himself toward the side, but his canvas shoes slipped on the muck and he sprawled forward. Above him came the heavy clang of metal striking metal.

The beams are coming down! Get out of here! His mind froze on the thought as he scrambled on all fours over the slick surface, like a man running in a dream, straining every muscle, yet getting nowhere. He reached the piling, pulled himself past it. *I've made it.... Another couple of feet—*

Something pushed down suddenly against his right ankle, sending a shock of pain up his leg. It held him fast, and he could hear himself screaming out against the pain. Then there was silence for a moment, and something dropped with a belated splash into the edge of the creek, like the period at the end of a paragraph.

Garvin lay with his face down against the wet muck, his fists clenched, his eyes tightly shut, trying to overcome the pain in the ankle. *The leg is broken. The damned beams fell through, and now my leg is broken ...*

"Ray! Ray!"

He raised his head and looked toward the bluff. Reed was hobbling down clumsily, slipping and sliding down the creekbank toward him.

"Ray! Are you all right!"

"I guess I didn't know may own strength," he said, trying to summon a smile. "A regular Samson."

Reed stopped beside him and looked down at the leg. "Can you—can you get your leg out?"

"I don't know." He raised the upper part of his body higher, propping himself on his elbows and turning his head so that he could see the ankle. One of the steel I-beams lay across the ankle, pressing it down into the muck. "I'll try ..." Garvin pulled, but again the pain seared up his leg. He groaned and let the leg to limp.

"The ankle's broken, I'm sure of that."

"I guess you were lucky," Reed said. "Two of the beams missed you."

"Sure, I was real lucky. Now get this thing off me."

Reed looked at him blankly. "Get it *off* you? That's a ten inch beam, Ray. It must weigh four hundred pounds or more. You're damn lucky it didn't cut your leg clean off, falling that far!"

"Will you stop telling me how lucky I am and *do* something?"

Reed shrugged and scratched his head. He knelt beside Garvin's foot and peered closely at the place where the beam lay across the leg. The end of the beam rested against the dock piling. He scratched his head again. "My gosh, Ray, you know this back of mine. No chance of me trying to lift this off you. It's a strain to lift a can of beer."

Garvin knew Lloyd's back, all right. Everybody knew about the back. It was Lloyd's claim to fame, the way he'd gotten it when he was a gunner aboard a B-17 and had to parachute out of the burning plane over the English Channel. It was also Lloyd's only source of steady income, his disability pension.

"I didn't mean to yell at you, Lloyd." He closed his eyes for a moment, trying to think. "Maybe you can dig out beneath the leg and then I can slide out."

"Sure! That ought to work!"

Reed began to dig down beside the ankle with both hands. He touched the leg once and Garvin stiffened.

"Sorry, Ray ..."

He went on digging at the thick muck, Garvin glanced to his right and saw that the skiff was now afloat where he had beached it only minutes before. "The tide's started in," he said. "I've got to get out of here."

"The tide?" Reed paused and moved back on his haunches. He looked at the creek, an odd expression sifting over his face. "Spring tide, too. With this northeaster it'll hit eleven feet—"

"For heaven's sake, Lloyd, will you shut up and get *busy!*"

He bent quickly to his task again, digging silently around the ankle. After a while he stopped. "Ray ..." He cleared his throat nervously. "Ray, there's something under your leg, an old timber or broken piling or something. That beam's got you pinned down against it."

Through the steady throb of pain, Garvin experienced, for the first time, a sudden small spurt of fear. He raised himself on his elbows, then pushed up with his hands until he was standing erect on his knees. The movement had brought with it excruciating pain, but now at least he was that much higher above the level of the water only a few inches to his right.

"What ... what'll we do?" Lloyd said.

If we can't go down, then we've got to come up. "We have to raise the I-beam somehow." He cast his gaze toward the bluff, his mind racing, trying to pick up some glimmer of an idea. Beyond the bluff he saw the top of Lloyd's car. There was power. Now, some way to transmit the power where it was needed ...

He looked up at the broken dock. The decking was gone where the beams had come through, but the side timber atop the piling seemed intact, and the cross beam that rested on it.

"Lloyd, run a rope over that beam. Tie one end to your car and the other we can slip beneath the I-beam. All we need to do is get it up a few inches—"

"Where's any rope?"

"Rope?" Garvin looked around quickly. He reached out to his right and snagged the painter of the skiff. "Here's some rope. It's not too old—"

Reed interrupted again. "That's not more than twenty or thirty feet long, Ray. We'll need at least a hundred to get to the car."

Garvin stared at the rope in his hand. Lloyd was right about it. It was not nearly long enough. He flung it away from him. "What about the car? Haven't you got any in the car?"

Reed shrugged and shook his head.

There was a new coil of half-inch manila in the trunk of Garvin's car, but they hadn't come in his car. No rope on the dock or around the new house. The eighteen foot outboard had a good long nylon anchor line aboard, but it was on its trailer in the garage in town.

He felt something against his knees and looked down. The creek was rising rapidly. An eleven foot tide Reed had said. Eleven feet in six and a half hours. Better than a foot and a half an hour. What is the distance from a man's knees to his nose? Four feet? That meant something like two and a half hours and if he wasn't out from under the steel beam . . .

"Lloyd . . ."

"You thought of something?"

Garvin turned his head and looked into Reed's eyes. "You've got to go for help. A couple of able-bodied men could lift the end of this thing high enough for me to slip my foot out."

Reed got to his feet, nodding. "I guess you're right. Let's see, it's only five or six miles into town. Maybe I can find Tom Forman. He's got a back like an ape. And Julius—"

"Lloyd," Garvin said slowly, rubbing one hand across his forehead. "Lloyd, this ankle hurts like merry hell. The tide is coming in. Will you please *go? Go!*"

"Yeah. Sure." He moved away, starting up the sloping creekbank. Halfway to the bluff he looked around. "I was going to tell you to wait here for me, but that wouldn't have been so funny, would it?" He slapped his shirt pocket quickly. "Hey! You got any cigarettes? Want me to leave mine with you?"

Garvin reached inside the open jacket. The cigarettes were there in the pocket of his shirt, but when he had fallen forward they had been ruined by the muck. "I would like a cigarette before you go."

Reed came back down, gave Garvin the pack and his matches. "I'll be back, Ray. You just . . . well, you just take it easy, huh?"

"I'll be all right."

Reed made his way toward the bluff again, but Garvin called after him. "Lloyd, *you* take it easy. Nobody but you knows I'm stuck here . . ." He stopped, feeling a sudden regret for having said it.

"Check." Reed looked at him for a moment, turned and scrambled up the bluff and disappeared.

The car door slammed, the motor roared to life, and the car pulled away. The sound of it faded very quickly.

For a time silence seemed to descend on him, and then, gradually, as if his senses had been honed razor-sharp, Garvin became aware of the sound of the wind. The lonely restlessness as it moved through the live oaks along the bluff, the sibilant, whispering sound it made in the marsh grass across the creek. A feeling of isolation, of utter solitude and help-lessness, crept like a heavy hand over his heart.

He thought of Lloyd Reed. Given his choice of a man with whom to entrust his life, it occurred to him that Lloyd would have been far down the list. Yet, why did he feel this way? They had grown up together, known each other since earliest memory. Still, his final admonition had instantly brought on an odd sensation, a feeling of distrust. Friendship should be synonymous with trust.

Perhaps that was it. This relation with Lloyd Reed, was it really friendship, or merely an acquaintance of long standing?

He looked down. The water had already risen above his knees. The injured foot was completely covered. He lifted his arm and looked at his watch for the first time. The hands stood at eleven fifteen. Mary would be at church now with her sister Eleanor. Lloyd had been gone ten or fifteen minutes and that meant at least another twenty before he got back.

Somewhere across the creek a marshhen cackled, and another responded downstream toward the river. It would be a good tide for hunting. The water would cover the marsh.

But the familiar sounds of the birds served only to increase this feeling of being utterly alone. Even the mounting pain in the ankle, throbbing with each beat of his pulse, did not take his thoughts off . . . off what?

It was simply a matter of time. In a few minutes Lloyd would be back with help and they would take him to the hospital to have the ankle attended to. He'd have to wear a cast for a while, walk with crutches . . .

He lifted the watch again. The minute hand was straight down. Eleven thirty. Garvin lowered his arm, realizing as he did so that the fingers now touched the water. He cocked his head, listening for some sound above the wind and water.

Nothing.

He turned his face up to the sky. Beneath the high gray overcast of the northeaster a lone gull angled off on the wind, gliding toward some roost to wait out the storm, or until hunger forced him aloft again.

Garvin shifted his weight, trying to bring his good leg up, but stopping as the movement brought a new burst of pain. It couldn't be much longer now. Lloyd had been gone at least half an hour.

He pulled the front of the muck-spattered jacket together and buttoned it against the chill that crept up his body from the water. This was typical of Lloyd, never on time, completely undependable. Lloyd had never married, and seldom held a job over six months. He lived carelessly, worked sloppily, didn't seem to have a care or ambition beyond the present moment.

Damn it! Can't he realize what I'm going through!

Garvin's face grew thoughtful. Was Lloyd really the way he seemed? Or was it a front that had been developed over the years? He recalled an incident that had taken place only a few weeks ago. Lloyd was in the office and Mary had come in. They had just bought this property and were involved in all the plans for the new house.

Garvin remembered how Lloyd sat quietly on the corner of the desk, listening to Mary's excited chatter about materials and colors and landscaping, and Ray's plans for the monorail for the boat.

Lloyd had watched Mary when she left, and after a moment turned around to face Garvin with a strange, lonely look. "You're lucky, Ray. I wonder if you really know how damn lucky you are—a good wife, good business, new house, dough in the bank." He lowered his eyes, picked up a pencil and slowly tapped it on the desktop. "Time gets away from you." When he looked up again there had been something like bitterness in his voice, "I envy you, boy."

But the mood had been ephemeral, and immediately he fell back into character.

"Come on, close the joint up! Everything's perfect for trout this afternoon! They ought to practically jump into the boat!"

Had it been something noted and said on the spur of the moment? Maybe it had been Mary. Lloyd had dated her the last two years they were in high school. Perhaps for a moment he glimpsed that which all men see fleetingly from time to time; what might have been.

Until now, Garvin had thought nothing of it. Again he looked at his watch and saw that Lloyd had been gone forty-five minutes. The creek had risen with surprising rapidity and the water now reached the top of his thighs. What could have happened to him? He could have had a flat, or run out of gas.

There was quite obviously nothing to do but wait, and Garvin tried to occupy his mind with ideas about a new dock.

But by noon, with the water swirling about his hips, he told himself the thing that had crawled slowly up from the depths of his mind. *He is not coming back. Lloyd is going to leave me here to die* . . .

Out in the open it was coldly logical. An opportunity, completely unforeseen and thus completely unplanned, had arisen. With a bit of luck Lloyd could take over Ray Garvin's life, lock, stock, and barrel. He could pick it up where Garvin left off, the way a relay runner takes the baton and moves ahead, taking with him all the advantage that has been built up to that point.

Mary liked him. The fact was, nobody *disliked* Lloyd Reed. But Mary and Lloyd had sort of gone steady in school and it was not at all inconceivable that with Garvin dead the old romance could be slowly rekindled. Mary was not a woman meant to live alone. After a proper interval, with gentle insistence from Lloyd . . .

Garvin suddenly struck the water with his fist. A deadening sense of impotence swept over him. His own survival palled. Somehow he had to leave a warning for Mary, tell her in some way this thing was not wholly an accident.

Yet, could he be wrong? *Had* something happened to Lloyd?

The hands of the watch stood at ten minutes past twelve. The water was at his waist. In less than an hour and a half it wouldn't matter if Lloyd got back with help or not.

He took another cigarette from Lloyd's pack. His hands shook and the pack dropped into the water.

"Damn—"

He watched the pack drift away on the tide, turning in the little swirls made by his own body. He lit the cigarette and threw the rest of the matches after the cigarettes.

Well, this must be it. He took a long, deep drag on the cigarette, watching the wind tear the smoke away as he exhaled. *A last smoke for the condemned man.*

What was Lloyd Reed doing now? Right this minute. Was he somewhere keeping an eye on the time, figuring the rise of the water and waiting? Could he really *do* it?

There were so many things yet to do. Garvin was thirty-six. He had worked hard, made headway, been neither miserly nor wasteful and was within sight of many of his goals. This place, this was one of the big ones.

With all that lay ahead, to be here trapped like an animal, watching the minutes slip past ...

He paused, the cigarette inches from his lips. *Like an animal?* He looked down quickly at the wate swirling about him just below his ribs, and he reached down tentatively, feeling the cold, heavy beam lying across his leg. He straightened again and took the jackknife from his pocket. He looked at the long blade, folded in against the handle. There were animals that would gnaw a leg off if it was caught in a trap. Could a man ... could a man actually *cut off his own foot* ...

Quickly he thrust the knife into the pocket of his jacket, repelled by the thought. There was time yet. He looked at the watch. Twenty minutes before one. But Lloyd had been gone more than an hour and a half. He was not coming back.

If I could see him afterwards, just for a moment, I would know. It would be there in his eyes. Perhaps Mary will see it.

The water climbed his chest. In less than an hour it would be above his chin, he would be straining upward for air, pulling against the trapped leg.

He felt for the knife again. It was the only way. The alternative was death.

He turned his eyes toward the shore, following the line of the bluff in the direction of the house. It stood there, out of sight, beneath the twin oaks near the turn of the creek, with a sweeping view of the broad marshlands and the distant blue of the sea. There would be nights, quiet windless nights, whey you would hear fish jumping in the creek, and the faint faraway thunder of the surf on the bar at the mouth of the sound.

A man with one leg would be able to hear that, see it. A dead man would hear and see nothing.

Suddenly he froze, cocking his head. Was it imagination, or had that been the sound of an engine? Maybe Lloyd *was* coming back after all ...

There it was again! It was a boat, on outboard by the high sound of it.

The sound came on the wind from the river. Only a fool would be fishing in a northeaster, but someone *was* out there.

His impulse was to call out, but the futility was obvious. The boat was upwind, at least a quarter of a mile away. A last wavering sound came on the wind and then it was gone, leaving a deeper void for its having existed at all.

After a while, when he was certain that the boat had gone, he lifted the knife from the water. *Can I do it? Maybe it will be so painful that I will pass out.*

He took the knife in both hands and pulled it open. He let his thumb move along the blade. The blade was sharp. A dull knife was little better than no knife at all.

If I can do it beneath the beam where the bone is broken . . .

There would be blood, quite a lot of it. He thought of the shark he had caught last summer less than a mile from this spot while he had been tarpon fishing. It had been something over eight feet long. Wasn't blood supposed to attract sharks? Maybe they weren't here this time of the year, or maybe the ones here were not man-eaters.

He reached down again and touched the trapped leg. The pain had become a dull throb and the ankle was swollen. The mere contact of his fingertips brought a great stab of pain.

Get on with it! Quit stalling! No one is coming here to help you . . . The tide is not going to wait!

Then he looked around, his eyes went to the dock above him and then to the knife in his hand, and strangely, a slow smile crept over his face. The tide! *The tide!* How could he have overlooked it. The smile broadened and after a moment Garvin began to laugh.

The dark water moved past the dock, swirling and eddying about the pilings, filling the bed of the creek. Gradually, an alien sound emerged above the wind. A car, traveling as fast as the twisting drive would allow, appeared through the trees. Tom Forman sat behind the wheel and beside him, Lloyd Reed, a white bandage wrapped about his head. In the rear of the car were Doc Sanders and Julius Mason.

The car pulled as close to the dock as it could get. The four doors flew open, the men piling out. Reed was the first to reach the dock, and he stopped short, his eyes scanning the creek. There was nothing, only the broken dock and the water.

We're too late! I knew it!"

"Where was he?" Forman said.

"Down there." He pointed. "See where the planking's smashed, that's where the steel beams went through. It was terrible. Ray was just underneath . . ."

"Hey!" a voice called.

The four men turned toward the sound. Ray Garvin sat below them at the edge of the creek bank, his back propped against the bluff. The jackknife was in his hand and the muck-smeared jacket lying over the lower portion of his legs.

"What took you so long, Lloyd?" he said.

"You're ... you're *alive* ...?" Reed's voice was little more than a hoarse whisper. He stared down at Garvin and his eyes moved to the jacket. "How ... how did you—"

"I asked you, Lloyd. What took so long?" Garvin said.

Doc Sanders moved to the edge of the bluff. "He said you were pinned under a steel beam, Ray. Somebody come along and help you out?"

"Nobody helped me out. I want to know what happened to Lloyd."

"I—I got to hurrying, Ray ... The car went off the road, smacked into a pine tree." He reached up quickly and touched the bandage. "Knocked me out. I was out for I don't know how long ..."

"I know how long. About three hours. You watch the time pretty closely when you're in the situation I was in. It'd surprise you just how fast the tide comes in when you don't want it do. You do a lot of thinking, you wonder how you're going to feel when the water starts lapping under your nose."

The doctor made his way down the bluff. When he reached Garvin he knelt by his side. "Let me take a look at that leg." He started to lift the jacket.

"Wait a minute, doc," Garvin said.

"But if it's broken—"

"In a minute." Garvin's eyes were on Lloyd Reed. "You think of all sorts of things. And while I was thinking, I thought of this." He held up the jackknife, the blade open and glinting dully. "I remembered stories of how some animals will chew off a leg that's caught in a trap."

Reed's mouth dropped open. He raised one hand, pointing toward the covered legs. "You mean ..." His eyes blinked rapidly, he swallowed. "You ... *you cut your foot off* ..."

The other men stared. Garvin folded the knife slowly. "I thought about it for a long time. I waited for somebody to come. I prayed. And all the time the water kept coming up. It reached my waist, my ribs, chest. I had to hold my arms up to keep them out of the water."

The doctor reached for the jacket. "You better let me see that, Ray—"

He pushed the doctor's hand aside, and went on. "I figured the bone was pretty well broken, so there'd be no problem with that. I wondered about the pain, and whether I could stay conscious while I was doing it—"

"*Oh my God* ..." Reed murmured.

Garvin smiled, folded the knife and pushed it into his pants pocket. "And then I thought about something else, something so simple that it made me laugh."

"What the devil *was* it?" Mason said.

"The skiff, it was tied up right beside me."

"It's not there now."

"It drifted around the bend a while ago."

"But how did—"

"It was tied up on the dock, but with the jackknife I reached as far up the line as I could and cut it."

The corners of Doc Sanders' eyes crinkled and he nodded. "You tied it to the beam, and when the tide rose, the skiff rose with it."

"And it ... it lifted the beam off you?" said Forman.

The doctor reached down and picked up the jakcet. Both feet were there, the right one bent over at an odd angle. "Get my bag out of the car, Tom," he said. "And one of you drive to a phone and get an ambulance." He looked at Garvin. "I think we'd better take you out of here on a stretcher, Ray."

"Sure, doc."

The black medical bag was brought down to the doctor. Garvin continued to look at Lloyd Reed. It was there in his eyes, the guilt. There was no disguising it.

The doctor held a syringe in his hand. He wiped a place on Garvin's arm and pushed the needle in.

"That'll ease the pain."

Garvin nodded absently. "Lloyd?"

"Ray ... I ..." His gaze wavered, his face grew pale.

What good was an accusation? The wound on Reed's head would be real enough, it would have to be, for without it there would be doubt in the minds of the others.

But the two of them knew what had happened.

"Lloyd ..." *Let me live with it.* "The cigarettes got wet, Lloyd. Got any more?" *Let him live with it. If he can ...*

Richard Deming

Number One Suspect

The new bread man asked, "How many loaves do you usually take, Mr. Jones?"

Before Henry Jones could reply, his fat wife bustled from the rear of the grocery store and said, "Another new man on the bread truck? What's the matter with your company, they can't keep a man on this route?"

"He asked for a transfer," the bread man said. He turned back to Jones. "How many did you say, Mr. Jones?"

Hazel Jones said testily, "I do the ordering around here, mister. Henry, go mark those soup cans like I told you. How many times I got to tell you to do something before it gets done?" Returning her attention to the bread man, she said, "Two dozen. And be sure you take the old ones out. Don't let me catch you putting the stale ones on top, and don't try giving me stale loaves you took out of some other store. You hear?"

"Yes, ma'am," the bread man said in a pained voice.

Picking the four remaining loaves of yesterday's bread from the bakery shelf, the man carried them out to his truck. At a glare from his wife, Henry Jones scurried over to the canned goods section, picked up a stamp pad and price stamp, and began stamping price marks on soup cans.

Delivery men all asked for transfers to some other route after a month or two of dealing with his virago of a wife, Henry thought. It was too bad husbands couldn't ask for transfers. Twenty years of being treated like a stockboy, doing all the menial work, while Hazel strutted importantly around giving orders. If she actually did something, it wouldn't be so bad, he thought. But she wouldn't even wait on customers. She was the executive type, good only for telling other people what to do.

If she only knew what was in store for her tonight, he thought with grim satisfaction, viciously slamming the ink stamp onto the top of a can. It would shock her speechless to realize even the lowest worm can turn.

The bread man returned carrying a double armload of loaves. He stacked them on the empty shelf to the accompaniment of a steady tirade of criticism of the bakery's service, the quality of its product, and its unreasonable prices. When he finished, he silently handed Hazel the slip to sign and went out without saying goodbye.

He would be asking for a different route in a week, Henry thought. Then he paused with the stamp upraised and mentally corrected himself. The man wouldn't ask for a transfer at all, because after today he wouldn't ever have to deal with Hazal again.

Behind him Hazel's rasping voice said, "You posing for a statue, bonehead? Hurry up and get that marking done. We need soap powder from the stockroom."

With a spastic movement Henry brought the stamp down on the can it was poised over.

Henry Jones was a mild looking little man in his late forties with a slight paunch and a fringe of sparse hair about his ears. The eyes behind his rimless glassess always seemed to be faintly apologetic, as though he were constantly asking the world's pardon for existing. He looked as little like a potential murderer as it is possible to look, and knew it. He considered this his best defense, for he had read enough true crime stories to know the husband is always automatically a suspect when a wife is murdered, even when all clues point to someone else.

All clues *would* point to someone else in this case. And he banked on his widespread reputation for softheartedness as insurance against the police giving him more than cursory consideration. He could visualize the neighbors and customers scoffing at police questions. "Henry Jones?" they would say in unison. "Why, Henry wouldn't swat a mosquito he caught in the act of biting him."

The neatest thing about it was that the police would find no one anywhere to negate the neighborhood picture of him as a softhearted man, because he really was one. With the exception of human beings, there wasn't a living thing Henry could have brought himself to hurt. Up to now there had never been an occasion when it was necessary for him to express his poor opinion of the human race. Even now he wouldn't have dreamed of harming Hazel if there were any other solution. But he had exhausted all alternate plans. He suspected that if he suggested divorce, Hazel would kill *him*. Running away and changing his identity meant losing his beloved store. The only other alternative, that of continuing to put up with her domineering after twenty years of subservence, was unthinkable. Henry had had it.

It was to be that night.

Jones' Grocery Store stayed open until nine nightly six days a week in order to compete with the chain stores, which closed at six. The routine at closing time was always the same. Henry would follow the last customer to the door and lock it after him in deference to Hazel's chronic fear of holdup men. Then, as Hazel counted the money and, in this case, a Saturday night, bagged the week's receipts in a night-deposit bag, Henry covered vegetables and, if it didn't look like rain, carried the trash can out to empty into the burner, so that it would be ready for a match in the morning.

Tonight Henry deliberately departed from routine. When the last customer, Mrs. Hoffman from up the street, left the store, he pretended to be busy rearrranging the contents of a shelf until she was out of sight. This was important to his plan because he couldn't afford to have the last customer testify that he had locked the door behind her.

Hazel called, "What's the matter, you don't lock the door, bonehead? You want some holdup man to walk in while we're all alone and take our money?"

"Sorry," Henry muttered. Hurrying over, he locked the door and dropped the keys in his pocket.

A moment later he departed from routine again by starting out back with the trash can before covering the vegetables.

"You in a trance or something?" Hazel yelled after him. "You never covered the vegetables."

Henry didn't have time to cover the vegetable bins. The chore usually took a good ten minutes, and he wanted to act as soon after Mrs. Hoffman's departure as feasible.

He said in an apologetic tone, "As soon as I come back in, Hazel. It doesn't make any difference which I do first, so long as it gets done, does it?"

"Well, just don't forget," Hazel said irritably.

Just outside the back door Henry set down the trash can and opened the lid of one of a number of cardboard boxes piled against the rear of the store. Groping inside, he drew out the nickel-plated hammerless revolver he had bought in a pawnshop six months before and thrust it into his belt under his apron. He reached inside again and drew out a small pinch bar. He picked up the trash can, one hand holding both a side of the can and the pinch bar, and carried it to the incinerator near the back fence at a rapid trot. Quickly dumping it, he set down the can, pushed open the rear gate, and stepped into the alley.

The only light back here came from a green-shaded bulb over the store's rear door, which cast a circle of light on the ground only about fifteen feet across. The reflected glow from this was just enough to make for bare visibility in the alley. It was sufficient for Henry to make out the broad metal disk embedded in the alley's center.

Kneeling, he used the pinch bar to pry up one side of the manhole cover. Getting his fingers under it, be dragged it partially off the manhole, just enough to leave an opening about six inches wide. He dropped the pinch bar through the hole and, after a moment, heard a satisfying splash some distance below.

Uttering a silent prayer that no automobile would drive up the alley during the next few minutes and wreck both itself and his plans by dropping a wheel into the manhole, he pushed back through the gate, picked up the trash can, and hurried back into the store.

As he set the can down in its accustomed place, Hazel said, "You took long enough. You been walking around in a daze all day."

She had finished bagging the money and the night-deposit bag lay next to the register. Glancing through the front windows at the street, Henry saw that no one was in sight.

"Did any customers try to get in while I was outside?" he inquired, and held his breath for the answer. If some late-arriving customer had tried the locked door, all plans would have to be put off for tonight. He couldn't afford having a possible witness who could testify that Hazel had still been alive after the door was locked.

"You crazy?" Hazel said. "Everybody knows we close at nine."

Henry went over to the door, took the keys from his pocket, and unlocked it. He pocketed the keys again.

"You in your second childhood?" Hazel yelled at him. "You think it's morning, we should be opening up already?"

Henry made no reply. Walking toward her until only the counter separated them, he drew the nickel-plated gun from under his apron. Hazel's eyes widened in shocked disbelief when he pointed it at her.

Henry shot her in the chest three times.

Hazel's body had hardly hit the floor when he was racing behind the counter. Thrusting the nickel-plated gun into his hip pocket, he jerked open the drawer in the counter immediately beneath the cash register and drew out a blue-steel .38 revolver. Kneeling, he grasped the dead woman's right wrist, placed the gun in her hand, and curled her fingers around the stock. Then he pulled it from her hand again, closed his own fingers around the butt, and rose to his feet. The whole operation took no more than thirty seconds.

A glance through the front windows told him the street was still deserted. But he knew it wouldn't be within thirty more seconds. In this quiet neighborhood the blast of pistol shots would bring curious neighbors to investigate from all directions.

Sweeping the night-deposit bag into his left hand, Henry sped for the rear door and outside. He made the back gate at a dead run, slammed through it, and stooped over the manhole. The night-deposit bag went in first, then the nickel-plated gun. With his heel he pushed the manhole cover back into place.

Straightening, he aimed the blue-barreled pistol down the alley in the direction of the street and fired two spaced shots. Then he turned and slowly plodded back inside.

When he re-entered the store, elderly Tom Bower, who lived in one of the apartments next door, was leaning over the counter staring down in horror at Hazel. Mrs. Caskin, from the apartment house on the other side of the store, was just coming in. Behind her other neighbors were converging from all directions.

Henry said in a deliberately dull voice, "I think I hit him, but he got away."

Bower gulped and looked at the gun in Henry's hand.

Seeing that the old man hadn't comprehended what he said, Henry made it clearer. By now Mrs. Caskin and several other neighbors were in the store, and he spoke for their collective benefit.

"It was a holdup man, Mr. Bower. I forgot to lock the front door and he got in while I was out back emptying the trash. When I came back in, he was pointing a gun at Hazel. He turned to cover me and ordered me behind the counter with Hazel. When he turned his head, Hazel jerked open the drawer beneath the register, where we keep a gun." He held up the gun in his hand. "This one. When she pulled it out, he shot her. Then he picked up the money bag and ran out the back way. Hazel had dropped the gun on the floor. I grabbed it up and chased him. I shot at him twice while he was running down the alley, and I think the second shot hit him because he staggered. But he kept running and disappeared around the corner toward Grand Avenue."

A dozen people had crowded into the store by the time he finished the explanation. Those who had arrived too late to catch the first part of it asked earlier arrivals what it was all about. The babble of low-toned voices kept increasing as the first to arrive repeated the story and it was relayed on to others still coming in.

Mrs. Caskin moved behind the counter and knelt over Hazel. Rising, she said in an awed voice, "I think she's dead."

Setting his pistol on the counter, Henry leaned over to look down at Hazel. Then he let his shoulders slump and buried his face in his hands.

There was a moment of silence before someone said awkwardly, "Maybe we better call a doctor. And the police."

One of the neighbors went after old Doc Mauser, who was only a block away over on Eichelberger. The doctor got there at the same time a one-man radio car arrived with a uniformed officer driving it. There was nothing Dr. Mauser could do for Hazel, except pronounce her dead, so he turned his attention to the bereaved widower. Henry had managed to work up a pretty convincing state of shock, only half simulated. The doctor gave him a tranquilizer.

By the time Henry had swallowed his tranquilizer, the uniformed policeman had managed to sort out the simultaneous explanations thrown at him by a dozen neighbors. He asked Henry for a description of the bandit. This was easy because Henry had been memorizing a description for months.

"He was big," Henry said in a low, grief-crushed voice. "Six one, I'd say, and maybe two hundred pounds. I'd guess he was around thirty-five years old. He was wearing a brown felt hat, a tan jacket, and brown slacks. He had a swarthy complexion, a big, hooked nose, dark hair, and there was something wrong with his left eye. The lid drooped lower than the right one. There was a black mole on his right cheek with hair growing out of it and a red scar running from his left ear clear down to the corner of his mouth. It made that side of his mouth kind of pucker up."

The policeman looked impressed by this detailed description. He went out to his car to call it in over his radio and have a dragnet thrown around the area.

When he returned, he contented himself with making a list of everyone present, including the corpse. He didn't ask Henry anything else, seeming to feel that in his upset state it was better to leave the principal witness to the experienced hands of the homicide squad.

A Sergeant Harry Newton from Homicide showed up about a quarter of ten. He was a stolid, square-faced man of middle age with deceptively sleepy eyes which never missed a thing. He had with him a thin, lanky man in civilian clothes who carried a laboratory kit and a flash camera. Sergeant Newton addressed the man as Mac, and Henry got the impression he was a civilian employee of the police lab.

Meantime an ambulance had arrived and was standing by to take Hazel to the morgue when the homicide officer released her body.

Sergeant Newton first listened to the uniformed officer's account of what had happened. After a bare glance at Henry, now seated in a chair someone had thoughtfully brought from the back room, he turned to Dr. Mauser.

"What's the dope, doc?" he inquired.

"There's almost no bleeding, sergeant, so she must have died instantly. Any of the three bullets could have done it. All three hit her directly in the heart."

The sergeant glanced around. "Any of you people know anything you haven't told the officer here?"

When no one said anything, he asked, "Which one of you was first one the scene?"

"I was," old Tom Bower told him.

"Okay," the sergeant said. "What's your story?"

Bower explained that he lived in a downstairs apartment next door and had been sitting in his front room, which had its windows open because of the warmth of the night. He said that when he heard the shots, he knew instantly they were gunshots and not merely backfires.

"How come?" Newton asked.

"Well, they sounded like they came from inside. I don't know how I knew, because the way they sounded, you couldn't tell what direction they came from. But I was sure they came from over here. Right away I thought of a holdup and I came running."

The sergeant thoughtfully tugged at an earlobe. "Why'd you think of a holdup?"

"Mrs. Jones was always afraid the store would be held up some night. Lots of times when I was the last customer out, she'd yell for Henry to lock the front door when I was only halfway to it. If he didn't move sharp, she'd make some crack like did he want a holdup man to walk in on them alone and take their money. I knew she kept that gun in the drawer under the register, and what I really thought was that she'd blasted some bandit. Didn't even occur to me he'd blasted her. If it had, I wouldn't of been in such a hurry to get over here."

Sergeant Newton emitted a noncommittal grunt.

"The front door was unlocked when I got here," Bower continued. "I couldn't see anybody inside, so I come on in. When I got to the counter,

I seen Mrs. Jones lying on the floor behind it. About then a couple more shots sounded out back and a minute later Henry come in by the back door with a gun in his hand. He told me what happened."

The sergeant looked around at the circle of faces, but no one had any further details to offer. To his general inquiry as to what time the shots had been heard, the consensus was that the first three had sounded about five after nine, the ones in the alley only about a minute later.

"You got all these people's names and addresses?" Newton asked the man in uniform.

"Sure, sarge."

"Then all of you please clear out of here," the homicide officer directed "Give us some room to work. You can leave too, doc."

Reluctantly the assemblage drifted outside. But no one, with the sole exception of Dr. Mauser, went home. The rest stood on the sidewalk watching the goings on inside through the front windows.

At Sergeant Newton's direction the thin man named Mac snapped pictures of the corpse from several angles. Then Newton told him to dust the gun for prints.

All this time Henry had been sitting dully in his chair, apparently paying little attention to what was going on around him. Now he roused himself.

"Why do you want to check that gun for fingerprints?" he inquired. "It isn't the one the holdup man used. That's ours—the one Hazel kept in the drawer."

"Just covering all bets," the sergeant said laconically.

After carefully dusting the gun with a silver-colored powder, the lab man used inch-wide Scotch tape to lift the fingerprints which appeared. When he had fixed the tape to some white cards, he had a permanent record of the prints.

"Take his prints," Newton said, pointing at Henry. "Then the dead woman's."

Laying an ink pad on the counter, the lab man motioned Henry over. Henry put a puzzled expression on his face, but he made no objection. Docilely he allowed his fingers one at a time to be rolled over the pad, then gently rolled over a white card.

When the process was completed, Sergeant Newton asked, "Got any place to wash up here?"

"Upstairs," Henry said. "Our apartment is right over the store."

The sergeant permitted him to go upstairs to wash the ink from his hands while Hazel was being fingerprinted. When he returned, the lab man was comparing the two sets of prints with the ones he had lifted from the gun.

"Checks out," he said to the homicide officer. "A clear set of his superimposed over hers. Hers are mostly smudged, but a couple partials are good enough for comparison purposes."

Henry was thankful that he had taken the precaution of closing

Hazel's hand around the pistol grip. While he hadn't been sure the gun would even be checked for fingerprints, he had read enough not to want to risk the lack of Hazel's prints on the stock.

Sergeant Newton said, "Stick that gun in your kit to take back to ballistics, Mac." Then he said to the man in uniform, "Tell those guys out front they can have the body now."

As the policeman went out to relay this message to the ambulance attendants, Newton finally turned his attention to Henry.

For the next twenty minutes Henry repeated his story, answered questions, re-described the bandit and, finally, went out back with the sergeant to show him exactly where he had been standing when he fired at the fleeing robber and just where the man had been when he staggered as though hit.

Back inside again Henry noted that Hazel's body was now gone and that the ambulance was missing from in front. The crowd on the sidewalk still lingered, however.

Sergeant Newton asked, "How much money did he get?"

"The duplicate deposit slip should be in the register," Henry said. "It was quite a lot because it was a full week's receipts. We make a night deposit on Saturday night, you see, so that money isn't lying around over the weekend. Do you think he may have been watching the place for some time, and knew the most money would be here on Saturday night?"

"He probably had the job cased," Newton agreed.

Walking behind the counter, carefully avoiding stepping where Hazel's body had lain, Henry opened the register and lifted out the duplicate slip Hazel had left there. He winced slightly when he saw the total. It was a lot of money to have thrown down a hole, but he hadn't dared risk hiding it somewhere. He had decided in advance to leave no loose ends whatever lying around for him to trip over accidentally. It was this planning which had made him pick Saturday night for the crime, despite the cost involved. Having a logical mind himself, it had seemed to him more plausible for a professional holdup man to strike at a time when the take would be greatest.

"Fourteen hundred and twenty-eigth dollars and seventeen cents," he said in a low voice. "Let's see. There's three—almost four hundred in checks, which I suppose I can get people to stop payment on. But it's still over a thousand in cash."

"Describe the bag."

"It was a regular night-deposit bag," Henry said. "With SECURITY NATIONAL stamped on its side. The keys to the bag and the night vault must be in Hazel's pocket. I always drove her over and waited in the car while she made the deposit."

Sergeant Newton was silent for a moment, apparently going over all the testimony in his mind and mentally checking to see if there were any questions he had missed. Presently he glanced about the store.

"Where's the empty trash can you were carrying when you came in from out back?" he inquired.

Henry pointed to where it stood against the wall over by the meat counter.

Newton's sleepy-looking eyes dropped half shut. "How'd it get way over there? That's halfway across the store from the back door and also from the register. When he ordered you behind the counter with your wife, did you carry the trash can clear over there first?"

Henry's stomach gave a lurch. Thinking furiously, he said, "I—I guess I just reacted automatically. For so many years I've been carrying that empty can in the back door and setting it down in the same place, I went right ahead and carried it over where it belonged when he pointed the gun at me and told me to put it down. That's when Hazel made her break. He had to turn half away from her in order to keep me covered."

This explanation seemed to satisfy the sergeant, for he didn't pursue the matter. Turning to the uniformed policeman, who was still standing by, he said, "Get on your radio and find out if the dragnet has pulled anything in. If it hasn't, have a half dozen officers report to me here. I want that alley scoured for the two bullets Mr. Jones fired."

He returned his attention to Henry. "I guess that's all we can do here tonight, Mr. Jones. As soon as my assistants get here and I set them to work, you can lock up and we'll go down to headquarters."

"Headquarters?" Henry repeated, his stomach lurching again. "What for?"

"Want you to look at some pictures," the sergeant said mildly.

Relief flooded over Henry. For one terrible moment he had thought he was under arrest.

It was well past midnight before Henry got back from downtown. In the interim he had looked at hundreds of mug shots of men with records of armed robbery. He had identified none, of course. To make it look good, though, he had hesitated over one or two before finally moving his head in definite negatives.

Sergeant Newton drove him home and told him he would get in touch with him as soon as there were any developments.

On Sunday Henry phoned a funeral director to make arrangements for Hazel's interment. When he explained the circumstances of his wife's death and that her body was presently at the city morgue, the mortician told him that a date couldn't be set until they learned when the morgue planned to release the body. He told Henry not to worry about it, however, as he would contact the morgue himself and let Henry know.

In the middle of the night it started to rain. When Henry arose Monday morning it was coming down in such solid sheets, he could barely see the other side of the street from his front room windows. A river of water gushed along the gutter out front, piling up at the intersection to form a small lake because the curb sewer slots there couldn't drain off fast enough.

Just as Henry finished breakfast Sergeant Harry Newton dropped in. The detective wore a raincoat and rubbers, but they hadn't been adequate protection against the deluge. When he shed his rubbers and raincoat in the upstairs hall, the lower legs of his trousers were soaked through and his shoes sloshed when he walked.

"Want to dry your trousers and shoes over the kitchen range?" Henry asked solicitously. "I'll lend you a robe while they're drying."

The homicide officer shook his head. "They'd only get wet again when I went back outside. This is going to last all day."

Sloshing into the front room, he carefully seated himself on the sofa so that the damp lower part of his trousers didn't touch the upholstery.

At first it appeared to Henry that the only purpose of the man's visit was to brief him on developments. He told Henry that the three bullets recovered from Hazel's body were all good enough specimens so that ballistics would readily be able to identify the murder weapon if it ever turned up. He added casually that they hadn't been fired from the gun Henry had used, and weren't even the same caliber, as the murder weapon had been a .32 instead of a .38.

"We recovered one of the bullets you fired from a telegraph pole in the alley," the sergeant went on. "We couldn't find the other, so maybe you did wing the guy. We've issued his description to all area doctors, in case he tries to get a wound patched up. I spent yesterday talking to a lot of your neighbors."

"Oh?" Henry said, a trifle confused by the abrupt switch of subject.

"Uh-huh. Seems to be general knowledge that your wife was kind of a shrew. Always on your back. Nobody thinks you'll grieve over her very long."

Flushing, Henry said nothing.

"On the other hand, everybody says you're the most softhearted guy in the world, that you wouldn't even set a trap for a mouse. Let alone kill a human."

Henry felt his stomach turn over. In a faint voice he said, "You mean—you mean—" and couldn't get any more out.

"I mean we haven't swallowed your story whole," Newton finished for him. "Not that you're under more than routine suspicion. We always automatically suspect the husband when a wife is murdered."

"But in a case like this!" Henry protested.

"It wouldn't be the first time a guy rigged a robbery to cover uxoricide. That's wife-murder, in case you don't know the word. We haven't got any concrete evidence that you did, but there are a couple of angles we don't like."

"What?" Henry managed.

"One is your description of the bandit. You must have a photographic mind, it's so complete. I'm not saying you made him up. All I'm saying is you might have. It's the sort of description an amateur murderer might dream up, thinking the more complete it was, the more convincing it would be. Another thing is the location of that trash basket. Maybe things happened like you say, but it's hard to imagine a bandit letting you walk clear across the store like that. Seems more likely he would have ordered you to drop it right where you were and get behind the counter with your wife."

"It's the way it happened," Henry insisted, sweating.

"We can't prove it didn't, Mr. Jones. The thing I have most trouble swallowing is your chasing the guy and shooting at him. Doesn't seem in character for a mild guy like you."

Henry said faintly, "He'd—he'd just shot my wife. I guess I saw red."

"Maybe," the sergeant conceded. "People do odd things under stress. But I have to ask you this question, because it's part of our routine. Did you kill your wife and rig this robbery?"

"Of course not," Henry said with forced indignation.

"Well, if you did, you'll probably get away with it," Newton said.

"Henry stared at the man in fascination. The homicide officer stared back at him speculatively.

"Why do you say that?" Henry finally got out.

"What can we prove? You've got a pretty good story. And if it was rigged, you did a thorough job. Even down to such details as your wife's prints being on that gun under yours. I imagine you'd be smart enough to dispose of the other gun and money bag so we'd never find them. We looked, of course. We sifted every ashpit, garbage can, and trash can in that alley. If you did kill her, we'd never prove it in a million years, unless we got a confession."

As Henry stared at him numbly, Sergeant Newton said, "This is just routine suspicion, of course. It doesn't mean I think you killed her. It just means I think you might have. I hope I haven't upset you. As I said before, we always consider the husband as a possibility."

With that he rose, bid Henry a laconic goodbye, and sloshed out into the hall to put back on his dripping raincoat and useless rubbers. It was a half hour after he left before Henry stopped shaking.

During the next two nights he had trouble sleeping. Partly this was because the rain continued to come down in torrents and its steady beating on the roof disturbed him. But mostly it was because he kept visualizing being dragged down to headquarters and questioned for hours on end with a white light in his face. He wondered if the local police employed rubber hoses to make suspects talk.

But when he heard nothing further from Sergeant Newton, his alarm gradually subsided. It *had* been just routine suspicion, he decided, and the sergeant merely had an unsettling way of expressing himself.

For several reasons Henry didn't open the store during this time. For one thing he felt a period of mourning would be expected of him. For another, funeral arrangements and the funeral itself took up so much time. For a third, there would have been little business anyway because the torrential rain kept everyone indoors except those who had vital errands.

Fortunately Henry's basement was so well sealed he only got dribbles of water in it. But according to news reports, many basements were flooded to the rafters. The city streets became shallow rivers, with water reaching to the hubcaps of the few automobiles whose drivers were brave enough to venture onto them. The mayor declared a state of emergency and business came to a virtual standstill as the city waited for the downpour to stop.

It stopped abruptly on Wednesday morning and the sun came out hot and bright. By noon the overtaxed sewers had drained away the surface water and the streets were steaming moisture.

Hazel's funeral had been tentatively scheduled for Wednesday afternoon, depending on the weather. With the streets now unflooded, it took place as scheduled. Henry managed to look appropriately sad during the service.

By Thursday morning the sun had backed the streets dry and the only evidence of the fifty-five-hour deluge was a few rapidly evaporating puddles on lawns where there were low spots. Henry engaged young Thad Bower, Tom Bower's grandson, to help out as a combination clerk and stockboy, and opened for business.

He still heard nothing more from the police.

Friday morning, when Henry went out back to set a match to the trash deposited in the incinerator the night before, he found a truck marked DEPARTMENT OF STREETS AND SEWERS parked in the alley. A tall, lean man wearing hip boots and a cap with a miner's lamp on it was prying up the manhole cover with a crowbar. A stolid, middle-aged man in a rumpled brown suit stood watching him. Henry's heart began to thump when he recognized the latter as Sergeant Harry Newton.

Henry forgot the incinerator. Pushing open the gate, he stepped into the alley.

The homicide officer glanced at him with sleepy eyes. "Morning," he said in an unnaturally husky voice.

Henry said, "What—what's going on?"

Sergeant Newton drew out a handkerchief and blew his nose. "Had a cold all week," he said hoarsely. "Guess I should have dried out my shoes like you suggested. Just making a routine check."

"On what?"

The sergeant blew his nose again, put the handkerchief away. "Fellow named Lischer came in to make a report last night. Seems he drove up this alley the night your wife was killed. His headlights hit this manhole just in time to save him from running a wheel into it. He says it was partway open. He managed to swerve enough to straddle it, and he drove on with his heart in his mouth. He only lives over on Delor, a couple of blocks from here. He was pulling into his garage when it occurred to him he should have stopped and shoved the cover back in place so nobody else would wreck a car. So he backed out again and drove back here. He says he was back within ten minutes, but by then somebody had replaced the cover. He figures he arrived the second time about a quarter after nine. He didn't hear any shots either time he drove through the alley, so all the shooting must have taken place between his two trips. He drove back home and forgot about it until he read about the robbery-murder."

Henry didn't say anything. He was watching the man in hip boots, who now had the cover off and was placing a circular metal guard rail around the open hole. When this was in place, the man drew a garden rake from the rear of the truck and descended into the hole.

Sergeant Newton said, "When Lischer read about the murder, he got to thinking about the open manhole and wondered if there was any connection. He wasn't sure your store was in the same block as the manhole, so he decided to drive over and take a look before saying anything. But the rain kept him indoors the first part of the week. Like a lot of people, he didn't even make it to work. And Wednesday he just didn't get around to it. On his way home from work yesterday he drove past your store, then around into the alley. When he saw the manhole was directly behind your place, he came in and told us about it."

Henry swallowed a couple of times before managing, "What do you suppose it means, sergeant?"

The homicide officer shrugged. "With all the water that's been rushing through the sewers since that night, anything dropped down there has probably been washed for blocks. There's twenty blocks of sewer pipe between here and the River Des Peres. But there's also ten manholes. A Department of Streets and Sewers worker is climbing into each of those holes with a rake right now. Whatever's down there, we'll find."

Henry felt ill. He said, "I'd better get back to the store. I've got a brand new clerk I don't like to leave alone."

He pushed back through the gate, forgetting to set a match to the trash as he passed the incinerator. Inside he collapsed into a chair in the back room and stared helplessly into space.

Ten minutes later young Thad Bower came back hunting for him to ask the price of potatoes. Rousing himself, Henry accompanied the boy out front and took over the waiting-on of the customer himself.

For the rest of the morning Henry functioned automatically, his lips smiling at customers but his insides churning. Every time there was a lull in business, he went to the back room to glance out at the alley. The city truck was still parked there.

At noon Henry sent his new clerk home to lunch. Ten minutes later Sergeant Harry Newton came in the back door. Henry's heart rose to his throat when he saw what the sergeant carried. In one hand he held a small pinch bar, in the other a nickel-plated revolver with spots of rust on it.

"We found this a block away," the homicide officer said, hefting the pinch bar. "The gun was two blocks away. They could both have been dropped through the manhole out back and carried that far by the rushing water."

Henry gulped.

"The other guys didn't find a thing," the sergeant said. "Or at least nothing we can connect to the robbery. They turned up a lot of miscellaneous junk ranging from flashlight batteries to a set of tire chains. I was hoping we'd find that night-deposit bag, but it must have washed clear to the river."

"Why did you expect that to be in the sewer?" Henry asked in a squeaky voice.

"Seems obvious what happened," the sergeant said. "Or at least two alternatives are obvious. The first is that the bandit opened the manhole just before he pulled the job, so that he'd have a place to dump the bag after removing the money. He'd know about the bag, if he had the job properly cased, and he'd want to get rid of incriminating evidence as soon as possible. After using the gun, he'd want to get rid of that, too. So it could be that when he ran out back, he cut open the bag with a pocket knife—he'd have to cut it because it was locked and the keys were in your wife's pocket—took out the money and dumped the bag and checks down the sewer along with the gun. He'd have time to do that and kick the cover back in place while you were scrambling around for the gun your wife dropped. Maybe that's what delayed him enough for you to get a couple of shots at him. If we had found the cut bag, it would tend to support that alternative."

"I see," Henry said, afraid to ask what the other alternative was.

Sergeant Newton told him anyway. "Then it could be that there never was a bandit, that you rigged the whole thing and dropped the murder weapon and the bag down the hole yourself. If we'd found the bag uncut and with the money still in it, we'd know you rigged it."

Henry managed to ask in a relatively steady voice, "Which do you think happened?"

The sergeant shrugged. "Without the bag showing, it could be either way. This may not even be the murder weapon, of course. But if ballistics says it is, we can probably trace the gun."

"How?" Henry asked, relatively secure on that point because he had given the pawnbroker a fake name when he purchased the gun six months before.

"We'll send the serial number to the manufacturer and get its original retail outlet. The outlet will have the name of the original purchaser recorded, and we'll let him explain what he did with it. We've traced guns through a half dozen different owners that way. We won't even have to go to all that trouble if it turns out the gun was bought in some local pawnshop."

"Oh? Why not?"

"It'll be registered at headquarters. A city ordinance requires pawnbrokers to report the purchase and sale of all small arms."

Henry's feeling of security began to evaporate.

"If the gun came from a pawnbroker, it will be a snap," the sergeant went on. "Even if it was bought under an assumed name. Pawnbrokers have a remarkable memory for faces. Particularly for the faces of gun buyers, because they get questioned about them so often. We'll give him a description of the bandit and show you to him. He should be able to tell us which of you bought it."

Henry was unable to make any comment whatever. He just stood there numbly.

Sergeant Newton didn't appear to notice Henry's reaction. With a final remark that he would keep Henry informed of any developments, he left by the same way he had entered.

When the back door closed, Henry started doing some furious thinking. Fortunately no customers came in during the next few minutes, so he was able to devote his full attention to the problem. The solution came to him quite suddenly.

The police still had possession of the .38 revolver which Hazel had kept in the drawer beneath the cash register, but there was still a box of .38 caliber shells in the drawer. Henry pocketed six.

When Thad Bower returned from lunch at one P.M., Henry announced that he would now take his lunch break, added that he planned to take a brief nap after eating, and requested the boy not to disturb him during the next hour.

"If you don't know the price of something, make a guess," he said. "Don't be running upstairs to wake me every five minutes."

"Yes, sir," the boy said. "I'll manage all right."

Henry went up the front stairs, walked through the apartment and quietly descended the back stairs. He eased his car from the garage into the alley and let it roll backward to the side street.

Twenty minutes later he parked in front of a pawnshop on Franklin Avenue.

It was a little cubbyhole of a place, and no one was in it but the same bent and wizened old man who had sold him the .32 six months before.

When Henry asked, "Do you have any .38 caliber handguns?" the old man peered at him with a flicker of recognition.

"Didn't you buy a gun here once before?" he asked.

The question dispelled any doubts Henry may have had about what had to be done. It was also reassuring to his conscience that the man was so old and looked vaguely ill. He told himself that it would be a blessing to the old man to be put out of his misery.

"I was in a few months back," Henry said in a steady voice.

The pawnbroker unlocked a case beneath the counter and brought out a .38 police special. Handing it to Henry, he said, "Here's a fine buy. Hardly been fired and not a spot of rust on it."

Breaking open the cylinder, Henry peered down the barrel. Then he drew the six shells from his pocket and thumbed them into the cylinder one at a time, keeping his eyes fixed on the old man as he performed the operation. The pawnbroker's expression grew increasingly worried. He started to open his mouth, then closed it again when Henry clicked the cylinder back into place and pointed the gun at him.

"Get into the back room," Henry ordered.

"The money's in the cage," the old man said, nodding toward a steel-latticed cage at the end of the counter.

"Get into the back room," Henry repeated.

Shrugging, the pawnbroker came from behind the counter and shuffled through the open door to the back room. Following, Henry closed the door behind him.

When the old man turned around with an inquiring look on his face, Henry pressed the gun muzzle against his heart and fired.

The muzzle, being directly against the man's body, muffled the explosion to a dull roar, loud enough in the small room to make Henry wince but hardly loud enough to carry through two closed doors to the street. Henry felt reasonably sure that it couldn't have been heard outdoors.

The old man fell on his back without a sound and lay there with his mouth open and an expression of indignant surprise on his face.

Whipping out a handkerchief, Henry rapidly wiped off the gun. Kneeling, he wrapped the dead man's fingers around the stock.

The front room was still empty when he peeped out. Carefully he wiped both knobs of the back room door and pulled the door shut behind him with his handkerchief over the knob. He used his handkerchief again to open the street door, paused to glance up and down the street, then wiped the outer handle before letting the door click shut behind him.

The only person on the street was a man on the other side looking into another pawnshop window with his back to Henry. Climbing into his car, Henry drove away.

Twenty minutes later he eased his car back into the garage, crossed the rear yard, and quietly climbed the rear stairs. It was five minutes until two.

In lieu of lunch he drank two glasses of cold milk from the refrigerator, descended the front stairs and re-entered the store at exactly two P.M.

"Everything went fine," young Thad told him. "I'm catching on pretty good. Have your nap?"

"A little one," Henry said. "Better get some canned peas from the stockroom. We're running low on the shelf."

Just before the nine o'clock closing hour Sergeant Harry Newton phoned.

"That gun we fished out of the sewer was the murder weapon all right," he reported. "We traced it to a pawnshop on Franklin."

"Oh?" Henry said.

"It was registered as having been sold to a George Williams at a nonexistent address up on the north side. Obviously a fake name, since the address was fake. But unfortunately we can't get a description of the buyer from the pawnbroker."

"Why not?"

"He committed suicide this afternoon. I'd be suspicious of the timing if circumstances didn't make it suicide for certain."

"What circumstances?"

"He used one of his own guns. Since they were kept in a locked case, unloaded, a killer could hardly have gotten at it. And he had a motive. A week ago he found out he had cancer and had only a matter of months to live. It would have been a pretty painful death."

Henry felt pleased. Actually he had performed the old man a favor.

"Anyway it brings us to a dead end," the sergeant said. "If you rigged your wife's death, I guess you get away with it."

"I'm getting a little tired of your implications, sergeant," Henry said.

"I'm not very subtle," the sergeant admitted. "Sorry if I offended you. As I've said before, you were never under more than routine suspicion. There's still an A.P.B. out on your scar-faced bandit. If we net him, you'll hear from us. Otherwise I probably won't be talking to you again."

"I hope you catch him," Henry said a trifle stiffly. "Goodbye, sergeant."

Hanging up, he said to Thad Bower, "You can empty the trash while I check out the register." He tossed the boy his key ring. "Lock the front door first. We don't want any more bandits walking in to hold us up."

Charles Willeford
Some Lucky License

The first hour of waiting was bad enough; then I ran out of cigarettes. Any second now I would be called into the committee room where three serious members of the Board of Inquiry—the Honorable Police Commissioner J. D. Mathews, presiding—were determining my fate, my future, my life's work. I simply could not chance going downstairs to the cigarette machine. Instead, I tried to picture in my mind the order of brands in the machine from right to left across the glass-faced panel. I discovered to my surprise that I was unable to make an intelligent guess. Some detective you are, I thought in wry disgust; so much for your keenly developed powers of observation.

At this moment Chief Garland Carey ("Gar" to his friends, and I was purported to be one of them) entered the anteroom, lumbered over to the closed double doors leading into the chamber of deliberations, and paused with his hand on the doorknob to look at me. I rose, of course, as he entered, and the movement made it almost impossible for him not to acknowledge my presence. But he did the next thing to it. With his right hand on the knob, holding a slip of yellow paper in his left hand, he looked through me and said, "Sergeant." With that, he was through the doors. They closed quietly behind him.

Not "Bill" or "William" or "Hartigan," but the impersonal word "sergeant." And what was written on the little slip of paper?

It was my fault that Chief Carey was wearing his dress uniform this morning instead of his preferred costume, the sober charcoal gray suit. And, with silver eagles shining on his shoulders, he was more self-consciously my commander than he was my friend; or my supervisor, to whom a detective-sergeant addresses oral and written reports. I could sense that he didn't like me very well at the moment.

I still didn't know what was written on the slip of paper. I was tired of waiting, so I ran downstairs to the cigarette machine. I hurried back up the stairs, taking them three at a time, arriving in the antechamber just as Gar came out of the committee room. I held out the pack.

"Thanks." He took a cigarette, lighted up, turned his head away from me, expelled a thin column of smoke, and said, "The Brett kid died."

These four words changed the picture and the channel. Section 1277 of the Criminal Code was no longer an abstract paragraph to be learned and forgotten during one's stint at the police academy. It was a real live issue and, depending upon its interpretation by the board, could not be applied to me. In a way, however, I was glad that the Brett kid had died; now the issue would be resolved one way or another, once and for all.

Succinctly, Section 1277 states that any police officer who fatally shoots six persons—in line of duty or no—will be separated from the force, and will not be reinstated. The section is known unofficially among policemen as the "trigger-happy" rule. The mental processes by which the drafters of the Code arrived at the cut-off number of six defy reason. The idea behind Section 1277 was that if a police officer shot and killed six men he had somehow violated the laws of "chance" and he was therefore "trigger-happy." As an incipient killer, he should not be retained on the force. Logically, one can shoot a good many holes in the rule. Every time a police officer shoots and kills a man in line of duty he must be cleared by a board of inquiry anyway, so technically, as long as he has been cleared each time, as I had been cleared on the first four men I had shot and wounded fatally in line of duty, what difference did it make if I shot and killed ten, twenty, or even a hundred men? But the squeeze that put Section 1277 into the Code was determined by public and political pressure, not by the prescribed policeman's duty. On the other hand, perhaps a statute like this was needed; if not for me, perhaps for some policeman who was truly trigger-happy.

Now, with the death of the second kid, Tommy Brett, the three-man board deciding my future was being faced with a disturbing technicality that made their decision even more difficult than it had been before. If they followed the Code religiously, my case did not come under Section 1277. I had shot and killed Joseph E. Craig; I had *not* shot Tommy Brett. Brett had been a passenger in the stolen car being driven by Joseph E. Craig, and his death had been caused by the accident that followed, after the driverless car zoomed into a giant elm shading the lawn in front of 1507 West Crescent Drive. Craig had died instantly when I shot him through the left temple. Brett and still been alive, without any bullets in him, when we pulled him out of the wreck, and he had been kept alive for five dramatic days in the hospital—choosing an even more dramatic moment to cash out. The news of his demise in the hospital was the information Chief Gar Carey had scribbled on the note he had taken into the board before I dashed downstrairs for cigarettes.

Would they or would they not count Tommy Brett as my sixth victim? If they did, I was through as a policeman. Certainly, mine had been a line of duty shot. We had chased Craig for fully five miles at high speeds; the fear-maddened youth in the stolen car was endangering the lives of countless innocent citizens; and I had fired two warning shots before sending the third bullet into his temple. But I know, and so did Chief Carey, that the board was going to charge me with both deaths. Such is the irony of being an overly conscientious police officer. The citizens, those I had tried to protect, were clamoring for my badge; the newspapers had recapitulated all of my previous fatal shootings, and they were calling me William "Trigger-Happy" Hartigan. This pressure was being felt by the board of inquiry, and Brett's death made their decision tougher.

Joseph E. Craig had been fourteen years old when I shot him, and young Tommy Brett, his equally guilty passenger, had been thirteen. My fifteen years on the force, my excellent record of arrests, and my good name were being weighed against the ages of the two teenaged victims, not against their crime.

At any rate, being something of a fatalist, I decided to hope for the best. And the best I could come up with was that I would now be forced into half-retirement with about a hundred and fifty dollars a month, thanks to my fifteen years of honorable service on the force. Not only was one fifty a big comedown from my monthly salary of six hundred, but if I were forced into retirement under the trigger-happy law, I wouldn't be able to get another policeman's job anywhere. All I knew was police work. Somehow, I had to hang on for the next ten years to get my regular retirement pay of two fifty a month for twenty-five years of service.

"Well?" Gar said, breaking into my dismal reverie. "Haven't you anything to say—about the Brett kid?"

I shrugged. "It's a tough break for me; what else should I say? Do you want me to say I'm sorry for him? He was a thief, just as much of a thief as Craig, so now there are two less thieves in town instead of one less."

"You talk to the board in that tone of voice and you'll be bounced out right on your ear."

"Don't kid me, Gar. I'm going to be bounced anyway illegally, but politically, and you know it."

"Maybe not. I just gave them an alternative way out. Play along with them when they call you in. Show some humility and contriteness whether you feel it or not, and they might just accept my suggestion. Lieutenant Morris did a brilliant job defending your record; so his recommendation, together with mine, should carry some weight with the board."

"What's the alternative?"

"If they accept it, you'll be told. Just wait and see. But I gave them a way out."

I nodded. "Don't worry, Gar," I said, softening. "I know how to perform for them. This is my fifth stellar appearance." I grinned.

"I know," he said grimly. "And if they take my suggestion, it will be your last."

Chief Gar Carey's so-called alternative was accepted. I wasn't keen on it, but the ugly moment of truth I had faced in the waiting room more or less forced me to accept the board's decision with an outward show of good grace. I even went so far as to thank the members of the board of inquiry.

I was still a sergeant, but I was no longer a plainclothes detective. I drew a sergeant's pay, and I was given an administrative position as "police force" jailer, a job that did not require me to wear a gun; in fact, I was now forbidden to wear a gun. I hated the job. There was nothing for me to do, and I had too much rank to be a mere assistant to the official city jailer, Mr. Malcolm. I was merely there, in Mr. Malcolm's office, in a "made" position.

I sat at a desk in Mr. Malcolm's office from eight to five. A precedent had been set for this sinecure several years before when an aging patrolman with arthritic feet had been allowed to sit quietly in the city jailer's office for three years to sweat out his retirement. Gar, playing on my good record, had sold the idea to the board.

However, I'll say this for Mr. Malcolm: he ran an efficient, no-foolishness lockup. He had everything down to a tight methodical schedule, and the simplicity of his system made the prisoners fear him. His impersonality toward the prisoners was deadly. He counted them six times daily, including Saturdays and Sundays, counted them as if they were cards in a newly opened deck; he wasn't concerned with their faces, only their backs and the accuracy of the count. Except for the trusty, Thomas "Mary Ellen" Wolgast, who cleaned the offices downstairs and waited upon us, I doubt if Mr. Malcom knew any of the prisoners by name.

I had no paperwork to do. When I volunteered to help Mr. Malcolm with some of his, he merely shook his head. "No, there ain't that much."

A few days later, I offered to count the prisoners for him. He thought this over, and pulled on his nose. "No, Sergeant Hartigan," he said, finally. "It would upset my routine. I'd rather do it myself."

Mr. Malcolm needed the excuse of counting prisoners to get away from his desk several times a day. Most of the time we merely sat in the cramped little office, smoking and drinking coffee. We had tried to talk to each other at first, but neither one of us was much for small talk. The trusty, "Mary Ellen" Wolgast, brought us coffee, cake, sandwiches, or ran errands, whenever we hollered for him, and the turnkeys, all of them well past middle age, needed no supervision.

The turnkeys were ex-police officers or ex-deputies. Obviously, Mr. Malcolm had selected them with great care. They were as silent and colorless as Mr. Malcolm himself. They did their work quietly, and treated the prisoners firmly but fairly. I snooped around a little, naturally, but none of the turnkeys was violating any of Mr. Malcolm's rules. The prisoners who had money on the books were allowed to send out for cigarettes, candy, and restaurant meals, and the turnkey who made the outside trip charged the flat rate of fifty cents for every delivery, whether it was a pack of cigarettes or a hamburger.

After three weeks of sitting in the city jailer's office doing nothing, I gained seven pounds. The following Monday morning I called on Chief Gar Carey in his office.

He grinned as I entered. "Morning, Bill. I expected to see you sooner or later."

"This isn't working out," I said bitterly. "It's worse than being a prisoner."

He nodded. "I know it's tough on an active man, Bill, just sitting over there. But you'll simply have to sweat it out until things blow over. The public has a short memory, and after a year or so—"

"A year or so!"

"I'd say at least a year. But if you're willing to wait it out, I'll be able to get you a rehearing, and—"

I shook my head. "Gar, I can't do it. If I sit in that office for a full year I'll be as stir-simple as Mr. Malcolm."

Gar shrugged. "Okay. You were officially cleared on the Craig and Brett shooting—"

"Craig only," I quickly reminded him. "Brett died as the result of an automobile accident."

He ignored my interruption. "—so you're prefectly justified to resign from the force at any time. You aren't quitting under fire, and if you want to leave I'll give you an excellent recommendation if you want to work on another police force in some other city."

"Thanks. Thanks a lot," I said dryly. "If I resign, what happens to my retirement?"

He raised his shaggy gray eyebrows in mock surprise. "You lose it, of course, as you very well know. You only get the half-retirement pittance when you're forced out because of circumstances beyond your control, on a line of duty basis, naturally."

"Fifteen good years down the drain, or another ten years sitting in the city jailer's office. This is some choice to give a man with my proven ability."

Gar's face reddened. "I did you a favor, and you grabbed it because you damned well had to! Don't come sniveling to me because you're drawing six hundred bucks a month for sitting out your time."

"I didn't mean it that way, Gar, and you don't have any call to get hot at me, either. I just thought . . ."

"All right, then, face the facts. In another year, I can probably get you a rehearing and a reinstatement on your old job. If you're turned down the first time, you'll get back on active duty the second or third year. These things blow over eventually; you have to give them time."

"Sure, Gar. I understand. Thanks for seeing me this morning, and thanks for the time."

In the slow days that followed, my mind worked overtime in an effort to find a way out. But the restrictions imposed by the board, I soon learned, went beyond the simple denial of my carrying a pistol. I called the commandant of the police academy, volunteering to teach a course to police cadets. He was delighted. An hour later he called me back to tell me he was sorry, but he had a full complement of instructors and couldn't use me after all. I got the idea. The board, as well as Chief Carey, wanted me out of sight and mind for the months it would take the public to forget about me; and they didn't consider me a good example for rookie cops, either.

There was only one sure way out of my problem, and that was to become a hero. And the only way I could become a hero was to make a spectacular arrest of some kind without, of course, having a pistol or firing a shot. But the regulations were particularly strict in this area; any policeman who made an arrest when he was unarmed would be suspended immediately, and he would then meet a board to see if he had enough marbles in his head to be retained on the force.

Then I got stubborn. I decided to do my time just like any other prisoner with a long stretch, one day at a time.

To keep my mind from going dull, I worked the daily chess problem in the newspaper each morning, and studied the rest of the day in preparation for the annual exam coming up for lieutenant. I was eligible to take the exam, and the idea pleased me. If I made the highest score on the exam—and I had a good chance, with nothing to do but study all day—the promotion board would be shaken up when they had to refuse a promotion to the brightest member of the force, a highly trained police officer who was doing absolutely nothing for his monthly salary. The irony of the situation cheered me up considerably, and each morning I arrived at the office eager to hit the books.

This was about as far as I could go in making a break for myself without any outside help. But when the real break came, I very nearly missed it.

At nine thirty A.M. I told Mary Ellen, the trusty, to bring me a ham sandwich and a cup of coffee from the kitchen upstairs. Mr. Malcolm ordered black coffee only. I had figured out the final move on my chess board by the time Mary Ellen returned to the office with the tray. Two bites later my teeth bit into a piece of paper. I pulled out the slip of paper and tossed it into my wastebasket, making a mental note to chew Mary Ellen out later for being so careless when he made my sandwich. Not until I had finished the sandwich and started on the coffee did I realize that Mary Ellen would not be likely to make a mistake of that nature. He was too neat to leave a piece of paper on the ham.

Watching Mr. Malcolm out of the corner of my eye, I dumped my ashtray into the wastebasket, retrieving the piece of paper at the same time. Holding it in my lap, I read the faintly printed message: SGT. HARTIGAN, IMPORTANT! MEET ME IN DOWNSTAIRS JOHN DURING 11 A.M. COUNT.

The note wasn't signed, but it had to be from Mary Ellen Wolgast; he was the only prisoner excused from Mr. Malcolm's count.

At five minutes to eleven, Mr. Malcolm and I left the office together. I headed down the corridor to the men's room; he had his clipboard, and took the self-operated elevator upstairs to make his count. Wolgast was already in the latrine, swishing a damp mop over the vinyl-tiled floor.

"Intrigue, Mary Ellen?" I asked.

He didn't smile; he was too frightened. Chewing nervously on his lip, he leaned the mop handle against the wall and, with difficulty, fished a folded twenty dollar bill out of his pocket. He handed the bill to me and said, "I'm in a jam, Sergeant Hartigan, a real jam."

"This isn't supposed to be a bribe, is it?" I grinned.

"No, sir. Not to you—to me; and I don't want any part of it! Bert Gulick gave it to me to—to help him escape." Close to tears, he ran his long fingers through his lank blond hair.

"Go ahead," I encouraged him, "tell me about it. And don't worry about Gulick finding out you told me." I was interested, keenly interested.

Wolgast nodded, and his bulging Adam's apple bobbed convulsively for more air. "I didn't know what else to do. Bert Gulick's got a good plan worked out that will get him out of here tonight, but he couldn't get away without my help. I don't want to get involved and lose my good time. I only got forty days to go," he whined.

"Get on with it," I said impatiently.

"But if you catch him, he'll beat me up. I know he will!"

"No," I shook my head, "I guarantee you that he won't touch you. That's a promise."

"I don't have any choice, anyway. You know the corridor from the elevator to the back door of the kitchen on the second floor? After supper at night I usually get a volunteer to help me bring down the trays. If nobody volunteers I have to wash 'em myself, but I usually get somebody because it gets a man away from the tank for an hour, and the cook always gives us a sandwich or something to take with us when we finish up. Anyway, the wire-mesh screen at the end of the corridor by the fire escape is only set in there with screws, and for the last three nights Bert Gulick's been helping me, loosening up the screws while we wait for the elevator. Tonight, when we come down, I'm supposed to tell the cook I couldn't get any volunteer to help me. But Gulick'll come down with me, take off the screen, and go down the back fire escape. He'll have at least an hour's advantage, but they'll know I had to lie and—"

"Never mind about that. You're in the clear already. What time do you bring down the dirty trays?"

"Well, we bring them down on the cart about six, but it'll only take Gulick a second to take out the screen and raise the window. The screws are just barely in there now."

"Doesn't a turnkey come down with you?"

"No. We're checked out upstairs when we get in the elevator. Without the elevator key, the elevator won't come down to the first floor, it's locked and set only to go to the second, so nobody needs to go to the kitchen with us. The turnkey, Mr. Conroy, has the key, and he unlocks the elevator when the cook goes home at night."

"Okay, Wolgast, I get the setup. And don't worry about it. I'll take care of things from now on. Just go ahead as you've planned it, and say nothing to Bert Gulick." I unfolded the twenty. "This twenty, and another one just like it, will be put on the books for you to draw on." I grinned. "If you spend a dollar a day, you can be flat broke when you're released."

"If Gulick ever finds out that I—"

"I told you not to worry. Your name won't be mentioned. Just go ahead with it, and keep your mouth shut."

At five o'clock I left the office, went to my car in the back lot, and got my pistol out of the glove compartment. It felt nice and heavy in my hand. I smoked a cigarette, waved goodbye to Mr. Malcolm as he spluttered out of the lot on his ancient motorcycle, and looked through the windshield at the lovely darkening sky. It wouldn't be completely dark until well after six but, thanks to a low overcast of purple rain-clouds, dusk would be darker than it usually was at this time of year.

There was more than one way for me to handle the situation. For publicity purposes it would be much better for me to apprehend Gulick in the act of escaping than it would be simply to plug up the escape route and prevent a "possible" breakout. After I picked Bert Gulick up at the bottom of the ladder, I could then march him around to the front of the building and make a dramatic entrance with him. My picture would be in the morning newspapers. There would be a photo of me around back, pointing up at the fire escape and the raised window and, with luck, there might even be a posed shot of me holding my pistol on Gulick in the downstairs outer office. The fact that I had picked him up without shooting him would carry a lot of weight with the board.

I was quite pleased with myself when I took my position in the shadowy recessed delivery doorway beneath the back fire escape. I didn't worry about Bert Gulick; he was a wife beater, not a strong-arm boy. Although he might be armed with a knife, he certainly didn't have a gun. I hoped he had a knife; it would be that much better for me when I took it away from him.

I didn't hear the noise of the screen being removed, but I heard the squeal of the tight window as he pushed it up. The rusty iron steps rattled and shook as Gulick backed down them as noiselessly as he could. I waited until he was midway between the second floor and the ground before stepping out of the dark doorway.

"Freeze, Gulick," I said sharply. "This is Hartigan."

He froze all right, not moving a muscle, with his back to me; and he was so frightened by my name that he clung there trembling and rattling the metal ladder. All I had to do now was to back him down a step at a time, put the cuffs on him, and march him around the building to the front entrance. With a spectacular arrest to my credit, I'd be back on my old job within a few weeks, doing what I wanted to do.

And what did I really want to do?

The realization hit me for the first time. I honestly hadn't known it until this very minute. I wanted to shoot and kill men like Gulick; that's what I really wanted to do! And with Bert Gulick as Number Six. I would be retired on a hundred and fifty a month for life. Why not Gulick? Why should I wait for someone else at a later date? Sooner or later I was going to get a sixth victim anyway. And because Gulick was my last free one, the last man I would be able to shoot legally before I lost my shooting license, my hand was never steadier as I squeezed the trigger.

Robert Edmond Alter
A Habit for the Voyage

The moment Krueger stepped aboard the steamer he was aware of a vague sense of something gone wrong. He had never understood the atavism behind these instinctive warnings, but he had had them before and usually he had been right.

He paused at the head of the gangplank, standing stockstill on the little bit of railed deck overlooking the after well deck. Down in the well, the Brazilian stevedores were just finishing with the last of the cargo. The steward was standing just inside a door marked DE SEGUNDA CLASE with Krueger's shabby suitcase in his hand. He looked back at Krueger with an air of incurious impatience.

Krueger took a last look around, saw nothing out of the ordinary, and stepped across the deck to follow the steward.

It came again—a last split-second premonition of danger—so sharply that he actually flinched. Then, as a black blurred mass hurtled by his vision, he threw himself to one side, and the object, whatever it was, smacked the deck with an appalling crash, right at his feet.

He shot one glance at it—a metal deck bucket filled to the brim with nuts and bolts and other nameless, greasy odds and ends. He moved again, rooting his hand under and around to the back of his raincoat to get at the snub-nosed pistol in his right hip pocket, staring upward at the shadowy promenade deck just above him and at the railed edge of the boat deck above that.

He couldn't see anyone. Nothing moved up there.

The steward was coming back with a look of shocked disbelief.

"Nombre de Dios, señor! Que pasa?"

Krueger realized that the stevedores were also watching him from below. He quickly withdrew his empty hand from under his coat.

"Some idiot almost killed me with that bucket! That's what happened!"

The steward stared at the loaded bucket wonderingly. "Those deck-hands are careless dogs."

Krueger was getting back his breath. The steward was right; it had been an accident, of course.

Krueger was a linguist. He felt perfectly at home with seven languages; it was important in his business. He said, *"Lleveme usted a mi camarote."* The steward nodded and led him down a sickly-lit corridor to his second class stateroom.

It was on the starboard and there wasn't much to it. A verdigris-crusted porthole, a sink on the right, a wardrobe on the left, and one uncomfortable looking bunk. That was that.

Krueger gave the steward a moderate tip and sat down on the bunk with a sigh, as though prepared to relax and enjoy his voyage. He always maintained a calm, bland air in front of the serving class. Stewards, pursers, waiters, and desk clerks had an annoying way of being able to recall certain little mannerisms about you when questioned later.

The steward said, "*Gracias, señor*," and closed the door after himself. Krueger stayed where he was for a moment, then he got up and went over to bolt the door. But there was no bolt. He could see the holes where the screws had once been driven into the woodwork of the door, but the bolt had been removed.

That was the trouble with second class travel. Nothing was ever in its entirety; nothing ever functioned properly. The bunks were lumpy, the hot-water tap ran lukewarm, the portholes always stuck. Krueger had had to put up with this nonsense all his life. The Party's rigorous belief that a penny saved was a penny earned was frequently an annoying pain in the neck to Krueger. Still—they were his best clients.

He took a paper matchbook from his pocket and wedged it under the door. It just did the trick. He opened his case and got out a roll of adhesive tape, cut four eight-inch strips, then got down on his knees and placed his pistol up underneath the sink and taped it there. Second class stewards also had a habit of going through your things when you were out of your compartment.

He never relied upon a firearm for his work. It was messy, and much too obvious. He was a man who arranged innocent-looking accidents. The pistol was purely a weapon of self-defense, in case there was a hitch and he had to fight his way out, which had happened more than once in his checkered career.

He was fifty-three, balding, inclined to be stout, and had a face as bland as a third-rate stockbroker's, unless you looked closely at his eyes, which he seldom allowed anyone to do. He had worked at his trade for thirty years. He was an assassin.

He sat back in his bunk and thought about the man he was going to kill aboard this ship.

Unconsciously his right hand went up to his ear and he began to tug at the lobe gently. Catching himself at it, he hurriedly snatched his hand away. That was a bad habit with him, one that he had to watch. They were dangerous in his line of work, bad habits, exceedingly dangerous. They pinpointed you, gave you away, gave an enemy agent a chance to spot you. It was like walking around in public wearing a sign reading: *I Am Krueger the Assassin!*

He remembered only too vividly what had happened to his old friend Delchev. *He* had unconsciously developed a bad habit—the simple, involuntary gesture of tugging his tieknot and collar away from his Adam's apple with his forefinger. Through the years the word had gotten around; the habit had been noted and renoted. It went into all the world's many secret service files. He was earmarked by his habit. No matter what alias or disguise or cover he adopted, sooner or later his habit gave him away. And they had nailed him in the end.

Krueger had known of another agent who used to break cigarettes in half, and still another who picked his ear, always the same ear. Both dead now—by arranged accidents.

And there was one colorful fellow who went by so many aliases that he was simply referred to by those in the business as Mister M. Krueger had always felt that he could have tracked M down within six months, had someone offered to make it worth his while. Because there was a notation in the dossiers on M of a bad habit that simply screamed for attention. M always tabbed himself by marking paper matchbooks with his thumbnail, orderly-spaced little indentations all up and down the four edges.

Well, at least tugging your earlobe wasn't that bad. But it was bad enough and Krueger knew it. He must be more attentive to his idio-syncracies in the future. He had to weed all mannerisms out of his character until he became as bland as a mud wall.

The distant clang of a ship's bell reached him. The deck began to vibrate. Then the engines went astern with a rattle that he felt up his spine. A pause and then the engines went ahead, throbbing peacefully.

All right. Time to go to work. Time to view the future victim.

The dining room adjoined the saloon and they were both very dingy affairs. Cramped, too. And you could see rust streaks down the white walls at the corners of the windows. It all added up to greasy, over-seasoned, poorly prepared food. But Krueger remained calm and benign; never call attention to yourself by being a complainer.

He sandwiched himself between a fat lady and a Latin priest, picked up his napkin and started to tuck it in his collar, but caught himself in time and put it on his lap instead.

Watch it; watch that sort of thing. You were the napkin-in-the collar type on the last assignment. Never repeat the same mannerisms! He smiled at the man across the table, saying, "Pass the menu if you will, please."

The man addressed was in ineffectual looking little fellow of about forty, with thinning hair and spectacles. His name was Amos Bicker and he was slated for a fatal accident—arranged by Krueger.

Krueger studied him surreptitiously. He certainly didn't look like the sort who needed killing. He had that civil employee aspect. However, some way or another, innocent or not, he must have placed himself in this position of jeopardy by getting in the Party's path. Krueger's instructions had called for Immediate Elimination. So be it. Now for the means. . . .

He caught his hand halfway to his ear. *Dammit!* He carried the gesture through, switching its course to scratch the back of his neck. Then he studied the menu. Two of his favorites were there: oyster cocktail and New York cut. He ordered them, then turned to the priest, trying him first in Spanish, which worked. Actually he was thinking about the man across the table, Bicker, and the permanent removal of same.

Krueger always favored obvious accidents. So, when aboard ships, man overboard. This could be handled in a variety of ways. One, make friends with the victim, suggest a late stroll along the promenade deck; then a quick judo blow and ... Two, again make friends and (if the victim were a drinking man) drink him under the table, and then ... Or three (and this method had great appeal to Krueger because it eliminated public observance of his contact with the victim), slip into the victim's room in the wee hours of the morning and jab him with a small syringe which induced quick and total unconsciousness, and after that ... well, that followed was simple enough. Man overboard.

The steward brought Krueger his oyster cocktail. Krueger reached for his small fork and gave a start. Something was rubbing his left leg under the table. He leaned back in his chair and raised the cloth. A mangy looking old cat—ship's cat probably—was busy stropping himself against Krueger's thick leg.

"Kitty kitty," Krueger said. He loved animals, Had he led a more sedentary life, he would have had a home, and the home would have been filled with pets. And a wife, too, of course.

A minor ship's officer appeared in the starboard doorway. *"Donde está Señor Werfel?"* he asked at large.

"Here!" Krueger called. That was one thing he never slipped on; he could pick up and drop an alias like the snap of fingers.

"The captain wishes to see you for a moment, señor."

A multitude of why's came clamoring alive in Krueger's brain. Then he caught the obvious answer and stood up, smiling. That accident with the bucket. It was annoying because the incident called undue attention to him—the steward, the stevedores, this officer, all the passengers, and now the captain.

He met the captain on the starboard wing of the flying bridge. The captain, originally some conglomeration of Mediterranean blood, was profuse in his apologies regarding the accident. Krueger laughed it off. It was nothing, truly. Those things happened. He wished the captain would put it out of his mind, really. He shook the captain's hand, he accepted the captain's cigar. He even allowed the captain to allow him to inspect the bridge.

He returned to the dining room wearing his professional bland smile. But something had happened during his absence.

The passengers were against the walls. The cook and his assistants and the steward formed a more central ring. But the star of the scene was on the floor in the exact center of the room. It was the ship's cat and it was stretched out to an incredible length and going through the most grotesque mouth-foaming convulsions.

"Ohh, Mr. *Werfel!"* the fat lady who had been seated next to Krueger cried. "I did a *terrible* thing! No! Come to think of it, it was fortunate that

I did! Certainly fortunate for *you!*"

"What?" Krueger said sharply, his eyes fixed on the convulsed cat. "What did you do?"

"That *poor* little dear jumped up on your seat after you left. He wanted your oysters! Of course I held him off, but you were so long in returning, and there are so many flies in here, you know."

"You gave him my oysters," Krueger said.

"Yes! I finally did! And before any of us knew it, the poor little thing went into those *awful* ..."

"I'd better put the poor thing out of its misery," the priest said, coming forward. No one offered to help him.

Krueger stalled for an interval, until the passengers had thinned out, then he led the steward aside. "What was wrong with those oysters?" he demanded.

The steward seemed utterly flabbergasted. "Señor, I don't know! Ptomaine, you think? They were canned, of course."

"Let's see the can," Krueger said.

There was a faint scent of taint to the can—if held close to a sensitive nose. Krueger put it down and looked at the steward.

"Anyone else order oysters?"

"No, señor. Only yourself."

Krueger forced up a smile. "Well, accidents will happen." But he certainly wished there were some way he could have had that can, more especially the dead cat, analyzed. He returned to his stateroom more angry than shaken.

Well, that had been close. Too close. Look at it either way you wanted to, he had been a very lucky man. Of course it *could* have been ptomaine ... those things happened ... but when you coupled it with the business about the bucket ...

He went over to the sink and reached under for his gun.

It wasn't there. The tape was there, neatly, but not the gun.

Now wait, he warned himself, pulling at his earlobe. A sailor could have kicked over the bucket by accident. Bolts are frequently missing from doors in rumdum ships like this. Ptomaine does occur in carelessly canned meats. And stewards do rifle compartments.

But the combination still spelled suspicion. Yet supposing his suspicions were right, what could he do about it? He couldn't disprove that the bucket and food poisoning were accidents; and if questioned about the missing pistol, the steward would appear to be the epitome of innocence.

I must tread carefully, he thought. Very, very carefully, until this business is over. It's just possible that the Party slipped up somewhere on this assignment. Or was it possible that the Party ...

No! That was absurd. He had always given them faithful service; they *knew* that. And they knew, too, that he was one of the best in the business. No. No. Tugging furiously at his ear. Absurd.

He replaced the match folder under the door and, not satisfied with that, put his suitcase before it, flat, and, using the adhesive tape again, taped it to the deck. A man could get in, yes, but he would make a lot of noise doing it. He turned out the light and undressed and got into his bunk.

At first he thought it must be the wool blanket scratching him. Then he remembered that he had a sheet between his body and the blanket. Then he was really sure that it wasn't the blanket, because it moved when he didn't!

He felt the soft rasp of straggly fuzz across his bare belly, crawling sluggishly under the weight of the blanket, as a thing gorged with food. He started to raise the upper edge of the blanket and the thing, whatever it was, scrabbled anxiously toward his navel. He froze, sucking his breath, scared to move a muscle.

It stopped, too, as if waiting for the man to make the first decisive move. He could feel it on his naked stomach, squatting there, poised expectantly. It was alive, whatever it was . . . it started moving again, he could feel the tiny feet (many of them) scuttling up toward his ribcage, the dry hairy fat little legs tickling his goose-fleshed skin which rippled with loathsome revulsion.

He'd had it. With movements perfectly coordinated out of pure terror, he threw the blanket and sheet aside with his left and took a sweeping thrust across his stomach with his right forearm—as he rolled from the bunk to the deck.

He was up instantly and frantically fumbling for the light switch.

The thing scurried across the white desert of the bottom sheet—a thick-legged tarantula species, hideous, its furry body as fat as a bird's. Krueger snatched up a shoe and beat the thing over and over, and because of the give of the mattress the spider died the long, slow, frenziedly wiggly way.

Krueger threw the shoe aside and went to the sink to wash the clammy sweat from his face.

There was no call-button in the stateroom. He unbarricaded his door and shouted, *"Camarero!"*

A few minutes later the steward looked in with a sleepy smile. *"Sí, señor! Que desea usted?"*

Krueger pointed at the crushed spider on his bed. The steward came over and looked at it. He made a face and grunted. He didn't seem overly surprised.

"Sí, it happens. It is the cargo, señor. The bananas. They come aboard in the fruit. Some of these *diablos* find their way amidships."

It was the kind of answer Krueger had expected, a reasonable explanation that left no room for argument. But it was getting to be too much. The tarantula was the last straw. He took his hand away from his earlobe and started getting into his clothes.

"Quisiera hablor con el capitan," he said flatly.

The steward shrugged fatalistically. If the unreasonable gringo wanted to bother the captain at this time of night, it was none of his concern.

Krueger shoved by the steward rudely, saying, "I won't need you to find him. You're about as much help as a third leg." He was starting to forget all of his rules.

The captain was no help at all. He repeated all of the old sad-apple excuses: clumsy seamen, careless canning, the bothersome little hazards of shipping on a cargo steamer hauling bananas . . .

"Now look here, captain," Krueger said, angrily pulling at his ear. "I'm a reasonable man and I'll go along with everyday accidents, as long as they stay within the limits of probability. But all of these accidents have happened to *me*. Within one day."

"What is it that you're trying to say, Mr. Werfel? Surely you're not implying that someone aboard this ship is trying to kill you, are you? You don't have enemies, do you?"

Krueger balked at that. It was a subject that he wanted to stay away from. To get into it would be wading into a thick sea of endless, embarrassing explanations. He hedged.

"I said no such thing, captain. All I'm saying is that these things keep happening to me aboard your ship, and I expect you to protect me from them."

"Certainly, Mr. Werfel. Let me see . . . yes! I can give you your choice of any of my officers' cabins. My own included. I can even assign a competent man to stay by your—"

"No, no, no!" Krueger said hastily. "That isn't at all necessary, captain. I don't intend to act like a prisoner aboard this ship. Just assign me a new cabin, one with a lock and bolt on the door."

Leaving the navigation deck, Krueger decided that he needed a drink. He would go down and see if the saloon was still open. His nerves were getting out of hand, and no wonder! The whole game was going very badly, turning sour on him. He was breaking all his time-tested rules, calling more attention to himself than a brass band.

He paused on the companionway overlooking the dark, gusty boat deck. Someone was down there on the deck, someone familiar, leaning at the rail just to the stern of Number One starboard lifeboat.

Krueger took a quick swipe at his face, wiping away the tiny, moist needle-fingers of the sea mist, and came down another step . . . but quietly, ever so quietly. The man on the boat back was Amos Bicker. He was mooning out at the black rambling sea, his forearms cocked up on the damp rail, his thin back to Krueger.

Krueger came down another quiet step, his narrowed eyes quickly checking out the points of professional interest.

Bicker had taken a position just inside the aft boat davit, to stand in the sheltering lee of the lifeboat's stern. He was leaning about a yard from the extreme corner of the rail; beyond that was nothing. There weren't even guard-chains, only the vacant space through which the davits swung the lifeboat. Below was the open sea.

Made to order. Krueger could finish the business here and now. Then he could concentrate all his wits on his own survival, guard himself against those recurring accidents . . . if that's what they were.

He came down on the last step and put both feet on the boat deck.

Krueger and the victim were quite alone in the whispering sea-running night. And the unsuspecting victim thought he was all alone. It wouldn't take much; just a sudden short rush and a bit of a push, catching Bicker on his side, and propelling him sideways right out into that empty waiting space.

Grinning tightly, Krueger broke into a cat-footed, avid rush.

All the lifeboats had returned and the captain had received their reports. Shaking his head, he re-entered his office and went behind his desk and resumed his seat.

"Well," he said, "this is certainly a sorry business. Unfortunate that you had to be subjected to it, Mr. Bicker."

Amos Bicker was sitting hunched and drawn in his chair facing the desk. The first mate had given him a shot of whisky but it didn't seem to be doing him much good. He was obviously in a bad state of nerves. His hands trembled, his voice too.

"You didn't recover the—uh—"

"Not a sign," the captain said. "Must have gone down like a stone. But please, Mr. Bicker, please do not let it prey upon you. You couldn't have done more than you did. You cried *man overboard* the moment it happened, and you even had the presence of mind to throw over a life-ring. You behaved admirably."

Mr. Bicker shivered and wrapped both hands about the empty shot glass. It was just possible, the captain thought, that he was going into shock. "Have a smoke, Mr. Bicker," he offered solicitously, passing over a cigarette box and matches.

Mr. Bicker had trouble lighting up, his hands shook so.

"He must have been made—deranged," he said finally, hoarsely. "I didn't know the man, had never seen him except in the dining room this evening. I was just standing there at the rail minding my own business, watching the sea without a thought in my head and—and then I heard a—a movement, a sort of quiet rushing motion, and I looked around and there he was. Coming right at me! And the look on his face!"

"Yes, yes, Mr. Bicker," the captain said sympathetically, "we quite understand. There's no doubt in anyone's mind that there was something—well, odd, in Mr. Werfel's behavior. I have reason to believe that the poor devil actually thought that someone aboard this ship was trying to kill him. Mental delusion. Lucky for you that you reacted by stepping backwards instead of sideways or he might have taken you over with him."

Mr. Bicker nodded, staring at the carpets. One of his thumbnails absent-mindedly was making orderly-spaced little indentations down one edge of the captain's paper matchbook.

Michael Zuroy

Diminishing Wife

"Henry," Thelma Elwick said to her husband, "these chairs seem to be
sinking."

Henry looked up from his paper to stare across the living room at the
large form of his wife. Seated in the upholstered chair, her thick sturdy
limbs firmly planted on the floor, her wide face bearing its usual competent expression, she did not look like a nervous or overly imaginative
woman. Henry knew that she was not. With Thelma, facts were facts.

"Sinking, dear?" Henry said. "How do you mean sinking?"

"Sinking. Getting lower. Closer to the floor."

There was a silence. Henry blinked. "Which chairs, dear? Which
chairs seem to be acting this way?"

"All the chairs," Thelma said. "The living room chairs. The dining
room chairs. The kitchen chairs. I've tried them all. They're all sinking."

"Well, that is peculiar," Henry said. "Are they doing it now? This
minute?"

"I can't feel it *happening*, if that's what you mean. But for possibly two
or three weeks I've had the definite impression that they're getting
steadily shorter."

Henry jumped up. "I'll get the yardstick . . ."

Thelma interrupted him. "I've already done that. Naturally. They
don't seem to measure any shorter. But I feel that they are."

A worried look appeared in Henry's eyes. "Are you sure you're quite
all right, dear?"

"Henry," his wife said evenly, "stop looking at me that way. Of
course I'm all right."

"Of course. But maybe you've been working too hard, dear. Too
many late hours at the office. I mean *I* don't notice anything about the
chairs. A sinking feeling, a feeling that things are getting shorter . . . I
don't like that. I don't like it at all. Something negative about it."

"Henry," his wife snapped, "shut up. Stop worrying. There's
nothing wrong with me. There must be a perfectly rational explanation."

"But—"

"I said, shut up." She glared at him.

But anyway, Henry thought, there was a hint of perplexity in her
eyes.

"What I don't understand," Altmeyer Thogg, Henry's park bench
crony puzzled, "is how you made her feel that the chairs are getting
shorter. And why?"

"Very simple." Henry scratched his back against the slats of the bench. "Thelma feels the chairs are getting shorter because they *are*."

"I don't get you."

"Sandpaper," Henry explained. "Every day, while Thelma's at the office, I sandpaper all the leg bottoms. Just a touch. Take off maybe a thousandth of an inch or two. Nothing you could measure without precision instruments, but it's steady. Every day the chairs are a hair shorter. Thelma, being a very exact person, senses the change, though she can't see it."

"All right," Altmeyer said dubiously, "but why? I can understand a gun. Or a knife. Or poison. If you could get away with it. But what's this going to do?"

"Ah." Henry pursed his lips and sucked his long cheeks in between his upper and lower teeth while he considered the question. "Will you grant that a positive person can't survive when forced to turn negative?"

"Hey?"

"I read it in a book by a professor," Henry said. "But let me put it this way. Thelma is a very positive woman. Self-assured. Domineering."

"Like mine," Altmeyer muttered with bitterness.

"What I got to do is throw her in reverse. Follow?"

"No."

"Well, look," Henry said, "suppose things start happening to her that can't be happening? In a negative way? Like chairs shrinking. Sooner or later, it's bound to shake her, isn't it? Make her worry about herself. About her health. About her stability. Make her less and less positive. Now do you follow?"

"Professors," muttered Altmeyer. "Sometimes their ideas just ain't practical. Me, I like poison."

"All right," Henry said. "Let's see how it turns out."

Henry rose and sauntered out of the park, a lanky stooping man with deep lines at the sides of his nose. He did the day's shopping at the supermarket, standing patiently in the long line of women at the counter. Then he went home to do some housework and prepare the evening meal.

Henry Elwick, like his friend Altmeyer Thogg, was a permanently unemployed husband.

Not because they couldn't find work. The fact was that they did't look. And they were not disabled, nor independently wealthy. No, it was because their wives wore the pants in the family that they didn't work.

It was the wives who were gainfully employed. It was the wives who were the ambitious, energetic, and aggressive ones. The husbands, like others of their order, remained home and did the domestic chores. In good weather, they spent much of their leisure hours on the park benches. Henry and Altmeyer had met each other there.

They were alike in their lethargic attitude towards life. They were alike in hating their wives, inwardly blaiming them for the breakdown of their masculine fiber.

Therefore, Altmeyer was not surprised at Henry's project.

The meal on the stove, Henry went into the living room and flopped into a chair. He looked around the apartment with his usual disgust. All Thelma's taste. Nothing of his own. And a fourth floor walk-up, too. What did Thelma care that he had to trudge up and down those stairs carrying heavy packages? She like the apartment. She wouldn't move. "Female dictator," Henry muttered. "Everything's got to be her way. Everything."

Of course, Henry had considered divorce. But if he divorced Thelma, he would lose her support. In fact, it was usually the man who paid alimony. This definitely did not appeal to Henry.

If something should happen to Thelma, however . . . well, she had savings, investments, and insurance that added up to a tidy sum. A nice inheritance. Enough to keep him in comfort for a long time.

And then, of course, the resentment had been with him too many years. He had not let Thelma see it, but it was there. Something had to be done about it.

When Thelma came home she ate her meal appreciatively. "Your cooking is excellent, as usual, Henry," she said. "Nice to come home to after a hard day at the office."

"What happened today, dear?" Henry asked.

"Well, that John Cummings—you know, I told you about him, the new advertising manager—he wanted to . . ."

Henry maintained a listening attitude while he washed the dishes, although he never actually heard much of Thelma's monologues. He had to suffer them every day, and the sooner this one was done with the better.

Thelma came up behind him and gave him a slobbery kiss on the neck. Henry felt his insides clench. She was in a genial, affectionate mood now. He hated her affectionate moods.

Later Henry observed Thelma walking around the house with the yardstick, shaking her head and frowning at the chairs.

In bed, listening to her robust snoring, a secret grin crossed Henry's face.

One evening, about a week later, Thelma said to Henry, "I'm losing weight, Henry."

"That so?"

"I've lost four pounds."

"Good. Women like to lose weight, don't they?"

"You don't understand. I haven't been under a hundred and seventy-five pounds in years. I'm not trying to lose weight."

An expression of concern came into Henry's eyes. "That doesn't sound quite normal, dear."

"I'm not dieting, as you know. I shouldn't be losing weight."

"No," Henry said. "You shouldn't. You certainly eat enough." He looked at her thoughtfully, went on gently, "Maybe you *are* working too hard, dear. I mean that sinking feeling. And now this. Shouldn't you see a doctor?"

"Damn it, Henry, I'm perfectly all right," Thelma ground out. "Stop fussing. I feel fine. It's just that I don't understand how ..."

A week later, Thelma announced grimly, "I've lost more weight. Almost three pounds."

'Oh, my," Henry said.

"I'm eating as much as ever."

"Maybe you ought to eat more, dear," Henry suggested. "Really load up. I'll make all the things you like."

"So tell me," Altmeyer said to Henry as they sat on the park bench. "How are you managing to make her lose weight gradually?"

"Nothing to it," Henry said. "I make her breakfasts and suppers, don't I?"

"So?"

"Calorie control. Low calorie foods where she can't notice it. Dietetic foods. She can eat all she wants, she's got to lose weight."

"I see," said Altmeyer.

"Henry," said Thelma a couple of weeks later, "the light seems to be growing dimmer."

Henry looked at his wife. Her loss of weight had become perceptible. Wrinkles were beginning to appear in her normally sleek skin. Her arms were less massive. "Light?" Henry said. "Growing dimmer. How do you mean, dear?"

"The lamps," Thelma said. "For some time they seem to have been slowly and steadily losing strength. I get the impression that the apartment is getting darker and darker. I get the feeling of having to strain my eyes more and more when I read."

"But, dear, I don't notice anything. It's not dark in here."

"I suppose not. But it seems to be *growing* darker. I would like to know what the hell is going on."

"I'm sure I don't know," Henry said gently. "Perhaps your eyes?"

"It's not my eyes. How about the bulbs, Henry? Maybe the bulbs are getting old. Put in new bulbs tomorrow."

"Is it better with the new bulbs?" Henry asked another night.

"No," Thelma said. "The light still seems to be fading."

They looked at each other. The perplexity in Thelma's eyes was now more evident. Stronger. "Could it be your eyesight, dear?" Henry asked sympathetically. "Do you notice anything like this during the day?"

"I don't know. It's hard to tell during the daytime." Thelma rose and paced about the room. She stopped and faced him. "Henry, something's wrong."

"It looks that way, dear."

"We've got to face the facts," she said grimly. "Facts are facts. Let's not try to duck the facts, Henry. These are the facts. I'm losing weight. I'm eating well, better than ever, but still I'm losing weight. I get this sinking feeling in chairs. But only at home, Henry. Not at the office. I wonder why not at the office?"

"I suppose there you're too busy to feel it. Too much going on."

"Hmn. Possibly. But to continue. There's nothing wrong with the chairs. I've checked them. Ten times. And now the light seems to be fading. Even with the brand new light bulbs, it seems to be fading. Can't be anything wrong with all those light bulbs. It's physically impossible."

"That's right," Henry agreed, regretfully.

"Only one explanation fits all the facts," Thelma said. "However much we dislike it, we're forced to the conclusion that there's something wrong with me. Loss of weight. Sinking feelings. Failing eyesight. Henry, I'm going to the doctor for a checkup."

"I think that's wise, dear," Henry murmured.

"Okay," Altmeyer said. "How did you do it?"

"A cinch," Henry said. "A mere gadget. You send away for it. It's advertised in the mechanics magazines, which Thelma never reads. Hook it on to a circuit and turn a knob and you can dim or brighten the circuit at will. I got 'em on all the circuits in the fuse box, inside the foyer wall. Thelma doesn't even know there is a fuse box."

"So you dim the lights a little more every day?"

"A hair. I just turn the knob a hair. You can hardly notice the total difference, but Thelma feels the change."

"Okay, but what's happening? Is all this getting you any place?"

"I think so," Henry said. "Thelma's positive factor is decreasing. Her negative one is rising. Takes time, of course."

The physical examination was thorough and detailed. The doctor and oculist were competent men. "From the oculist's report and my own findings," Dr. Blackburn told them, "I would say there is no evidence of anything organically wrong. Vision seems normal. What we have here is possibly a nervous condition."

"I have never been a nervous woman, doctor," Thelma bristled.

"Nevertheless, I suggest that you try to relax more. Slow down. If that doesn't help, come back. We'll make some hospital tests. Possibly have an alienist check you."

"Hospital," Thelma said. "Alienist."

"Meanwhile, just relax."

"Relax," Thelma said. "You want me to relax."

"I guess there's nothing seriously wrong," Henry remarked on the way home. "Unless it's too insidious to be detected by ordinary examination. The main thing is not to worry."

Henry found Thelma's attempts to relax highly interesting. She pursued this goal with her characteristic vigor and determination. Doggedly, she forced herself to remain quiet, watching television or keeping her eyes glued to a book. But often, Henry noted, she ended up staring into space. Henry fussed over her when she was home, putting pillows behind her head to make her more comfortable, bringing her tempting snacks and pastries prepared by himself—all low calorie. Grimly, Thelma swallowed tranquilizer pills. She came home early from the office. She towed Henry to shows, concerts, and bowling alleys, although at times Henry murmured, "I think this is a little too exciting for you, dear."

The symptoms of her trouble were not mentioned between them now, but Henry knew that she was keenly aware of them. A brooding look would come into her eyes as she sat in a chair with a book. She would hold the book a little closer or change her seat. At times she would grow morose and irritable, barking orders at Henry, and he would always comply meekly.

Sometimes she would seem unnaturally jovial, as though she had forgotten the whole thing. A strange excitement would come into her manner. She would laugh heartily at nothing.

And more and more frequently she was subject to periods of, for her, unusual lethargy, her heartiness and vigor vanishing. During these periods, her eyes would show veiled fear, their whites growing more prominent. She was, at these times, oddly submissive. "If I could only understand it," Henry heard her mumble. "If it was something I could cope with."

Then she would bounce back for a while.

Henry waited.

At last, she spoke of it. "Henry, there's no change."

"Ah," Henry said. "You still get those sinking feelings?"

"Yes." Thelma's voice was not quite steady.

"And you're still losing weight, I can see. And your eyes?"

"I don't care what the oculist says. There is something wrong with my eyes. Henry, there's something wrong with my eyes."

"Mmn. Perhaps. And perhaps these are only delusions."

"Delusions, Henry?"

"Hallucinations."

"But the weight, Henry?"

"Loss of weight frequently accompanies . . . a nervous disturbance. And then again, the whole thing may be completely physical . . . Are you sure you're trying to relax?"

"I've been trying very hard, Henry."

That night, Henry felt Thelma's hand shaking him. "Huh," he said from the depths of the pillow.

"Henry, wake up." There was fear in her voice.

"What is it?"

"Henry, I'm shrinking."

"You're what?"

"Shrinking. Lately , after I go to bed, I've been getting this feeling that I'm getting shorter and shorter. I've tried to disregard it, hoping it would go away. But I still feel I'm getting shorter and shorter."

"Let me get this straight, dear. First it was the chairs, now it's you. But that isn't possible, is it, dear?"

"I've been checking my height," Thelma whispered hoarsely. "It hasn't changed. But every night in bed this feeling hits me. I'm getting shorter. And shorter. Henry, what's the matter with me?" Suddenly a sob escaped Thelma. The bed shook. It was the first sob Henry had ever heard from his wife.

"You'll have to go back to the doctor," Henry said. "Meanwhile, try not to think about it. Try to sleep."

"Sleep," Thelma said dully.

"So how did you pull this one?" Altmeyer asked.

"Easy. Just lengthened the bedcovers every day. A fraction of an inch. Opened them up, put a new hem on. Her covers grew longer, she felt shorter."

"I see." There was a grudging admiration in Altmeyer's voice.

"I think she's about over the line," Henry said. "Turned negative. Of course, her positive side's still there, underneath, so I've got to be careful. According to the professor's book, a personality that gets hit by something that's too much for it goes way under. I sure hope he's right."

The next day, Henry whistled as he went about his household tasks. He did the laundry. He ironed. He dusted. He vacuumed. He prepared a tempting meal for Thelma.

When she was home from work and fed, Henry looked closely at his wife. Her once sturdy form was now bony. The skin of her face and neck was loose and wrinkled. Her complexion was haggard. Her ordinarily perfectly groomed hair showed signs of neglect. An anxious stare was in her eyes.

"Well, Thelma," Henry said, "we got to face the facts."

"Facts." Thelma grasped at the word.

"You've lost thirty-three pounds. The sinking feeling and failing eyesight you still have with you."

"I'm beginning to doubt my hearing now." Thelma's voice had a wild note. "I'm beginning to doubt everything."

"And the shrinking's still there?"

"Still there."

Henry tapped the edge of his chair thoughtfully. "Make me a drink, will you, Thelma?" he said experimentally.

"I'll be damned if I—" She stopped and passed her hand over her eyes. "A drink, Henry? All right, Henry. I . . . I don't know what gets into me. Sometimes I feel like I'm two people." Weeks ago she would have responded to this insane request with contemptuous fury. Now, she obediently mixed the drink.

"Ah," he breathed, sipping it. "Now, my slippers, there's a good girl."

She brought him his slippers.

"You'll have to go into the hospital for tests," Henry said. "Mental and physical. I hope they can help you." Henry shook his head gloomily. "I hope they can."

"You mean ..."

"I don't know." Henry kept shaking his head. "I don't like it. We have to face the truth, Thelma. Dr. Blackburn didn't understand your symptoms at all, and he's a highly competent physician. If they can't help you ... well, we'll have to prepare ourselves, I'm afraid."

"Prepare ourselves?"

"For the worst. For further deterioration. Mental and physical. You may be suffering from a rare and wasting ailment. These symptoms may be only the beginning."

"Oh, no!" Thelma cried. "I couldn't stand that."

"Courage," Henry said. "You must have courage. It wouldn't be brave to take the easy way out."

"The easy way?"

"Suicide. Try not to think of that, Thelma. Try not to."

"Oh!"

"Freedom from your complaints. Rest. No black future to face. Try not to think about this, Thelma."

"I'll ... try," Thelma said dully.

Henry reached into his pocket and brought out an empty pack of cigarettes. He explored it with a finger. "Out of smokes. I'll have to go out and buy some. Unless ... Thelma, would you ...?"

There was silence. Thelma's staring eyes didn't leave his face. She said suddenly, almost eagerly, "Yes, Henry, I'll go out and get you some cigarettes."

"You might take a little walk while you're out." Henry's tone grew soothing and suggestive. "Get some air. Be good for you. Why don't you stroll as far as the bridge? Just a pleasant walk."

"The ... bridge, Henry?"

"Very fine view from the bridge," Henry said. "The water is so ... peaceful. There's always a nice breeze at the bridge. Yes, why don't you walk to the bridge, Thelma? If I were you I would walk to the bridge."

"The bridge," Thelma said. "Yes." At the door, she turned and looked at Henry. "Goodbye, Henry," she whispered.

"Goodbye," Henry said.

"Well," Henry remarked to Altmeyer on the park bench the next day. "That's that."

"You don't mean . . ."

"Yep," Henry said complacently. "All over."

The two cronies sat in silence for a while, basking in the sun. At last, Altmeyer said, "Any trouble?"

"No trouble," Henry answered. "I'm in the clear. She jumped off a bridge while I was home."

There was another long silence. Altmeyer seemed lost in thought. "Smart feller, that professor." he remarked finally.

"Yep."

"Say, Henry," Altmeyer said, "you got any of that sandpaper left?"

Douglas Craig
Jambalaya

Vince Savoy is going to the chair this morning at Angola. That's the way it's got to be, Vince being what he is—an ex-trooper who went bad and brought shame on us all.

I'm no kin to Vince Savoy and I keep telling myself that I've no more pity for him than I'd feel for a mad dog loose in a schoolyard. And yet, while I sit here waiting for the dawn light to come crawling over the marshes, I'm plagued by the thought that there's somebody else who ought to be going with him. Me.

We grew up together in the bayous of Louisiana, in the shadow of oak and cypress that drip long gray moss like the tears of the dead. We rassled 'gators and dodged quicksands together, baying the moon on white nights. Girls were no problem between us in those days, and we got a big laugh out of it when they passed us up for some type in a tin hat, a *texien* from the oil rigs in the Gulf, or a well-heeled tripper from up north. Women, Vince used to say, brought trouble on nobody but themselves.

There were a couple of exceptions though, and the main one was Clo Ronsard. We'd have died for her any time, either one of us. But as things worked out it was worse than that. When I think of the years stretching out ahead of me now, I get sick.

My name is Mike Logan and I'm a trooper myself. What's more, I'm married to a girl that's too good for me. Her name is Felice. No kids yet, maybe never. That's not for me to say now.

It never crossed my mind that Felice would get hurt by anything I ever did. But I think she knew what was wrong with me, long before I was assigned to the Savoy case.

The first hint I had of it was that same night, when it struck me for the first time since my marriage that I didn't feel like going home. I hung around headquarters until everybody else was gone and then I went over to Ti'Jean's bar and leaned on that for a while. I didn't get drunk. It just seemed all of a sudden as if life was pretty raw, and I put away a few cherry flips with a bourbon base to kind of improve matters.

But it didn't work. I was in a bad situation, and I knew it.

Vince had dropped out of sight all of a sudden like a 'gator into its hole, and headquarters picked on me to pole him out. I squawked bloody murder, but it stuck and they detailed Dubois to help me, which was no help at all. Dubois is a good kid, you understand, but heavy footed, the kind you don't trust in the swamps with those size sixteens of his. When he lifts one up, the other only sinks in deeper.

But my main problem was Clo. To get any kind of line on Vince I'd have to keep an eye on her day and night, and I wasn't sure how that would work out. Not sure at all.

I was well stirred up by the time I stomped out of Ti'Jean's place and up along the bayou to my own house, pulling up short at the foot of the steps to draw a deep breath. Then I went on up and the good smell of simmering gumbo came out to greet me and I felt like a dog.

"Felice—?" I said, "Felice—?"

She came out of the kitchen quickly and quietly, wiping her hands on her pink apron, and held up her cheek for me to kiss, a cool, smooth cheek that smelled of rosewater. Homemade rosewater, at that. Her eyes were smiling, but she shoved me away gently and said, "You're late, Mike. You must be hungry. Will you eat right now, or would you like a shower first?"

"Shower," I grunted, holding my breath so the blast of bourbon wouldn't drown out the rosewater. I pulled out my gun and parked it on the shelf behind the clock, as usual. "Tough day," I told her, heading for the bedroom door with my shirt half off before I got there. "They've put me on the Savoy case—what d'you think of that?" And then, before she could speak, I whirled around and saw the sudden shocked paleness of her face. "Don't tell me!" I yipped. "I don't want to hear!"

She didn't have to tell me. I could hear the words inside my skull under the roar of the shower in the old tin tub ... *but Mike, you can't—Vince is your friend ... and what about Clo?*

Sure, what about Clo? I wanted to know myself. There was a rumor that she'd left Vince. Did that mean she was through with him now, for keeps?

I wasn't proud of the notion. Not just because Vince had been my friend a long time ago—hell, he was nobody's friend these days! And it wasn't only on account of my wife. The thought of Clo was like a fresh wound, the pain of it banked down under the jab of a needle—then wham! It busts loose before you even get to the dressing station. That happened to me in Korea.

I tried to stare myself down in the wavy old mirror over the washbasin, but it wasn't easy. I dug out a clean shirt and buttoned it slowly, looking around the shabby little room that Felice had tried to fix up with bright curtains and a bedspread to match and odd bits of furniture that didn't. Shabby was the word, all right. It was a safe bet that Vince Savoy had done better by his woman. But maybe she didn't care where she slept, as long as—

"Mike, are you coming?" Felice called out from the kitchen.

The tone of her voice made me prick up my ears. It sounded different. I remembered suddenly that she never had much to say about the Savoys, one way or another, since they got married, except once. Just once, when she turned to me in the night with a queer little sob and said, "Mike—wait—there's something I want to ask you. Mike—are you still in love with Clo?"

That knocked the breath out of me, but I said something fast and convincing like, "Hell, no—what ever gave you such a crazy idea?"

But she didn't say. Felice is the only woman I ever knew who never had much to say about anything. It could be restful, if you didn't start wondering what was going on inside her head.

"Coming," I called back, and a minute later I was digging into a dish of gumbo while she brought the coffee pot and a crusty hunk of bread with garlic butter that she'd been keeping hot in the oven. A meal for a king, as usual. "Great stuff, honey," I mumbled. "You never lose the touch."

"As a matter of fact," Felice said coolly, "it isn't very good tonight. Dubois was here a while ago and I gave him a plate, but he left half of it."

I quit eating. "Dubois?" I said. "What did *he* want?"

"You," said Felice. "He said he'd be back after supper." Her voice had a catch in it.

"Is that all?" I snapped suspiciously. "Did he say anything else?"

She thought about that for a second. "If you mean, did he tell me anything he shouldn't, no," she said. "I think you're too hard on Dubois, Mike. He's young, but he's a good policeman, too."

"Did he—" I was going to ask her if he'd said anything about the Savoy case but I shoved back my plate, instead, and reached for a cup of coffee.

"You see?" Felice said sadly. "It isn't very good, I'm sorry, Mike. I think I'll go and lie down for a little before I wash up. I have a small headache."

"You're not sick?" I asked quickly, but she'd slipped into the bedroom, closing the door behind her.

It's Clo, I thought. She's heard something about Clo. That dumb ape of a Dubois! But it didn't have to be Dubois. Everybody up and down the bayou knew that the four of us had grown up together, but that things had changed between us. That was enough for the busybodies with the knack of putting two and two together and making five out of it.

Vince and I had married the Ronsard girls, Clothilde and Felice. They were cousins, no kin to either Vince or me, and that's something in our part of the country.

There's no use denying that I'd been in love with Clo as far back as I can remember. But Vince was more her type. She saw him as some kind of hero, like the great old pirate, Jean Lafitte, whose raiding crews used to roam the Gulf, sacking and burning as they went.

Felice was different, the gentle kind, blonde as an angel. She thought the old time pirates were very bloody and sad, poor fellows. What were they, after all, but criminals and lost souls? But you could see the hero worship in Clo's big dark eyes when she looked at Vince. I used to wonder what went on behind those eyes that had come down to her through a long line of Cajun grandmothers, blazing and sultry by turns, loaded with dreams that she kept to herself.

But I could never see myself in any of those dreams, and Vince was my friend. So I married Felice. I got the best girl in the world, bar none. But Vince got the girl we'd both wanted from the time we found out what wanting was.

Felice and I settled down in a comfortable old house close enough to headquarters for me to report in any kind of weather, because we have some fast winds down here in the hurricane season. And we were happy. Maybe it wasn't all fire and honey, as the old folks say, but it was good, even when Felice held back a little. She felt that married love had a good deal of sinfulness in it, and that kind of put the damper on sometimes.

I hate to admit it, but I used to ask myself sometimes if a man didn't make a mistake to marry a woman who was so damned *good*. If only she'd leave off braiding her pretty hair into two tight pigtails every night, and maybe sew a bit of ribbon and lacy stuff into her nightgown. But what kind of animal would want to change a good wife into something that was half hussy?

Vince wouldn't settle for a quiet life, no matter how you sliced it. He transferred to one of the new oil and shrimp towns on the Gulf, where things weren't so tame. Clo had the same streak of wildness in her, I guess. She was crazy for the change.

They bought a modern, ranch-type house, all brick and glass, with a TV aerial as tall as an oil derrick, and an outside freezer that packed the kind of food they liked to eat these days. That freezer really tore it for the folks back home on the bayou, the old time *habitants* who still eat better than any other people in the world, and know it.

There was an ugly rumor that Clo Savoy wouldn't even cook for her husband. Least of all the gumbo and jambalaya that no real man could live without. And her coffee—! It was only a pinch of brown powder that melted away at the touch of hot water. Where were the grounds? The dark, rich, useful grounds that held up the pot on the back of the stove from one day to the next?

Most of it was woman-talk that Felice picked up when she went visiting up and down the bayou, but I kept half an ear cocked, just in case. God forgive me, I was listening for worse, for some hint that the Savoys weren't getting along nearly as well as they might.

After awhile, though, there was another kind of buzz down at headquarters and I gave both ears to that one.

Vince had always been wild, with a sort of blind courage that drove him into every clip joint and dope den along the coast, and more times than not he got the man he was after. He barged deep into the marshlands on the trail of smugglers and hijackers that lived off the muskrat trappers and raided the payboats that were heavy with dough in a good season.

The trouble was that Vince was a smart money man himself, and they don't last. He started out on the force in a blaze of fireworks, but the show winked out in a smelly smudge of damp powder.

That's when the bad breaks began. And it wasn't the sweating taxpayer who squawked about Vince to headquarters—it was the crooks.

The first time it was a payroll job. Somebody knocked off an elderly Chinese who made a fortune drying shrimp in the old fashioned Cantonese way. He couldn't add up to ten without one of those rattling bead counters they call an abacus, and he still paid off his help in silver dollars, the way his grandpa used to do.

One payday somebody plugged him in the back of the head and took off with the cash. We never found out for sure who actually pulled the job or how he got rid of the proceeds. Our real headache was who thought it up? The brains behind it, so to speak.

Of course, there weren't any. We tried it for size on all the "known criminals" in the parish, but all we pulled in was a mess of hurt feelings. Nobody, but nobody, was going to own up to a corny, hamstrung job like that! Some of the biggest thugs in three states were so shocked and embarrassed professionally that they were ready to tell what they knew. It made quite a story. So simple.

A state trooper had planned this one, they told us. An "amachoor," what else? His name? Sure, sure—his name was Vince Savoy.

It was the laugh of the year, that picture of Vince staggering around under a load of hot silver dollars. He laughed himself when he was called down to headquarters for routine questioning. "Crazy, man —crazy!"

But it started me wondering. The Savoys were living high off the hog these days, and his pay was the same as my own. How did he do it?"

A wealthy shipbuilder was the next to go. No silver cartwheels this time, just green paper currency, although some of it might be hard to pass. The man had been shot in the back and had fallen forward across his pay table. The stuff must have been soaked with his blood. Nobody tried to pin this on Vince, but the Savoys came out with a fancy car as long as a deep-sea lugger, and I stopped wondering. I knew.

The big surprise came when Vince quit the force of his own accord. The whisper got around that he'd rigged himself up a neat little syndicate, a protection racket based on all he'd discovered while he was in uniform. The slimy roots of it reached up from the muck at the bottom to the top where the politics grow.

Vince was playing pirates for real now, I thought that night, as I paced up and down in front of my house, waiting for Dubois. I wondered how Clo was taking it.

A voice came to me through the half-dark, along with the crunch of heavy boots. "Logan?" This would be Dubois turning up after supper, as promised. "Sorry if I kept you waiting."

"Think nothing of it," I said. "Maybe we could stroll over to Ti'Jean's for a couple of beers." And then, when we were out of range of the bedroom window, I let him have it. "What the hell did you say to my wife?"

"So help me, nothin'!" Dubois yelped like a kicked pup. "I just asked her if she'd seen Clo Savoy since she got back to the bayou—"

"You did, did you?" I snapped. My tongue was thick in my mouth. Clo—back on the bayou with the old folks on their camp boat. Clo skinning muskrats and running the bloody pelts through a wringer, the way she had to when she was a kid. What kind of life was that? In spite of myself, I said gruffly, "What did she say? Felice, I mean."

"Nothin'," Dubois said glumly.

I laughed. "That sounds about right," I said, but when we got to Ti'Jean's place I was still sweating.

Dubois chattered along for a while over his beer, but I didn't pay him much mind until I heard that name again and I snapped at it. "What's that about Savoy? If you've got any fresh dope, spill it!"

He shook his head. "It's all just say-so. You know."

It was never any more than that. Nobody had ever pinned anything on Vince, and maybe we never would. It wasn't even our job to pick him up unless we caught him standing over a body with a gun in his fist. Knowing Vince, that didn't seem likely. I said so, and Dubois tried to look tough, flattered to be talked to like a grownup policeman. It was pretty funny and I was trying to wipe a sour grin off my face when he let drop something that hit a nerve.

"That gal of his," Dubois said, looking wise. "She's mad like hell at him. Maybe she'd talk."

"Clo?" I said. "You're crazy. She'd feed herself to the sharks first!"

"Not her—not Mrs. Savoy!" Dubois cut in. He was shocked. "The other one. That doll he took up with after his wife left him."

There was a queer lurch inside me. Another woman, eh? I'd never heard a breath about another woman. "I don't believe it," I said. "Whoever she is, she's lying."

"He's been seen with her a couple of times," Dubois said hopefully. "But it wasn't long before he gave her the air."

I whistled. That made sense. No other woman could get Clo off his mind. Nobody but Clo could do that. I knew . . . But this briefing was getting out of hand. I was supposed to be filling in a rookie on a tough new case, and here I was with my head stuck through a sheet while he fired coconuts at me.

"Okay," I said, tossing a bill on the bar. "Let's pack it in for tonight. See you in the morning."

"Well, th-thanks—" Dubois mumbled, blinking, and I clapped him on the shoulder, sorry for catching him off balance. "You'll rack up a medal for this job, kid," I told him. And with that I headed home by myself, thinking sixteen to the dozen. Another woman! Well, well, well. . . .

I wasn't drunk, but I wasn't sober either. I stumbled on the front steps and barged in with a heavier tread than I meant to. I'd forgotten Felice had a headache. But there she was, sitting in her own chair under the lamp, with a pile of mending beside her. She was sewing buttons on a shirt.

I stopped short. My gun was lying on the table next to her.

She looked up at me and bit off a thread. "I think you ought to be more careful, Mike," she said quietly. "You keep forgetting your gun."

That was all, and God knows it wasn't much. I'd always been careless about my gun, and there was more than one crook from the waterprairies who would have jumped at the chance to pick me off unarmed. Felice had a right to be worried, but tonight I took it as a personal insult.

"When I need your advice, I'll ask for it!" I yelled. "And as for that shirt, it's old enough to throw away—I won't wear it!"

She didn't answer. Her face was still pale but while she put the needle through the hole of a button there was the ghost of a smile on her lips. It took some of the fight out of me. I sat down and started to take off my shoes.

"Well, say something," I growled. "Tell me I'm drunk. Tell me I'm some trooper to be running around in the dark without my gun. Tell me you curse the day you married me—"

"All that?" she asked, the needle flashing into a new hole. "It doesn't sound much like me, does it? Besides, it's none of it true."

I kicked my shoes across the room and rested my head on my fists. I knew I ought to come up with some kind of apology for my rough talk, but I didn't feel like it. I felt like staying mad.

"Mike," Felice said softly.

"Yeah?"

"It's Clo, isn't it? It always has been. Oh, Mike, why did you marry me? It must have been hard—hard for you, I mean."

"Woman," I said, when I could speak at all. "You are out of your mind."

But she shook her head. "You know I'm not," she told me.

I opened my mouth to say something, but she beat me to it. "I don't suppose it's ever occurred to you that I might get tired of playing second fiddle—oh, not to anybody else! Not even Clo. Just to some crazy dream that never had an earthly chance of coming true!"

If there was an answer to that, I didn't know what it was. But I tried. "Since you're talking about Clo," I said, "it's true that I had a bad case on her once—puppy love, I guess you'd call it. But that's long over."

Felice laughed, a thin, silvery sound like ice in a glass. "Oh, Mike, you do try to hard! You're so honest—*policeman* honest—in all the things that don't count! Goodnight, Mike, I'm going to bed."

She stood up and reached for my gun. I suppose she was going to put it back behind the clock, but I jumped.

"Lay off that!" I barked. "You could hurt yourself with that thing!"

Felice gave it to me, but after she'd gone into the bedroom I sat there holding it, my hands slippery with sweat. I'd better find another place for it, someplace she didn't even know about. If she got hurt, I'd never forgive myself—never. I ended up by putting it on a shelf in the china closet, behind the wedding plates we never used, and turned the key in the lock of the glass door.

I was too stirred up to feel like sleeping, so I went out on the *galerie* and smoked a while, looking up and down the bayou where the lights were winking out one by one. Clo was up there somewhere, living on the campboat with the old people, the way she did when we were kids.

I strolled along the old footpath that was seldom used these days. There was a new paved road lying behind the houses, running all the way from the Gulf. You could make time on that road with a motorcycle or a squard car, but it was just as useful for a fast getaway—

That's what I was thinking when I saw the headlights of a big car that came roaring down toward the coast. I was surprised when it pulled up short and a voice came to me from between two old Cajun houses that were pretty much like my own.

" 'Allo, you there—Mike! Mike Logan!"

All the blood in me turned cool and slow, sluggish as the dark stream of the bayou beside me. I'd known it all my life, that voice. It belonged to Vince Savoy.

" 'Allo yourself," I said. I didn't have to yell because there he was already, out of the car and coming towards me, tall and thin and swaggering, like the great old pirate Jean Lafitte himself. It was the first I'd seem him in a couple of years.

We didn't shake hands, and somehow that bothered me. There was a little matter of mayhem and murder, sure, and me assigned to tail him from here to hell and back, on account of I was a trooper and he was a crook—but for some reason that didn't stack up very high at the moment. Damn it, I was glad to see him! Still and all, I didn't hold out my hand, and neither did he. Presently the feeling flickered out between us like a tallow candle at the grave of something dead and gone.

"Are you lookin' for me, Mike?" Vince said. His voice sounded light and kind of jeering, like a mockingbird.

"I'm lookin' for you, all right," I said. "But it don't do me much good at the moment. As you very well know."

He laughed. "Man, don't I just! Would I be here if I had fresh blood on my hands?"

"Probably not," I said. "But keep lookin' over your shoulder, boy. I'll be there some day, right behind you."

I couldn't see his face, only the gleam of his strange, light-colored eyes. Maybe he was smiling, but I couldn't prove that either. "Thanks for the tip, Mike. I'll bear it in mind. Where are you headin'?"

"I'm not," I told him. "Just ramblin' along, lookin' around."

But he seemed to want to toss the ball back and forth, just for kicks.

"An evenin' stroll, eh?" Vince said. "For instance, you didn't know that Clo's folks have got their campboat tied up a short piece from here, up the bayou?"

"What's it to me? I've got nothin' on her either."

"That's right, you haven't," he said thoughtfully. "They've worked her over at headquarters already. I guess you know that."

"Well, you guess wrong," I snapped. I was getting mad now. "They'd no business doing that. What's she got to do with the crazy way you act?"

"Not a thing," Vince told me smoothly. "They found that out. She made like them three monkeys—no talk, no hear, no see. You know Clo."

"How is Clo?" I said, to be saying something. And there was a long silence between us, heavy as lead.

"I wouldn't know," he said finally. "She won't talk to me. So long, Mike—see you around." And he was heading back to his car before I could speak again. I stood there staring after him and the haze of light and dust that kept getting smaller as he burned up the new road at ninety or more. The fool thought came into my head that it would be tough luck if he got pulled in for speeding. Then my mind switched back to Clo.

So she wouldn't talk to him. But why would he tell *me* that?

The answer was right there. I couldn't miss it. The four of us had grown up together, he and I, and Clo and Felice. It wouldn't have crossed his mind to lie to me about a personal matter like that. He still believed I was his friend. It doesn't make me feel any better, let me tell you that.

They say there's nothing like an uneasy conscience to turn a man uglier than he is already. I was sure in no mood to go home. I felt stubborn, mean, and I started walking again, only this time I knew where I was going. I'd been assigned to the Savoy case, hadn't I? That meant keeping tabs on the two of them, didn't it? Okay. That's what I was doing.

The old campboat was tied up under a tent of long gray moss that hung down from a big, black cypress. I was standing in the shadow of it when I saw her come out of the deckhouse and look towards me, shielding her eyes against the glare of the deck light.

"Who's there?" she asked sharply.

I went forward, afraid of the change I'd see in her. She was wearing a green dress cinched in at the waist and a flowery apron over it. Her figure was a little fuller, that's all. Maybe richer is a better word. Her dark hair lifted in the light breeze and blew across her forehead just the way it used to, and her feet were bare.

"Mike!" she cried, and she sounded glad. "Oh, Mike, it's been such a long time!" She ran to me as I stepped over the low deckrail, but not all the way. I saw the quick color whip into her face as she checked herself.

"I came close to hugging you," she told me, smiling. "But that would never do. What would Felice say?"

"Likewise Vince," I said, and the tone of it was none too pleasant. "How're things with you, Clo?"

"As if you didn't know," she said. Her face changed. A look of sadness came over it. "You won't ask me any questions, will you, Mike? They tried that at headquarters. It didn't work."

"I'm off duty," I said. There was no such thing as being off duty on a case like this, and she knew it, but she let it go by.

"Will you take some coffee, Mike? For old times' sake? The old folks have gone to church, so I'm alone."

"Just a drop, maybe," I said. "Then I'll be on my way."

Well, the busybodies had lied about her coffee. It was hot and strong enough to stand alone. I tossed it off, knowing I'd best get out of there fast. The crazy dream Felice had been talking about wasn't just a dream any more. Clo was near enough now for me to feel the warmth of her and the darkness around us rocked with the sweet smell of oleander. Not far off a bull 'gator bellowed and threshed in the slow water, sending a little scurry of ripples along the side of the boat. Clo shivered, wrapping her arms about herself like a kid that feels cold or scared.

"You know, I'd forgotten—" Clo said softly. "I'd forgotten it was so beautiful back here—and so *awful*—"

She was scared! It was a real shock to me. I'd seen her mad when we were kids, spitting mad and ready to take out her spite on anybody, the same as Vince. But I'd never seen a look of fear on her face before.

I was so close to reaching for her that I took a step back and hit the deckhouse wall. A kind of rank bitterness welled up in me. "You like it better in Roux City with the neon signs and the jukeboxes, eh?" I said. "Well, why don't you go back to him? You won't be seeing much of him when he starts doing time."

"Mike, don't *talk* like that!"

"Like what? I'm up to the nose myself with muskrats and mosquitoes. Maybe I'll give the job a heave and stake myself to a lugger and a stretch of clean salt water. I always thought I had the makings of a jumbo man—"

"Stop—please ... stop!" She grabbed my arm hard and her small fingers felt like the claws of a bird. "That's the way *he* used to talk! And where did it get us? You and Felice would end up the way we—we—" Her voice broke in a dry little sob. "He's changed so, Mike. You've no idea! But you don't just stop loving people."

"That's a fact," I said. Before I knew it my arm went around her, pulling her close to me, and she buried her face in my shoulder and cried and cried. So help me, there was nothing worse in me at that moment than pity for her.

Finally she pulled away, lifting her apron to mop up the tears. "I'll never go back to him, Mike. But I left everything behind me, all my clothes, everything—" her voice trailed off and I knew that she was thinking about her things too. Women are funny. Even Felice, with that old shirt she kept mending and never could bring herself to throw away.

"Well," I said. "I'll be on my way."

"Don't get mad, Mike," Clo said, very low. "You're sore and unhappy, I know. Honest, I *know*. There's never been anybody but Vince for me, but if there was, if there ever could be. ..." She stopped.

That was more than I could take.

I grabbed her by the shoulders and shook her until her head fell back and she set her teeth in her lip to keep from crying out. "You can't devil me like that! If it was anybody but him, who would it be—who?"

The answer was so soft I hardly caught it. "You, Mike—you."

I let go of her. I knew I'd go crazy if I didn't. But I was past being polite, or even careful. "Suppose he two-timed you? What then?"

She looked as if I'd run a knife into her. "He'd better not," she said quietly. "I'd cut his heart out. The same as he would mine."

I cursed myself for a dumb ox. I'd come close to telling her about the other woman. I was getting as bad as Dubois. But there was one more thing to be said, so I said it. "If I can pin anything on him, Clo, I'll pick him up. But I won't hurt him—not if I can help it."

She nodded without saying anything, and I climbed over the side of the campboat, stepping carefully over the wet mud so I wouldn't sprawl on my face in front of her.

Then I went on home.

After that night I tried to put Clo out of my mind for good. But she was in my blood. It was worst of all when I was with Felice. There was kind of a wall between us, and it shamed me to find I couldn't beat it.

You don't just stop loving people, Clo had said. That's the truth. But there was more to it than that. You don't lie to somebody you love, either, and I loved my wife.

I tried to make it up to her in little ways, like the bunch of store-bought roses I had sent from town for her birthday, and the king-size box of pralines I had shipped over from N.O., and I talked her into spending a few extra bucks on something new and pretty to wear. But I couldn't forget what she'd said that night about "all the things that don't count," and the hurt was there in her eyes, no matter how hard she tried to hide it.

Meanwhile, Vince kept himself out of sight. He didn't need to, as far as headquarters was concerned. He wasn't even on the "wanted" list. But I was curious. Then the word got around that he'd left the parish altogether and I figured he had some big job lined up and wanted to be far, far away when they pulled it off. As it turned out, I was right. Vince had a good organization.

It was Dubois who picked up the information that Vince was having himself a time in New Orleans, and that he had taken a woman along with him. No, not Clo. The other one.

"You can't pick him up for that," I said.

"Maybe not, but she's madder than a wet hen," Dubois told me, happy to be in the know. "Savoy gave her the air again. That's twice, now. She's ready to talk."

"Don't make me laugh," I said, burying my nose in a pint of beer. "If that baby had anything on Vince, he wouldn't let her out of his sight."

But Dubois had dreamed up a different angle. "This doll wants to be friendly," he explained. "If anything breaks, she'd be on the side of the law."

"That's the place to be," I said. "Is something going to break?"

"There's one person who might know." Dubois leaned across the bar and scooped himself a handful of boiled shrimp, feeding them into his face slowly, one by one. It made me feel kind of sick.

"Okay," I asked. "Who?"

"Mrs. Savoy," he said, grinning.

I had to hold down my right fist hard to keep from pasting him one. "I told you before, she won't squawk." But Dubois continued.

"Not even if this other dame gets to her with a lot of stuff about Savoy, personal stuff that only another woman would know?"

"You slimy slug," I said to my trusty sidekick. "You dirty—"

"Hold it!" Dubois gulped down the last shrimp and backed away from me. "This doll hit town an hour ago and I just got through dropping her at the campboat to pay a call on Savoy's wife. What's the harm in that?"

I shoved past him and headed home, sick as a pup. But I still didn't believe it would work. Clo wouldn't talk—I'd have bet my soul on it. She'd find some other way to get even, maybe, but not that!

When I got home I found the place a litter of boxes and white tissue paper and Felice trying on the new stuff she'd bought on a shopping trip to town that afternoon. It looked as if she'd bought out a store, and I almost said so, habit being what it is.

Her eyes were bright and her cheeks pink with excitement as she held the things up in front of her, showing them off to me. There was a real pretty dress with bright flowers all over it, and a yellow one with a big skirt that stood out like a dancing girl's, and she'd had something done to her hair. It was shorter and curled around her face. She'd bought shoes, and a lot of underwear, some plain, some kind of lacy. I stood there gawking while I felt my face get red and the queer, sick feeling grew in the pit of my stomach. I remembered the times I'd wished she'd do something like this—fix herself up a little, make like life was more worth living—I don't know how to say it even now.

The thing was, it was too late! She looked pretty as a valentine, but nothing stirred in me. Nothing. And she knew it. I suppose a woman always does.

I saw the color drain out of her face and she started folding the things up and tucking them away in the tissue paper without looking at me. "Silly—silly—" I heard her whisper to herself, as if I weren't even there, and then she went off into the bedroom and put the boxes away on a high shelf in the closet.

"Aren't you going to wear them?" I said gruffly. "Honey—?"

But the bedroom door banged in my face and presently I heard the creak of bedsprings and the muffled sound of her sobbing. But I didn't go and try to comfort her. I knew I'd make a mess of it. Instead I went into the kitchen and broke out the bottle of bourbon we kept for company and went to work on that, cussin' myself.

That was a long night. I stayed out on the *galerie*, smoking, my head thick with drink and disgust with myself and with Dubois, wondering what had happened on the campboat between Clo and that other woman of Savoy's. I wouldn't have put it past Clo to kill her if the notion took her. Even that didn't seem as bad as Clo there facing up to scolding chatter of the old folks, Clo with her pride smashed, living out her days in the ruins of it. . . . But there didn't seem to be any police action indicated that night, so I finished the bottle.

Next day headquarters filled me in. Dubois had picked up Savoy's ex-doll, crying, but all in one piece, when Clo put her off the campboat. She was having second thoughts and now she wanted protective custody. She didn't say whether she was scared of Vince or Clo, but we obliged by locking her up. It brightened up the old jailhouse a good deal for a few days. Then we forgot about her.

The fuse had been lit for the biggest bank robbery the state had ever seen, and it blew up right in our faces, vault and all, netting close to two hundred grand. As usual, there wasn't a jot of evidence to connect it with Vince Savoy.

Two cashiers were killed, both women. Likewise the president of the bank, who was seventy-one, and his favorite grandson, aged nine, who was playing checkers with grandpa in the private office at the time. All four were tossed through the plate glass window into the street. It looked like a massacre, which it was.

We were all put to work on it, every trooper that wasn't nailed down, and pretty soon the F.B.I. came swarming in, with press, radio, and TV right on their tail.

We put Savoy's ex-dollie over the hurdles once more, but she was a complete washout and we let her go, limp as a dishrag and still whimpering for police protection.

Then it was Clo's turn again. We still didn't have anything on her, or Vince, and when we asked her to stop by headquarters for a small chat, she came.

It was the same old story. Nothing. But when I saw her coming out afterward her face told me that she might know plenty. Horror and despair were cut deeply into it, and the look in those great, dark Cajun eyes was a look out of hell.

She went past me without a word.

I could be wrong, I thought. Maybe it was the mark that woman left on her, with her dirty tales about Vince. Maybe the bank job was as much of a surprise to Clo as it was to the bank. But something made me go after her.

The street was shaded by big trees and when she moved from one black shadow to the next it looked as if she'd gone underground. I walked faster and caught up with her.

"What do you want, Mike?" she asked, not even turning her head.

"Mostly I want you to know I had no part in that lousy deal."

She pulled away from the hand I laid on her arm, but not before I felt the chill of her flesh. "That woman? No, Mike, I know you didn't."

Then suddenly she started running. I never knew a girl who could move so fast. She always could when she was a skinny little kid, high-stepping it through the marshes like a heron. Where was she heading now?

Dubois pulled up alongside me in his old jalopy and I got in. "You want us to chase her?" Dubois asked me, every inch the trooper.

"You try that," I said, "and I'll kick your brains out. Run me home."

I felt in my bones that Vince Savoy was the one we wanted, but there wasn't a crack in the big silence that wrapped up his whole organization. I kept thinking he'd come back and answer the headquarters call for routine questioning, the way he had in that silver payroll job a long time ago. Having been a trooper himself, he knew all the right answers, and it sure would look better for him if he showed up of his own accord. But he didn't.

Meanwhile the public was getting pretty wrought up about the kid who'd died. They wanted some kind of police action, any kind, but fast.

It felt like a storm building up. You can smell it and feel it and see it in the queer light over everything, but you never know how bad it's going to be until it hits, and then maybe it's too late. That's how things were the night I got the call from Roux City.

There was a strong wind brewing in the Gulf, driving inland in gusts that churned up the sluggish water of the bayou, but it didn't budge the heavy heat that hung over everything like steam.

Felice had a lot of nice cold stuff ready for the table, nothing hot except the coffee. We were in the middle of supper when the phone rang. "I'll get it—" Felice said. But after she did her voice turned cold as the food on the plates. "It's Clo, Mike."

It was Clo all right, her voice thick and queerly choked. "Mike, I'm back in the house in Roux City."

"That's nice," I said sarcastically. "That's dandy. Am I the first to know?"

"No—no—it's not what you think—" She was close to crying. "I only came back to get some of my things. There's nobody here but me. I've got to see you, Mike—now, tonight! Please, please ..."

"Okay," I said. "I'll be there." I hung up and turned to find Felice standing close by, her eyes dark with hurt and something that looked like fear.

"You're not going?" she whispered. "What right does she have to call you like that? Don't go, Mike."

"It's my job," I said flatly. "You know that."

"Clo? Clo's part of your job?"

"You know she is! You married a trooper," I reminded her.

Felice called something after me, but I didn't hear what it was as I took the front steps three at a time on my way to headquarters to connect with a motorcycle, and less than an hour later I rolled into Roux City on the tail end of a rain squall that flooded the streets.

I found the address of the Savoy house in my notebook. I'd put a red ring around it the day I got my assignment and now the ink ran under the rain, leaving a red smear on the page and on my fingers.

The house stood out from the junk heaps around it like a dimestore diamond in a can of bait. Too flashy for my taste, but it wasn't my house. I ran the bike around to the side and parked it behind some bushes. Then I went to the front door and rang the bell.

That's when I got my first jolt. My hand went back to where my gun ought to be, and wasn't. It flashed over me that that's what Felice had called after me when I left. I'd forgotten it again. I'm one fine trooper.

The door opened and Clo stood there. "You got here fast, Mike."

"That's what you wanted," I said, looking around. It was quite a place. Better furniture than I ever saw outside of a catalogue; lamps and bright colored rugs and drapes that hung all the way down to the floor. I whistled. "Say, this is something."

She nodded. "Vince likes to live good. I used to, too, when I thought it was on the up and up."

"Come off it," I said. "Don't tell me you thought he struck oil?"

I was looking her over now, thinking she was like one of those movie queens that look as if they don't care if they get caught in the rain. She had on a little short black dress with no sleeves to it, and no makeup. Her hair was slicked back, showing every line and bone of her face, dead white, the eyes half shut and the mouth narrowed down to a thin line. She didn't seem like the girl on the campboat with dark hair blowing in the wind. This was somebody strange. She looked as if she'd just been pulled out of the river.

"You need a drink," she said, quietly. "It's still bourbon, isn't it?"

"Thanks." I took the drink she held out to me. "Why did you want to see me?"

She curled up on the big sofa, her long legs drawn up under her. "Sit down, Mike—no, here beside me—that's better—" And then, "This is your big break, Mike. I'm telling all I know."

"You're lyin'," I said. "This is some kind of runaround."

She shook her head slowly. "No. You still haven't got anything on him, I know that. But you will have when I tell you what I know."

I stared at her. No shame, nothing but a kind of frozen pain.

"Why the switch?" I asked her finally. "When they had you down at headquarters, you wouldn't talk. I don't get it."

She had her hands twisted together in her lap, tight enough to hurt, and her eyes kind of veered off mine for a second. "That child—that little boy in the bank—Vince shouldn't have let that happen."

So that was it. Or was it?

"Who says he did?" I said carefully.

"He planned that bank job," she told me. "He worked on it for months. I thought it was just another of his crazy schemes. Vince always has to have something cooking . . ." She stopped.

There was that look again, the one I'd seen on her when she came out of headquarters. That look of the damned.

"You're sure that's what's eatin' you?" I asked her. It wasn't nice, but I had to know. "You're sure it's the bank job that's botherin' you and not that other doll he's been carryin' on with?"

"I—I don't know what you mean." It was hardly a whisper, hardly a sound at all.

"I think you do. You told me that night on the campboat that you'd cut his heart out if he two-timed you. That's what you're doin'. And you know what he'll do to you if you rat on him."

"Why shouldn't I?" she cried out. "He's killed everything I ever felt for him. *Why shouldn't I?*"

"Take it easy," I said, putting my big paw over her locked fingers, trying to warm the ice out of them. "You don't have to be the one to sell him out. Some day we'll catch him dropping slugs in a pay phone and that'll be it. We can't miss."

"You can—you can!" she almost screamed at me. "While you're playing cops and robbers, he'll do something worse!"

"Okay, okay, take it easy."

She sat quiet for a long minute, that look frozen on her face, while a dull ugly anger rose up in me and I choked on it. I thought, it's still Vince, Vince, Vince—!

When she started talking again I was slow to tune in.

"—I guess you're right, Mike. I can't do it, after all. I thought I could when I phoned you, but now it's all died out inside me. I'm glad you came, though. I did want to see you again, just one more time."

She leaned back against the cushions, looking at me with those big dark eyes, and the hard whiteness of her face seemed to soften a little. There was a kind of sweetness about her now. Maybe it was remembering old times, I don't know. But it took the breath out of me. When she held out both hands to me I thought for a flash that maybe I had it doped right, that she felt the same about me as I had about her, for half of our lives.

Her hands were still cold and shaking when I took them, but not for long. She came into my arms with a sob, like a tired kid coming home, and the warmth and sweetness of her overwhelmed me. I couldn't have stopped myself if I'd tried, and nobody could have stopped me.

What happened between us in that fine flashy house of Savoy's that night was like the old dream come true. We didn't stay there in the living room long. I lifted her up and carried her into a big, dim bedroom next to it, and once, when she turned her face away from mine for a moment, wondered if she was remembering him. But it was too late then.

It wasn't long before Clo fell asleep. She lay curled up on the big bed like a ten-year-old, with one hand under her cheek and her dark hair spread out on the pillow. I didn't remember any crying, but there were tears on her cheeks.

I pulled the silk spread partly over her before I went into the bathroom, leaving the door open a crack.

I heard Vince when he set his key in the front door and the slam of it after him. Queer as it seems, at a time like that, my first thought was that he'd played it smart—he'd come back for questioning.

He came straight through to the bedroom, shoving his keys back into his pocket. Then he saw Clo and stopped short.

It was plain that the last thing on earth he expected was seeing her there. At first he looked surprised and glad, but then his face turned dark. It's hard to put it, but the place wasn't neat—the way it would have been if she'd been alone. He knew.

Vince's right hand slid back to his gun just as I swung open the bathroom door and came out. He rocked back a step and swung the gun around to cover me. "So it's you! Stay where you are, Mike!" He nodded towards the bed. "Who was with her?"

"Me," I said.

I was watching him close and I saw what was in his mind. I dived into him. There was that one lunge and a jab or two before we locked, but it wasn't me he wanted. He was holding his gun arm free, but not for me. The gun exploded and we both stood there staring at what he'd done. She never even woke up.

The room started swinging around me and there was a thick, roaring noise inside my head. When I could speak, I said, "Okay, Vince. It's my turn. Get it over."

He laughed. If you could call it a laugh. It was more like the snarl of a dog that's been kicked in the belly. He was kind of bent over, looking up at me out of the tops of his eyes, and I saw then that he was gone—all gone. The craziness that used to come and go in those queer light eyes of his had moved in to stay.

"There's no hurry about you, Mike. I'd as soon see you sweat a while."

He went over to the bed and pulled up the spread to cover the horror and ruin of Clo's face. As he did, I dived again. This time the gun fell to the floor at my feet. When I picked it up, all the fight went out of him. It must have been some kind of reflex. He shook his head a couple of times, as if it needed that to clear it.

"Man, oh man," Vince said, "I wouldn't want to be in your shoes. No, sirree. You've got to go on living—maybe for a long, long time."

I motioned him into the front room and called headquarters.

When I put down the phone Vince asked me for a smoke. I shook a couple loose in the pack and he broke out a fancy lighter, gold. We sat there smoking until we heard the screech of the sirens.

Later, when they had him booked, I asked him if he wanted anything and he said, "Hell, no. Not any more."

"You could put up an argument," I said. "The unwritten law, all that stuff. I wouldn't contest it."

He even smiled a little. "Thanks just as much, Mike. Say hello to Felice." He turned his back to me. But when I was leaving he swung around on his heels and stopped me. "Don't get the notion Clo was in love with you," he snarled. "There was another dame and Clo found out about her. It was a spite job! You hear me? A spite job!"

"Sure," I said. If it made him feel any better to think that, okay. Me, I wasn't so sure.

At the trial Vince clammed up completely. He wouldn't tell them anything they wanted to know about his organization, but it will come out sooner or later. Without him it will fall apart, and a few prominent citizens are going to start doing time along with the hoods. It's just a question of when.

He wouldn't defend himself against the murder charge either. He said he killed her, that's all. He wouldn't say why. Vince wasn't the kind of man to tell the world his wife had cheated on him. He left that job to me.

It was in my official report, all of it. What else could I do from inside a uniform? I'm a policeman.

They grilled me for three days in the back room at headquarters, hoping against hope that there was some terrible mistake. But when all was said and done, I was the fair-haired trooper who'd picked up Vince Savoy on a charge that would stick. They settled on some kind of disciplinary action "to be determined later."

What worried me sick was Felice. She'd stuck by me through it all, tight-lipped and dry-eyed. But she never said a word. Felice isn't much of a talker.

The old dream died with Clo, the "crazy dream that never had an earthly chance of coming true." It's my job now to make up to Felice for the hurt I've given her, to prove I love her in the ways that count.

Harold Rolseth
Tight Fix

Arly Minto was a successful businessman. He lived in a shack on the fringe of the city dump and, for his services of watching out for fires and shooing scavengers away, he was granted by the authorities sole scavenging rights to the dump himself.

With the exception of food, everything that Arly needed was supplied by the dump. Arly never ceased to marvel at the valuable things people threw away. Take the trousers he was wearing, for example. They were of excellent material and practically new, and why they should ever have been discarded was beyond comprehension.

The fact that they were a vivid blue and had been designed for a robust six foot figure, while Arly was slightly over five feet and scarcely cast a shadow, had not deterred him from using them. Arly had merely snipped off a foot or so from each leg and pinned six inch tucks on each side and with these alterations found they fit him perfectly.

The dump not only supplied Arly with necessities but with luxuries as well. A Persian rug covered the floor of his shack, and although stains of many sorts superimposed a second pattern over the original one, it was nevertheless a genuine Persian product.

Even Arly's liquid refreshments were supplied by the dump. Bottles from the city's taverns and night clubs were deposited in vast quantities, and a goodly portion of Arly's day was spent in emptying the few drops of liquid these bottles frequently contained into a gallon jug colorfully labeled *Fleur-de-Lis Burgundy*.

Arly did not discriminate among the various liquids he trickled into his jug. Whisky, rum, gin, and wine were all equally acceptable. Lemon extract Arly also regarded with favor, and certain hair tonics whose labels indicated a high alcoholic content. And there was a vivid purple concoction known as Scripp's Wonder Tonic which Arly held in high esteem. Quite frequently he found almost full bottles of Scripp's, an indication, perhaps, that the purchasers had discovered after one swallow that their afflictions were much easier to endure than the tonic.

Arly had to admit that, taken straight, Scripp's was not especially refreshing, but when combined with an assortment of other fluids, much of its unpleasantness was submerged. And there was no question but that it gave a splendid color and sparkle to the otherwise drab contents of the jug.

Arly was not a lone drinker. He carefully hoarded each week's collection of liquor for Friday evening when he acted as host to his intimate friend, Joseph J. Jeffwick, better known as Jay-Jay.

Jay-Jay lived in the basement of the city jail next to the morgue and considered himself a valued member of the police force, although this was not precisely the case. The truth was that the police had become so weary of hauling him in on drunk and disorderly charges that they had finally provided him with quarters in the basement in return for sundry odd jobs. Jay-Jay was permitted to come and go as he saw fit provided he did not go too far out of bounds with his drinking. This, except for his bouts with Arly, he could not often do, since he had no income.

There was a deep bond between the two old men. Jay-Jay loved Arly for his lavish Friday night hospitality, and Arly treasured Jay-Jay for his worldly wisdom and companionship. For Jay-Jay, living as he did under the jail and only a step or two from the morgue, was a gold mine of grisly and morbid tales.

On this particular Friday night, Arly awaited his friend with a high degree of anticipation. A half tumbler sample of his brew had convinced him that this week he had made a perfect blend. The burning sensation as it went down his throat and the lurch his stomach gave as it entered were undeniable proof of this. Also, without question, Jay-Jay would have a wealth of detailed information since, during the week, there had been a bank robbery and a brutal murder in the city. Arly anticipated a fine evening.

Jay-Jay arrived promptly at seven. Over the years, his entry into Arly's shack had assumed a ritual-like procedure. Jay-Jay gave one rap on the door, which was wise since the door could not have withstood more. Then, without waiting, he thrust his head in the doorway. "Anyone to home?" he inquired.

"Well, well," Arly exclaimed as though surprised at the intrusion. "Come in, come in."

The two shook hands in a formal manner, and Arly with a courtly gesture motioned to a chair at the table. Jay-Jay sat down and dropped his hat on the floor.

"Care for a little nip?" Arly asked casually.

"Don't mind, don't mind a bit," said Jay-Jay, clearing his throat in anticipation.

Arly produced two tumblers and filled them to the brim. He watched closely as his friend closed his eyes and rolled the liquor about in his mouth. Jay-Jay held the liquor in his mouth for several moments in blissful contentment and then, tilting his head back, allowed it to flow down his throat.

"Arly," he said, "this time you've come up with a genuwine connysewers item."

Arly beamed and took a deep swallow from his glass, but modesty forbade his making any comments about his masterpiece. "I hear you've been pretty busy this past week," he said.

Jay-Jay shook his head. "Arly, you don't have no idea what I've been through these last few days. What with the chief running to me every five minutes for advice, and me intergating prisoners all day and night, I tell you it's been tough."

Admiration showed strong in Arly's eyes. "You sure lead an exciting life, Jay-Jay. Tell me about the morgue."

Jay-Jay shuddered and drained his tumbler to fortify himself. "A syndicate job," he said. "A human sieve this poor victim was. I never seen a more complete job of murder."

Arly shivered deliciously. "Plenty of blood, I suppose."

Jay-Jay shook his head. "Nope. Nary a drop. The victim was drained clean dry with all them holes." He took a deep swallow and went on, "Them kind are even worse than the bloody ones. Just like white marble statues they are, except for the holes."

"Why'd they do it, Jay-Jay?" asked Arly eagerly.

"Squealing, that's why," said Jay-Jay. "The syndicate won't stand for it." He shook a finger at Arly. "You remember that case I cracked five, six years ago?"

Arly struggled to unfocus his eyes from Jay-Jay's finger and direct his mind back into the past. Jay-Jay drained his glass and filled it again.

"That one was a squealer, too," he said, after he had allowed Arly several minutes in which to think.

"Which one?" asked Arly, whose mind had become lost in its musings.

"The tall one."

"Oh, I thought it was the short one."

"No, that one was an accident case."

"Accidents will happen," said Arly profoundly.

"Right," said Jay-Jay. "And here's another thing I've noticed, Arly . . . accidents always happen to people who have accidents. That's a funny thing."

"It sure is, Jay-Jay. And accidents just don't happen to people that don't have accidents. That's funny, too. Now why do you suppose that is?"

Jay-Jay opened his mouth to explain why this was when without warning the door burst open and two enormous guns came in with two men behind them.

"Huh. Two old geezers guzzling wine," said one, a mean-looking young man with stringy blond hair, and watery blue eyes.

"Hey, we ain't done nothing," said Arly indignantly. "What's the idea busting into my home?"

"Home he calls it," the blond gunman cackled, turning to the other who stood staring with beady black eyes at Arly and Jay-Jay.

Arly rose to better protest this insult, but Jay-Jay reached across the table and pushed him back into his chair. "Shh . . . Arly," he said in a whisper that could be heard a city block. "Take it easy. These are syndicate guys. Play along with them."

Arly considered this soberly. "Jay-Jay, you're absolutely right," he said. "I'll get some cards and we'll play along."

The blond man stared at the two in angry bewilderment. "Are you two nuts or something?" he demanded. "Talking behind our backs like that right in front of us?"

The other gunman spoke for the first time. "Drunk," he said. "Just a couple of winos."

"Yeah," said the blond one. He stepped forward and studied the label on the jug. "Floor de Less Burgundy. Looks like good stuff, too." He looked at Arly and Jay-Jay accusingly. "Living in a dump like this and drinking high class stuff like Floor de Less. You oughta be ashamed."

He went to a wall cupboard and took two water glasses and filled them from the jug. He handed one to his companion who took it with a brief smile.

"Okay, Jerry," the blond hood said, "let's show these old clowns how to drink. Bottoms up."

In unison the two put the glasses to their lips and gulped deeply.

The next moment was electrifying. The two gunmen dropped their guns and their glasses, and, gasping for air, stared at each other in shocked horror. Then, as the mixture took command of their stomachs, they fell writhing to the floor.

"Oh, Jeez, get a doctor," yelled the blond man.

"Two doctors," corrected his companion with an anguished wail.

Arly and Jay-Jay stared at each other in bewilderment.

"What's the matter with them?" asked Arly.

"Drug attics," said Jay-Jay professionally. "It hits some of them like that. What they need is a fix-it."

"I don't have no fix-its on hand," said Arly regretfully. He turned to the two twisting, moaning figures on the floor. "Hey, you guys, why don't you go out and get yourselfs some fix-its? You'd feel a lot better."

"Doctor, doctor," the two on the floor moaned.

Jay-Jay poured himself a drink and gazed down at the two thoughtfully. "You know, Arly," he said. "These two guys are illegal."

"Yeah?" said Arly, shocked.

"Yeah," said Jay-Jay. "Didn't they point guns at us? That's contrary to the jurisdiction."

"Sure it is," said Arly. "And besides what did we ever do to them?"

They were interrupted in their discussion by the wail of a siren. A moment later two uniformed policemen burst into the room with guns drawn, ready for duty.

"You see a couple of ..." one began and then noticed the two limp figures on the floor. "Well, by George!" he exclaimed. "Here they are. But what's happened to them?"

"We didn't do it officer," said Arly. "They just got sick all of a sudden. They come in here with guns real tough and then ..."

"Well, they don't look real tough now," one of the officers said. "We better get them to a hospital. We don't mind if they croak, but we want a confession on that bank robbery first. You guys will have to come along and tell your story at the station."

A few minutes later Arly and Jay-Jay were seated across a table from the chief of police and a stenographer.

"Now you old geez ... gentlemen, just relax. You aren't implicated in the bank robbery in any way. Creepy James and Jerry Baines were just trying to hide out. So tell us what happened and then you can go."

"Here's how it was, chief," Jay-Jay began.

"Better let Arly tell it, Jay-Jay," the chief interrupted not unkindly. "We can assume that Arly isn't drunk, but we sure can't ever assume that with you. Now, Arly, go right ahead."

Arly cleared his throat, but before he could say anything an officer rushed into the room.

"Chief, we got signed confessions from both of them," he said. "And not only for the bank job, but for three or four other heists as well. They thought they were going to die for sure, and spilled everything." The officer handed the chief a form. "Here's the doc's report. They'll live, he says, but they'll have weak stomachs the rest of their days. The doc can't figure out what the stuff is they drank, but it was sure powerful."

The chief turned to Arly. "What was this stuff they drank?"

Arly squirmed. "Well... it was just some stuff I found in the dump." "That's pretty dangerous stuff to have around, isn't it? What were you going to do with it?"

Arly turned to Jay-Jay for help just as a fly lit on Jay-Jay's red nose.

"Bugs," Arly said in a burst of inspiration. "It's for killing bugs. Ain't it, Jay-Jay?"

"Yeah," said Jay-Jay, staring cross-eyed at the fly on his nose. "Remember, Arly, how them cockroaches turned white like corpses that time I poured some on them?"

"Call it insect spray," the chief directed the stenographer. He turned to Arly again. "Now how did you get them to drink this poisonous insect spray?"

"They thought it was Floor de Less Burgundy," Arly explained.

"Floor de Less?" The chief pondered this for several moments, then shrugging hopelessly, he instructed the stenographer, "Say they mistook the insect spray for an alcoholic beverage."

There were several minutes of waiting while the stenographer typed out his notes. During this time the chief studied Arly and Jay-Jay as though he were trying to come to some decision about them.

When the statements were finished, Arly and Jay-Jay signed them without question, and Arly asked, "Can we go now?"

The chief motioned them to remain seated. "One more thing, men. I didn't mention it before but there's a five thousand dollar reward for those two crooks. Your claim to the reward is clear."

The chief leaned forward. "Now here's what I've been thinking. This reward money is enough to put you both in a home for retired people. There's a fine one right here in the city. An uncle of mine lives there and loves it. Lots of nice friendly old folks around, good meals, a clean, airy room, a bath every day ..."

"A bath every day?" asked Arly.

"Two a day if you want them." The chief studied his fingernails.

"Chief," said Arly, "I don't think Jay-Jay and me are entitled to this reward. Ain't that right, Jay-Jay?"

"That's a fact, chief," said Jay-Jay emphatically. "We don't deserve no reward for what we done. Why, them two crooks were just getting ready to get the drop on us when your men came to the rescue."

"It's your men should get the reward, chief," said Arly. "They done all the work."

The chief shook his head. "Against regulations." He thought deeply for a moment. "There is one way out, though. You two could accept the reward and then sign it over to the Police Welfare Fund. Is that agreeable to you?"

It was more than agreeable. Arly and Jay-Jay signed the documents that were given them with audible sighs of relief.

The chief called a police car to take them back to Arly's shack, and as they left the room, he said to the stenographer, "Al, I think I did them a good turn. An old folks home would be plain hell for them. I don't believe they'd live out a year. And I doubt if they could handle five thousand dollars' worth of booze, even if they did spike it with that insect spray of theirs."

Back in Arly's shack, the two friends worked diligently at catching up on their drinking.

"I shiver yet to think of the tight fix we were in," said Arly. "Just think ... a bath every day." He drank deeply to erase the horror of it from his mind.

"And living in a joint full of old coots," said Jay-Jay. "What chance would you have to mixing up a fine drink like this?"

"The chief sure got brains to figure a way out of it like he done."

"The chief always looks out for his men," said Jay-Jay proudly. "And naturally, you being my friend, he looked out for you, too."

"Let's talk about something pleasant," said Arly. "Tell me some more about that syndicate guy in the morgue."

Lawrence Treat

Homicide, Maybe

Around nine o'clock that morning, give or take a few minutes, Magruder came trudging up the steps of the precinct house and went inside. It was the new one, only built six or seven years ago and it had tan marbled flooring and the plywood on the rear wall was tinted, and he still wasn't used to the place.

Charlie, in iniform and sitting at the desk, said, "Morning, Mac. Lieutenant wants to see you."

Magruder nodded and kept on walking. "Sure," he said. "Soon as I get set."

"Mac!" Charlie's voice, sharp and brittle, stopped Magruder cold. "He's got his long drawers on and something's up. Something big."

Magruder frowned, gave a kind of shrug with his big, heavy shoulders and swung left. The door of the lieutenant's office was partly open and Magruder went in.

The lieutenant, a tense, stringy guy, was sweating away at the phone and taking it on the chin from somebody he couldn't talk back to. When it was over, he slammed the phone down and gave the metal waste paper basket a solid kick. It slid across the room, hit the wall with a resounding bong, and tilted over. The mess of cigarette butts, torn envelopes, and crumpled police forms settled him down a little, but not enough.

"We got trouble," he said crisply. "Look." And he shoved a report at Magruder. It was headed "Medical Examiner's Office," and the subject was Marian Reed.

"I thought we had that one wrapped up," Magruder said. "What's the matter? Isn't a confession good enough?"

"No. He denied it this morning, claims he didn't know what he signed, that you tricked him and beat him up. And he has a black eye to prove it."

"We told you about that, "Magruder said. "He resisted arrest, and I had to take a poke at him. Sid knows—"

"That's the least of it," the lieutenant said. "I can hold off the D.A., but what about the medical examiner? He says nobody hit her, nobody beat her up. She died of carbon monoxide poisoning. She fell and rolled under the bed and had convulsions. He thinks that's how she banged her head. Read it."

Magruder glanced at the M.E.'s report. "Multiple bruises over extended area—typical cherry-red tissue-carboxyhemoglobin, 40%— Van Slyke test—conclusion, asphyxiation due to carbon monoxide, probably generated by defective refrigerator."

"About those bruises," Magruder said slowly. "It says here that some of them may have occurred a good twelve hours before death."

"But they didn't kill her, so what's the point?"

"I don't know."

"I do," the lieutenant said. "We arrest her husband, an innocent man, and we charge him with murder and get a confession. Wait till the papers get hold of that. The commissioner's down my throat, says we can't tell an accident when we see one and he's going to get to the bottom of this."

"Yeah," Magruder said. "Sid come in yet?"

"He's upstairs. I figured I'd drop the boom on you, first. You can take it."

"Thanks," Magruder said dryly. "Me and Sid, huh?"

"I back up my men," the lieutenant said, "but we got to do something about this. A defective gas refrigerator, and we book a man for murder."

Magruder rubbed the side of his face and felt a small patch of stubble that his razor had missed. "Reed was in the same room as his wife," he said. "Why didn't he kick off, too, and make things easy for us?"

"The M.E. says people react differently, and parts of the room can have different concentrations of gas, on account of the drafts. He thinks Reed was knocked out by it, that Reed shows the typical effects of carbon monoxide poisoning—general confusion and loss of memory. He's in the hospital now, for examination, and he may have permanent brain injury."

"Anybody fix the refrigerator yet?"

"No, nobody's been in. We've got a man at the apartment, outside."

"I'll get hold of Sid and take a run over there. Maybe—" Magruder searched his mind and found nothing.

"Maybe what?" the lieutenant asked.

"Nothing, except that maybe he did beat her up, and not by accident. So something's screwy." He yawned and added casually, "Too bad we can't hang it on somebody."

Something in the way the lieutenant grunted made Magruder spin around, and for a couple of seconds the two of them looked at each other. If they could get a fall guy, twist somebody's arm, dress this up as a homicide, they'd be off the hook. And they could do it.

They wouldn't, of course. They were honest cops, decent guys. They didn't railroad people or manufacture evidence, but the idea crossed both their minds at the same time, and they knew it.

Neither of them smiled. The lieutenant said, "Let me know what's cooking," and Magruder said, "Yeah, sure," and he turned and went out, closing the door.

He winked at Charlie, sitting at the desk, and he crossed the big room and climbed the stairs to the squad room. There, he spotted Sid Kohacky.

"We got a little problem," Magruder said. "On the Reed case. I'll tell you on the way over."

Marguder drove, because he liked to, and Sid sat next to him and kept jerking his knee impatiently. He was all fired up, and Magruder wasn't.

Magruder was an old man, as cops go. In his fifties. Big, slow-moving, grizzled, maybe a little tired. And Sid was a tall, quick, rangy kid, a year out of college where he'd studied police work. He had plenty of ambition and a lot to learn, and he was supposed to learn it from Magruder.

"We went wrong somewhere, "Sid said, "but so did everybody else. What do you figure we can find out now?"

"Probably nothing," Magruder said, "but we'll give it a try, anyhow. Think it over, Sid. Anything we missed?"

It had happened yesterday. In the morning, they'd finished going over the inventory of some stuff that had been taken in a jewel robbery. They'd left the jewelry store and were sitting in the car and looking over the forms they'd filled out when they got the call. A woman had been found dead, Apartment 4E, 1829 North Whitman, and a uniformed cop was there, waiting. So the pair of them rolled.

The address was a five story brick building, built just after the war and in fair condition. There was no elevator, and Magruder hauled himself up the stairs while Sid bounced behind him.

Patrolman Joe Chambers was outside the door of 4E, along with a young, bony, dark-haired guy and a middle-aged piece of pudge wearing a beret. Joe identified them.

"They found the body. George Elwin, the super," he said, pointing to the pudgy guy. "And Bellini, from the refrigerator people. He came to fix something, and Elwin let him in. They say they didn't touch anything except a blanket. They almost tripped over it, so they pulled it back. That's how they happened to see her, under the bed. Otherwise, they wouldn't have noticed."

Magruder glanced at them. They both looked a little sore, as if they'd been having some kind of an argument.

"Who is she?" Magruder said to the superintendent.

"Marian Reed," fat stuff answered in a rasping voice. "Her husband's a truck driver. He's probably at work."

"Where?"

"I got the address downstairs, somewhere. You want it?"

"Later on," Magruder said. He put his hand on the knob and pushed the door open. "Come on, Sid," he said, and walked in.

It was a big one-room apartment with a kind of recessed alcove for the kitchen. A Murphy bed, double-size, covered the far side of the room. The bedding was rumpled, a chair was knocked over, and an empty whisky bottle was lying next to it. The bare leg sticking out from under the bed showed where the body was, and the blue blanket that had concealed it had been shoved against the night-table.

Magruder sniffed at the odor of stale blood. "Better open a window," he said, and he went over to examine the body. He had to get down on his hands and knees to see it under the bed.

Her pink, frilly nightgown was ripped down the front, and you could see some of the body bruises. She was blonde and she must have been quite a piece, a few hours ago and before she'd been hit on the head.

Magruder turned away. The closet was around three feet to the right of him and the doorknob had blood on it. He figured they'd find a few blonde hairs and that would be it.

While he crouched there with his joints stiffening up, he could hear the argument going on outside. The refrigerator man wanted to be paid for his service call, and the super refused because they guy hadn't done anything. They'd apparently been at it for quite a while, and neither of them would give in.

Magruder made a mental note to find out all he could about that service call. He felt a little drowsy, and he kept hearing the voices outside. He rubbed his forehead, pulled back, then rose slowly to his feet.

"Tell Joe Chambers to put in signal four-eight," he said to Sid. That was the one that would bring in the experts and the lab men and the big brass, all the complicated machinery that goes to work on a homicide. "Then bring those guys in. The super first."

"Sure," Sid said. "You think—" He broke off. They'd probably told him in school that you don't jump to conclusions, you do your investigating no matter how obvious the set up looks. "Sure," he said again, and went out.

Magruder moved heavily around the room, studying it section by section. His head ached and he had to force himself to concentrate. On the table he found a crumpled up delivery sheet headed Acme Express. The initials, H. R., were scrawled on the bottom, so Acme Express was where Reed worked. Magruder copied the address on his pad. Then he walked over to the kitchenette.

The dishes hadn't been washed. A couple of glasses were broken, and there was a highball glass that smelled of watered whisky, as if somebody hadn't finished his drink and then the ice had melted down. The sink and the gas refrigerator looked new. More or less, everything added up in Magruder's mind. The case seemed to him pretty well cut and dried, nothing to it but leg work.

Sid came back with the super and Magruder let him stand there, pulling uncomfortably at his beret and not too sure of himself. His black eyes kept shifting to the bare leg of the dead woman, as if he couldn't tear them away from the sight.

"What was the trouble with the refrigerator?" Magruder asked.

"She said it smoked" the super answered. "But you better ask that guy outside. He's the expert, that's why I had him come and look it over."

"When did he do that?"

"Yesterday, while I was away."

"Where'd you go?"

"To my sister's. She lives in the country and I stayed there overnight."

"Go away often?" Magruder asked.

"I get lonely," the super said. "My wife left me a couple of months ago. I don't like being alone, so I visit my sister."

"If the guy fixed it yesterday, what is he doing here now?"

"Claims he wanted to check up, and he range the bell but nobody answered, so he called me. I went up with him and opened the door with my pass key." His eyes bugged up. "I called the police right away."

"How did the Reeds get along?"

The super shrugged. "I wouldn't know. They were just tenants."

"When did you see them last?"

"Her?" the super said. "I don't remember. But funny thing—when I got back from my sister's this morning, it was around ten, I saw him leaving. On his way to the bus stop, just like nothing had happened."

"Yeah," Magruder said. He rubbed his forehead, but the fuzziness was still there. He said, "Anything else, Sid?"

Kohacky nodded and spoke to the super. "What's your sister's name?" He jotted it down along with the address, and looked pleased with himself.

They took Bellini, the service man, next. He had the roving eye of a Romeo and he was nervous, and Magruder threw it straight at him.

"What went on when you were here yesterday?"

Bellini stared at the carpet. "I fixed the refrigerator," he said sullenly.

"Fix her, too?" Magruder demanded.

Bellini didn't look up. Magruder said, "How long were you here?" Bellini shrugged, shifted his weight from one foot to the other. Magruder said, "I can find out easy, your work sheet will show it. How long?"

"Maybe an hour," Bellini mumbled, as if talking hurt him somewhere in the stomach.

"An hour," Magruder said, thinking about it. "And do you always go back the next day to check on your jobs—it's a rule or something?"

"I wanted to be sure," Bellini said.

"Of her?" Magruder snapped, hoping to catch the guy off balance.

Bellini finally looked up. "Lay off me," he said angrily. "Between you and that skinflint of a super that won't fork up, I'm losing a day's pay. Lay off."

"What about this morning?" Magruder asked. "Where'd you go before you got here?"

"I left home at seven thirty, same as always, and I stopped in at the shop and I made two service calls before I came here."

Magruder turned to Kohacky. "Better get it all down," he said. "We can check it later on."

Sid was making notes on the alibi when the lieutenant arrived. The fingerprint men and the photographers showed up right after that, and then the medical examiner and a deputy commissioner.

Magruder fed them what he'd found out. the medical examiner lifted the bed and decided she'd probably been killed when the metal rail of the Murphy bed had dropped down on her, by accident or design. He put the time of death in the early morning, say between midnight and six A.M., although he couldn't be certain, yet. Later on, he decided it was around four A.M.

"Looks like Reed is our man," the lieutenant said. It didn't take any brains to guess that Reed had beaten up his wife and killed her, maybe because he'd found out she'd been monkeying around. "I'll get those alibis checked, the super's and what's-his-name—"

"Bellini," Magruder said.

"Yeah, Bellini. You and Kohacky better go down to that trucking place and pick up Reed. Slap him with it right off. You may get a fast confession. Chances are he doesn't even know the body was found."

"The way I see it," Magruder said, "he went to work as usual and figured he'd come back for the body. He has a truck. He could lug the body downstairs and then take it some place to dispose of it."

"Right," the lieutenant said. "He may show here, of course, and if he does, I'll handle him. Better get moving."

Magruder and Sid went out, and for once in his life it seemed to Magruder that there were more stairs going down than up.

"I got a headache," he said, rubbing his forehead. And up till then, that was about the only clue anybody had that carbon monoxide was involved.

Out in the fresh air, the headache went away, and by the time Magruder and Kohacky got down to the Acme Express, Magruder was feeling fine.

The place was mostly garage, with a section in the back where they kept crates and packing materials, and with a small office in front where the dispatcher spent most of the day doing nothing. He was a stubby little guy who hated being alive, but he got a lift out of the idea of Harry Reed's being in some kind of trouble.

"Don't surprise me none," he said. "What did he do on that binge of his?"

"How do you know he was on a binge?" Magruder asked.

"You shoulda seen the hangover he had this morning. Showed up an hour late, and needed help backing out of the garage. He must have tied one on last night."

"Did he ever do that before?" Magruder asked.

"They all do," the dispatcher said. "They drive you crazy, they don't give a damn."

"I'm asking about Harry Reed," Magruder said. "Ever see him drunk?"

"Well," the dispatcher said. He couldn't quite come out with anything that might help a guy.

Magruder and Kohacky left and sat across the street in the squad car. It was a long wait. They talked about some of the boys in the precinct and then about food and then Magruder told about a cop named Putnam who had a phenomenal memory. In particular, he remembered numbers, he could rattle off the license plates of every car that was ever reported stolen. He could go back years, and still remember. They used to quiz him and check up, and he was never wrong. He was in the department for ten years and he never came across a stolen car. Not once.

Around four in the afternoon an Acme truck with a dented fender came in. The driver was wearing a zipper jacket. He was a big, broadshouldered guy with a thick neck and plenty of flesh, and the dispatcher signaled to the pair of cops, this was Reed.

They got out of the car and walked over, and Reed was trying to explain the fender. It was just one of those things, he was saying. Never happened before. There was something the matter with the wheel, maybe. How else could he swerve like that and clip a hydrant? There was something wrong with the steering.

Magruder interrupted. "You're Harry Reed? We want to talk to you." And Magruder flashed his shield.

The dispatcher was peeved because he wasn't in on this, but at least Reed was in hot water, and so things could have been worse.

Magruder and Kohacky brought Reed over to the squad car and stood him against the door. "You know why we're here," Magruder said. "Just tell us about it, and it'll be a lot easier for you."

Reed blinked. His eyes were dark and set deep, and there was scar tissue around them, as if he'd spent a few years in the ring. "Last night?" he said. "What did I do?"

"You killed your wife. What for? What reason did you have?"

"Me?" Reed said. "Why, you son of a—" His eyes went small and mean, and his left hook came around so fast that it caught Magruder in the ribs. He was jolted back, puffing heavily and aware of the slowness of his reactions.

Sid charged, grabbed Reed's arm and spun him around before he could get a haymaker in on Magruder. Then the two cops waded in. Sid grabbed Reed's jacket and twisted it, and Reed lunged and ducked into Magruder's punch and caught it in the eye. Reed staggered back against the car, hit it with a bang and shook his head groggily.

"Well?" Magruder said. He had his hand on his gun, but he didn't pull it out.

"The slut," Reed said. "She walked out on me."

"What did you kill her for?" Magruder said.

"Me?" Reed said. "You're kidding, you don't mean it." The two cops glared, and Reed let out a kind of sob. "I don't know what's the matter with me," he said. He raised his left hand and looked at the fist. "I'm getting slow with those dukes of mine," he said. "A few years ago, and

I'da knocked you cold."

"Like your wife?" Magruder said.

"Where is she?" Reed said. "Who'd she run off with?"

"Just tell us about last night," Magruder said.

"I don't know," Reed said. "I don't know. We had a drink when I got home, I guess we killed the bottle, and I woke up this morning with one hell of a hangover. But I couldn't have gotten that stoned on one bottle."

"Then you had more than one," Magruder said.

Reed didn't argue. "I must have," he said, "because when I woke up, I was still dressed and I'd been sleeping in the green chair, and it was almost ten o'clock. I didn't even have breakfast. I just washed up and went to work."

"What about your wife?"

"I didn't see her. I figured she'd taken a powder on me."

"You slammed her around, knocked her to the floor, then conked her real good with that bed rail."

"Did I? I don't know. I can't remember."

"Let's go down to headquarters," Magruder said. "You and me, we'll sit in back and talk."

Magruder didn't get very far. Reed cried a little, then he perked up and laughed a little, not hysterical, but just saying it was funny, he was kind of mixed up on everything.

Down at the precinct, they brought him into the interrogation room and went to work. The lieutenant helped out, and he had the medical examiner's preliminary findings. Marian Reed had been killed early in the morning, around four. Apparent cause of death was violent contact with the metal rail of the bed, although the autopsy was not yet complete.

Reed kept insisting that he remembered nothing, and it was pretty clear that he'd killed her in a drunken frenzy.

"Ever hit her before?" Magruder asked.

"I got a temper, I get sore easy, and she'd been playing around with somebody. I know that much." Reed rocked as if he was in pain, and his eyes had a blank look. "Sure, I hit her every once in a while, but not hard. Never like that."

Magruder turned to Sid. "The guy can't even think straight. Better type out a statement. He'll sign."

Sid typed it out, the bare essentials of what must have happened, and he and Magruder read it aloud to Reed a couple of times and asked him to sign, and he did. Then they went home.

So that was the way it had gone yesterday, and the two cops hashed it over now on their way to the apartment, enumerating details.

"Let's ask around," Magruder said. "I'd like to find out if either of them left the house. It might help."

They made a door to door canvass, ringing bells and looking for somebody who had seen the Reeds recently. Nobody had. Then they tried the neighborhood stores, and they drew blank until they hit the druggist.

"She was here," he said. "She was upset, she had a wild look in her eyes. She asked for some ointment to take care of a bruise."

"When was that?" Magruder asked.

"Day before yesterday. In the afternoon."

"What was she wearing?"

"She had a coat on. She kept it closed and held it up to her neck. And every once in a while she kind of moaned."

Magruder almost smiled as he said, "Thanks," and went out.

On the street, he rubbed his jaw and tried to remember on which side of his face that patch of stubble was. "I got a feeling we're onto something," he said.

Sid perked up. He'd heard about those hunches of Magruder's, and he kept studying Magruder and waiting for him to come out with something. But all Magruder did was rub the other side of his face and look up at the fourth floor. He sighed as he thought of all those stairs.

"May as well go up," he said finally.

The cop on duty told them the gas had been turned off, and Magruder and Kohacky went into the room. The windows were wide open. Sections of the table and refrigerator and all the door jambs were splotched with fingerprint powder. The Murphy bed had been stripped, probably for a lab examination. There were chalk marks on the carpet under the bed showing where the body had been. Otherwise, the apartment was pretty much the same as it had been yesterday.

"Nice rug," Magruder said. "Good, heavy pile. Feel it."

Sid rubbed his shoe into the nap. "So?" he said.

"So it's a nice rug," Magruder said. Then, in a kind of explosion, he erupted.

"Just think of it," he said bitterly. "From what the M.E. says, Reed came home, had a couple of drinks with his wife and ate dinner, and then killed the bottle and went to bed, and all the time they were inhaling that stuff. They got groggy and passed out, and she had convulsions and rolled under the bed and hit her head, and she finally died. He must have staggered over to the chair, it wasn't so bad there. Anyhow he pulled out of it and managed to get up the next morning. Out in the fresh air he shook off the worst of it, but he can't remember anything and maybe he never will."

It was quite a speech for him, he wouldn't have come out with it to anybody else. Just Sid. Still, after all those words, Magruder wanted to be by himself. So he went into the bathroom and found the tube of ointment that Marian had bought from the neighborhood druggist. Then he opened her closet and examined her dresses, one at a time.

He pulled the green one out and held it up. "Look," he said. He pointed to the rips on the front and to the missing buttons. "She had a bad time with somebody." Magruder said. "After she fought him off, she went down to the drugstore. The way the druggist described her, she was still in a state of shock."

Sid said, "And whoever assaulted her was scared she'd talk, either to the police or else to her husband. Reed would just about kill anybody for fooling around with his wife."

"Easy enough to sneak each into the apartment while she was downstairs," Magruder said. "Romeo could slip the catch on his way out, the super could use his pass key."

"It could still be an accident," Sid said. "And if it wasn't, how do we find out who monkeyed around with the refrigerator?"

"A little common sense ought to do it," Magruder said. "Let's go see the super, that's the first step."

The superintendent was fixing lunch in his basement apartment when they walked in, and he was in a bad mood.

"A thing like that," he said, "it gives the place a bad name. Who wants to rent an apartment where a man killed his wife?"

"He didn't kill her," Magruder said. "She was asphyxiated. By the refrigerator."

"That makes it worse," the super said glumly. "A defective refrigerator—nobody'll take a chance on that apartment. They'll be scared of another accident."

"It was no accident," Magruder said. "Somebody fiddled with the gas jet and changed the adjustment. Somebody who knew about refrigerators."

The super stared and pulled his beret down on his head. "Bellini?" he said. "The guy must have been off his rocker."

"Who said it was Bellini?" Magruder asked.

"Who else?" said the super.

"You."

The super gave a short, surprised grunt as if he'd been socked in that round belly of his. Then he twisted his lips. "I hardly knew her," he said. "Never even spoke to her."

"Sure you did," Magruder said. "Your wife had left you, and there was an attractive tenant upstairs and you figured she wasn't fussy, so you tried. Only it didn't work out, and you were in a hole and scared of a beating, so you fixed the refrigerator adjustment and went away overnight. It must have been quite a surprise when you saw Reed calmly walking down to the bus."

"You're crazy," the super said. "I wasn't even in that apartment."

Magruder didn't exactly smile, but he had a friendly expression as his hand whipped up and knocked the beret off the super's head. The wound on his temple was reddish, the scratch marks were vivid.

"So that's where she clawed you," Magruder said. "I figured a dame like her, she'd fight back."

"I fell in the shower," the super said. "Banged my head. And if anybody attacked her, it must have been Bellini, the young bully."

"A young, goodlooking guy like him?" Magruder said. "She'd be a pushover for him. But you?" He snorted, needling the guy. "Who would fall for you?"

"Even if you were right," the super said in a low voice, "even if I made a pass at her, so what? She didn't die from it, did she? She died because Bellini did a lousy job on the refrigerator."

"And you refused to pay him. But that was yesterday morning, and you'd just come back from staying overnight with your sister, remember? How did you know the refrigerator was still defective?"

"Something Bellini said. I don't remember I—I—"

"Yeah, you, you," Magruder said. "You're our boy and we won't have much trouble proving it. So why don't you make it easy on yourself and tell us about it?"

It took Magruder and Sid a little over two hours to get the confession. Which was about average, Magruder figured. Just about average for a routine case like this one.

James Holding
The Sunburned Fisherman

At a quarter to six on Sunday morning, Randall found Dalton's body. He cut the outboard at once and drifted up on the small fishing skiff for which he had been searching Lake Doncon ever since midnight.

A call had come in from Mrs. Dalton. She said her husband was missing. He'd gone fishing alone at six Saturday morning, intending to stay on the lake all day. But here it was midnight, she said, and Mr. Dalton wasn't home yet. She was worried. Could the police do anything?

So Randall had been assigned by the lieutenant to take this corny outboard job and comb Lake Doncon's surface for the missing fisherman in the darkness. And only twenty-four square miles of lake to search! Randall had done his best, but had nothing to show for his trouble except a stiff back. Until now.

The fishing skiff was floating like a sleeping water bug on the dawn-flushed mirror of Hance's Cove, about fifty yards from shore. Hance's Cove was partially screened from the rest of the lake by an archipelago of trees that curved across its mouth. No wonder Randall hadn't located the skiff until daylight. If it *was* Dalton's skiff.

When he drifted close enough, Randall reached out a hand, grasped the skiff's gunwale, and half stood up in his own boat to look inside the other.

Dalton was there, all right, lying sprawled in a dreadful mess on the bottom. He had been violently sick all over himself and the skiff's interior. The exposed skin of his face and arms was pink with sunburn. His mouth was stretched to one side, half-open in a rictus of agony. And he was obviously as dead as the three northern pike that lay on the strakes beside him.

Randall swore, thinking of Mrs. Dalton. He noted automatically that Dalton's lunchbox, dip net, tackle box, and live bait containers were still in the boat under the thwarts, although one oar was missing and there was no sign of Dalton's fishing rod. Lost overboard, Randall thought, when Dalton was taken violently sick. He reached across and felt for a pulse in Dalton's wrist, but it was just a formality. Dalton was dead.

After debating for a moment, Randall took Dalton's skiff in tow. The sound of his outboard bounced back at him from the dense woods that lined the cove's borders. With the skiff and its grisly burden trailing behind him, he left the cove and headed for Dalton's home on the south shore of the lake. That was as close as any place else to find a phone at this time in the morning.

Like almost everybody in the not-so-large town of Doncon, Randall knew something about William Dalton. He was an attorney, a successful one. It was common knowledge that he was deeply in love with his beautiful wife. He was well-liked in the community. And in his spare time, he was an enthusiastic fisherman, like Randall himself. Randall had often spoken to him at the local fishing club meetings. Randall knew where he lived, a modest white house about three miles out of town, on the shore of Lake Doncon where he did his fishing. He had his own skiff, boathouse, and dock.

Approaching the Dalton house from the lake, Randall could see lights in the kitchen, pale now in the daylight. She's still up, waiting for word of her husband, Randall thought bleakly. He hated to be the messenger that brought bad news. Especially to Mrs. Dalton, who was a real doll with red hair and green eyes and a pleasant smile.

He tied up his boat, and then Dalton's skiff, at the dock, and stepped ashore. Mrs. Dalton had seen him coming. She ran out of the back door and down to the dock to meet him. She was wearing a dark green dressing gown and bedroom slippers, but she hadn't been to bed, Randall guessed. Her eyes were tired and dark-ringed, and an anxious frown creased her forehead.

"Is it William?" she asked as she ran out on the dock. "Did you find him? Is he all right, officer?"

"I found him, yes," Randall caught her and held her for a second. "I'm afraid though ..."

She broke loose, darted past Randall to the dock edge and looked into her husband's skiff. She gave a subdued scream, and gasped, "He's sick! William's sick, officer. Get a doctor, oh, please! Dr. Gerson next door ..."

Randall put a hand on her arm and said, "I'm sorry, Mrs. Dalton," just as she keeled over in a dead faint.

Well, a doctor would never do Dalton any good again, but Dalton's pretty wife was something else. Randall carried her into the house, through the kitchen into the living room, and deposited her on the sofa there. Then he ran next door to the only house close enough to deserve that term, and pounded on the door until a bleary-eyed man in striped pajamas answered his knock and grumpily admitted he was Dr. Gerson.

"Police," said Randall tersely," can you come next door right away? Dalton is dead and his wife has fainted. We need you."

Gerson snapped awake. "Five minutes," he said, turning from the door. "I need my bag and a bathrobe. Get back to her, officer. I'll be right over."

Randall went back to Dalton's house. Mrs. Dalton was still out of things, lying pale and beautiful on the sofa. Randall didn't have much success in rousing her by rubbing her wrists and putting a cold cloth on her head. So he went to the telephone in the front hall and called headquarters, reporting the finding of Dalton's body and the circumstances. He told them they could call in the other searchers for Dalton's boat, if any, although he knew very well the tiny police department of

Doncon hadn't been able to spare anybody but him for the search job. The police department only had one boat, as a matter of fact. But Randall enjoyed needling the lieutenant.

By the time he got back to the living room, Dr. Gerson was there, having come in through the back door. He was waving something under Mrs. Dalton's nose. She stirred and groaned a little almost immediately, and came out of her faint. "Take it easy, Thelma," Gerson murmured to her when she opened her eyes. Evidently a friend of the Daltons as well as a doctor. "I'm going to give you a mild sedative . . ."

"Is William dead?" she asked, remembered horror in her expression.

Gerson looked at Randall who nodded. "The officer says so," Gerson said gently. "I haven't seen him yet, Thelma. I just arrived. But if you'll promise to lie here quietly until the sedative takes effect, I'll take a look at William."

Mrs. Dalton nodded her head in numb acquiescence.

Randall and Gerson carried Dalton in from his skiff up to a bedroom on the second floor. After a quick examination, the doctor said to Randall, "It looks like food poisoning to me. He's gone, all right. Let's talk to Mrs. Dalton before she goes under."

They went downstairs. Dr. Gerson said to Mrs. Dalton, who was lying on the sofa with her eyes closed as directed, "What did William take with him in the boat for lunch yesterday, Thelma?"

She said, "A can of baked beans. A hunk of Italian bread. A can of tuna fish. Three hardboiled eggs and a can of beer. The same as usual."

Randall couldn't help saying, "The same as usual?"

"Yes," Mrs. Dalton said, "William loved cold baked beans on bread. And he loved canned tuna fish with hardboiled eggs." She began to cry quietly.

"Then it was the tuna fish that killed him," Gerson said. "It must have been crawling with bacteria, Thelma. William has all the symptoms of botulism. Violent digestive disturbance. Dilated pupils. Signs of ptosis and respiratory paralysis . . ." He stopped talking abruptly when he saw the expression on Mrs. Dalton's face. "I'm sorry, Thelma," he apologized then. He patted her shoulder. "Get some rest. I'll handle things here for a while."

Randall called in again to report the cause of death. This time the lieutenant himself took the call. He said, "Did you look over Dalton's skiff?"

"Yes, sir," Randall said. "Generally. One oar, bait containers, tackle box, dip net still in it. No fishing rod."

"Not that," the lieutenant said with exasperation. "The guy died of tainted tuna fish, Randall. Is the empty can around? Public Health will want the brand and the batch to warn the public against it."

"Oh," said Randall. "I'll take another look down at the boat."

"Do that. Unless Mrs. Dalton is in shape to tell you herself?"

"She's out of it now. Doc Gerson gave her a shot."

"Then search the boat. It might save time for Public Health."

Randall hung up and went out and searched the fishing skiff thoroughly. There were no empty cans in it anywhere. Randall even looked in the empty lunchbox, the tackle box, the bait containers. Apparently Dalton had tossed all his luncheon debris overboard after eating.

Dr. Gerson was using Dalton's telephone to call the Doncon Funeral Home when Randall left.

That was Sunday morning. On Wednesday, Randall got off duty at three in the afternoon, and went out to Swensen's Tackle and Bait Shop on the lake shore near Dalton's house to look at a new fishing reel they were touting.

Swensen, the proprietor, showed him the reel. Then he said, "It was you who found Mr. Dalton last weekend, wasn't it? When he died? I saw it in the paper."

"Yeah."

"He was one of my best customers. Nice guy."

Randall twirled the handle of the reel with the drag off. It spun in a silent whirring blur. "He certainly was sick before he died," Randall said idly. "You never know, do you? Guy eats a can of tuna fish, and bingo!"

"He looked in good shape when he stopped in here at six fifteen Saturday morning," Swensen said. "Fit as a fiddle. Except the complained of feeling tired lately. And then he was dead by the next morning."

"He stopped here on Saturday before he went out on the lake?"

"Yeah, for his minnies and worms and hellgrammites. Dalton was a fisherman who didn't care what bait he used as long as he caught fish, you know? Lures, spoons, jigs, flies, live bait . . . he always went out with all of them. So Saturday morning I sold him his live bait, as usual."

"Anything else?" Randall joked. "Such as a can of tainted tuna fish?"

"Huh-uh," Swensen said. "I asked him if he needed anything else, though. That's when he told me about the sinkers."

"Sinkers?"

"I asked him if he needed any sinkers. He laughed and said no, he had plenty. In fact, he said, he had some better sinkers in his tackle box than I'd ever stocked. And he was going to use one that day if the water was active enough to need a fairly heavy sinker on the line. And it was choppy that day."

"What kind of sinkers were they?" Randall asked curiously.

Swensen said, "That's what I asked Mr. Dalton. And you know what they were? Curtain weights, of all things!" Swensen was disgusted. "He took one out of his tackle box and showed me."

"What was it like?"

"Little metal cylinder less'n an inch long, shiny, with a six inch wire attached to the end, like a leader. Mr. Dalton said he found a batch of them in his boathouse several weeks ago in a box of old clothes and curtains and other trash. The minute he saw them, he thought they'd make dandy sinkers for heavy water when he's fishing live bait. He asks his wife what the things are, and she tells him they're the corner weights out of some old living room drapes she's giving to the church rummage sale." Swensen laughed. "Curtain weights! A fisherman'll use anything. Dalton stuck 'em in his tackle box and kept 'em." He sobered. "No use for 'em now, though."

"No," Randall agreed.

That's when Randall went to see the lieutenant.

"There weren't any drapery-weight sinkers in Dalton's tackle box when I searched the skiff Sunday for the tuna fish can," he said.

The lieutenant sighed. "So he used 'em up. Lost 'em overboard. Found they weren't any good and threw them away. What the heck!"

"I don't believe it." Randall's sulphur-yellow eyes stared challengingly at his superior.

The lieutenant said, "The guy died of botulism, Randall. The death certificate, filed by Dr. Gerson, says so. And he's already buried! So what's eating you?"

"I wonder where those sinkers went."

"Forget it. Food poisoning isn't police business."

"Can I nose around a little on my own?"

"Play detective? On your own time, I can't stop you, I guess. But let that widow alone. She's had enough trouble without a screwy cop bothering her with stupid questions."

"Okay. I'll leave her alone." Randall got up to go. "I'm a fisherman, too, lieutenant. I got a feeling there's something funny about the disappearance of Dalton's drapery-weight sinkers."

"Nuts," the grayhaired lieutenant grunted. "Now get out of here. I'm busy."

Randall got his first encouragement from the part-time medical examiner attached to the Doncon police department. "The guy was sunburned," Randall recalled, describing Dalton's appearance when found in his fishing skiff. "And he'd been plenty sick all over the boat. And . . ."

"Sunburned?" the M.E. asked, indulging Randall.

"Yeah."

"There wasn't a whole lot of sun that Saturday," the M.E. said with a grin. "I had my family on the beach for a picnic that day, and I remember it was overcast most of the time."

"Well," Randall said, "that may mean something. But what I really want to know is this: could Dalton have died of anything else besides botulism, do you think? Discounting Dr. Gerson's statement, and going only on my own visual evidence?"

The M.E. looked shocked. "Are you questioning Dr. Gerson's diagnosis?"

"I'm merely asking you if you think Dalton could have died of something besides botulism."

"He *could* have, I suppose. A lot of fatal ailments are accompanied by violent nausea and vomiting and so on."

"Thanks," said Randall.

Superficial research revealed that Dr. Gerson was a bachelor whose lakeside household was ordered by a middle-aged housekeeper who went home nights. He was attached to the staff of Municipal Hospital and had an excellent reputation, professionally. More significant, Mrs. Dalton and Dr. Gerson seemed to be more deeply interested in each other than their mere proximity as neighbors might account for. A bartender at the Cameron Tavern, a road-house at the edge of town on Route 70, told Randall that Dr. Gerson, who was known to him, and a handsome woman with red hair and green eyes, who was not, had been frequent patrons of the place on Saturday and Sunday afternoons for some months ... drinking, dining, and dancing there together while William Dalton, presumably, was out on the lake at his everlasting weekend fishing.

Thereupon, Randall made it a point to date a young nurse of his acquaintance who worked at Municipal Hospital. Over lobster tails and drawn butter, he plied her with apparently aimless questions about the hospital, its staff and procedures.

Then he went back to the lieutenant.

"It's more than a possibility," he said. "I think it's a dead-sure thing."

"Nonsense," said the lieutenant automatically. Then, "What is?" He put down his ball point pen on his desk blotter with resignation.

"That William Dalton didn't die of botulism. That he was murdered."

The lieutenant grunted. "That's strong talk." He stuffed and lit his pipe. "If Dalton didn't die of botulism, what did he die of?"

"Radiation sickness."

"What!"

"The M.E. says it could have been that as well as botulism. Especially with the sunburn Dalton had. That could have been radiation burn."

The lieutenant sucked loudly on his pipe stem. "Dalton was a lawyer, you dope. Not a scientist. So how come he'd be messing around with atoms and get radiation sickness?"

"He wasn't messing with atoms," Randall said seriously. "He'd been messing with drapery weights, the way I figure it."

The lieutenant stared.

"Those so-called drapery-weight sinkers Dalton had in his tackle box weren't curtain weights," Randall went on. "I think Mrs. Dalton lied to her husband about that."

"What were they, then?"

Randall said, "Heyman's capsules?"

"What on earth are Heyman's capsules?"

"They're metal alloy cylinders about an inch long and a quarter-inch in diameter with a screw-off end. And they contain needle-thin gold-colored sticks of stuff as dangerous as cobra venom."

"What is it?"

"Radium, sir."

"Radium!"

"Yes, sir. Each capsule might have held, say, twenty or thirty milligrams of the stuff. All together, that would be pretty hot. I think for several weeks, every time Dalton went fishing in the evening or on weekends, he sat next to a tackle box loaded with death rays. And the last massive dose on his all-day fishing trip last Saturday finished him off. That's what I think."

The lieutenant, shaken from his lethargy, shouted, "You think! You think! You got any kind of evidence?"

"Not yet," Randall said, "but we may get lucky."

"We better! Supposing you're right ... that Mrs. Dalton's drapery weights were really radium capsules. Then she deliberately lied to her husband about them when he found them in his boathouse and asked her about them? Is that it?"

"It has to be that way. She knew he was a devoted fisherman, an inventive one. She was sure he wouldn't pass up anything that looked as perfect for fishing line sinkers as those capsules. She meant murder, that pretty woman, lieutenant. And she faked a beautiful faint for me when I brought her husband's body to his home."

The lieutenant ruminated, "She and Dr. Gerson, then?"

"They're in it up to their necks. They've been carrying on behind Dalton's back. That I can prove."

"So why not a divorce instead of a murder?"

Randall shrugged. "Dalton loved his wife, everybody agrees. And there was a religious angle. On both counts, his wife assumed he wouldn't countenance a divorce."

"Maybe. But where did the radium come from? You can't buy it at the corner drugstore. The hospital?"

Randall nodded. "Sure. Dr. Gerson is the radiologist at Municipal. As such, he's in sole charge of the hospital's supply of radium he uses to treat malignancies. He could have borrowed the capsules of radium from the hospital and not reported their absence. Nobody else would know they were missing."

"You can't just stick radium in your pants pocket," the lieutenant objected, "and carry it around like loose change."

"Not if you want to stay healthy. But the radium safe at the hospital where Gerson stores his radium capsules is a flat leaden box with wheels and a handle, perfectly mobile. Looks something like a carpet sweeper, I understand. He could have wheeled it out to his car, driven to Dalton's place, taken the capsules of radium out of the lead safe, and planted them in Dalton's boathouse. Handling the capsules briefly without lead shielding, say five minutes or so, wouldn't do the doctor any harm. It takes longer exposure to hurt or kill. In the boathouse, Gerson and Mrs. Dalton knew that nobody but Dalton would be likely to go near the unshielded capsules. Yet Dalton would almost certainly come across them there, and appropriate them for fishing. This was a very slick set-up."

Judiciously now, the lieutenant said, "Those curtain weights, or radium capsules, or whatever they were—can you explain why they turned up missing when you searched Dalton's tackle box that morning? That's the question that bugged you in the first place."

"What if Gerson stopped out back of Dalton's at the dock on Sunday morning, when he was on his way over to tend to Mrs. Dalton's faint? And took the radium capsules out of Dalton's tackle box and put them back in the boathouse, say? It wouldn't have taken forty seconds. I was in the front hall telephoning and wouldn't have seen. He could return the radium capsules to the hospital safe at his convenience after that."

"That's simple enough to be true. But radiation poisoning, Randall! That's too complicated."

"Why? There's a superficial similarity between botulism and radiation sickness. Enough to get poor Dalton buried and out of sight before anybody could get a good look at him except Gerson. There's one thing I know, for sure, that could point to radiation, sir. Dalton told Swensen on Saturday morning that he was feeling tired lately. That's characteristic, doc says."

The lieutenant leaned back in his chair. It squeaked under his two hundred pounds.

"What do you want next?"

"An exhumation order, lieutenant?"

The lieutenant shook his head decisively. "Huh-uh. Not on what you've got. It takes more than a half-baked suspicion to get a man dug up out of his grave. Get me something solid, just one piece of solid evidence, and I'll go after Gerson and Mrs. Dalton as hard as anybody. But not until."

Randall's yellow eyes blinked equably. "I was afraid you'd say that. Can I use our boat?"

"On your own time. And providing nobody else is using it." The lieutenant grinned at his protégé.

"Good enough."

Randall went out.

So at a quarter to six on Sunday morning, exactly a week to the minute since he had found Dalton's body, Randall was cruising at a snail's pace in the police outboard up and down and across the lightening waters of Hance's Cove.

Behind and below his boat, he trailed an unseen apparatus whose weighted hooks explored the cove bottom with slow patience.

Just inside the mouth of the cove, a quarter mile from shore, Randall's sensitive fisherman's fingers felt a weight come on the drag line suddenly. Not a very heavy weight. But heavy enough, Randall judged.

He was tempted to rush into a flurry of activity, to jerk up the drag as though it were a hooked muskie he had down there. But he deliberately slowed his movements, exercised infinite care as he pulled up the drag line for the eighteenth time in the last hour, not hopeful, exactly, but not hopeless, either. Probably just another snag, he thought, another old boot, another six-pack of empty beer cans.

It wasn't until the cork handle and attached reel of an expensive glass fishing rod broke the surface of the water that Randall allowed himself a tight and knowing smile.

Gingerly he grasped the wet handle of the fishing rod, disengaged it from the grapple teeth, and slowly raised it until he felt the thin fishing line threaded through its keepers come freely up through the water. Then he used the dripping reel to wind in line, carefully.

The line came in. From the feel of it, Randall thought there was a sinker on it. When the sinker came up with a spatter of water drops and flashed back a spark at the new sun, Randall abruptly stopped reeling in.

For just a split second he looked at the shiny little metal cylinder attached to Dalton's fishing line—the drapery-weight sinker that was neither a drapery weight nor a sinker—and hurriedly let out line again, almost in a panic. He licked his lips.

Then he kicked his outboard into higher speed and headed up the lake, trailing behind him at an exaggerated distance the "one piece of solid evidence" that would convict two people of murder.

Elijah Ellis

The Sheriff's Rainy Day

The sheriff pulled the county car off the highway and came to a stop on the muddy shoulder of the road, just behind the blue and white highway patrol cruiser. The wreck up ahead didn't look too bad. The two cars involved sat at drunken angles to each other across the highway's center line. Their front ends were pretty well crumpled, and there was a scatter of broken glass and twisted bits of metal strewn across the rain-slick road.

But I'd seen worse. I glanced at Sheriff Ed Carson. He was gripping the steering wheel of our car so tightly his knuckles stood out taut and white. I could guess what his thoughts were as he looked at the wrecked cars ahead.

I coughed uneasily. "Well, at least the rain's let up."

"What? Oh, yeah. So it has." Carson gave a tug to the brim of his hat, opened his door, and got out, his ancient rubber slicker crackling as he moved.

I slid across the seat and followed him out. Harry Shelley of the highway patron had spotted us and walked toward us through the bleak, misty-gray afternoon. His partner stayed over by the wreck, taking pictures of the two cars. I noticed another man leaning against the back fender of one of the cars. He was puffing at a cigarette as if his life depended on it.

Harry Shelley reached us, shook hands, and asked, "What brought you fellas out here?"

"We were out in the county, seeing some people about a case, when we heard your call to patrol headquarters over the squawkbox," I told him. "Thought we'd drive over and see what'd happened."

Shelley nodded. "Good. I got a prisoner for you." He waggled a thumb toward the man leaning against the wrecked car. "Speeding, reckless drivin', not to mention he'd been hittin' the bottle."

Carson made an angry sound. "Who was hurt? We passed the ambulance heading into town, few miles down the road in a hurry."

"Well, the old lady drivin' the other car got bunged up some. Cracked ribs, busted nose, maybe internal injuries, accordin' to Doc Johnson. He won't know till he gets her to the hospital in Monroe. If she'd just been wearin' a seatbelt she'd have been all right. But these darn fool people just won't believe—"

The patrolman suddenly broke off. He glanced at Ed Carson. His broad face turned red. "Sorry, sheriff. I wasn't thinking ..."

"It's all right, Harry. Go on with what happened."

"Well. Same old story. That guy was headed north, makin' too much time for the road conditions. He topped that rise down there and hit a slick spot. Skidded across the center line and smacked into the old lady's car. I came along not more'n a minute or two after it happened. Good thing, too, I'm thinking."

"What do you mean?" I asked.

"Well, me and my partner both got the idea that fella was about to take off for the woods, afoot. He'd crossed the ditch and was standin' by the fence borderin' the field yonder when we drove up. When he seen us, he started holdin' his head and actin' like he didn't know what he was doing." Shelley paused to wave a passing car on by. "But he knew, all right," he said then, calmly.

"Was he hurt?" Carson put in.

"Nah. Old Doc Johnson looked him over. Not a mark on him. Not even a bruise." Shelley laughed shortly. "He was wearin' a seatbelt. Wouldn't you know it?"

The three of us were walking slowly along the edge of the highway toward the accident. A wrecker had just arrived from Monroe and was jockeying into position behind the nearer of the damaged cars.

"What's this guy's name? I don't recognize him," I said to Shelley.

"No, he ain't from around here. Transient. Name's Milton Cord, or so his driver's license says. He claims he's been workin' down in the south part of the state, and now he's headed up into Tennessee to take another job."

The man called Cord stood on the far shoulder of the road with Shelley's partner, watching the wrecker crew work at the smashed cars. He turned as we approached, his close-set gray eyes flicking nervously over Carson and myself.

Shelley ignored him. The two patrolmen drew away a few yards and discussed the accident report the second patrolman had filled in. The drizzle had thickened into a shower, and Shelley held the skirt of his raincoat up as a shield for the clipboard the other man had in his hands.

"Who're you guys?" Cord asked now. He was a tall, slender man with a mop of greasy black hair, and skin as white and soft-looking as a baby's. He wore a short khaki jacket with the collar turned up, and a pair of wrinkled slacks.

"This is Sheriff Carson," I said. "My name is Gates. I'm the Pokochobee county attorney."

For a moment Cord didn't move. What little color there was in his face drained away. His eyes darted from side to side like those of a trapped animal. Then he gave an uneasy laugh. "The sheriff and the county attorney? Geez, why didn't you bring along the governor?"

Ed Carson asked quietly, "What happened here?"

"Nothing. I mean, it was just an accident. I don't know why all the fuss. It wasn't my fault. That old woman in the other car, she swerved right into me—"

"That ain't the way the patrolmen tell it," Carson said, still speaking quietly. Too quietly.

"Ah, what do they know? Just because I'm a stranger, and that old gal lives around here, they figure they'll stick me with some bum rap." Cord spat on the pavement. "Nuts."

Harry Shelley rejoined us now. "If that lady should up and die, you'll think 'nuts,'" he prophesied.

Cord burst out, "What the heck, it was her fault—damn woman driver, got no business on the highway."

The sheriff abruptly turned and walked away.

"What's the matter with him?" Cord asked.

I took time to light a cigarette. Then I said, "About a week ago, his wife was driving to a store in town. At an intersection a drunk slammed into her car broadside. Mrs. Carson was killed."

"Well, that's nothing to do with me," Cord whined.

"No. But if I were you, I'd keep my mouth shut about women drivers," I told him.

Cord shrugged. "Nuts."

It was raining harder. The wrecker crew had the damaged cars off the highway. A man was sweeping up the broken glass and other debris. Shelley said, "Let's wrap this up."

The sheriff walked back toward us. There was no expression at all on his leathery face. But I noticed the ridge of muscle standing out along the line of his jaw. "Ready to go?"

"Before long," Shelley said. "Why don't you take Cord on in, now? No use all of us gettin' soaked."

Carson nodded. Cord made a few halfhearted protests, but no one paid any attention. The sheriff, Cord, and myself started toward the county car. Then Harry Shelley called, "Hey, Lon?"

I turned. "Yeah?"

"Listen, would you mind waitin', and ridin' into town with me? I'd like to talk to you about that trial I'm supposed to testify at next week."

I hesitated. I didn't particularly like the idea of Carson taking the prisoner in alone. But what the heck, the sheriff could handle Cord if he made any trouble.

"Well, okay," I said. "Ed, you go on."

Carson nodded, and a few moments later the county car made a U turn and headed for Monroe, Milton Cord sitting on the front seat beside the sheriff.

"Old Ed sure took it hard, didn't he, about his wife," Harry Shelley said.

"Yeah. They'd been married—what? Twenty-five years?"

Shelley nodded. "Well. He'll get over it, I guess."

I tried to imagine how I'd feel if it had been my wife crushed to a bloody pulp in a senseless accident. "I doubt it," I said then. "I doubt he'll ever get over it ..."

The patrolmen finished their work, and we started for town, driving slowly because of the rain. We reached downtown Monroe and the courthouse square about half an hour behind Carson.

Leaving the patrol cruiser in the parking lot, we hurried across the open ground and into the ancient courthouse. We went along the dingy corridor to the sheriff's office on the ground floor. A deputy was on the phone at one of the desks in the big outer office. Carson was alone in his private cubbyhole, leaning back at his desk with his feet up, a paper cut in his hand.

The sheriff lifted the cup in greeting. "How about a drink?"

Shelley shook his head. I got a cup from the rack and helped myself from the bottle Carson kept in the bottom drawer of his desk. After a quick one, I asked, "Any trouble?"

"No ..." The sheriff looked puzzled. "Cord was as quiet as a mouse all the way in. No problem a'tall. Got his prints here in the office, then I took him on over to the jail. An' I'll be damned. The jailer and me had no more got him in a cell, than he started blubberin' and yellin', and beggin' the jailer not to leave him alone with me. You never heard the like."

"What brought that on?" I asked.

The sheriff tugged at one end of his shaggy pepper-and-salt mustache. "Don't ask me, Lon. Durndest thing I ever seen. Feller didn't have a word to say, up till he started yellin' there in his jail cell."

I poured myself another short one. "I'm beginning to get some ideas about Mr. Milton Cord. None of them good."

"Uh-huh. Well, we'll get his prints and description off to the state bureau here directly. Old Jack out there is on the phone to them now. Maybe they'll have something on Cord."

The phone on Carson's desk rang. He leaned forward, picked it up. He said, "Yes?" He listened a moment. A frown crossed his lined, weather-beaten face. He said, "Okay," and slowly replaced the phone.

"What now?" I asked.

"That was the jailer. Said I'd better get over there in a hurry. Somethin' to do with Cord ..."

The sheriff rose, reached for his hat. He walked quickly out the office. Harry Shelley and I tagged along behind him. We went out the back door, trotted across the wide parking lot to the jail. It was raining harder than ever.

The jailer, Pete Tillman, was waiting just inside the heavy jail door. He licked his lips nervously when he saw Shelley and me trooping in after the sheriff. "Ah, Ed—maybe I better see you alone for a minute—"

"It's all right, Pete," the sheriff said. "What's up?"

Tillman shuffled from one foot to the other. "Well, it's that Cord feller you brung in while ago." He hesitated, then burst out, "He claims you beat him on the way into town, Ed. And that you threatened to kill him if he said anything about it."

The sheriff blinked at the jailer, than at me. He shook his head as if to clear it. I snorted, "Oh, for—surely he doesn't think he can pull something like that?"

Tillman glanced at me, and quickly away. "Maybe you all better see him, Mr. Gates."

"That's a right good idea," Carson snapped angrily.

As we trooped along the musty-smelling hallway to the cell block, Tillman muttered to the sheriff, "Cord asked me to call him a doctor. But I figured you'd want to see—"

"Yeah," Carson replied. "I sure do want to see."

The lights were on in the cell block. Cord was lying face down on the iron bunk in the center cell. He turned his head to look at us. When he saw Carson, he cringed away, pressing his back against the brick wall.

"No," he wailed. "Don't let him—please, don't let him near me—"

"What is this, Cord?" the sheriff asked.

"You know what it is," Cord said. He got to his feet. He was shaking like a leaf, and his white face was wet with tears. He looked beseechingly toward me, then Harry Shelley. "He said he'd kill me if I told—but I couldn't hold out. The pain—"

"Ah, come off it," I said disgustedly. "Pain from what?"

With trembling fingers Cord unbuttoned his shirt, stripped it down over his shoulders. The overhead light beat down on his bare chest and belly. The white flesh was crisscrossed with angry reddish-purple welts.

For a long moment, no one spoke. Then Harry Shelley said in a shaken voice, "For heaven's sake, sheriff."

Carson was staring at Cord with unbelieving eyes. He opened his mouth to speak, then shut it again.

"Now do you believe me?" Cord said. Slowly he pulled his shirt back up over his shoulders. He gulped, winced, and went on, "It—it happened when we were about halfway into town. He stopped the car, and pulled his gun on me. He made me take off my jacket and open my shirt. Then he—he took out a blackjack and started hitting me and hitting me, all the time cursing at the top of his voice, about how I'd killed his wife ... He's crazy, I tell you!"

Harry Shelley swore under his breath.

The sheriff stammered, "He's lyin', you all know that. I didn't touch the man."

I felt sick. I remembered Shelley telling us that Dr. Johnson had examined Cord and hadn't found a bruise on him. But now—

I turned to the jailer. "Go call Doc Johnson. You'll probably catch him at the hospital. Tell him to get over here as fast as he can."

Tillman glanced at the sheriff. But Carson appeared to be in a daze. The jailer hurried away down the corridor toward the office.

Cord was sitting down on his bunk, his face buried in his hands. He didn't move when I asked, "What really happened, Cord? How'd you manage to get beat up like that?"

In a muffled voice he said, "I told you."

I looked in through the bars at the small cell, the bare iron bunk. On the opposite wall was a wash basin, and a toilet in the corner. Otherwise the cell was empty. Nothing was there that Cord could have possibly used to inflict the injuries on himself. There was only one other prisoner in the block, and he was way down at the far end, several cells distant from Cord.

I tried to think of some way, any way, out of the belief that Ed Carson had beaten a helpless prisoner. But there was no way out of it. No way at all.

The sheriff looked twenty years old than he had a few minutes ago. He turned his head and met my glance with dull, unseeing eyes. He didn't speak. Neither did I.

Harry Shelley muttered, "Damn, sheriff. We all knowed you was upset about your wife dyin', and all, and you ain't really been yourself since it happened a week ago. But this—"

Carson shook his head, turned away. He walked slowly along the hallway toward the front of the building. After a moment, Shelley and I followed. We stood around the little office waiting for the doctor. No one had anything to say.

Doc Johnson arrived about ten minutes later. He waddled in, took off his hat and shook rain from it, looked around inquiringly. He wiped his big, red, jowly face on a bandanna, and wheezed, "Well, Mrs. Dickens, the woman in the wreck, will be all right. She's a tough old hen. I'd just barely got through tapin' up her cracked ribs when she was wantin' to get home. What's goin' on here?"

"Back here," I said, and led the way into the cell block. Shelley came along. The sheriff and Tillman stayed in the office.

The fat doctor entered Cord's cell when I unlocked the door. "Well? Well?" Doc Johnson puffed. "What's ailin' you? Don't try to tell me you was hurt in that wreck, 'cause I know better."

Cord silently took off his shirt. The door breathed, "My God, boy."

In a minute or two he turned, glared at me.

"He claims Ed Carson beat him up," I said.

"Somebody sure did," Doc Johnson snapped. Then he blinked. "But—Ed?"

I nodded. "That's what this guy says."

"Don't believe it," the doctor snorted. He opened his medical bag, delved inside, came out with a bottle of antiseptic and a couple of cotton tipped swabs.

As he worked on the angry welts on Cord's chest, I heard a stir in the corridor and turned to see a short, pudgy man wearing an old fashioned raincape bustling toward us. I groaned silently. Jeremiah Walton. The editor of the Monroe *Herald-Gazette*, and a bitter political enemy of both Ed Carson and myself. The very last man on earth I wanted to see.

Walton gave me a toothy smile, while his narrow, shoebutton eyes darted curiously toward the doctor and Cord. "Well, Lon, howdy, I was over at the courthouse, and heard there'd been an accident out north of town. Thought I'd—"

He suddenly broke off. Dr. Johnson had moved aside, giving the editor a clear view of Cord.

Walton said softly. "Well, well. Just what have we here?"

He soon found out, once Cord understood who he was.

The editor stormed out of the jail, leaving a volley of promises. He'd have the best lawyer in the county for Cord. The best medical care. He'd tell the world of this infamy. In the jail office he paused long enough to give Carson a withering glance. He said, with ill concealed glee, "You finally done it. Finally hanged yourself!"

Carson lunged toward the pudgy editor." Get out of here.

Walton hurriedly left, chortling to himself.

"There's going to be hell to pay now," I said. No one disagreed with me.

Harry Shelley left, pointedly ignoring the sheriff. Tillman went back to the jail's kitchen to prepare supper for the prisoners. Carson and I sat in the little office.

Finally Carson looked up at me. "Go ahead and say it."

"What's to say?"

"You think I beat up that man, too. But I swear to you, I didn't touch him."

I sighed, drummed my fingertips on the scarred desk. "Then what happened?"

Carson scrubbed his hands over his face. "I don't know."

"He was fine when you left the wreck out there for town. You got here, put him in a cell. There's not a thing back there he could have used to hurt himself like that. No one went near him, except old Pete; and he certainly didn't take a club to the guy. So . . ."

I looked at him hesitantly. Then I went on, "Ed, you've been under a real rough strain here. Not sleeping enough, not eating. And there's a similarity between this accident today and last week, when your wife—well. I was thinking, maybe you kind of blacked out. You know? Just for a couple of minutes. It could happen."

The sheriff stared down at his clenched fists. He shook his head slowly. "No. I remember every minute of the ride into town. I'm as positive I didn't lay a finger on him as I've ever been of anything in my life."

"Then what's left?"

Before Carson could answer, we heard a call from the cell block. It was Cord. When we got back there, he was leaning against the bars of his cell, nervously tapping a ballpoint pen against the crossbar of the cell's door.

"Listen," he said. He paused, cleared his throat. "Listen, I don't want to cause no trouble—"

Carson gave a short, bitter laugh.

"No, I mean it. All I want is out of here. I heard you talking when the doc was here, about how that old woman was okay, not that it was my fault she got hurt, anyhow. But anyway, just let me take off. I'll be out of this county, out of the state, so quick it'll make your head swim. You forget about these two-bit charges against me, and I'll forget about this." He tapped a finger against his chest. "How about it?"

Carson didn't answer. I stared at the prisoner, then said, "It's a little late to make a deal, isn't it? After the way you shot off your mouth to Jeremiah Walton."

Cord grinned uneasily. "Ah, what the heck! What can he do, if I ain't around to back him up? I promise you. Just open this door, give me my billfold and stuff, and I'll be out of your stinkin' town in fifteen minutes. You can keep that old car, it's not worth me bothering with it."

I believed him. But—

"We'll think about it," I said.

Carson and I walked away. Behind us, Cord said, "Think quick, mister. I might just change my mind, and blast the both of you right out of office, you know?"

I was getting more and more confused, if that was possible, about this whole business. The Milton Cord we had just talked to was not at all the same quivering, frightened man who had blubbered on Jeremiah Walton's shoulder.

But there was no way to get around the fact that he had been beaten up. I was going in circles.

"I need a drink," I said.

Carson grunted absently. We left the jail, crossed the wide, muddy lot to the back door of the courthouse. The rain had stopped and the clouds were breaking overhead. It would be dark soon.

When we were in Carson's private office with paper cups full of bourbon in our hands, I asked, "What about it, Ed? You want to spring Cord? He's right, you know. With him gone, we can spike Walton's guns and forget the whole thing."

Carson slammed a palm down on his desk. "No. You know better than that."

I breathed a sigh of relief. "Okay, then."

"But how the heck did he do it?" Carson growled. "How did he get those blasted marks on him?"

"Maybe he did it with that ballpoint pen he was playing with," I said. I chewed my lower lip a moment. "Ed, if it comes to it, will you be willing to take a lie detector test?"

He frowned. "Yes. You bet I will.'

A few minutes later the phone rang. It was the State Crime Bureau. I went into the outer office, picked up an extension phone, and listened in. Carson was saying, "Yeah, go ahead."

A crisp, businesslike voice said, "Well, about this man you're holding, one Milton Cord. From the description your deputy gave us earlier, he sounds like a fellow we're very interested in finding. Of course, we won't know for sure until we get his prints from you."

"We sent them off, special delivery," Carson said. "You ought to get them first mail in the morning."

"Good. In any case, hang on to him. If it's the man we want, he has an armed robbery and a murder count waiting for him, over in Beckham County. He held up a gas station, and shot the attendant four times when the attendant tried to jump him. Poor guy lived long enough to identify the suspect. His real name's Martin Curtis—not at all a nice fellow. Got a record long as your arm."

No wonder Cord wanted to make a deal, I thought.

The state bureau man went on, "We traced this character through the country, and lost him. Then last week we got a line on him again. He was working with a touring carnival, down in the southern part of the state. A thing called Reid Brothers Greater Shows, or the like. But by the time we could get there, he'd taken off. That was day before yesterday. He just took off in the middle of the night, when the carnival was playing at Thomasville."

I did some rapid figuring. Thomasville was about three hundred miles southwest of Monore. If Cord, or Curtis, had hold up somewhere around Thomasville until this morning, then headed north, it would put him in Monroe just about the right time to be involved in an accident on the highway north of Monroe this afternoon.

"I kind of think you've got the right man, sheriff," the bureau agent said. "I'd almost bet on it. You see, Martin Curtis used a phony name at the carnival."

"What's that?" Carson asked.

The agent gave a discreet chuckle. "Milton Cord."

Moments later, we hung up. I went back to Carson's cubbyhole, sank into the chair beside his desk, and reached for my drink. "Well," I said.

"Yeah," Carson agreed. "How abou that?"

"That pretty well explains Milton-Martin Cord-Curtis, why he'd try to frame you, claiming you belted him around, and why he was so anxious to get out of jail and be on his way. And if that didn't work, he had Jeremiah Walton in reserve to complain about 'police brutality,' which just might have some effect on his trial for the murder rap, even though it's in another part of the state. You know how juries are, at any hint that a suspect has been slapped around, no matter what the suspect has done."

Carson was up, pacing back and forth. He swore angrily. "I'm a good mind to go over to the jail and really let him have it. At least I'd have that comfort when I get run out of the county."

I went around behind Carson's desk, sat down and picked up his phone, and asked for long distance. He stopped packing, looked at me questioningly.

"I'm going to call Thomasville," I said. "Try to talk to somebody at that carnival who knew Cord."

"What good is that?" Carson snorted. "What happened happened here, not clear down in Thomasville."

I agreed. But I couldn't think of anything else to do. Eventually I got through to the manager of the Reid Brothers Show, at the hotel in Thomasville. His name was Ludlow, and he was not overjoyed to hear from me, especially when I mentioned Milton Cord.

"There's not a thing I can tell you, sir," he snapped. "I hardly knew the man. He traveled with us only a couple of weeks. When he left, everyone here said good riddance."

"I understand that," I said. "Just what did he do with your show?"

"Ah, he worked as a stick-man at some of the games, general stuff. Then he had his crummy little act he worked sometimes in the freak tent."

This was getting us nowhere. I was about to thank Ludlow and hang up. But instead I asked, "What kind of act?"

"Nothing to write home about. This Cord, or whatever his name is, had some kind of skin condition. Something called 'dermo' something or other."

I suddenly sat forward in the chair. "What was that? Explain what you mean, Mr. Ludlow."

"Heck, I don't know," he said, in a surprised voice. "He just had this whatever it was wrong with his skin. His act was, he'd let the marks write their names on his bare chest, with the blunt end of a pencil, or whatever. In a few seconds, where they had written would light up like a neon sign, you know? The names would stand out in big long welts across his skin. Some of the rubes got a big charge out of it. He billed himself as The Great Dermo."

"How long did these—these welts last?" I shouted.

"Why I don't know. Couple or three hours, I guess."

"Thank you, Mr. Ludlow. Thank you very much."

I hung up, looked at Ed Carson. I started laughing. "You know what? We've got a celebrity in jail. The Great Dermo, of all people."

Ed stared. He said anxiously, "Lon, maybe you better go home and have dinner. Get some rest—"

But I was already on the phone again, calling Doc Johnson. "Yes," Doc said slowly, when I explained what I wanted to know. "Yes, I've heard of it. Never seen a case, though. I think it's called 'dermatographia,'" which is just another way of sayin' 'skin-writing.'" Why do you ask?"

I told him. He said he'd be right over. By now, Ed Carson knew what was going on. For the first time in days there was a smile, if a somewhat grim one, on his face.

When Doc Johnson arrived, we trooped over to the jail. We went along the corridor. We stopped at Cord's cell. He rose from his bunk, looked at us apprehensively.

"Come over here a moment, son." Doc Johnson said.

Cord walked to the cell door. "What the—"

Dr. Johnson suddenly reached a big hand through the bars, tore open Cord's shirt. The doctor had a ballpoint pen in his free hand, the ball retracted into the body of the pen, just like the pen Cord had been playing with earlier. Dr. Johnson dragged the pen across Cord's chest.

Cord yelled and tried to pull fee, but the doctor held on. For several seconds nothing happened. Then a red line appeared on Cord's chest, and rapidly widened and swelled into an angry reddish-purple welt.

Sheriff Ed Carson said softly, "How are you—Dermo?"

One look at the man's crumpling face was enough to tell us that The Great Dermo had given his last performance.

Max Van Derveer

Hijack

Sergeants Pierce and Anderson were rewarded for their patience three minutes after the ten ten streamliner from Seattle arrived at ten forty that hot July night. The man they wanted was in one of the crowds surging through the doors into the station from the debarkation platform. Pierce gauged the description while Anderson, the chain smoker, lit a fresh cigarette. The man was Caucasian, looked twenty-eight, was about five ten, one hundred and sixty pounds, and moved with a slight limp, right leg. His disguise was amateurish, dyed red hair and dyed red brush mustache, both near a burnt orange color.

Pierce nodded to Anderson, and the two detectives from Central Police Headquarters edged through the mushrooming crowd expertly to flank the man. "Mr. Greene?" Pierce inquired in a firmly polite voice.

The man jerked and halted. His head pivoted between Pierce and Anderson. Pierce identified himself and the man paled immediately. Flesh pinched at the edges of eyes that became fear-coated.

"Your left forearm, please, Mr. Greene," Pierce said.

The man remained frozen.

Anderson took the arm, pushed up the coat sleeve, and opened the cuff button of the shirt. Pierce grunted with satisfaction when he saw the tattoo on the underside of the forearm, the naked girl entwined in a snake.

The man looked ready to bolt.

"Don't," Pierce said in an even voice. "Seattle police picked up Mrs. Flora at the air terminal before she boarded her plane. They are holding her now. She will not be waiting for you. She provided your description, Mr. Greene, and she has also admitted her part in the slaying of her husband, naming you the accomplice."

"I love her," Mr. Greene said in a voice that was a low whisper of defeat.

Pierce took his suitcase, and the two detectives escorted him toward the exit doors. Pierce was looking forward to fresh air. The air in the station was dead and pressing in. He felt wet and he wondered why some people found it necessary to hurry on such a hot night. The man ahead of them was hurrying. He was forty feet in front of them perhaps, a small man, neatly attired and carrying two new suitcases. He was moving toward the idle, uniformed policeman near the street doors with short, quick steps.

Pierce saw the two youths slide in on the man and knew immediate premonition.

One of the youths bumped the man on the right. The other hit him from the left. The youth on the left brought the edge of a stiff hand down hard against the back of the man's neck. The man cried out. Each youth grabbed a suitcase. The man went down on his knees. His hat sailed from his head and rolled across the station floor as the youths bolted toward the street door. The startled uniformed policeman stood here flatfooted for a moment, then moved to block the escape route.

The sound of the gunshot was echoingly thunderous in the station. Somewhere a man chortled an oath of surprise, and a woman screamed as the uniformed policeman went up on his toes, his face caught in an expression of astonishment.

The youths burst past him. One of them hit his shoulder, and the policeman half turned and went down.

Pierce shoved Greene into Anderson. "Hold him, Andy!"

Pierce bolted from the station, but he was too late. A sports car carrying the two youths leaped from a stall in the parking area and bounced toward the avenue, then skidded into the glut of traffic and was gone.

Greene was in a cell, awaiting the arrival of Seattle police, and a cop had been slain.

The pall in the shopworn squad room at Central Police Headquarters that hot July night was a blanket. The quick death of one of them was not new. Collectively, they were subconsciously aware of Death's shadowed presence. It hung over them day and night, week in and week out, as an imagined halo hangs over an altar boy. It was a hazard of their occupation, yet none was prepared for the reality that came with Death's happening. None could quite accept, even with the reality, a new weight on their shoulders.

Sergeant Hugh Pierce, twenty-six, powerfully constructed, with dark good looks that made him a hellion with women, a member of the detective division ten months now, sat slumped at his desk. He had shed his suit coat and was in shirtsleeves, the sleeves rolled back from massive wrists. The fingers of his right hand were wrapped around a paper coffee cup, his constant companion, as he stared bleakly on the broad back of Sergeant Crocker.

Crocker, ill-dressed and lumpy, stood at an opened, smoke-filmed window, looking out on the night. His pudgy hands were locked behind him, and Pierce watched the fleshy fingers twitch reflexively. Crocker had been at the window almost five minutes now. He hadn't spoken since Pierce and Anderson had escorted the natty man who had been slugged at the train station into the squad room. Crocker had heard about the uniformed cop's death by the time they had arrived and was already in a black mood. No one, not even the boys on the night trick who now hung in the background, could blame him. At forty-seven, he was a veteran in police work. He knew many of the men in the service—beat patrolmen, car patrolmen, desk men, detectives—and he had viewed, but never had accepted, many deaths. Each was a blow to him even if he did not know the victim. But the killing this night had a personal touch. The dead cop was a veteran, too. Crocker had served with him, walked a companion beat in their early years on the force.

"Gentlemen, may I inquire why I am being detained?"

The natty man sat calm in a straight back chair near Pierce's desk. He had fitted a cigarette into a long, black holder, and now he held the holder almost delicately between two fingers of a manicured hand that rested on a carefully crossed knee.

Pierce lifted an eyebrow at Anderson. The chain smoker lit a fresh cigarette from the butt in his fingers and ground out the butt. Behind him, the night trick boys stood silent and grim-faced, some braced against the wall, some one-hipped on the corner of vacant desks. No one said a word. They just waited for Crocker to explode.

Crocker did not oblige. He turned his bulk slowly from the open window and fixed a gelid stare on the natty man. "You say your name is Nathan Moss?" His voice was flat.

"That's right."

"And you came in from Butte, Montana?"

"Again correct."

"You're a salesman?"

"I made my statement, sergeant."

"You sell maps to schools."

Nathan Moss drew on the cigarette holder, exhaled. "May I be released?"

"You're a cool customer, Moss. Let me remind you, a police officer has been killed."

Nathan Moss drew more smoke. "Yes. I saw the man die."

"So maybe you can tell me why those two punks wanted your suitcases?"

"Again I say, one contained clothing, one contained a supply of world maps I was prepared to present in an effort to sell your city schools. You drew the conclusions. This is my first journey to your city—and I hope my last."

"You'll have to stay in town a few days."

"Why?"

"I want you to identify the punks when we pick 'em up."

"Then apparently you are on optimist. How can you be so sure?"

"We've been known to apprehend a man or two."

Nathan Moss became coldly sarcastic. He looked Crocker straight in the eye. "Perhaps you should concentrate on a quarter of a million dollar armored car robbery?"

The detectives reacted simultaneously. Most stiffened and eyed the natty man with cold stares. Some shifted nervously and cast quick glances at each other. Crocker became a lump of rooted speculation. But before any of them could say a word, Nathan Moss continued, "I read newspapers in my spare time. An armored car robbery occurred in your city last week. A quarter of a million was stolen. That is a large enough amount to make a news story, even in Butte, Montana."

"Beat it, Moss," Crocker snapped.

"Thank you."

"But stay in town."

"Certainly."

All eyes in the squad room watched the natty man stand and snub out his cigarette carefully in an ashtray on Pierce's desk. He smiled at Pierce as he removed the butt from the holder, but the smile did not mean a thing. He dropped the butt into the tray. "Gentlemen," he said in departure, and then he was through the railing that separated the working area from the entry and was gone.

"Pierce," Crocker snapped. "I want to know where he goes."

Nathan Moss went straight to a downtown hotel. He left a cab and marched across the sidewalk and into the lobby of the hotel as if he were expected. Pierce watched him from a distance as he registered. Then Nathan Moss obtained a handful of change and stepped into a pay telephone booth. He was in the booth almost five minutes. Pierce wondered why he preferred the inconvenience of the pay phone over the telephone in his room. Was it because he did not want a record of the call?

Nathan Moss left the phone booth, crossed the lobby and disappeared into an elevator. Pierce waited until the door had closed on him, then he found the registration clerk polite and efficient. Moss had registered as a resident of 1023 Bowie Street, Butte, Montana. He had told the clerk he would be retaining his room several days, and then he had asked for change, enough to make a long distance call to San Francisco.

When Pierce returned to Central Police Headquarters, queries were sent to police departments in Butte and San Francisco.

Wednesday was another brilliant and hot day, and Sergeant Gilbert Crocker was in a sour mood when Pierce arrived in the squad room. Pierce put the paper cup of coffee he had taken from the vending machine on his desk, shed his coat, and rolled up his sleeves. Lieutenant Gifford, the blintz addict, arrived at eight thirty. He was angry. The death of the uniformed patrolman had been senseless. He wanted the two youths apprehended fast. He also wanted action on the armored car robbery. There was only one hood in town big enough to pull the job. Everyone knew Courtney Klane had engineered the hijack and Klane had been interrogated thoroughly, but Klane was also free. Not one shred of evidence pointed a finger at him. Only speculation pointed the finger. There was no evidence. The cops were stuck high and dry on this one, so far.

"Pierce and Anderson take the slaying," Lieutenant Gifford decided. "Gil, the heist. Get me something. All of you."

Crocker grunted and Gifford turned of Pierce. "I want those kids in here, sergeant. *Someone* has to know them. Hit every tipster in the city."

"They aren't pros. I'd stake my last dollar on that."

"Why?" Gifford asked bluntly.

Pierce shrugged. "They were twenty, twenty-one maybe, well dressed. Anyway, pros would have let Moss get out of the station, out where it was shadowed and there was less chance of being tripped up by a gutty bystander."

"One of them is a cop killer," Gifford said penetratingly.

"I'll find them, lieutenant."

An answer to their Butte query arrived at nine forty. Butte police had no record of a Nathan Moss of that city. He was not listed in the telephone book, city directory, or with the driver's license division, and 1023 Bowie Street was a fictitious address. As fictitious as a mapmaking company. There were no mapmaking firms in Butte.

San Francisco police provided the link. Nathan Moss was an alias used by Nathaniel Logger, a syndicate man who had been known to transport large sums of money from one section of the country to another. San Franciso's description of Nathaniel Logger fit Nathan Moss perfectly.

Crocker growled, "So now we know why two suitcases were so damned valuable."

"Moss ... er, Logger was bringing in money?" Pierce frowned.

"Small, used bills to be exchanged for some of the armored car stuff. I'll bet on that, sergeant. Two suitcases—I'd say that'd be about fifty thousand, just as an estimate."

"But how would two kids know about a syndicate operation?"

"*How* isn't important. The important things at the moment are Moss and the fence."

"Jerold Bishop?"

"Do you know a bigger fence in the city?"

"No."

"Let's bring 'em in."

But Nathan Moss had checked out of the downtown hotel and vanished.

Pierce and Crocker drove in silence into the newly-named Kennedy section of the city. Neither cherished returning to headquarters and Liuetenant Gifford's wrath when they would be forced to tell him of Moss's disappearance. Pierce braked the official sedan at the curbing in front of book store in the quietly substantial neighborhood. The store occupied the ground floor of a huge stone edifice. Jerold Bishop, fence and store proprietor, was a softly polite little man of thirty-five years with a thick mane of gray-black hair, bushy eyebrows, and a hearing aid. Bishop acted as though he didn't have a care in the world. He greeted the sergeants amiably.

"Get off the dime."

"Jerold."

"Hot."

"Very."

Bishop adjusted the hearing aid with his fingertips and led them back through the bookshelves and air-conditioned comfort to richly appointed bachelor quarters. He offered them brandy, which they refused, and put them in deep chairs. He sat opposite them, lit a large cigar, and waited politely.

Crocker said, "We talked to a friend of yours last night, as you undoubtedly have heard. We'd like to talk to him again, but he has taken a flyer."

"Friend?" Jerold Bishop arched a bushy brow.

"Nathan Moss, or maybe you know him as Nathaniel Logger."

"Moss? Logger?" Bishop's face didn't change. "Never heard of him, sergeant."

"Get off the dime."

Bishop shrugged. "Sorry."

"He was bringing in exchange money. You've heard of exchange money, haven't you, Mr. Bishop?"

"I've never heard of Moss—or Logger."

Crocker stood up. His voice hardened. "Okay, Jerold, let's go downtown."

Bishop didn't move in his chair, "Why?"

"In our books, there's only one guy in town who can move a quarter of a million."

"I believe you gentlemen have talked to Mr. Klane about that."

"Right now, I'm talking to you, Jerold—about you."

"I've never seen a quarter of a million in my life, sergeant."

"Damnit, creep, a police officer was killed!"

Bishop's face changed this time. He looked sad as he studied the growing ash on the light tip of the large cigar. "Yeah, I heard about that, Crocker. Tough."

"Out of the chair, creep."

"Maybe you should try College Boy."

Crocker glowered. Pierce inventoried Bishop carefully. College Boy. His name was Peter Ambler. He belonged to Courtney Klane.

"College Boy is in trouble," Bishop continued. "Deep trouble, I hear. There's a stable. You know, a guy with his looks has gotta have a stable. There's a doll named Billie. Another'n named Cynthia. Others. That kind of stable—and horses—all require green."

"How much green?" Crocker snapped.

Bishop shrugged and puffed on the cigar. "I hear about fifty thou."

"Where?"

"The Shark."

"The juice man?"

"Who else has dough these days, sergeant? Not banks."

Crocker looked at Pierce. The young detective was thinking rapidly.

It could figure. Klane could have pulled off the heist, Klane could have arranged the exchange. College Boy would be on the inside. He'd know who was coming in with the money. He'd know *when*. And he might be just fool enough to stage the hijack. It would be suicide when Klane caught up with him, but College Boy might be a big enough fool to . . .

"The punks, Bishop," Crocker was saying. "Who are the punks?"

Bishop shrugged. "Things happen in town, sergeant, even I don't know about." He left his chair then, stood neat and at ease before Crocker. "Are we still going downtown?"

"We want them. Fast."

"I can't help you."

"If I find out you're lying to me, creep—"

"I'm not."

Crocker measured him for a long time. "So it's College Boy, eh?"

"Try him, sergeant."

"Like I say, creep, if I find out you're lying . . ."

He let the words dribble off as Jerold Bishop calmly turned off his hearing aid. He stared at Bishop, and then he turned and stomped out of the bachelor quarters. Pierce trailed after him. Pierce knew a tremendous urge to yank the hearing aid from Bishop's ear and stuff it down his throat.

In the heat of the sun again, Pierce asked, "So how do we find Peter Ambler, sergeant?"

"Alive—I hope," Crocker said sourly.

"Then we'd better get to him before Klane does."

But that Wednesday was not a day designed for cops or search. It became a day of almost unbearable heat, greasy bodies, short tempers, and futile search. The detectives did not find Peter Ambler, nor were they able to pigenhole Courtney Klane when they finally turned their humanized radar beams on him. By late afternoon they felt as if a poniard had been stuck in their bodies, individually. Then the poniard was twisted. A pick up order for Jerold Bishop was sent out. But Bishop had disappeared, too.

Crocker swore harshly, and the night trick boys who had come on duty at six P.M. wisely remained in the background. Only Pierce and Anderson met Crocker's wrath head-on. And Pierce felt like swearing back at him.

"We should have brought him in this morning," he said flatly.

"Yeah," Crocker growled. "We could've saved his shyster a trip, too. Right, sergeant? We could've swung around and picked *him* up on the way downtown."

Anderson lit a fresh cigarette, snapped the used match to the scarred floor. "Maybe we're going at this thing wrong, Gil. Maybe we should be concentrating on the two punks."

"Concentratin' on em!" Crocker exploded. "Hell, we don't even know 'em!"

Pierce went out into the hall and got a new cup of coffee from the vending machine. He was tired, dog-tired, and he felt soiled. He suddenly wanted a bath and the soothing equanimity of his wife, Nancy. The equanimity was a quality about her he treasured. Nancy knew his moods, his frustrations. More important, she knew the salve.

He looked up at the ancient wall clock as he returned to his desk. Ten minutes before nine o'clock. Nancy could be ironing, reading, or merely waiting. He decided he needed her this very minute. He said, "How 'bout calling it a day, sergeant?"

Crocker ignored him and answered the jangled demand of the telephone on his desk. He grunted, listened. His scowl deepened. And Pierce watched him with a queasy feeling of impending doom. Pierce could not hear the words being rattled into Crocker's ear, but he knew the message was not good.

Crocker slammed the phone together and sat swearing as he fixed Pierce and Anderson from eyes that gleamed with determination. "Another'," he said in a viciously soft voice. "Another cop has been killed."

Silence hung in the squad room.

"Patrol car," Crocker continued, the words coming as if they were being churned out by a machine. "One dead, one wounded. Two kids in a sports car. Drunk. Our boys attempted to stop them."

It was a long time before Pierce ventured: "Two kids in a sports car?"

Wednesday night became a long and horrendous night for Pierce. Not even Nancy's placations could reach him. He smoked cigarettes, drank coffee, paced, pondered, damned, vowed, tossed in their bed, wanted to shout at the muscle spasms in his legs. And Thursday came too soon, dawned too hot. He got up with a dull throb between his eyes. Coffee had a dishwater taste. Cigarette smoke burned his lungs. Crocker was a sore boil.

A ballistics report received at ten twenty in the morning only heaped misery on misery. Bullets from the same gun had killed the beat patrolman in the train station and the car patrolman who had attempted to halt a pair of drunks.

Then Peter Ambler was found. Bruised, wire-bound, and dead, Peter Ambler was fished from the river.

College Boy had been graduated. The only trouble was, he was not wearing the traditional cap and gown in the photographs used by the afternoon newspapers.

Lieutenant Gifford had slid beyond the edge of caution when he addressed Pierce, Crocker, and Anderson in the squad room. His thoughts were no longer with shysters, adverse publicity for the department, or the ire of his superiors if he was wrong. His face was a mask. His words were terse. "Bring in Courtney Klane. I don't care if you find him in Anchorage—bring him in."

The three detectives stood quiet.

A girl fractured the silence. "Is this ... this the Detective Division?" she asked in a voice that was a combination of uncertainty and desperation, almost whispered.

She was tall and lithe, with gold-blonde hair framing an Hellenic face, a girl on the brink of full-blown womanhood who looked nineteen but probably was twenty-five. She wore a fresh white blouse and a fitted gabardine skirt, and she stood at the railing that divided the room, long fingers of one hand twitching against the top edge of the gate, dark eyes dancing pleadingly.

Pierce knew an instinctive liking for the girl, and a deep-seated desire to set her at ease, give her peace of mind. Some of both stemmed from a taunt. She was vaguely familiar; far back in his catalogued memory, she was an image. He attempted an appearance of nonchalance and an easy grin.

"Can we help you, Miss ..." He let it hang purposely.

"Weatherly," the girl said quickly. She came through the gate. The dark eyes became rooted on him. "Lucy Weatherly."

"This is the Detective Division, Miss Weatherly," he said, nodding. "I am Sergeant Pierce." He forced the grin to remain alive over disturbing curiosity. He had her with the name.

"I came here to ..." She hesitated. The dark eyes danced away in a moment of indecision, flashed back and held with fresh determination. "A desk sergeant downstairs said you might be able to help me."

"Yes?" Pierce said patiently.

"It's about ... Peter Ambler." Perfect white teeth caught her lower lip briefly, but the eyes remained steady. "At least the afternoon newspapers said Peter Ambler was his name. I knew him as Danny Sloan."

Pierce was unable to stem the sudden tenseness of his muscles, but he managed to resist the magnetic impulse to flash looks at Gifford, Crocker, and Anderson.

"What about Peter Ambler, Miss Weatherly?"

"Well ... I just don't understand."

Pierce waited.

"I mean—Danny Sloan, Peter Ambler, College Boy—what the newspapers say he is ... was ..." She caught the lower lip again. "Please ... I'm confused."

"He was Peter Ambler and he was everything the newspapers said," Pierce said, wishing he was on the sidelines and listening to Gifford or Anderson or any other detective.

The hurt appeared in her eyes, but it did not push out acceptance. "How did you know Peter—er, Danny Sloan, Miss Weatherly?"

She met his look and he knew an even greater liking for her. "We dated."

"Isn't your father Arnold Weatherly?"

"Yes."

"Was he acquainted with Ambler—Sloan?"

"No. Father and Danny never met."

"By design?"

"I—don't understand."

"Perhaps you didn't want them to meet, Miss Weatherly."

Her eyes changed suddenly. Pierce didn't like what he found there now. "It wasn't that at all, sergeant," she said, clipping the words slightly. "Danny Sloan was not like the man described in the newspapers this afternoon. The only reason he and Father did not meet was, my father is quite busy these days. He seldom is home for very long periods of time."

"I believe he is about to announce that he will be a candidate for the U.S. Senate."

"He is."

"Would he have approved of Danny Sloan?"

"He would have."

"Peter Ambler?"

"I—" She stopped. Her nostrils flared slightly. "No. Father would not have approved of Peter Ambler." Her words were suddenly soft.

"I'm sorry things worked out this way for you, Miss Weatherly."

"Thank you."

She turned. Pierce remained silent.

"Just a minute, Pierce."

Lieutenant Gifford's voice was hard and the muscles in his face were set when Pierce looked at him. "Perhaps there are some things Miss Weatherly can tell us about Ambler," he said. He eyes rooted on her. "Understand. Miss Weatherly, two of our officers have been killed and we have reason to think Ambler knew about those murdered."

"Yes," she said, her voice just above a whisper.

Pierce boiled inside as he stared at Gifford. The girl had reached him. No one in his right mind could possibly conceive that she would have any knowledge of Peter Ambler's—Danny Sloan's, or whatever you wanted to call him—true self. No one could even *think* she might know anything about murder or gangland slayings or armed robbery. Yet here was Gifford bulldozing into her as if she had been taken from a lineup of street girls.

Pierce swelled but managed to hold himself.

After all, the lieutenant was being a police officer. He was investigating murder. Three murders.

They used the privacy of Gifford's officer for the interrogation. His questions were polite but pointed, the questions of an expert at work. But, surprisingly, Lucy Weatherly was an expert, too. She refuted, fended, and defended beautifully. And Pierce found himself gradually slipping into the role of an entertained spectator as he remained in the background and allowed his initial irritation to fade before the tide of admiration for the foes. He was witnessing a classic in query and answer, a running conflict of clever mind against clever mind. And it was dusk before the foes backed off and surveyed their opponents anew. Each had earned the respect of the other, and each saw the futility of continuance.

Gifford said, "I think that will be all, Miss Weatherly."

"Please do not *think*, lieutenant," she said calmly. "I do not wish to return."

"That will be all, Miss Weatherly."

"Thank you."

She stood, smoothed the gabardine skirt across her hips, and left the office as if she were leaving a beauty salon.

Pierce went after her, expecting a sharp summons from Gifford. None came. "Miss Weatherly?"

"Yes?" She stood at the railing, half-turned.

"Do you have transportation?"

"I came in a cab."

He grinned. "Then I'll give you a lift."

"It isn't necessary, sergeant."

Pierce opened the railing gate for her.

"More questions?" she asked.

"No questions," he grinned.

She rode beside him in the front seat of his dented sedan as if it was natural for her to be there. Their conversation was idle and exploratory, and Pierce was conscious of her oblique inventory as he piloted the sedan expertly through the city traffic and into a residential district. The Weatherly home was a massive stone stucture in the dusk of evening, set far back from a quiet street on a sculptured lawn. Pierce braked on the curving concrete drive behind a topdown sport convertible, and Lucy Wealtherly left the sedan with an economy of movement.

She leaned in the open door. "Thank you, sergeant," she said with a genuine smile.

He sat stonefaced, suddenly gripping the steering wheel hard, as a blond boy who looked twenty came out of the stone house and ran down the front steps. The boy was neat in dark sports coat and slacks and white bucks. He danced between the front of the sedan and the back of the sports car with a lifted arm.

"Sis," he said in greeting.

And then he was inside the convertible and the motor came to life.

"What's the matter, sergeant?" Lucy Weatherly's face was pleated with a frown.

"Your brother?" Pierce asked, bobbing his head toward the car that was moving away now.

"Bernie? Yes."

"Good evening, Miss Weatherly."

She straightened slowly, shut the door of the sedan, and Pierce knew she was deeply troubled, but he did not have time for explanations now. Anyway, she wouldn't like the explanations if he gave them.

He drove after the sports car. He wasn't sure that he actually had recognized the car. But he was sure about the youth. Bernard Weatherly had been one of the youths who had grabbed a suitcase from Nathan Moss in the train depot.

The car was not difficult to follow, but Pierce was cautious. He was positive about Bernard Weatherly and the train station, yet the connection was difficult to accept. His mind churned. Bernard Weatherly was from a family of wealth and stature. Why would he hijack a man? Why would he steal? Why would he kill?

Had Bernard Weatherly killed?

Pierce was forced to admit he did not know which one of the two youths had fired the fatal shot.

His thoughts leaped to the now dead Peter Ambler. Bernard Weatherly's association with College Boy was easy—Lucy. Which, in turn, almost had to mean Bernard had discovered *who* Peter Ambler really had been, and *what* he had been. And this meant Bernard had hoodwinked his sister and probably the rest of his family, if Lucy Weatherly had told the truth during the squad room interrogation.

Pierce shook his head. He didn't like the thoughts, the possibility that Lucy Weatherly might have lied to them.

Taillights on the convertible flashed. Pierce slowed the sedan and watched it turn through an iron gate. He braked at a curbing. He had a clear view over a thick hedge of a driveway and a sprawling redwood house. He watched Bernard Weatherly swing the car through a U turn in a large, vacant carport and stop. Another youth, also neatly attired, popped out of the house and jumped into the front seat on the small car beside Weatherly. The car shot down the drive, hit the street, and turned away from Pierce.

He followed it across the city. If Weatherly and his companion knew they were being tailed, they were not concerned. They slowed, turned from the street into a parking lot beside a cocktail lounge. Pierce eased his sedan into a slot at the curbing and sat watching the two youths leave the lot to enter the lounge. He looked around. It was dark now, a hot night. He recognized the area of the city. It was on the edge of the warehouse district.

He went into the carpeted dimness of the neat lounge. Business was slow and he saw his quarry immediately. They were in swivel chair-stools at the bar. He knew he should call into the squad room. On the other hand, he had not had a good look at Bernard Weatherly's companion yet. And what if he were wrong about Bernard?

He sat alone at a table near the street door and ordered a bourbon and water. He did not touch the drink as he inventoried the youths. Bernard's companion was the right build, the same as the second youth at the train depot.

Pierce backoned his waiter again. "Those two at the bar," he said. Do you know them?"

"Mr. Weatherly and Mr. Poswold," the waiter said crisply.

"How often do they come in here?"

"Nightly."

"Tuesday night?"

The waiter hesitated. "No, now that you ask, they were not in last night."

"I know the Weatherly boy. What about the other one? Poswold?"

The waiter was frowning now. "I don't believe, sir, that I should say—"

Pierce identified himself and the waiter decided to become neutral. "Mr. Randy Poswold, sir. His father is Judge Poswold, I believe."

"Thanks."

Pierce waved the waiter away and sat for a long time wrestling with his thoughts. Judge Poswold, huh? He knew the jurist by reputation.

He kept an eye on the waiter and noted with satisfaction the man remained away from other employees and from the youths at the bar. It was a good move on the waiter's part. Communication with others would have called for immediate action from Pierce, and he was not yet ready to move in. He still had not had a good look at the Poswold youth.

Well, there was only one way to get that look.

He left his untouched drink and went to the bar. He knew an immediate need for wariness as he met the direct looks of Bernard Weatherly and Randy Poswold. He wanted both.

"Hey ..." Bernard Weatherly let it fade as he stiffened and stared hard at Pierce.

The detective knew the youth was struggling for recognition, was unsure. He attempted to keep him off-balance. "Sergeant Pierce. Central Police Headquarters." He moved his hand. He was in position to take out his gun quickly. And watching the eyes of the youths, some of the tension left him. Both had noted the move, both knew what it meant.

"My sister," Bernard Weatherly breathed. "He was with my sister ..." He let it trail off.

Randy Poswold was stone. His expression was black, his eyes glittering with hardness, but he did not move. He said, "What do you want with us, copper?" He spoke almost without moving his lips.

Pierce bobbed his head toward the street door.

Neither youth moved.

Pierce stepped back, waited, ready for anything. Poswold turned on the swivel seat of the chair-stool, stood. Bernard Weatherly followed quickly. They walked side by side toward the street door. Pierce trailed them, his confidence swelling with each step. He'd cuff them outside, before they got into his sedan. He didn't want to stir the other customers in the lounge.

Suddenly Poswold hunched, whirled, and shot a fist straight into Pierce. The fist drove him back with a gasp of breath. Blows pounded his body. He heard others. He struggled to get his hand to his gun. And then a fist came up under his jaw and snapped back his head. He knew he was reeling. He heard his own hoarse shout. His heels caught something. He sat down jarringly.

The room swirled, cleared quickly. He shook his head. The youths were not in sight. Hands caught his armpits. He struggled up, shrugged off the hands, and lunged toward the door unsteadily. He hit the sidewalk. The sports car bounced out of the parking lot. Street traffic swerved and squealed. The car roared through a sharp turn in front of a careening police patrol car. And then the sound of a shot filled the night. Pierce heard the whine of the bullet, went down on the sidewalk and rolled. The wail of a siren started low, took on stature. And Pierce was on his feet again and racing to his sedan.

He drove through the spread traffic expertly, using the path cleared by the siren and flashing red light of the patrol car ahead of him. He heard what sounded like gunshots. The sounds came again. He saw the police car weave and shoot at an angle into the opposite lane of traffic to smash head-on into a parked car. He saw the back of the police car lift off the street and start to come around, then he was past the wreck and his eyes were glued on the taillights of a weaving convertible. It had slowed, seemed out of control.

When the body spilled from the driver's side onto the street, he knew why.

It required all of his skill to miss the body. He used his brakes to start into a side skid. He cut the steering wheel at the final second. The back end of the sedan whipped back and he was skidding in the opposite direction, but he had managed to slide around the prostrate form. He eased off the accelerator, allowed the sedan to right itself, then he shot after the sports car that was now widening the distance between them rapidly.

They roared into the warehouse district. Good. They had lost the benefit of a siren or red light to warn traffic now. They had weaved in and out crazily. But in the warehouse district, the traffic thinned abruptly and Pierce was able to concentrate on closing the distance between the two vehicles.

Suddenly he saw the convertible go into a turn and he shouted an involuntary warning. He knew the car would never navigate the intersection corner at its speed. He saw the small car swing wide, hit the curbing, bounce, go up on the sidewalk and then into the skid.

And then he was past the intersection and sliding to a stop. He hadn't even tried to make the same turn. It would have been suicide.

Rolling from the sedan, he stumbled, righted himself, drew his gun, and raced back to the corner of the building. The sports car was folded around a street lamp pole, the pole seemingly protruding from the driver's seat, but instead of the driver being limp inside the car, Pierce saw him pounding down the middle of the street, racing into the heavy shadows of the squat warehouses.

He shouted and ran after the fleeing figure. He did not know whom he was chasing, Bernard Weatherly or Randy Poswold, but he knew now that he had a chance. In the auto chase he had been at a distinct disadvantage. The small car was faster than his sedan, maneuverable. In the hands of an expert, it could have lost him easily by using corner turns. But the driver had not been an expert, had not seized his advantage. And now the odds had narrowed considerably.

Pierce saw the youth turn a corner and disappear. He slowed, slammed into a brick wall. He had no desire to burst around that same corner and into a barrage of bullets. With his gun gripped in his right hand, he gasped for breath and eased his head out from the building. The street and sidewalks ahead were dark with shadows and vacant.

He stepped out from the protection of the building, stood silent. Nothing stirred in the shadows. He moved forward cautiously. His slow steps sounded unusually loud in the still, hot night. Sweat poured from his pores. He felt on fire. He stopped in stride when he saw the light. It came from a door that was wide and open, a vehicle door in one of the warehouses. Was the youth inside the warehouse? Pierce knew he would be exposed to almost any kind of attack when he stepped into the patch of light. He stood at its edge, breathing heavily, listening intently, but there were only the normal night sounds of the city.

He drew in a deep breath, held it, and stepped quickly into the warehouse, gun poised, ready for anything.

The warehouse seemed empty of humanity. That was odd. Had someone carelessly departed without locking up? Or would he find men working in the far reaches of the large structure?

His eyes moved constantly. To his right and left were solid, stacked wooden crates. Straight ahead was a wide gap, wide enough to accommodate large trucks easily. There were no vehicles in the building. He listened again for men at work. Nothing. He moved slowly into the building.

The hiss of indrawn breath was his warning.

Pierce hunched, whirled, and took the blow on his shoulder. His gun flipped from his fingers and clattered against the concrete floor. He clutched futilely at the youth's shirt front as his knees came unhinged. The youth was armed. He brought the gun down on Pierce's left wrist. Pierce sprawled on his hands and knees, knowing that Randy Poswold had come out from a hidden aisle behind the stacked crates.

All he could see now was the polished toes of Poswold's shoes as Poswold let him hang there for a long time. Pierce blinked hard against the pain in his shoulder and wrist. His left arm was numbed. Scrambled thoughts whirled through his head. He remembered the body sprawled in the street. It had to be Bernard Weatherly. Was Weatherly dead?

He remembered the hard glitter of Randy Poswold's eyes when he had approached the two youths in the cocktail lounge. Now he saw that glitter as Death. And he remembered Sergeant Crocker's time-worn warning, "Never take a punk alone, sergeant!"

Randy Poswold shuffled his feet. "Up."

The command jerked at Pierce. He forced his head up slowly. Poswold stood about four feet away, ugly and taut with youthful ferocity.

Wasn't there anyone else in the warehouse? Why didn't they show?

"Up," Poswold repeated loudly.

"Take it easy, Randy."

Poswold grinned and stepped forward as Pierce pushed back on his knees. Pierce saw the gun flash but he was unable to pull his face out of the way. The gun slashed against his mouth and the yell of protest was jammed back in his throat. He spilled back and then on his side. He could taste the blood through the blinding pain and he knew that one of his lips, perhaps both, had been split against his teeth.

"How do you like it, copper?"

The words came from far away. Pierce shook his head, attempted to get the youth in focus.

"You coppers shouldn't have killed Bernie."

Pierce pushed up into a sitting position. Everything whirled. He moved his legs under his body, remained still. His head was clearing slowly. Pain was taking over. His mouth felt swollen all out of proportion. He couldn't feel his teeth with his tongue. Maybe those teeth were gone. But he didn't remember spitting them.

"You shouldn't have killed Bernie!" Poswold repeated with animal shrillness.

Pierce got him in focus. He pushed up on his knees, planted a foot and stood slowly. He bobbed, but he could feel the strength flowing back into his muscles.

Poswold held the gun steady in his right hand. His mouth was wire-tight, his eyes narrowed and gleaming. Pierce saw his own gun on the concrete floor. It was ten feet away.

Suddenly Poswold's lips thinned in a grin that wasn't a grin at all. His eyes flicked to Pierce's gun, came back. "You're in a jam, huh, copper?"

"Are you going to kill me, Randy?"

"You damn right I'm going to kill you!"

"Just like you killed the others."

"Just like you coppers killed Bernie."

"You've already killed two police officers and College Boy. You've already—"

"Not Ambler!" Poswold was actually grinning now.

"You and Bernie and College Boy. The three of you. College Boy knew the money was coming into town with Nathan Moss. He set up you and Bernie. He had to cut you two in. Nathan Moss would recognize College Boy but not you two. He—"

Poswold opened his gun, looked in the chamber, snapped the gun together again, laughed deep in his throat. "One slug, copper. This is gonna be fun." He leveled the gun on Pierce. "A little Russian roulette, huh?"

It hit Pierce hard. He'd been stalling, attempting to gain an advantage.

He saw the gun quiver and he knew Poswold was squeezing the trigger.

The snap of the firing pin striking the empty chamber was loud in the stillness of the warehouse.

Pierce jerked reflexively.

Poswold laughed.

The gun quivered again.

And Pierce leaped. He shot a large fist into the megalomaniac's face. The fist hit home with the second empty click of the gun and Poswold went back with a howl. Pierce followed with a looping uppercut that struck Poswold's wrist and brought his arm up. The gun left his fingers and sailed back over his shoulder. Pierce drove a right jab into the youth's stomach and sent him down to the concrete with a looping left. He was over the groveling body quickly and wrenching Poswold's wrists back to his spine. He whipped on the handcuffs and then he stood erect and spread-legged over the youth, taking in air with huge gulps.

He found a man in a sweat-stained shirt and pants and checkered cap gaping at him round-eyed from fifty feet away.

The man was frightened and cooperative. The warehouse door had been open because he had been expecting a delivery truck in to load. He had been working at the back of the building, had heard voices, had thought the expected truck had arrived, but had come up front to find Pierce smashing Poswold into the concrete.

Randy Poswold was sullen and silent. He refused to say more than to give his name and address and demand permission to telephone a lawyer. Sergeant Crocker suggested calling his father. The youth told Crocker to "go to hell."

Poswold was hustled downstairs and into a cell to cool, the warehouse man was dismissed, and the newspaper boys were given their story.

Crocker fixed Pierce with a steady look. "How're you feelin'?"

"Like hell."

"You look like hell. How many times have I told you never to take a punk alone?"

"I figured I could handle him."

"Sure."

Even the night trick boys flinched under the sarcasm.

Pierce asked, "The Weatherlys know about their son?"

"Yeah."

"How 'bout our boys?"

"One wounded, the other smashed up in the wreck, but both will make it, doc says. Speaking of docs, you'd better see one."

"My wife will take care of me."

"Yeah," Crocker grunted, and Pierce walked out of the squad room. He found the night still hot, but he felt better inside. A job had been completed. He touched his swollen mouth with his fingertips, tasted new blood on the split in his upper lip. His shoulder was sore and his wrist ached. He drove slowly across town to the modest apartment. He was thinking about Lucy Weatherly and the shock of her brother's death to her and the family. The man seated in the front room of his apartment caught him unprepared. The man held a gun on Nancy.

Pierce became rooted two steps inside the open door.

"Close it," Jerold Bishop said without looking at him.

Pierce kicked the door shut. "What's with you, creep?"

"He's been here almost thirty minutes," Nancy said. "What happened to your mouth?"

She was calm, but slightly wide-eyed as she stared at him. She sat on a large footstool near an ironing board. She was in shorts. The lone signs of tension were in the way she pressed her knees together and clenched her fist on her thighs. Across the room the television set was turned off now, probably at Bishop's demand, but Pierce knew that earlier his wife had been ironing in the front room so that she might also watch the video shows.

"I got the flash on the radio," Bishop said.

Pierce attempted to hide his ignorance. "Yeah?"

Bishop shrugged without taking his eyes or gun from Nancy. "So I gotta have a way out of town. Figures?"

"Maybe."

Bishop's laugh was a grunt. "No cat and mouse, sergeant, please. The Weatherly kid is dead, and you've got Randy Poswold in the clink. I know the punk. I've been dealing with him for a couple of years now, although, thinking back, I don't know why. The kid always was potential trouble. But he came in with some good stuff to move. His stuff always had class. I don't know where he got it. I never asked. It brought a good price, so I handled it. That was a mistake. I can see it now."

Some of the jumbled thoughts began to straighten out in Pierce's mind, but he stalled. "You fenced for him, eh, creep?"

"I never should have. He always smelled of trouble."

"And then Courtney Klane hit the armored car and came to you to set up the money exchange."

"Fifty thousand is big dough, sergeant."

"You needed a couple of guys to hit Nathan Moss, somebody Moss wouldn't recognize. That'd be Poswold and Weatherly."

"Randy brought in Weatherly. I never saw the kid in my life until this setup."

"Let's see—their cut would be about five thousand."

"Ten. They came high, but I couldn't quibble. It had to be quick."

"College Boy?"

Bishop flicked Pierce a glance, grinned. "A sucker. You and Crocker were pressing so I gave him to you to keep you off my back."

"And then killed him so he couldn't talk."

"College Boy always did have a big mouth when there was a squeeze."

"But tonight we got Randy Poswold."

"Yeah. Let's quit stalling, sergeant. I know punks. They bleat. You know all of this, so let's quit stalling. I gotta get out of town. Klane ain't gonna like me now. Nor you guys. That's where you and your doll come in. You're gonna take me. I figure that by this time your boys have got the exits plugged, waiting for me to make my move. Well, I'm making it—but with you and the doll. You two are gonna drive me out, nice and quiet-like. Get it?"

"Yeah."

Bishop got out of the chair suddenly, fingering his hearing aid. "So let's roll."

The reflexiveness of domesticity never ceased to amaze Pierce, and all he could do was shake his head when his wife stood and said, "You'll excuse me a moment, Mr. Bishop?"

She wet the tip of a forefinger and touched the bottom of the iron upended on the board. The iron sizzled. She gave Bishop a tiny smile. "See, the place could burn down while we are gone."

"Yeah," he grunted. He swung his gun on Pierce, kept it there.

Pierce saw his wife lean over the board and pull the cord from the wall plug. When she turned from the board, Bishop was in profile to her. The movement was smooth. She swept up the not iron as she took the step to join her husband. She brought the iron up and around fast. Bishop flinched, but she managed to slap the iron against his cheek. He howled. His gun boomed.

And then Pierce was on him, driving a fist deep into his stomach and catching the gun wrist. Pierce whirled, brought up his knee, and smashed Bishop's wrist down across his thigh. The gun flipped from his fingers. Bishop stiffened with another howl and when Pierce looked, he found Nancy pressing the flat of the iron against Bishop's spine.

Pierce spun Bishop across the room and followed with his fist. Bishop went down on the carpeting and Pierce was on him fast, cuffing him.

It was a long time before he looked up at Nancy. She stood slightly spread-legged, the iron still clutched in her hand. She was half turned, staring at the new bullet hole in their plastered wall. She faced him. He shook his head in amazement. "You're dangerous with that thing, love."

She hefted the iron, held it aloft. And then a grin spread over her face. "Remember that, darling."

C. B. Gilford
Dream of a Murder

Harvey Fenster had committed murder, plain and simple. The crime hadn't been detected. His wife Beryl was dead and in the ground, and they'd called it an accident. The police weren't bothering him. Nobody blamed him. In fact, what few acquaintances he had, sympathized with him. Poor old Harvey. An accident. And now he was all alone. Plain and simple. That was the kind of murder it had been. And that was why it had succeeded.

The only trouble was, Harvey Fenster dreamed.

The first dream started with the murder. It was so clear, so detailed, and so accurate, that it was just like committing the crime all over again. Once had been bad enough.

"Harvey, I've just got to have a new washing machine." It was a whine of complaint, like everything she said.

He let his newspaper fall to his lap, and glanced up at his wife. She was standing there, wringing her hands as usual, her pale face sad, wisps of gray hair falling over her forehead; scarcely forty, and already looking like an old woman.

"What's the matter with the washing machine?" he asked her, and he didn't try to make the question sound friendly.

"Take a look at it, will you, Harvey? I got another shock from it today. Honestly, I'm going to be electrocuted sometime for sure."

He went down to the basement unwillingly. The washing machine loomed out of the dim light, high and huge, like an old Model T. There were more places where the paint had chipped off, he noticed. Obviously Beryl hadn't taken proper care of it. He squatted down to take a preliminary look, and he saw what the trouble was right away. The wire was worn, just where it went under the machine to the motor. The insulation had dried and cracked, that was all.

What should he do? Replace the cord? No, just some electrician's tape. He went to the tool chest and rummaged around. No tape. He remembered now. He'd asked for some at the hardware store, and when the clerk told him it cost seventy-nine cents for that skimpy little roll, he'd refused to buy it and walked out. He wondered now if it were worth even seventy-nine cents to keep Beryl from getting electrocuted.

And then he knew the answer to that question.

She was only an expense. If he tried to divorce her, he'd have to pay alimony. And he was tired of the nagging, the complaints; fix this, buy me that, this is so old, that's worn out. He wanted silence, blessed silence.

His preparations for murder were simple and straightforward. The machine was unplugged, so he could work with the wire in safety. He bent it back and forth dozens of times at the place of wear, then scraped it patiently on the bottom rim of the machine till the copper strands gleamed bright and bare. Then he wedged it up under the rim so that the wire would be in contact with the metal of the machine itself. Finally he plugged it in. Now the whole washer was "hot," waiting. Last of all, he doused water on the concrete floor. The "ground" was waiting, too.

Near the bottom of the steps was the pair of old shoes his wife always wore while washing in the basement where she might get her feet wet. He picked up the shoes, examined the soles. Both, he saw, were almost worn through. Calmly, carefully, he dug at the thin, crumbling leather with a fingernail. He kept at it till there was a clear hole the size of a nickel.

After that, it was only a matter of getting her downstairs to try the machine. She was difficult, as she often was.

"I think I've fixed it and I want you to try it," he called up to her.

"I wasn't planning to do a washing tonight ..."

"Well, I want you to try it anyway. If it doesn't act right, then we'll think about replacing it."

The promise, vague as it was, lured her. She came obediently down the stairs. Her legs, he noted, were bare. Automatically she changed into her work shoes. With her mind on the washing machine, she seemed unaware that the skin of the sole of her foot was in direct contact with the floor. At least, she didn't wince.

"How'd everything get so wet?" she asked him.

"I was testing," he assured her.

He knew his plan wasn't a certain thing. Electrical shorts are tricky, unpredictable. She mightn't be killed, only injured, or possibly not harmed at all. But he felt lucky, somehow, and about time!

He watched her. She approached the machine gingerly, as if doubtful, or even afraid. Her feet were in the film of water that clung to the floor around the drain. She reached out to touch the machine with both hands, like a child exploring a new toy. He waited in an agony of suspense, the moment elongating into a near eternity.

And then her hands were gripping the rim of the metal tub, gripping it and could not let go. Shudders and spasms racked her body. What sounds did he hear? Did he actually hear the crackling of the electric current? And what sounds came from Beryl? A scream or a moan? Or did she make any sound at all? Was it his own voice instead, uttering an inarticulate cry of triumph? On and on ...

Until another sound interrupted it, louder and more insistent, a buzz like a terrible swift jackhammer, clamoring right in his ear. He reached out a hand, partially to ward off this sound, partially to stifle it. Finally, he did the latter. His groping hand found the alarm clock on the bedside table, his numb fingers reached the button and pressed it.

By that time he was fully awake, wide-eyed and shaking and sweating, with the clock in his lap, pulled to the full length of its cord. Tremblingly he replaced the thing on the table, then wiped his perspiring face with a pajama sleeve.

But it was a time before he fully recovered from the experience. Afraid of getting a chill, he burrowed back under the blanket, and stayed there until his quivering body was still. This was the way he had reacted when he saw Beryl die, he remembered now. His body had jerked and shuddered just as hers had, the two almost in tune.

It had been only a dream, hadn't it? But how could a dream of a murder, real as it might have seemed, affect him more deeply than the actual murder itself? Anyway, the thing was over with now. Done. Finished. He was safe again in the waking world. He smiled.

Harvey Fenster's day was busy, ordinary, untroubled, work-filled. In the evening he watched television, which was more pleasurable now that he didn't have to argue with Beryl over the selection of programs, and went, at last, to bed.

He wasn't expecting to dream.

But it happened. A dream . . .

"Harvey, I've just got to have a new washing machine" . . . till Beryl's body shuddered in the grip of the electric current. Her cry—or his.

What then? Yes, he had gone upstairs. And he was going now. In a voice broken by grief and terror, he called a doctor, an ambulance, and the police.

The last arrived first, two uniformed officers in a patrol car who acted with the efficiency and compassion of men who had seen things like this happen before. It was one of them who told him that his wife was dead.

The policemen handled everything. Harvey stood dumbly by the front door and watched the sheeted corpse being carried out on a stretcher. He answered a few questions automatically, stunned.

In all the time between the death and the funeral, the only one who seemed unkind was a plainclothes police officer named Godney. Joe Godney had a sharp face, thick brows, and under them, black, piercing eyes.

Godney hinted that Harvery Fenster should have known about the condition of the washing machine, and Harvey kept answering that he certainly would have attended to it had Beryl ever mentioned the matter. Then an accusation finally came out in words. "You know, Mr. Fenster, I'd call it almost criminal negligence on your part."

He didn't crack. He didn't even start guiltily. "Don't you think I haven't thought about it myself? Don't you think I've blamed myself? That washer was pretty old. I should have checked it over once in a while. But it never gave any trouble . . ."

"Okay. Okay, Mr. Fenster. I'm not trying to make a case out of it."

Godney's face looked very sharp, honed like an axe blade, his eyes glittered malevolently, and he added a strange remark. "Not that I wouldn't like to."

What was ringing? The phone? Or the doorbell? Harvey tried to rise from his chair, anything to escape from Godney's accusing stare. His hands reached, to clutch something to help him . . .

And he was wrestling with the alarm clock again, pulling at it, almost pulling it out of the wall. But now, as he awakened, he knew enough to press the button to shut off that persistent ringing.

Shaking in every extremity, sweating profusely, he sought refuge like an animal in its lair, and dived under the blankets. But in the warm dark it was a long time before the shaking stopped and his sweat dried.

"Criminal negligence." What was it anyway? Maybe something you accuse a homicidal driver of, or maybe a doctor who was careless during an operation. But him, Harvey Fenster, for harboring a beatup washing machine? He laughed.

But at the bank that day, he made a mistake that took him hours to locate. And in the evening he watched television grimly, until the last late-late show was finished, until the final weather report, until the screen went blank. Then he stared at the blankness for a while.

He succumbed finally, however. Weariness forced his surrender. He staggered into bed, letting his eyes close, hoping he wouldn't dream.

"Harvey, I've just got to have a new washing machine . . . Your wife is dead, Mr. Fenster . . . Criminal negligence . . . not that I wouldn't like to."

A knock at the door. It had happened before . . . A dream? He didn't know who was knocking. Too late to run. The house was surrounded.

"Hello, Mr. Fenster. Sit down, Mr. Fenster." Godney smiled when he opened the door. Two other plainclothesmen came in and disappeared somewhere on mysterious errands. Harvey sat down, but he sat on the edge of his chair, fearfully. Godney sat in Harvey's easy chair, made himself comfortable, and took a long time in lighting a curved-stem pipe.

"I've just remembered something, Mr. Fenster, a circumstance of your wife's death. I know the memory is accurate because I checked with several other people who were on the scene. It's been bothering me all this time, but just today it started to make sense. A funny thing. Very funny."

"What's funny? What . . ."

"When we found your wife, the cement floor of the basement was all wet. Do you know what was funny about that? Just this. Your wife hadn't been in the middle of doing a washing. No wet clothes. The inside of the tub wasn't wet either. Only one thing was wet. The floor."

Why hadn't he thought of that?

"Can you explain that, Mr. Fenster?"

He tried to speak, but had no voice. But even if he had, what was he to say?

One of the other plainclothesman entered from the bedroom. He was carrying Beryl's old shoe, and he handed it to Godney.

"I remember looking at your wife's corpse," Godney went on. "On the sole of her right foot there was a deep burn, about the size of a nickel. Yes, this was the shoe she'd been wearing." Godney turned the shoe over and was staring at the bottom of it. The hole was there, about the size of a nickel. "A very curious hole, this. Looks like it's been picked at. Looks like somebody was trying to enlarge it. This hole was manufactured, Mr. Fenster. It's perfectly obvious."

Harvey mouthed words, silent, voiceless, futile words.

Godney tossed the shoe to the man who'd brought it in. "Label that 'Exhibit A.'"

Now the second plainclothesman appeared, coming from the basement. "I've checked the washing machine, Joe."

"And what did you find?"

"Fenster's fingerprints all over it."

Godney chewed happily at his pipestem.

"Not only that, but Fenster's prints are on the frayed wire, too."

"Yes? Yes? Yes!"

"And there's been some funny business with that wire, Joe."

"I think that should be enough," Godney said. "More than enough. Label that washing machine 'Exhibit B.' What do you say now, Mr. Fenster? Ready to confess?"

"No!" His own scream burst inside his skull. Did anyone else hear it?

Harvey leaped out of the chair and tried to run. But quickly strong arms seized him from either side. The front door opened, uniformed cops flooded in. A great mass of hostile bodies bore him to the floor by their very weight.

He reached out, groping, searching. He had it, wrestling with it in his bed as if it were a live thing, unil his eyes were fully open and he realized, with a vast sense of relief, that he was awake again. He was awake, and the clock was ringing. Fumbling, he found the button, pressed it.

But he didn't let go of the clock. This little box was his savior. Its cord going into the wall was his lifeline. He cuddled the little clock like he would an infant. And he waited there, fondling it, waiting for the awful fear to subside a little, for reality, the un-dream world, to establish itself once again.

What a frightening difference between this dream and those preceding it! The first two dreams had repeated events which had actually occurred. But this last dream was a fiction, an imagining. These things hadn't happened.

Godney hadn't connected the wet floor with the lack of wet clothes yet, but he might think of it in the future. If he did, he might come to look at the shoe and the washing machine. Warning ... Well, I'll do something about that!

Gleefully he hopped out of bed, replaced the alarm clock, got dressed quickly, ran down the basement stairs. Yes, there were the shoes.

It wasn't until then that he realized how fortunate he was. The shoes hadn't been carted away with the body. They had somehow dropped off, and then just lain here. He stuffed them into his pockets.

The washing machine wasn't so easily handled. Wrestling it into the car trunk took a lot of doing, for Harvey wasn't a big man. But he managed it because he had to. The trunk lid closed down far enough to conceal the contents, and he tied the lid handle to the bumper. Then he backed the car out and started driving.

He knew of only one sure place, the old quarry beyond town. The pit had filled with water, which people said was thirty or forty feet deep. Harvey drove there, and found the place abandoned. No one witnessed his strange actions, he was certain, as he lifted the machine out of the car trunk and pushed it over the cliff. It made a tremendous splash and sank reassuringly. He tossed the shoes in after it.

He was late in arriving at the bank that morning, but nobody questioned him. He worked so cheerfully and diligently that day he didn't fall behind in his job.

He was cheerful because he felt safe. All day.

"Harvey, I've just got to have a new washing machine." Her face, Beryl's face, leering accusingly down at him; her voice, not whining, but shrieking vindictively ...

"I'm innocent!" he shrieked in return.

But the white-haired judge, Lieutenant Godney in black robes, only sneered down at him from his high bench. And the twelve stern men in the jury box shook their heads in disbelief.

"Was this your wife's shoe?"

The lawyer—he was Godney, too—shoved the incriminating object in front of his face. Attached to it was a large tag, "Exhibit A." There was no sole to the shoe at all, no sole and no heel.

And then came the washing machine, carried into the courtroom by two men wearing diving helmets. The machine was rusted and still dripping with weeds and slime. Affixed to it was a clean, fresh tag saying, "Exhibit B."

"Mr. Fenster," Godney said, "your fingerprints were all over it, and on the wire where the insulation was scraped off."

"Impossible!" he shouted at them all. "This is a frame-up!"

But the twelve men didn't listen. Like a chorus they stood up together, and like a chorus, speaking with one voice, they announced their verdict, "Guilty!"

The judge beckoned Harvey to the bench. He hadn't the strength to

move, but the police dragged him, inert, like a gunnysack of straw.
Judge Godney extended a long arm, and the forefinger wagged in
Harvey's face. "I sentence you . . . to death . . . in the electric chair . . ."

But there was a bell somewhere, very distant, ringing weakly,
forlornly. Harvey reached for it . . . the alarm clock . . . more with his
desperate mind than with his helpless body; he leaped . . .

. . . And got it. Somehow . . . a little metal cube with rounded edges
that had an insistent buzz inside it.

"I love you . . . I love you . . ." He was saying it to the clock, and
covering the cold metal with wet, grateful kisses. And he didn't want to
press the button to silence the thing. The sound was too precious, too
beautiful, too reassuring.

The bell will wear out! No . . . no . . . Reluctantly, almost fearfully, he
did, at last, press the button . . . and then trembled in the dreadful
silence that followed.

A dream, that's all it was, Harvey Fenster, you imbecile, you idiot.
Don't you know the difference between waking and sleeping? Between
dreams and reality? This is the real world, the real thing, right now,
right here. You're in bed, alone. Beryl's dead, but they didn't find you
out. They didn't, really. The shoes are gone, and the washing machine
is gone, just like Beryl, gone. They can't come back . . . The electric
chair! Now they were going to get even with him and kill him with
electricity.

Who was going to do that? Who was they? The police? The police
couldn't touch him. No evidence. The shoe, the washing machine, the
fingerprints . . . And they'd convicted him! They were going to send him
to the electric chair! Would their electric chair be real?

It would only seem real. After all, it was a dream . . .

Which was the dream?

He didn't know!

"Harvey, I've just got to have a new washing machine."

He looked around for somewhere to run. Anywhere to escape that
shrill, nagging voice.

"Harvey, I've just got to have a new washing machine."

When he tried to run, he was stopped by the bars. No, not
bars—cords, electric cords—a maze of electric cords enclosing him like a
fly in a spider web.

"Take it easy, fella, you don't have very long to wait now."

"Let me out!"

"There's only one way out of here, fella. For you, that is. Through
that door. Just five more minutes. Can't you wait? What's your hurry?
Why can't you wait?"

They came for him. Two huge guards. He screamed and cringed into
the farthest corner. But they dragged him out of it, yelling and writhing.

The door opened, and it was a basement door, the door to his own basement. And there was the chair ... somehow like a chair ... but really ... a washing machine!

"No!"

"Relax, fella. That's all you have to do. The electricity will do the rest. As long as you stand in this water on the floor ..."

"I'm innocent!"

"Strap too tight, fella? It's just to keep you here till the juice comes on. Don't worry about it. It doesn't last too long."

"Beryl," he shrieked, "does it last long?"

But she didn't answer. She was already dead. Dead and gone.

"Left arm okay. Now let's have the other arm."

No, don't give them that other arm. Reach out! Reach hard! Reach far!

"Come on, fella ... Boy, that right arm of his is strong. What's he trying to reach for? What's he trying to hang onto? Trying to pull the cord out of the wall? Come on, fella, give up."

"No! No! Give me my alarm clock!"

"Give it to him, boys."

It's just a dream. That's all it is—a dream. This is my alarm clock, my own ...

Lieutenant Joe Godney looked down at the twisted, contorted body, and then stooped to untangle it. From the very middle of the tightly wrapped ball, and after prying away the rigid grip of the fingers, he drew an electric alarm clock. While the others looked on, he patiently examined the thing.

"Worn wire right at the terminal," he explained, showing them.

"Looks as if," said another plainclothesman, "he didn't let go as you ought to when you get a shock. He was holding on for dear life. You wouldn't call it suicide, would you, Joe?"

"Accidental death," was the judgement of Godney.

Arthur Porges
Blood Will Tell

"Breathes there a cop with hide so tough, he thinks four amendments aren't enough!"

Ulysses Price Middlebie, professor emeritus of the history and philosophy of science, and sometime consultant in criminology, smiled tightly at Sergeant Black's doggerel. "The Fifth Amendment," he said solemnly, "is a splendid conception, designed to prevent the taking of evidence under torture. It is no more to be blamed for being misused than the morphine which, instead of helping a cancer victim, gives some young fool a thrill."

"I know," Black said. "I was just letting off steam. It's damned frustrating to see a murderer get off scot-free, no matter how noble the Fifth Amendment itself might be. Besides, it isn't always clear to us cops just how the lawyers spread that one rule so ludicrously thin."

Middlebie sank deeper into his old leather armchair, and fixed luminous grey eyes on the young detective.

"I'm not a lawyer," he said, "so it's not at all plain to me what you expect here. In the purely scientific matters of crime detection, I've been able to help you out on several occasions. But if you're looking for loopholes in the Fifth Amendment, I must plead a total incapacity to offer advice."

"You have a point," Black admitted. "It's just that you are a problem-solver, and even though a legal aspect is involved, there may be some other approach I can't visualize. You might be able to succeed, judging from past performance. In any case, I'd like to disucss the situation with you—okay?"

"By all means. Your cases are usually quite interesting. Or possibly you don't bring me the other kind."

"That's right, I don't. I come to you only when I'm in a bind. I'm a pretty good detective," he added, without false modesty, "but you've made a specialty of logical deduction, and have fifty years of experience in practicing what you preach. I know it wasn't crime consultations, but more of a Ph.D. doctor—a man who could help almost any young research student over a bad block in his project. There isn't such a difference. Your work on past cases proves that."

"Thanks," Middlebie said dryly. "But any more butter, and I'll need a serum cholesterol test!" Then he smiled in a way that removed any sting from the reproach. "I know you meant that as a sincere compliment, but it's difficult for an old curmudgeon like me to accept praise gracefully. Now, about the case—or rather," he punned outrageously, "the fifth!"

"Well, it's basically a simple matter. There's a skunk by the name of Carleton Chambers Dell—at least, that's his current one—who has almost certainly disposed of three wives for their insurance and possessions. They were murdered in other states, by the way. Now he's killed a fourth one here and, luckily for us, got a little careless. It seems that wife number four got in a good swing at his nose, which is hard to miss, and he spilled several ounces of blood at the scene of the crime. It was meant to look like an accident, but he goofed, and the death was called murder."

He paused, and Middlebie asked: "Where does the Fifth Amendment come in? It would seem to be a clear case of first degree homicide."

"Ordinarily, yes, but Dell has the luck of the Devil. There are several possible suspects he didn't know existed, but we turned them up—not with any intention of helping him, you can bet! Just part of the routine investigation before we even knew about Dell's past record. In other words, we don't have a sure case against him—one that will really stand up in court, and against his lawyer, who's about the best around. As to the Fifth Amendment, did you know that it applies in this state to a blood test? That is, we can't force Dell to give us a sample of his blood. That pool near the victim undoubtedly came from his nose, which was known to be red and bruised the morning after the murder. It's the rarest type, the police lab says, and if we could state in court that Dell's blood is a match, I think we'd have him, because the other suspects are all different."

"I should think the elimination ought to be enough," Middlebie said.

"Not with Parks, his lawyer. He'll ring in another unknown killer and confuse the issue. Mrs. Dell was a weird one, and had a lot of off-beat friends. One of them *might* have done it."

"Are you sure it didn't happen that way?"

"Morally, yes, because of his past record. But we can't use that during the trial; that's never permitted. Plus the fact that he's obviously scared to death about giving any blood. He's claimed everything from religious objections—and he has about as much religion as the late Stalin—down to the Fifth Amendment. That did it. The court has warned us not to touch his sacred veins, or else."

"I suppose," Middlebie said, a wicked glint in his eyes, "you couldn't manage to have somebody, quite casually, punch his nose in public?"

"I thought of that," Black admitted ruefully. "But we'd be crucified in court. They'd make a martyr out of Dell. Too many complaints about abuse of police power these days. Some of it is justified," he added hastily, "but cops are human, and they like shortcuts as well as the next guy. When you see some punk sneering at the law, and practically daring you to make something stick, it's hard to remember civil liberties. That's not an excuse; just an explanation."

"We should all be careful about criticizing anybody until we've worn his shoes a few days," Middlebie said. "But surely Dell must have an army record, complete with blood type."

"Not that we can find. My guess is he ducked that one just as easily as he's ducked the law. Hid out in Mexico, faked a disease, or got an 'essential' job through bribery or pull—who knows?"

"What about hospitalization?"

"Nothing. Either he's in perfect health, or, more likely, used a phony name. So you see what I'm up against. No blood, no solid case. Either I let him go without bringing a murder charge, or pull him in, and risk losing in court because there's no proof the blood came from his big, bunged-up nose."

Middlebie was silent for a moment, his eyes blank. After a few moments he said: "Then I take it that if—and mind you I only say 'if'; I don't know how it could be done—but if you could get some of his blood without violence, even through fraud, you'd have your case."

"Provided we could prove in court our sample really came from Dell. Which means good, dependable medical evidence in the form of some reputable doctor." Black's face was grim. "It's a hopeless problem. Blood without violence. He's so cautious now that if Albert Schweitzer wanted to nick him for any reason, Dell would refuse automatically. Nobody's going to get any of his blood voluntarily, that's certain. And we can't take it by force. So I guess I've bent your ear for nothing. The problem can't have a solution."

"At the moment, I'd have to agree," the professor said. "But let me sleep on it. Occasionally an impossible problem has an obvious answer."

Black looked at him in wonder.

"You mean there might be a chance?" He shook his head several times. "You never say die, do you? Well, I know better than to bet against you, but I can't see a way out of this mess." He paused at the door. "Here's hoping I hear from you tomorrow."

"Wonderful stuff, blood," Middlebie said absently. "No wonder so many people hate the idea of losing any. I don't mean criminals, like Dell," he added. Then, with more resolution in his voice, "We can't let this wife-killer get away with only a punch in the nose!"

"He will, if you don't stop him," Black retored, and left.

When he was gone, the professor prepared a swig of his pet drink, a loathsome brew made up of bourbon, brown sugar, and bock beer, He sipped this with relish while reading a long article on the subject of blood. It told him more than he wanted to know, and none of the information promised to be of use in Black's dilemma. Until the part about sporozoan parasites ...

Late the next night, Middlebie, Sergeant Black, and a small, round, querulous man, known the world over as an authority on tropical medicine, moved with the air of conspirators up to the rear window of a certain motel apartment.

"This is the one," Black whispered.

"You're sure?" Middlebie husked in his very low monotone.

"Positive. Dell's asleep in there right now. You ready, Dr. Forrest?"

The small man said in a deep, frog-like croack, "Of course I'm ready. But if anybody except Middlebie asked me to participate in such a fool's trick—and in the middle of the night!" His voice faded away in an irritable mutter.

Quietly, with almost surgical skill, Black made a hole in the screen. It was a warm night, and the window was up several inches. A word from Middlebie, and Forrest held something over the hole. When he removed it some moments later, the sergeant stuffed cotton into the opening. Then the three men retreated.

"Two detectives will watch the place until morning," Black said, as they got to the car." As soon as it's light, I'll pick Dell up and, of course, I need you there too. My men can prove nobody else went into the room, but you'll have to vouch for the rest. It's going to work," he said gleefully. "It's got to!"

* * *

FROM THE TRIAL RECORD:
The State Vs. Carleton Chambers Dell

State's Attorney Brand: Please tell the court, in your own words, Professor Middlebie, just what happened on the night of June 18. Be as explicit as possible.

Middlebie: Dr. Forrest, Sergeant Black, and myself went to the Sea Foam Motel, found the rear window of the defendant's apartment, and cut a small hole in the screen. Through it, Dr. Forrest released fifty common mosquitoes, all with empty stomachs, and all dyed bright yellow with a harmless chemical pigment.

Brand: Would you explain those points—about the empty stomachs, and the dye?

Middlebie: Certainly. These female mosquitoes—the only kind that bite—were raised in the laboratory, in wire cages, for Dr. Forrest's work in parasitology. Consequently, and blood found in their stomachs in the morning must necessarily have come from the one warm-blooded inhabitant of that motel room. As for the dye, that insured our using only those insects released by us. That is, there was no chance of our capturing any—ah—mavericks that might have brought blood from somebody other than the defendant.

Brand: I see. And in the morning, you did subsequently recapture some of the dyed mosquitoes?

Middlebie: Yes, from the walls of the motel room. The blood in their stomachs was typed, both by Dr. Forrest and police technicians.

Brand: As to that, further testimony will show the blood to be of the relatively rare type spilled by the murderer in the victim's room . . .

"I never saw a more surprised man than Dell," Black said later. "The jury was flabbergasted enough, but Dell!—I almost felt sorry for him. The jury couldn't disregard the words of men like Middlebie and

Forrest. And how could *we* be blamed for the mosquitoes' 'force and violence'?"

"There's a certain subtle justice you may have overlooked," Professor Middlebie said. "Not only did Dell have a miserable night, what with fifty starved mosquitoes in that small place, but all his torture and the murder conviction—came from the females of the species."

Allen Lang

The Mark of Cain

"I was counting on those trees to see Art and young Jake through college," Harry Harbinger said. He gazed at the raw stump as though it were the corpse of one of his cows, shot by a careless hunter. "The army bought a few walnuts from me in the war," he said. "They wanted all the trees I had; but I told 'em what's the use of winning the war with walnut rifle-butts if you don't have a country with any walnut trees left? They were mighty careful with the trees they did take. Dug 'em up roots and all, not to waste a scrap of wood. Not like these sneaking tree thieves."

"What's a full-grown walnut tree worth, Harry?" I asked.

"Three, four hundred dollars," he said. "They put it on a lathe and peel off a veneer they can glue onto pine furniture to make it something to brag on. Get a two-hundred-foot strip of sixteenth-inch veneer out of one big tree. It isn't myself I mind so much for, Jake, except that a man don't cotton to being stole from. It's the boys. They don't go off and get an education, they won't amount to any more than I do, a rundown farmer on a rundown farm, with no future."

"I suppose hardwood poaching comes under my jurisdiction as game warden," I said. "Harry, I'll keep my eyes open. Maybe we can recover some of the money they got for your stolen trees."

"Just keep the rascals from stealing any more. That's all I ask." Harry stared out from his grove of walnuts, out onto the cornfield where inch-tall tufts were sprouting. Blackbirds clustered on the corn mounds like relatives at graveside. "I got crows and I got timber thieves," he said. "All I need is a tapeworm to support."

I scuffed my feet in the leaf mold and walnut hulls. "Something else you've got, Harry, is a fine crop of morels," I said, pointing out the tiny cone of a mushroom. "Mind if I harvest a few?"

"Go right ahead, Jake," Harry Harbinger said. I got out the plastic sack I carry around for woodsy panhandling and walked through the walnut trees to pick a couple of handfuls of the sponge mushrooms.

"These will go good for breakfast." I remarked. "My wife sautees 'em with butter and sherry wine, pours 'em on hot toast. Try it some time."

"I was never much for eatin' fungus," Harry Harbinger told me. "Look, there, Jake; it's a fire hangbird."

Like a flash of flame in the upper boughs of a solitary elm, a male oriole was patroling his nest. "Johnny, Joe, and Jim," he whistled, "Johnny, Joe, and Jim."

I peered at the nest, a grey, woven pouch twenty feet above us. "There's something Dan'l Boone never saw, Harry," I said, pointing. At the bottom of the oriole's nest, woven in with the knotted bits of string, red cellophane pulltabs from cigarette packs, grass stems, and flakes of beech bark, was a long green piece of paper. On that paper, peering down from the foundation of the oriole's hangnest, was Mr. Andrew Jackson.

"I seen people's houses hereabouts that didn't have that much money in 'em," Harry said.

The male Baltimore oriole had noticed our interest, and was worried about it. "Chichichichichi!" he chattered at us. His mate, olivegreen and yellow, fluttered down to the base of their home tree. One wing tucked back at an angle, she limped and scuttled in the rotting leaves, trying, with her broken-wing act, to lure us invaders away from the nest. "Don't mention this to anyone, Harry," I said. "Some folks might be mean enough to tear up those birds' happy home to get that twenty dollar bill."

"Not a word," Harry promised.

I jeeped him back to the farmhouse, half a mile down the gravel road from his cornfield and walnut grove, then turned around to head back to the north shore of Loon Lake, up where the cottages are.

The regular summer people hadn't shown up yet. The water was too cold for water skiing, and if you wanted to scuba dive, you'd need to wear a set of those black rubber longjohns. The folks who stay at Loon all year round don't go much for such active sports, being mostly my age. They ice-fish in winter, spudding down through two, three feet of ice to hook two pound crappies and ten inch yellow perch. The summer they spend out on the lake in rowboats, using their fishpoles as excuse for taking a nap, and waking up only to cuss the powerboats that splash too close.

One cabin had been rented out just a week ago. A couple of brothers, name of Bowling, had driven up, paid for a month, and retired inside with two rifles, four big suitcases, and a case of beer. They came out now and then to get fresh beer from Sim's store, or to line up their empty cans and plink 'em down with rifle fire. I figured they were waiting for visitors. They had the look of businessmen conspiring to fix prices, or con artists baiting the trap for a sucker.

There was a rifle blasting away at the Bowling cabin now. I walked over. One of the brothers was busy with his .22, potting away at the day's crop of empty beer cans. "Hi," he said, pointing the gun down like he had a grudge against his toes. I reached over and straightened the gun. "Oh," he said. "Thanks." He nodded at my badge. "Game warden?"

"That's right. Jake Binkley's the name."

"I'm Bill Bowling." We shook hands. "Nothing wrong shootin' beer cans, is there?" he asked.

"Open season on cans, all year round." I said. "But your spent bullets are flying a mile into a woods that holds, on the average summer Sunday, three troops of Boy Scouts and five pairs of lovers. You want to sharpen up your marksmanship, Bill, there's a hill down the road that's just right for a backstop. Okay?"

"Sure," Bill Bowling said. "I didn't think."

"Where's your brother?"

"Walt's sleeping," Bowling said. "Pretty dull vacation, if you ask me. We play cards and drink beer all night, sleep all day. I'd almost as soon be back at the office. You want a beer, Mr. Binkley?"

"No, thanks," I said. "Watch that gun, will you? I've got a brandnew first aid kit, and I'd hate to have to unwrap it."

"Sure thing."

I walked down to Sim's place for coffee and a sandwich. Sim sells bait and beer and canned goods. His business during the season would make a supermarket perk up. Now, though, with the ice gone and the sun not ripe enough for most vacationers, Sim was enjoying his slack time. I went into the bar-restaurant side and hung up my Smokey-the-Bear hat. "Here's ol' Turtle Sheriff," someone shouted.

I didn't have to look over to know that my greeter was Danny Doon, no special friend. The others said hello. Sim poured me a cup of coffee. Doon loomed up with his quart bottle of beer clutched like an Indian club and banged it down on my table. I'd as soon have a bear at the table with me. Bears don't use a deodorant, either; but they're honest. Doon sat down. "What's new out in the woods?" he demanded.

"Someone's been stealing lumber off Harry Harbinger," I said. "They've sawed down five fifty-year-old walnuts and dragged 'em out. That's about a thousand bucks out of Harry's pockets. School money for his two boys."

Sim brought me my Swiss on rye and the pot of horseradish. "Dirty shame," he said. "I heard about it."

Danny Doon rolled his empty quart bottle over toward the table edge. "Gimme 'nother," he said.

Sim caught the bottle. "Danny," he said, "I wouldn't be too tore up if you took your trade somewheres else."

Doon stood up to fish in the pockets of his denim overalls. He was a man as much like a beerkeg in build as in capacity. "Sim," he said, "you know dern well there ain't another beer joint closer'n the village. That's twelve miles off."

"Fine," Sim said.

Doon scattered silver and damp little wads of dollar bills on the table. "That makes me a customer here," he said.

"One more," Sim sighed and went back to get it.

A frowzled fellow, red-eyed, wearing crumpled chino pants and a T-shirt, came into the store. He looked as though he'd been jolted out of a deep sleep with electricity. "Case of the usual," he told Sim, slamming a bill on the bar.

This, I thought, must be Walt Bowling. Doon leaned over the table. "Those city guys from the end cabin seem to have all kinds loot, Jake," he said. "Maybe you should search their place. Bet you'd find two or three walnut logs under their bed."

"Whoever's stealing Harbinger's wood," I said, "I'll catch him. I expect to be visiting that walnut grove pretty regular, Danny."

"Lot of luck," Doon said. He grinned at me and tilted back his bottle.

I finished my sandwich quick, not caring for the company at my table, and went out to get my outboard started. This time of day I cruise around Loon Lake, partly because I'm supposed to keep an eye on my precinct, and partly because I purely enjoy the trip. Besides, the wife had told me to pick up a few special groceries to go with supper.

One of the little streams that empties into Loon is navigable up to my secret watercress ranch, a spread of plants that has supplied my family with salad greens every spring and summer since we left Chicago. I pinched off a couple of handfuls of the leaves and tucked them into my plastic bag with the mushrooms. Then I drifted back out into the lake to gather some cattail sprouts to add to our salad. Wild vitamins are best. I docked the boat, locked it, and headed home.

The weather was warmer the next few weeks, bringing out the leaves and the first fishermen, after the cats and bluegills. Our state hasn't got any closed season, creel or size limits on fish, which makes sense to me. Hook and rod hardly make any difference to the fish population, and who'd keep a half-pound crappie anyway? I kept an eye on the walnut grove; checked the patches of wild strawberries out by Indian Cemetery; looked in on my well-heeled Baltimore oriole family from time to time; and showed some kids who were fishing for pumpkinseed at Ranger Creek how to make whistles out of the willow twigs around them. I passed out a ticket to the first speeder on the lake, too; and warned a solitary scuba diver that he'd be safer with a buddy along as insurance. All standard stuff for a turtle sheriff in early spring.

The Bowling boys had visitors from time to time, sharp types from the city. What was their business? None of mine. The brothers drank their beer peaceably enough on the stoop of their cottage, or took out a rented boat to decorate the lake bottom with their empties. Since a cop is a cop, though, whether he's piloting an RMP down Cermak Road or jeeping a game warden's beat in the woods, I kept an eye on the Bowlings.

They had taken my advice about using a hill as backstop for their rifle practice. "Good shooting," I told Walt Bowling, after I'd watched him pick off a line of two dozen cans, one after the other, fast as he could fire.

"You got much crime up here at Loon Lake?" he asked me.

"Not very much," I said. "Why?"

"That's funny," Walt said. "Seems there'd be lots of crime, the way the only lawman around wastes his time where he ain't wanted."

"You are without doubt, Walter Bowling, the unfriendliest beast that ever set paw to earth," his brother said. "If you don't apologize to Jake this minute, I'm going back to town and to heck with your stupid vacation."

"Okay," Walt grumbled. "I didn't mean to offend you, Jake. Honest."

"No harm done," I said. "The game warden business doesn't get too active till about July, which is why I've got so much time to putter around. The reason I took on this job and this silly hat when I retired from the cops was that it's pretty much vacation here, outside of high summer."

"Cops?" Walt Bowling demanded, clutching his rifle to his chest. "Where were you on the cops?"

"Chicago," I said. "Me and the wife and kids used to spend my off days in the forest preserves. With the kids gone off, we decided to go native full time. Well, I'll see you boys."

I sauntered back to the jeep, whistling, with just a little prickle at the back of my neck to remind me that Walt, who hated policemen, still was holding his rifle.

It started raining, so I drove down to the county seat to check some pictures in the gallery at City Hall. Walt and Bill Bowling weren't there, and I didn't recognize any of the rough-looking businessmen who'd called on them. It gave me a chance for shoptalk with a few uniformed friends, though, before I went home.

In the morning, I stopped again at Harry Harbinger's walnut grove, carrying my plastic trick-or-treat bag. A spread of mushrooms is like a biggish bank account; you can keep collecting interest on it without cutting into the principal. The rain should have coaxed some more of my morels out of the ground.

I walked across the soggy cornfield. The crows, wet-feathered and mean, took off and fluttered away, impatient at having their conferences disturbed. Three or four didn't leave the ground. I nudged one of these with my foot. Shot. With a rifle. Good shooting, I thought. One lay with its wings sprawled wide. Whoever had shot this bird had picked him up to examine the body. Didn't know crows very well, whoever he was. I didn't pick up any of the bodies myself, not wishing to get a bad name amongst all the blackbirds in the county.

Right after this, I saw that I'd failed to do my duty to Harry Harbinger. All that thunder and rain yesterday evening had furnished perfect cover for the roar of a gasoline-powered saw. Four more walnut trees had been kidnapped. Their oozing stumps rebuked me. I walked deeper into the grove and discovered further evidence of a crime wave. The oriole's nest had been torn from its limb. Yolk and pencil-patterned eggshells lay on the soggy refuse of the nest. Andy Jackson's picture had been taken. The parent birds were nowhere to be seen, probably wouldn't return.

I was mad when I walked back to the jeep, cussing Danny Doon, whom I'd chosen as the wood thief without being able to prove it. I was madder at the guy who had destroyed the nestlings of one of the world's most beautiful birds. Maybe, I grumbled at myself, I should have retired all the way when I left the cops. Maybe I should have taken the old woman and gone to Florida to play bingo and swap lies with the other golden-agers.

Then I found the dead man, and slipped back into gear as a practicing policeman.

He'd been shot as neatly as the crows, one hole above his eyes square in the middle of his forehead. A .22 can do the job as well as a cannon, if the range is right. I eased the wallet from the dead man's jacket. The credentials made him a U.S. Treasury agent. A Secret Servant, slain in secret.

The Bowling brothers, hasty to be gone, tried to pass me on the gravel road to Loon Lake. They had their rifles and their suitcases in the car, and were in no mood to stop and talk. The shotgun I carry in the jeep persuaded them to turn around, though, and lead me to Sim's place, where I could phone for help.

"Turtle Sheriff!" Danny Doon cried out. "Wanna beer? On me?"

"Get out of my way." I herded Bill and Walt Bowling in under my shotgun. "Phone the town cops, Sim," I said. "We've got a killing at Loon Lake."

He didn't question me, but got right at it. Danny Doon, who had already had a hearty breakfast of beer, bellied up to the bar and demanded more. "I'm a customer," he said, "and I got money to prove it." He laid down a twenty.

"Get lost," Sim said. He turned to me. "They're on their way up," he said.

"One beer," Danny Doon insisted.

Sim grunted, decided that the principle wasn't worth the argument, and uncapped another quart. He picked up Doon's twenty and turned to the cash register. Then he stopped. "Look at this, Jake," he said, handing me the twenty dollar bill.

It wasn't a very good grade of snide. The gear-teeth around the Treasury seal were blunted; the mesh of the fishnet motif in the border hadn't been woven on the Bureau of Engraving's patent geometric lathe; the crosshatching behind Jackson was flawed. The bill was dirty, and smelled of feathers. "Where'd you get this phony bill, Doon?" I asked him, keeping my gun on the brothers Bowling.

"You'll never believe it, Jake ..." Doon began.

"Out of an oriole's nest," I said.

"How in the world do you know that?" Danny Doon demanded.

"I found the scattered eggshells, the ruined nest, and big ugly footprints," I explained. "I'm happy to remind you, Doon, that there's a hundred dollar fine for disturbing a songbird's clutch. And you'll have to surrender this counterfeit bill, or face a bigger fine and a stint in jail. One more thing, Doon. You weren't in Harry Harbinger's walnut grove just to rob the birds. You went in there after hard wood."

"Okay," he grunted. "So we dragged out a few trees. Harry wasn't getting any use out of 'em."

"You'll pay Harry back every cent you got for all that wood," I said, "or I'll personally rip big hairy strips off your hide."

"You should have burned those bills," Walt Bowling mumbled to his brother.

"You told me to bury the plates," Bill said. "Well, I did. And I buried the smudged bills, too. How did I know some stupid bird was gonna dig 'em up and build a nest out of 'em?"

"The rain washed out the buried bills," I said. "A Treasury agent—Secret Service man—found out about a treasure trove of counterfeit money, probably from some kid fisherman's old man. It doesn't matter much; under the law you're both guilty, but I'd like to know which of you fellows met the agent and shot him."

"It was Bill," Walt Bowling said.

"Walt," said Bill Bowling.

"Brothers!" Sim snorted.

"So were Cain and Abel," I reminded him. "Okay, boys. We've got witnesses to the shooting of the Treasury man. Soon as the town cops get here, we'll go see who they finger."

Neither brother replied. Only the murderer would know that no human had been in sight when he'd aimed his rifle at his victim's head.

"What were these guys doing up here at Loon?" Sim asked me.

"Selling snide at a markdown," I said. "You could buy maybe five thousand dollars' worth of their funny money for two hundred Federal bucks."

"One fifty," Walt said. "We ran a cut-rate operation."

"From the look of your product," I said, "you'd be lucky to pass it in a game of Monopoly."

When the cops arrived, I turned over Bill and Walt Bowling, and led the way in my jeep to the soggy cornfield where the dead man lay with his face in the mud.

We stood at the verge of the walnut grove, looking down at the victim. The police chief plucked out his wallet and examined it. "Like you say, Jake, he's a Fed," he said. "How'd you mean we'd find witnesses out here to the shooting?"

"Henry Ward Beecher, who was also partial to hens, said that if men had feathers and wings, very few of them would be clever enough to be crows," I said. Several of the blackbirds were circling the chief's sedan, inside which sat the Bowling brothers.

"Jake, I respect your experience," the chief said, "but right now you're a mite too woodsy for me. What we've got is a body, two counterfeiters, and that copper plate we found half buried back in the woods. We've got half a million dollars in phony twenties in the Bowlings' suitcases. What we don't have is the name of the man who shot this poor fellow. We'll get that from Ballistics at the state lab."

"Nope," I said. "Ballistics can identify the rifle, but not the man who fired it."

"Nitrite test on their hands?" he asked.

"The brothers have both been target shooting for the past three weeks," I said.

"So?"

"So I want to present the case to a jury of the birds," I said. "Let Walt and Bill Bowling get out of your car, where the crows can see 'em."

Sim had locked up his store and come along with me in the jeep. "What's with birds, Jake?" he asked. "We got a human corpse, which raises this case outside natural history."

"Sim, listen to me," I said. "I'm a Chicago cop gone rural, but I've spent more time watching wildlife than you've spent tending bar and sacking beans. Some of the smartest people I know are birds. Those crows up there can think rings around, say, Danny Doon."

"So could oysters," Sim observed.

"Get on with it, Jake," the police chief said. "This is my virgin murder. I want to get the big wheels rolling."

"Watch the crows," I told him. "Men can live with a murderer; crows can't. They've got a special mark-of-Cain call, even. It's a rattle, not like their normal *cawk!* What it means is, 'Here comes something with a dead crow in its beak."

The chief looked around the cornfield, at the dead crows lying in the furrows. "I'm not here to avenge dead birds," he said.

"Nor am I," I assured him. "Look, chief; whoever shot this man was out here potting crows. Okay? You do agree with that?"

"Not tight, but likely," he said.

"The killer had a rifle, and he saw a man walking toward the spot where the plates and the bad counterfeit bills were buried. He raised the rifle and shot the man as he'd shot the crows."

"Whoever shot the crows shot the Secret Service agent," the chief said. "That the extent of your theory, Jake?"

"Yes."

"All right. Who shot the crows?"

I turned to speak to the Bowling boys, who stood side by side under the earnest gaze of a town policeman. "Bill, you and Walt walk toward the woods," I said. "Slowly."

"You're gonna shoot us?" Walt demanded.

"That's not the local style," I said. "Just walk. You'll sleep tonight in a quiet cell, both of you. You've got my word for that."

"Four rude letters," Walt said.

"Come on," Bill told his brother. "What's the harm in getting a little mud on your shoes?"

The crows circled above us, impatient to get back to their business of rifling late-sprouting grains of Farmer Harbinger's corn. The Bowlings walked, followed by their guardian cop.

"Corp! Corp! Corp!" cried the crows, wheeling above the three men. "Corp! Corp! Corp!"

"Spread out!" I shouted at them.

They walked farther apart. The policeman kept his distance from the brothers, one hand careful on his pistol holster. The crows buzzed above Walt Bowling's head, swooping close beside his ears, cawing their corvine judgment.

Rattled by the rattling cry in his ears, panicked by the musty feathers beating against his head, fearful of the flash of those sharp, indicting beaks, Walt broke. "Help!" he yelled, his arms across his face to protect his eyes, running toward the woods. "Help me!"

He tripped over a walnut stump and lay in the mud like his victim, the crows rattling above him, his hands hugged over his head. "Pick him up," I shouted to the policeman who was bog-trotting up after him. "Pick the killer up."

Lee Millar and Wayne Hamilton

"A.C. from E.B."

For some strange reason people always think if you own a lot of property or land you're loaded. I only wish it were true. Ever heard of being property poor? Taxes, you know. Well, that was the situation I found myself in, or I wouldn't have considered selling that block of old buildings on the outskirts of the downtown area of the city. Not that they couldn't have condemned it, but I needed the cash, and the old block wasn't doing me any good, so when the City Fathers approached me with the idea of selling it to make way for the new civic center, I agreed.

Most of the stores were empty, and those that were still operating didn't pay much rent. The warehouse was still paying a little every month, as was the garage, but everything else was pretty well vacant and falling apart. The taxes had doubled in the previous year, so I was wondering what to do when they called on me.

When I agreed to their proposition they thought I was terribly civic minded. And by readily agreeing to their plans without argument, I found they would bend over backwards to any small demand I put on them, like giving me plenty of time to dispose of what furnishings were inside, and giving the few tenants proper eviction time.

The garage people gumbled a little, and the warehouse company got into a snit, but these were minor, and soon the buildings were vacant and ready for demolition.

Well, about four days before the wrecking job was to start, I decided to give the old dumps a last looking over, just in case something of value had been missed that I could sell. I wandered through the vacant stores and old tenements and finally came to the old cigar store. All the locks and doorknobs had been removed from the buildings, so the various doors swung loosely on old hinges, some of them squeaking as a slight wind moved them to and fro. I pushed the front door open and wandered in. I realized this was the first time I had ever been inside the place. When my uncle had left me the property in 1962, the store had been vacant, and from the one time I wiped the dirt away from the window and looked in, I knew it had been vacant for a long time. No one had ever inquired about renting it, so I hadn't thought about it since then.

Inside the musty store the display case was still there, but the glass top and front had been broken, and it didn't look salvageable.

I opened a door that led to a small storage room in the back and went in. There wasn't any window in there, so the only light was that which filtered through the grimy windows in the front. I looked around at the rubble and refuse, and was about to leave, when I saw there was another little doorway in the back. I almost didn't notice it because a stack of old crates and cartons stood between it and me. I made my way to the door, pushed the stuff away, and tried the knob. That was my first surprise, the knob! My workers had missed this door when they were setting about the job of removing the saleable hardware, just as I had almost missed it.

The second surprise was when I noticed the padlock. It was old and rusty, but didn't budge an inch when I tried to wiggle it open. I figured there might be something of value behind the door so I decided to get in. The jack handle from the trunk of my car did a good job of ripping the hasp from the rotten wood.

Just as I started to open the door, I noticed a small slit in it about eye level, maybe six inches long by three inches high. It was closed on the other side by a piece of wood paneling. I opened the door quickly. On the reverse side, a sliding panel covered the opening and was locked into place by a bolt. I quickly opened it and slid it to the side.

A thought started to nag at me, and I turned to try to see what was beyond the door, but all that met my gaze was the beginning of a flight of stairs downward and inky blackness below. But I was pretty sure I had stumbled upon an old speakeasy.

As I slid the panel back into place, I laughed to myself, visualizing what must have gone on many, many times when this place was in operation. A big burly thug inside, probably with a broken nose and maybe a knife wound running down one cheek, standing by the door, waiting for a familiar, knock, a signal. Then, outside in the cigar store, a nicely dressed couple would enter, to buy cigarettes, or a cigar. Quickly, when the coast was clear, the couple would be spirited through the door into the back room and over to the door with the panel in it. The man would knock on the door with the proper number of shorts and longs, and the panel would slide open. The thug inside would glare through the slit, sizing up the potential customer. Maybe the man would hesitate a moment when he saw the ferocious eyes, or maybe he was a regular, and wouldn't bat an eye. Anyway, he'd look at the thug and say, "Joe sent me," or something like that, and there they were in.

And then I thought I'd probably been watching too many old movies on the late show, and it wasn't what I thought it was at all. But I was sure going to find out.

The electricity had been turned on for the salvage job, so when I tried the switch in the cigar store, a bare light bulb burst into illumination.

Inside the back room was another switch. If I should say I turned it on casually, I would be lying, for my stomach was tied up in knots when I flicked it. I hadn't the vaguest idea what I would find down there; had even told myself it wouldn't be anything more than another empty room, but the knot in my stomach wasn't so wrong after all, for the sight I saw below me from the landing was incredible. I felt as though I had stumbled on a discarded movie set, for in the cellar was a complete nightclub.

I think I must have taken the stairs three at a time because only a moment later I was standing in the middle of the room looking around.

At least a dozen crystal chandeliers hung from various points in the ceiling, glittering like dirty jewels and throwing cobwebby shadows around the room. There was only one thing wrong; there weren't any people. This may sound funny because how could anyone expect to find people in a speakeasy that had been closed up for over thirty-five years? I have only one reason for saying this, and that's because it looked like people *should* be there.

On the many tables around the room were highball and cocktail glasses, crusted with evaporated drinks from another age. Bottles of whisky, gin, and scotch were in evidence, many still unopened.

At the foot of the stairs was a small cloakroom, and inside, on the racks, musty clothes still hung from decaying hangers: a woman's feather boa, three silk hats and a derby on the shelf, a man's velvet-lapeled topcoat. There was a pile of something in the corner that appeared to be fur.

I looked over the edge of the Dutch door. On the floor inside the cloakroom was a broken tray, obviously belonging to a one-time cigarette girl. The contents had spilled across the little room, and I could make out packages of Melachrinos and Fatimas among other more familiar names. There were even about six dried corsages, withered and ready to blow away at the first tiny breath of air.

At the far end of the room was a stage for entertainment. Thick red velvet drapes had once luxuriously graced the proscenium, but now they were hanging in the shreds of age and filth. On the stage was a set of drums and a small, upright piano. Chairs and music stands for about five other pieces were there, but the instruments were missing, although I did see a discarded clarinet case lying near the drums.

I stepped up onto the stage and went to the piano. Old, yellowed copies of sheet music were on it. I picked up the top selection, blew off the dust, and read the title, "Ain't She Sweet?"

The sharp sound of breaking glass brought me around quickly, and I faced the other end of the room, where the long, padded leather bar was rotting. There was no one in sight. I held my breath for an instant, my heart pounding. In this moment of silence, I heard a burbling sound coming from the bar, then saw a trickle of liquid making a tiny waterfall onto one of the dirty stools. My heart resumed its proper rhythm as I saw a long, sleek black rat move quickly among the bottles on the backbar, where it had knocked over the champagne that was quickly draining.

From my high vantage point on the stage I surveyed my surroundings, and the picture began to become clearer; things I had not noticed at first now were glaring. Chairs were overturned, a table or two on their sides. There was broken glass on the floor, remnants of bottles and glasses.

I stepped down and walked slowly around the room, taking in every little point of information. A long rope of beads lay broken under a table next to a beaded bag. I picked up the bag and opened it. Inside was a compact, lipstick, small hadkerchief, a money clip with five ones (the large, old fashioned kind) and a ten, a small change purse with some silver, a five dollar gold piece and some pennies, and an identification card case. It held only one thing, a driver's license.

The license had been issued to an Edna Balzer of 1710 Waring Street, who had blue eyes, blonde hair, fair complexion, and had been born on June 13, 1903. The expiration date was 1928.

I stuffed the contents back into the bag and slipped it into my pocket; might be kind of fun, I thought, to check this dame out, if at all possible.

Everything was now pretty clear; something had happened—a raid, probably, and everybody had left in one helluva hurry, not particularly caring what they had left behind, just as long as they didn't get mixed up in a speakeasy scandal, especially those who were there with the wrong wives and girlfriends.

But the more I thought about the raid, the more it bothered me. Sure, they had raids all the time in those blue-nose days, but usually somebody came back afterwards. Even when they got closed down, they came back, if only to auction off the fixtures.

No, I realized, there couldn't have been a raid, if only for one reason. The hootch was still intact, and everybody knows when the cops raid a speakeasy they always smash all the liquor. It had to be something else. Which brought a very good idea to mind. After all, I still owned everything in these buildings, so why not sample my own newfound stock of beverages?

There were a lot of labels I didn't know, but hootch was hootch, so I opened a bottle of scotch at random and took a swig. It was great, and I was beginning to feel I had me a real find. Then a door leading out of the main room caught my eye, so I started in that direction.

The door led to a hall and the restrooms, which I didn't bother to investigate immediately. Off the hall were four other doors. One led to a large storage room which, I noted with glee, was packed to the rafters with unopened cases of booze. Two led to dressing rooms (which I decided to investigate later) and the last one, to a very ornate and plushly furnished office.

Whoever had operated the club hadn't stinted himself on luxurious surroundings. Eveything had been of the best material and in the finest taste—for the twenties, that is.

There didn't seem to be anything of importance; the desk had been shoved up against one wall, and three chairs had been placed on top of it for some reason, and I could see that the drawers had been opened and emptied, also obviously in a hurry. Aside from the large desk, the only other furnishings consisted of sofas, chairs, tables, lamps, and the like. As I was leaving I noticed that a large picture on the wall was hanging at an odd angle, as though it were supported by hinges instead of wire. I checked it out and found a safe behind it. It was open and empty.

One of the dressing rooms was obviously for the band, as cardboards from shirts were lying around and cigar butts were in the ashtrays. Other than this, there wasn't anything to see but an empty closet with some hangers on the floor. The other dressing room was something else again.

Rotting on a clothes rack and in the closet were women's dresses and costumes—low-waistline things with much bugle beads and spangles. A couple of cloche hats were on a shelf next to three or four beaded bags. On the dressing table were a lot of tubes of makeup, jars of cold cream, towels, and all those other things chorus girls use.

Against the wall in one corner was a wardrobe trunk. It was locked but I pried it open. Inside there wasn't much to see, and I wondered why anybody had bothered to lock it in the first place. Strangely enough, it didn't contain women's clothes; inside were things belonging to a man. A couple of pinstriped suits, a pair of spats, a gold headed cane, several tuxedo shirts with wing collars, some expensive looking cufflinks, a gold stickpin with what later turned out to be a real diamond in it, and a topcoat. That was all, except for one very loud and expensive tie with the monogram "AC" on it.

The monogram set me to wondering, so I looked a little more carefully. I turned the cufflinks over and found there was engraving on the back. It read "A.C. from E.B." Of course, "E.B." immediately rang a bell, and I wondered if it could possibly stand for Edna Balzer, the lady whose purse I was carrying. Probably not, I thought, but it was worth trying to find out.

Two hours later I emerged into the sunlight of 1964, leaving the shadowy world of the Roaring Twenties below me in the darkness.

I suppose the city thought I was kind of kooky when I asked them to postpone the wrecking job, but when I explained what had happened, they agreed. Naturally, the newspapers heard of the story and it made the front pages for two days. They took pictures and interviewed me, and even a national magazine did an article. You probably remember.

It was a good thing I got all that publicity or I probably wouldn't have been able to dispose of that stuff as soon as I did. Lucky for me, some crazy millionaire decided a 1920's speakeasy was *just* what was needed as a tourist attraction between the movieland wax museum, Knott's Berry Farm, and Disneyland, so he bought the whole kit and caboodle.

While all this was going on, I decided to check out the old address of Edna Balzer's driver's license. I figured she wouldn't still be there, but I didn't have anything else to do.

The house looked pretty good in spite of all the gingerbread and folderol on it. The paint was fresh and the grounds had been kept up, so as I walked up to the door I thought maybe the Balzer woman did still live there.

A real doll opened the door, and for a moment I hesitated about asking for some woman who had lived there over thirty-five years ago. I figured she'd think I was crazy, but I asked her anyway—and she did.

It turned out that this doll was Anna Marie Balzer, the woman's niece. She was real nice and asked me in for coffee. Then she told me the whole story, or as much as she knew. It went something like this:

She had never known her Aunt Edna, and had inherited the Victorian monstrosity from her father, Edna's brother. Not that Edna had died. She had just disappeared in the late fall of 1928, and had never been heard from again. As Edna's only relative, the brother had received the house when the missing woman was declared legally dead in 1935, the proper seven years after her disappearance. Upon her father's death, it had come to Anna Marie.

There was still an old trunk that belonged to Aunt Edna in the attic, and I was given permission to look through it. I headed toward the stairs that led to the attic. There, in a forgotten corner of the attic, I found the steamer trunk. It was filled with the usual souvenirs and mementos; bundles of tied letters, a scrapbook, a pressed corsage, the photograph of a very pretty woman in a flapper costume, which I presumed to be Edna, and other trivia only important to the collector. I thumbed quickly through the stacks of letters until I came to the pile I was hoping would be there. They weren't in their envelopes, so the name "Al" was obvious as I riffled the stack. I untied the string and started to read the letter on top.

About two hours later, Anna Marie came up the stairs looking for me. She was dressed ready to go out, and seemed a little disappointed that I was so engrossed in the pile of letters I was reading that I didn't notice her until she spoke.

I gave her a quick smile, tied up the bundle of letters again, put them where they belonged, closed the trunk, and stood up.

She smiled back. "Find what you were looking for?"

I frowned, wondering if I had. "Maybe," I said. "I'll know more tomorrow when I can check with the police."

She seemed startled when she said, "The police?"

I realized she was suddenly afraid I was about to throw muddy clods and sully the family name, so I put her at ease. "Not Aunt Edna," I said, "A man she used to know—quite well."

I remember how wide her eyes opened when she asked, "Who?"

"Al Cartelli," I said.

Before checking on the Cartelli guy, I decided to see if I could find out who had rented the cigar store along about 1927 and '28. Probably be a phony name, but worth checking.

The first thing I did was get the police to let me take a look at their old records on speakeasies, where they had been and who had run them. That was a dead end, for there were no records of there ever having been one in my block, another thing that made me think my theory of "no raid" was correct.

City offices, archives, records, and morgues took up my next three days until I finally located the proper file for the cigar store. I paused for a moment before running my finger across the page to locate the name. I was positive it would be Al Cartelli. I was wrong—the name was Edna Balzer.

But I was still right. The "A.C." had to stand for Al Cartelli if Edna Balzer (obviously the "E.B." on the cufflinks) had operated the cigar store-speakeasy. So Cartelli was the next on the list.

Strangely enough, the police captain remembered Cartelli well; he had good reason. The captain had been the arresting officer when they grabbed Cartelli and sent him to Alcatraz for bootlegging and counterfeiting.

The captain's story was a long and interesting one. Cartelli had been paroled from "The Rock" in 1928, but had made the unfortunate mistake of announcing publicly that he would "get that lousy Mickey Foster if it's the last thing I do!" This statement proved to be very prophetic, as, so far as the world knew, it *was* the last thing Cartelli had done. It was common knowledge that Mickey Foster had "put the finger" on Cartelli, and had been responsible for Al's going to prison. Foster had been a little naive about Cartelli's threats because he had believed in the "Unwritten Underworld Law." ... "Ain't the head of a rival gang *supposed* to finger his opposition?" had been his private remark, although it had reached the ears of the police.

So it was only about two weeks after Al's release that a black sedan had whipped out of a side street and a machine gun from the car's back window had turned Foster into a human sieve.

Unfortunately Al had made the mistake of being seen by nine or ten passersby, who were perfectly willing to testify to this fact. And—that was the end of the story. Al Cartelli had never been seen or heard from again, despite the fact that the government put a five thousand dollar reward on his head, dead or alive. (The government had gotten into the act because it wasn't just a matter of killing Foster, but also the fact that, prior to the murder, Cartelli was circulating some of his old counterfeit cash again, probably from a cache they hadn't found the first time.)

Slowly, as the others were caught, Cartelli's name had risen on the "Ten Most Wanted Men" list, and as far as the police captain knew, it was still there, although nobody seemed to be looking for him any more.

"Probably living a respectable life as a banker or something in some small town somewhere," the captain smiled at me. Probably, I figured, it had happened before. And I thought about the letters of Edna's I had read, the love letters from Cartelli. Hadn't she disappeared at the same time? It figured. That also explained why no one had come back to the club, and why it had been left so quickly. I could see it easily.

The cops are after Al, and are getting close. He dashes into the club, tells Edna what's up, she rushes out into the club telling everyone there's a raid. They all get out fast, knocking over tables, drinks, bar stools, etc. The band rushes out, the clarinet player even forgetting his case; the chorus girls leave their costumes behind because they don't own them anyway; general pandemonium, but soon everyone is gone— except Al and Edna. Everything's fine now, the club's closed and quiet, so no one will come poking around and find Al, but they still have to hurry.

Edna skedaddles into the office, scoops up the dough in the safe, dumps the desk drawers into a suitcase, and off they go.

The pillars of some small town society, now, I thought. The mystery solved—over and out.

The one nice thing about it all was Anna Marie. If it hadn't been for that beaded bag, I might never have met her. Of course, when I had everything pretty well cleared up in my mind, I told her the whole story, and she was fascinated to learn that she was related to a gun moll.

Finally the day came when the wreckers started tearing down the old block. I decided I should show the old speakeasy to Anna Marie, even though it was only an empty room now.

They started banging away at the buildings on the other end of the block, so there was no reason why she and I shouldn't go into the club, despite the KEEP OUT signs that were posted.

We fumbled our way to the little door, and I opened it. We didn't have any electricity, but I had brought along my big torch, and Anna Marie had another, so everything was fine.

I escorted her around the place, pointing out various things. Where the stage had been was just a hole now, but she was able to visualize it all, especially having seen the magazine spread, and knowing that I was planning to take her to the reassembled club when it opened.

Back in the dressing room, the trunk was gone, donated to a local Little Theater, but I pointed to where it had rested. Then, very dramatically, I produced the cufflinks, tie pin, money clip, and gold piece from my pocket. I had planned to give them to her all along, but had decided to wait and give them to her in the place where I had found them and, more or less, her too. She was pleased as punch.

As we entered the office, we could hear the thudding, smashing noise in the distance, and felt a tremor pass through the building.

When another shudder went through the walls, I decided it was time we got out of there. With a building that old, who knew what could happen? Anyway, bits of plaster were already falling around us, so we started out fast. I think it was the strange creaking sound that made us stop and turn back.

Part of the office wall was slowly opening, and we suddenly realized it wasn't a wall at all but a secret door. This was the wall the desk had been pushed against. We stared in fascination as the vibrations in the building made the wall open wider and wider. Finally, it came to a standstill. After a moment, we made a move to enter the secret room. I led the way, but as I let my torch plough into the darkness I stopped quickly and turned to face Anna Marie. I guess the look on my face was pretty terrible because she almost screamed.

"Let's get out of here," I remember saying, and I took hold of her arm, dragging her toward the door. She didn't want to go at first, but I guess my attitude scared her enough to stop protesting and allow me to shove her bodily through the various doors, up the stairs, and into the sunlight.

When we were outside, she turned toward me, questions written all over her face, but before she could ask them I rushed for the nearest phone across the street. My dime brought the police captain and it wasn't long before the street was swarming with prowl cars and the wrecking was halted.

The first thing I said to the captain when he came out of the secret room was, "It's still in effect, isn't it?"

He sort of glared at me, then nodded. "Far as I know. One of those things people forget about, I guess."

I was delighted.

"Good for people," I said.

He turned and started toward the door, his crew of experts following.

There wasn't much left of the man or the woman. More than thirty-five years can do a lot to a body. But the tie with the large, fancy "A.C." on it made identification obvious, and tests could probably prove that the woman with him then had been Edna Balzer.

As the bodies were removed, I looked again into the secret room, watching a policeman scoop up hundreds of thousands of dollars scattered about.

It was obvious what had happened.

The safe in the office was a dummy, to fool rival gangs or cheap hoodlums. The real money was in this room, built on the inside like a small version of Fort Knox. Large safe-deposit boxes lined one wall and there were complicated wall safes from top to bottom. Each was open and empty, the contents strewn around the room.

The police were close, Edna and Al had thought. Their only chance to get away clean lay in the large vault in the office—enough money for the rest of their lives. They had opened the vault hastily, rushed in to clean out the money, but they hadn't taken the proper safety precautions and the door had closed behind them. There was no one who could hear their calls for help—not even the police they thought were right on their heels. It had become their tomb in a gay era.

I watched carefully as the policeman collected the scattered legal tender. After all, it was mine, my contract with the city read that way.

Yeah, it was all pretty exciting. Then, as the cop left, a creepy thought popped into my head; if that's what happened to Edna and Al, who had padlocked the door in the cigar store?

Then I thought of Foster's gang—revenge!

But then, I argued, if they had locked Edna and Cartelli into the vault and locked the outside door, why hadn't they taken all that money?

From the corner of my eye I saw a ten spot the cop had missed. I picked it up, turning it over and over.

I dropped the bill to the floor and sagged a little against the wall. Hundreds of thousands of dollars—all mine—and all phony. Foster's gang wasn't so dumb after all.

Oh, well, I thought, at least the five thousand dollar "dead or alive" money from Al Certelli would pay for one slambam honeymoon.

James H. Schmitz
Crime Buff

Jeff Clary stood halfway down the forested hillside at the edge of a short dropoff, studying the house on the cleared land below. It was a large two story house with a wing; Jeff thought it might contain as many as twenty-five to thirty rooms. There was an old fashioned, moneyed look about it, and the lawns around it seemed well-tended. It could have been an exclusive sanitarium as easily as a private residence. So far, there'd been no way to decide what, exactly, it was. In the time he'd been watching it, Jeff hadn't caught sight of a human being or noticed indications of current human activity.

What had riveted his attention at first glimpse wasn't so much the house itself as the gleaming blue and white airplane which stood some two hundred yards to the left of it. A small white structure next to the plane should be its hangar. The plane was pointed up a closely mowed field. It seemed a rather short runway even for so small a plane, but he didn't know much about airplanes. Specifically—importantly at the moment—he didn't know how to fly one.

That summed up the situation. A large number of people were engaged today in searching for Jeff Clary, but the blue and white plane could take him where he wanted to go in a few hours, safely, unnoticeably. He needed someone to handle it.

That someone might be in the house. It not, there should be one or more cars in the garage adjoining the house on the right. A car would be less desirable than the plane, but vastly superior to hiking on foot into the open countryside. If he could get to the city without being stopped, he'd have gained a new head start on the searchers. If he got there with a substantial stake as well, his chances of shaking them off for good would be considerably better than even.

Jeff scratched the dense bristles on his chin. There was a gun tucked into his belt, but he'd used the last bullet in it eight hours ago. A hunting knife was fastened to the belt's other side. A knife and a gun—even an empty gun—could get him a hostage to start with. He'd take it from there.

Shade trees and shrubbery grew up close to the sides of the building. It shouldn't be difficult to get inside before he was noticed. If it turned out there were dogs around, he'd come up openly—a footsore sportsman who'd got lost and spent half the night stumbling around in the rain-wet hills. As soon as anyone let him get close enough to start talking, he'd be as close as he needed to be.

He sent a last sweeping look around and started downhill, keeping to the cover of the trees. His feet hurt. The boots he wore were too small for him, as were the rest of his fishing clothes. Those items had belonged recently to another man who had no present use for them.

He reached the side of the house minutes later. No dogs had bayed an alarm, and he'd been only momentarily in sight of a few front windows of the building. He'd begun to doubt seriously that there was anybody home, but two of the upper-floor windows were open. If all the occupants had left, they should have remembered to close the windows on a day of uncertain weather like this.

He moved quickly over to a side door. Taking the empty gun from his belt, he turned the heavy brass doorknob cautiously. The door was unlocked. Jeff pushed it open a few inches, peering into the short passage beyond.

A moment later, he was inside with the door closed again. He walked softly along the tiled passageway, listening. Still no sound. The passage ended at a large, dimly lit central hall across from a stairwell. There were several rooms on either side of the hall, and most of the doors were open. What he could see of the furnishings seemed to match the outer appearance of the house—old fashioned, expensive, well cared for.

As he stood, briefly undecided, he heard sounds at last, from upstairs. Jeff slipped back into the passage, watching the head of the stairway. Nobody went by there, but after a few seconds the footsteps stopped. Then music suddenly was audible. A TV or radio set had been switched on.

That simplified matters.

Jeff moved across the hall and up the stairs, then followed the music along a second-floor passage to the right. Daylight and the music spilled into the passage through an open doorway. He stopped beside the door a moment, listening. He heard only the music. Cautiously he looked in.

A girl stood at one of the bedroom's two windows, looking out, back turned to Jeff; a dark-haired, slender girl of medium height, wearing candy-striped jeans with a white blouse. A portable TV set stood on a side table.

Jeff came soundlessly into the room, gun pointed at the girl, and drew the door shut behind him. There was a faint click as it closed. The girl turned.

"Don't make a sound," Jeff said softly. "I'd rather not hurt you. Understand?"

She stood motionless at sight of him. Now she swallowed, nodded, blue eyes wide. She looked younger than he'd expected, a smooth-featured teenager. There shouldn't be any trouble with her. He went to the TV, keeping the gun pointed at the girl, turned the set off.

"Come over here," he told her "Away from the window. I want to talk to you."

She nodded again, came warily toward him, eyes shifting between his face and the gun.

"Be very good, and I won't have to use it," Jeff said. "Who else is in the house?"

"Nobody right now." Her voice was unexpectedly steady. "They'll be coming in later, during the afternoon."

"Who'll be coming in?"

She shrugged. "Some of my family. There's to be a meeting tonight. I don't know just who it'll be this time—probably seven or eight of them." She glanced at the watch on her wrist, added, "Tracy should be back in around an hour and a half—about two o'clock. The others won't begin to show up before five."

"So Tracy should be back by two, eh? Who's Tracy?"

"Tracy Nichols. Sort of my cousin by marriage."

"You and she live here?"

The girl shook her head. "Nobody lives here permanently now. My Uncle George owns the place. At least, I think it's his property. It's used for meetings and so on."

"Who looks after it?"

"Mr. and Mrs. Wells are the caretakers. They left yesterday after they got everything set up, and they won't be back till tomorrow night when we're gone again."

"Why did they clear out?"

"They always do. The family doesn't want other people around when they have a meeting."

Jeff grunted. "You got secrets?"

The girl smiled. "Oh, there's a lot of talk about business and so on. You never know what's going to come up."

"Uh-huh. What's you name?"

"Brooke Cameron."

"Where do you live?"

"Place called Ranfrew College. Two hundred miles from here. You're Jeff Clary, aren't you?"

She'd added the question with no slightest change in inflection, and Jeff was jolted into momentary silence. Watching him, she nodded slowly, as if satisfied.

"Take away the beard—yes, that's who you are, of course!" Interest was kindling in her face. "Pictures of you were shown in the newscasts, you know. But you were supposed to be heading north."

Jeff had heard as much on a car radio ten hours ago.

"Pretty sharp, the way you walked out of that maximum security spot," Brooke Cameron went on. "They said it's only happened once before there."

"Maybe you talk a little too much," he told her. "If you know who I am, you should have sense enough not to play games."

Brooke shrugged. "I'm not playing a game. Of course, you *might* kill me, but I wouldn't be any use to you then. I'd like to help you."

"I bet you would."

"Really! I'm a sort of crime buff, and you're a very interesting criminal. That's not all, either!" Brooke smiled engagingly. "So, first, what do you need here? The plane's your best chance out, and it got a full tank this morning. Can you handle it?"

"No," Jeff said after a moment. "Can you?"

"Afraid not. They didn't want to let me learn how for another two years. But Tracy's flown it sometimes. She took it out today to get it gassed. You'll have to wait till she gets back."

"I could take your car," Jeff remarked, watching her.

"No car here now, Jeff. Tracy brought me in with her early this morning and went on to the city to pick up some stuff she ordered. Either way you want to go, you'll have to stay till she gets back. The only thing you'd find in the garage is an old bicycle, and that's probably got flat tires. You can go look for yourself."

"I might do that." Jeff studied her curiously. "You'd like to help me, eh?" He nodded. "Well, let's try you. This should be good hunting country. Any guns in the house?"

"Not sporting guns," Brooke said promptly. "But there could be a loaded revolver in Uncle George's desk. He usually keeps one there. His room's down the hall." Her gaze flicked over the gun in Jeff's hand. "Ammunition, too," she said. "But it won't fit the gun you have."

Jeff grunted. "You're wondering whether this one's empty?"

"Well, it might be." Her blue eyes regarded him steadily. "You put two bullets in the guard you shot, and you wouldn't have found any spare shells on him. There was more shooting, and then they must have been pushing you pretty hard for a time. If this isn't a gun the couple you kidnapped happened to have in their car, it could very well be empty."

Jeff grinned briefly. "Are you wondering now where that couple is?"

Brooke shook her head. "No, not much. I mean you're here by yourself, and I don't think you'd let them get away from you." She shrugged. "Let's go look in Uncle George's desk."

The revolver was in a desk drawer, a beautiful shop-new .38. Brooke looked on silently while Jeff checked it and dropped half a dozen spare shells into a jacket pocket.

"So now you have that," she remarked. "You want to shave and clean up next, or eat? A ham was sent in for dinner."

"What makes you think I want to do either?" Jeff asked dryly.

She shrugged. "We can go sit in a south room upstairs, of course," she said. "You can watch the road from there and wait for Tracy to drive up. But that'll be a while. She'll call, anyway, to let me know when she's ready to start back."

Jeff laughed. "That's convenient, isn't it? I'll try the ham."

He hadn't realized until he began to eat how ravenous he was. Then he concentrated savagely on the food, almost forgetting Brooke sitting across from him at the kitchen table. When he'd finished and looked over at her, he saw the worn brown wallet she'd laid on the table. Jeff stared at it, eyes widening.

"How—"

"I'm quite a good pickpocket," Brooke said absently. She frowned at the wallet. "Told you I'm a crime buff—and I don't just read about it." She touched one of three irregular dark stains on the wallet with a finger, looked at Jeff, and pushed the wallet across the table to him. "I got it while we were going to Uncle George's room. So Mr. and Mrs. Rambow didn't get away, did they?"

"No, they didn't get away," Jeff said harshly. He hadn't noticed her brushing against him or touching him in any manner as they went along the passage, and the thought of her doing it without letting him catch her made him uneasy. "And they shouldn't have tried," he went on. "Their car got smashed up enough while they were about it that I couldn't use it any more. It's down in a nice deep gully back in the hills where it isn't likely to be found very soon, and they're inside. Now you know."

Brooke brushed back her hair. "I really knew anyway," she said. "You have a sort of record, Jeff."

Anger faded into curiosity. "Aren't you scared?"

"Oh, yes, a little. But I'm useful to you—and I'm *not* trying to get away."

"I'd like to know what you are trying to do," Jeff admitted. "Whatever it is, there'd better be no more tricks like that."

"There won't be," Brooke said.

"All right." Jeff tugged at the shoulder of his jacket. "Are there clothes in this spooky house that could fit me?"

Brooke nodded. "Uncle Jason's just about your build. He's got a room unstairs, too. Let's go see."

Jeff stood up. "What kind of place is this?" he asked irritably. "A home away from home for any of you who happens to feel like it?"

"I guess it's used like that sometimes," Brooke said. "I don't know everything the family does."

Uncle Jason's room was at the south end of the house. It was equipped sparsely and with the neat impersonality of a hotel room. Several suits hung in plastic sheaths in the closet and two pairs of shoes stood in a plastic box on the closet shelf. The shoes would be a bit large for Jeff, but a relief after the cramping boots he'd been wearing. He decided any of the suits should fit well enough, and he found an electric shaver. He peered out a window. No vehicle was in sight, and anyone coming could be spotted minutes away. All good enough.

He hauled a straight-backed chair away from a table, turned it facing the window. "Come here and sit down," he told Brooke. She'd been watching him silently as he moved about, not stirring herself from the position she'd taken up near the passage door.

She came over now. "You want me to watch the road?"

"Just sit down."

She settled herself in the chair. Jeff said, "Now put your arms behind you." He fished a piece of rope out of a pocket.

"You don't have to do that," she said quickly.

"I'll be busy for a while," Jeff said. "I don't want to worry about you."

Brooke sighed, clasped her hands together behind the chair. Jeff looked down at her a moment. Brooke Cameron bothered him. The way she was acting didn't make sense. It wasn't just the matter of the wallet, though that had been startling. He'd suspected at first that she was trying to set a trap for him while pretending to be helpful, but he didn't see what she could attempt to do, and it didn't seem to fit in with telling him where he could find a loaded gun. Perhaps she was hoping help would arrive. He didn't feel too concerned about that possibility. He'd be ready for them.

He could put an abrupt end to anything she might have in mind by slipping the rope around her slender neck; but that would be stupid. If some unexpected trouble arose before he got out of here, a live hostage would be an immediate advantage, and he might still find her useful in other ways.

He fastened her wrists together, drawing the rope tight enough to make it hurt. She wriggled her shoulders a little but didn't complain. He knotted the end of the rope about a chair rung below the seat, grinned at her. "That'll keep you safe!"

He washed his hands and face, shaved carefully, and put on Uncle Jason's suit and shoes, interrupting what he was doing several times to come back to the window and study the empty road. When he'd finished, he went downstairs and found a door that opened into the garage. There was a bicycle there, as she'd said, and no car, though the garage had space enough for three of them. Jeff returned to the top floor.

Brooke looked around as he came into the room.

"I suppose you'll be going to Mexico," she remarked.

His eyes narrowed. At it again—and she happened to be right. "Sounds like a good first stop, doesn't it?" he said.

She studied him. "You'll need a good paper man to fix you up once you're down there."

Jeff laughed shortly. "I know where to find a good paper man down there."

"You do?" Got the kind of money he's going to want?"

"Not yet." There wasn't much more than a hundred dollars in the stained brown wallet. "Any suggestions?" he asked.

"Twenty-eight thousand in cash," Brooke said. "I keep telling you I want to help."

He stiffened. "*Twenty-eight*—where?"

She jerked her elbows impatiently. "Get me untied and I'll show you. It's downstairs."

He didn't believe her. He felt an angry flush rising in his cheeks. If it was a lie, she'd be sorry! But he released her.

She got up from the chair, rubbing her bruised wrists, said, "Come along. Have to get keys from my room," and went ahead of him into the passage.

Jeff followed watchfully, close on her heels, looked on as she took two keys from a purse. They went back to the stairway, down it to the central hall on the ground floor. Brooke used the larger of the keys to open a closet behind a section of the hall's polished oak paneling. A sizable black suitcase stood inside. Brooke nodded at the suitcase.

"The money's in there." She offered Jeff the other key. "You'll have to unlock it."

Jeff shook his head.

"We'll take it to your Uncle Jason's room before we look at the money," he told her. "I'll let you carry it."

"Sure," Brooke said agreeably. "I carried it in here."

She picked up the suit case, shut the closet, and walked ahead of Jeff to the stairs. The way she handled the suitcase indicated there was something inside, but something that wan't very heavy. It could be twenty-eight thousand dollars, but a variety of rather improbable speculations kept crossing Jeff's mind as he followed her upstairs. Was the thing rigged? Would something unpleasant have happened if he'd unlocked it just now? He shook his head. It wasn't at all like him to engage in nervous fantasies.

Nevertheless, he found himself moving a few steps back from the suitcase when he told Brooke to put it on the carpet and open it. She knelt beside it and unlocked it, and nothing remarkable occurred. She opened the suitcase and Jeff saw folds of furry green material. "What's that?" he asked.

"My cape. Dyed muskrat. The money's under the clothes." Brooke took out the green cape, laid it on the floor, added several other items while Jeff watched her motions closely.

"There's the money," she said finally.

Jeff nodded. "All right. Take it out and put it on the table."

Brooke glanced over at him with a quick grin. "Don't trust me yet, do you?"

"Not much," Jeff agreed.

"You should. That's my money I'm letting you have."

"Your money, eh?"

"Well—sort of. I stole it."

"That I can believe," Jeff said. "Get it up on the table."

Brooke took six slender stacks of bills from the suitcase, laid them side by side on the table, and moved back. "Count it!" she invited, then looked on as Jeff riffled slowly through the stacks.

"Where did you steal it?" he asked.

"Man named Harold Brownlee—city councilman. He has a home in the suburbs. The money was in his den safe. I picked it up two nights ago."

"Just like that, huh?"

"No, not just like that," she said. "It was worked out pretty carefully. Twenty-five thousand was bribe money on a land development racket. I don't know about the rest—probably just a little something Brownlee wanted to have on hand, like people do. We knew when the bribe payoff was to be and where he keeps that kind of cash between his trips out of town to get it deposited."

"How did you know?" Jeff put the last bundle down. It was twenty-eight thousand dollars and a little more.

She shrugged. "Family intelligence. How? They don't let me in on that kind of thing yet. But they did let me do the Brownlee job by myself—well, almost by myself. Tracy insisted on being a lookout at the country club where the Brownlees were that night. She'd have let me know if they started home before I finished." Brooke added with a trace of resentment, "It wasn't necessary. If they had come back early, they wouldn't have seen me."

Jeff was staring at her. An hour ago, he would have considered it a crazy story. Now he simply wasn't so sure. He was about to speak when he heard a tiny sound, like the tinkle of distant fairy chimes. "What was that?" he asked sharply.

"Just Tracy," said Brooke. "She wants to talk. I guess she's ready to start home." She tapped her wristwatch. "Two-way transmitter," she explained. "Tracy has one just like it. You want me to talk to her?"

Startled, Jeff hesitated. The chimes tinkled faintly again. Now it was clear that Brooke's little watch was producing the sound.

"Go ahead," he told her. He added, "You'd better remember what not to say."

Brooke smiled. "Don't worry! You'll have to stand close if you want to hear Tracy. They're made so you can talk privately." She slid a fingernail under a jeweled knob of the watch, lifting it a scant millimeter, gave it a twist. "Tracy?" she said, holding the watch a few inches from her ear. Jeff moved over to her.

"I'll be on my way back in just a few minutes," the watch whispered. "Have there been any calls?"

"No," Brooke said. "Didn't know you were expecting any." Her own voice was low but not a whisper.

"I'm not really expecting one," the ghostly little voice said from the watch. "But I remembered Ricardo wasn't sure he could make it tonight. He said he'd phone the house early if he couldn't come, so we'd be able to get someone else to give us a quorum."

Brooke winked at Jeff, said, "Well, he hasn't called yet, so he'll probably show up."

"Right. See you soon. 'Bye."

"'Bye," said Brooke. She pushed down the knob, told Jeff, "That switches it off again."

"Uh-huh." Jeff scratched his chin. "How long will it take Tracy to get here now?"

"Forty minutes probably. Not much more. It's a good road most of the way, and she drives fast."

"How old is she?"

"Twenty-four. Seven years eight months older than I am. Why?"

"Just wondering." Jeff held out his hand. "Let's see that thing."

"The two-way? Sure." Brooke slipped the instrument off her wrist, gave it to him. "Be careful with it," she cautioned. "It's mighty expensive."

"It should be!" Jeff turned it about in his fingers, studying it. A stylish little woman's wristwatch, and it was running. There was nothing at all to indicate it could be anything other than that, but he'd heard it in action. "Yes, very expensive!" he said thoughtfully. He placed the watch on the table beside the bills. "That sounds like a peculiar family you've got," he remarked. "You really weren't lying about the Brownlee job?"

Brooke smiled. "Take a look at what's inside the cape," she said. "That's my prowling outfit, or most of it."

Jeff laid the dyed muskrat cape on one end of the table, opened it, fur side down. There were a number of zippered pockets in the lining. Jeff located variously shaped objects in some of the pockets by touch, took them out and regarded them.

"Earphone," he said. "So this matchbox-sized gadget it's connected to should be another radio?"

Brooke nodded. "Local police calls."

"Yes, handy. And a fancy glass-cutter. The two keys?"

"Duplicates of the ones Brownlee had for his den safe."

"Which made that part of it simple, didn't it?" Jeff remarked. "And a pocket flash could be useful, of course. Why the cigarette case, if that's what it is?"

"Open it," Brooke told him.

He pressed the snap of the case, looked at the long-tipped narrow cigarettes clasped inside, a brand he didn't know. "Imports?" he asked.

"Uh-huh."

Jeff sniffed at the cigarettes. "Anything special about them?"

"Just their length. They taste lousy." Brooke put out her hand. "There's a back section, you see. Let me—"

"Just tell me what to do," Jeff said.

Opening the hidden inner section of the case turned out to be a more complicated operation than switching the wristwatch over to its transmitter function, even under Brooke's guidance, but after some fumbling Jeff accomplished it. He pursed his lips, considered a silk-packed row of thin metal rods in silence for a moment.

"Picks," he said then. "You any good at using them?"

"Pretty good, I think," Brooke said. "I should be able to open almost any ordinary lock with one or another of those."

"Look kind of light."

"Not too light, Jeff. That's beryllium—harder than steel."

"I suppose you know it can be worth ten years just to be found with a set of picks like those on you?"

"That's why it's a cigarette case," Brooke told him.

Jeff shook his head. "Where did you get all these things?"

"They were custom-made. For me."

Jeff snapped both sections of the cigarette case shut and put it down. "None of it really makes any sense!" he remarked. "Your people must have money."

"Plenty," Brooke agreed.

"Then why do you play around with stuff like this? Are you nuts who do it for kicks?"

"It's not for kicks," Brooke said. "It's training. The Brownlee job the other night was a test. It's a way of finding out if I can qualify for the fancy things the family does—that some of them do, anyway."

"And what do they do?" Jeff asked.

"I don't know that yet, so I can't tell you. The family operates on a theory."

"Okay. Let's hear the theory."

"If you decide to stay legal," Brooke said, "you give away too much advantage to people who don't care whether they do or not. But if you do things that aren't legal, you can get yourself and others into trouble. It takes a knack to be able to do it and keep on getting away with it. So it's only those who show they have the knack who get into the nonlegal side of the family. The others don't break laws and don't ask questions, so there's nothing they can spill. The family keeps getting richer, but everything looks legitimate. And most of it is."

Jeff shook his head again. "Just who is this family?"

"Oh, the Camerons and the Achtels and some Wylers and a few on the Nichols side. There could be others I don't know about." Brooke added, "The Wylers and Nicholses are kind of new, but the Camerons and Achtels have been working together a long time."

Jeff grunted. "Supposing you'd got caught at the Brownlee house?"

She shrugged. "That could have been *it* for me. Nothing much would have happened. The family's got pull here and there, and I'd have been a fool rich kid playing cops and robbers. But I'd never have got near a nonlegal operation after that. I'd have proved I didn't have the knack."

"What if it was just bad luck?"

"They've got no use for someone who has bad luck. It's too risky."

Jeff nodded. He watched her a moment, head tipped quizzically to the side. "Now, something else." He smiled. "Why are you pretending you want to help me?"

"I do want to help you." Brooke frowned. "After all, how likely is it you'd have come across the cash if I hadn't told you?"

Then what do you figure on getting out of it?"

"You're to take me to Mexico with you."

"You're out of your mind!" Jeff was honestly startled. "From what you've been telling me, you have it made here."

"You think so." Brooke turned to the suitcase. "There's something you haven't see yet."

"Hold it right there," Jeff said. "What's that something?"

"You can keep your gun pointed at me while I'm getting it out," she told him, half scornfully. "I picked up more than money at the Brownlee place."

He made no further move to check her than but kept close watch as she opened a side section of the suitcase and brought out a small leather bag. She loosened the bag's drawstrings and shook its contents out on the table. "What do you think of those?" she demanded.

Jeff looked at the tumbled, shining little pile and moistened his lips: "Nice stuff—if it's genuine."

"*If* it's genuine!" Brooke's eyes flashed. She reached for a string of pearls, swung it back and forth before his face. "If you knew pearls, you wouldn't be calling that just 'nice stuff'! You need someone like me, Jeff! For one thing, I do know pearls. They were in the safe with the money, and there was a very good reason for that."

She dropped the pearls back on the other jewelry. "But you know what would have happened if you hadn't come along today? The meeting at the house tonight was supposed to be about *me*. A quorum of the active side of the family was going to review the Brownlee job and decide if I was maybe good enough to go on to something a little bigger than I've been allowed to do so far. The job wasn't much for sure—I just went in and did what I was supposed to do—but I did everything *right*; there's nothing they can fault me on.

"So probably I'd pass. And then?" She waved her hand at the table. "I wouldn't see any of that again! Oh, sure, a third of what the haul's worth would be credited to my family account. When I'm twenty-one, I'll finally have a little something to say about that account. The rings and the watch and those lovely pearls and the rest of it would leave the house with Ricardo Achtel—he runs a jewelry firm for the family, imports, exports, manufacture. And they'd decide I could move up a notch. You know what that would mean?" She laughed. "I'd be working out with a lousy circus for a couple of years at least!"

Jeff blinked. "A circus?"

Brooke nodded. "Right! We've got one in Europe. It's a small circus, but putting in a hitch there while you're young is family tradition for active members. It goes back for generations." She grimaced. "There're all *kinds* of things you can learn at the circus that will be useful later on, they tell you!"

Jeff grinned warily. "Well, there might be."

Brooke tossed her head. "I don't need at that discipline. I don't want to be thinking about the family in everything I do. They're so cautious! Now, you're somebody who doesn't mind cutting corners fast when it's necessary. We'd be a team, Jeff!"

Jeff felt a touch of amazed merriment. "What about Tracy?" he asked.

"What about her? She takes us there; we ditch her. I sort of like Tracy, but she's sold on the family. She won't make trouble for us afterward, and neither will the others. They're too careful for that. They know the kind of trouble I could make for them. You have a place to go to down there?"

Jeff nodded. "Uh-huh. Friendly old pot rancher, fifty miles from the border. Nice quiet place. You know, I've been thinking, Brooke."

"Yes?" she said eagerly.

"You've got these cute miniatruized gadgets. A cigarette case that isn't really one, and a watch that's something else besides." Jeff picked up the pencil flash he'd discovered in Brooke's cape. "This looks custom-built, too."

Her eyes might have flickered for an instant. "It is," she said. "It's the best."

"The best what, aside from being a light?"

"Well—nothing. I want a light I can rely on, naturally."

"Uh-huh. But it's thicker at this end than it really needs to be, isn't it? As if something might be built in there." Jeff fingered the pencil flash. "And this little hole, you'll notice, points wherever you point the light. I don't see how the thing can be opened either."

"Opening it is a little tricky," Brooke said. "If you'll let—"

"No, don't bother." Jeff smiled. "Here's where you switch on the light—fine! So it is a flashlight. What does this ring do?" He turned the flash up, pointing it at Brooke's face.

"Twist it to the left, and it dims the beam," Brooke said, watching him.

"To the right?"

"That brightens it, of course. And—" Her breath caught. "Don't twist it too far, Jeff."

"Why not?"

"Well, don't point it at me then." She smiled quickly. "I'll explain."

"Sure, explain." Jeff lowered the flashlight.

Brooke was still smiling. "I didn't really know about you. You can see that."

"Uh-huh. I understand."

"So I didn't want to tell you about it yet. It's a tranquilizer gun."

Jeff raised his brows. "Doesn't look much like one."

"Family specialty. You couldn't buy that kind of transquilizer anywhere. I don't know what it is, of course, but we might be able to have it analyzed."

"Maybe we could," Jeff said. "What's its range?"

"You're not supposed to try to use over thirty feet. Indoors, that's likely to be as much range as you'll want."

"You've used it?"

"No," Brooke said. "I saw it used once, but it's only for a real emergency. The family doesn't want it to get out that someone makes a gun like that."

"What was the effect?"

Brooke grimaced. "Worked so fast it scared me! The man didn't even know he'd been hit, and he didn't move for another two hours. But it won't kill anyone, and there isn't supposed to be much after-effect. It's a little hollow needle."

Jeff nodded thoughtfully. "Very interesting. It seems now we have the explanation for your generous offer to finance me."

Brooke looked startled. "I told you—"

"You told me a lot of things. I even believe some of them—that this is a gun, for example. It's what you were working to get your hand on right from she start, wasn't it?"

Brooke said reluctantly, "I would have felt better if I'd had it. You see—"

"I know. You just weren't sure you could trust me. All right, obviously I can't be sure I can trust you either." Jeff raised the pencil flash, pointing it at her. "So why can't I see for myself what that little hollow needle does after it hits?"

Brooke shook her head. "You don't want to do that, Jeff."

"Why not?"

"Tracy's sort of slippery. If I'm awake and in the plane with you two she'll be a lot easier to handle. I can keep her conned. Whether you believe it or not, I do want to go to Mexico with you."

Jeff grinned and dropped the pencil flash into a coat pocket.

"And you're getting your wish!" he told her. "Go sit down in your chair."

He tied Brooke's hands behind the chair back, secured the rope to a rung, testing all knots carefully. Then he checked the time and said, "Keep your mouth shut from now on unless I ask you something."

Brooke nodded silently. Her expression indicated she might he frightened at last, and she might have reason for it. Jeff went to the window, studied the valley road. Nothing to be seen there yet. Rain-clouds drifted over the lower countryside though the sky remained clear above the house. There was a distant roll of of thunder. Jeff left the room, returned with a silk scarf. He laid the scarf on the table, restored the bundled bills, the jewelry, and Brooke's burglary equipment to the suitcase, except for the pencil flash, which stayed in his pocket along with the two-way watch. He covered the assortment in the suitcase with Brooke's cape, thinking there still might be stuff concealed in it that he hadn't discovered. If so, it could wait. He closed and locked the suitcase, pocketed the key. The clothes and boots he'd been wearing went into the closet from which he'd taken Uncle Jason's suit and shoes.

He returned to the window, stood looking out. He felt a little tense, just enough to keep him keyed up, which he didn't mind. He was always at his best when keyed up. He knew exactly what he was going to do, and it was unlikely that anything could go wrong. Even if Brooke happened to have lied about Tracy's ability to fly a plane, it wouldn't affect his plans seriously. He'd leave the two of them here, dead and stowed away where they shouldn't be found at once, and go off in Tracy's car. A few hours' start was all he needed now. The plane would be preferable, of course. If the two disappeared with him, he could work out a way to put heat on their precious family.

He'd been tempted to wait, to let that crew of cautious wealthy practitioners of crime start drifting in during the afternoon, nail them down as they arrived, and then see what he could make out of the overall situation, but that might be crowding his luck. He'd got a great deal more than he'd expected to get at the house, and he liked the way the setup looked now.

He inquired presently, "What color is Tracy's car?"

Brooke's tongue tip moistened her lips. "Red," she said. "Cherry red. Sports car. Is she coming?"

"In sight," Jeff said. "Still a few minutes away." He went to the table, picked up the silk scarf. "Let's make sure everything stays very quiet in here when she shows up!" He wrapped the scarf tightly around Brooke's mouth and jaw, knotted it behind her head, and came back to the window.

He stood away from it a little, though there was no real chance the sharpest of eyes could have spotted him from the road. Tracy he decided, did drive fast—and expertly. The little red car was flicked around the curves, accelerated again on the straight stretches. By the time the sound of the engine grew audible on the breeze, he could make out a few details about the driver: a woman, all right—goggled, bright green scarf covering her head, strands of blonde hair whipping out back of the scarf. She was coming to the house because there was nowhere else to go; the road stopped here. Satisfied, Jeff left the room, went unhurriedly downstairs. He'd made up his mind a while ago about the place where he'd wait for Tracy, and he was there a minute later. A side door opened on the garden near the angle formed by the house with the garage. The angle was landscaped with thick dark-green bushes, providing perfect cover. For the moment, he remained near the door. The chances were that Tracy would come directly to the garage; and if she did, he'd have the gun on her as soon as she stepped out of the car. If, instead, she drove around to the front entrance of the building, he'd slip back into the house through the side door and catch her inside. The rest would be simple. It shouldn't take long to make her realize what she had to do for her own sake and Brooke's, that Jeff didn't really need either of them, and that if she didn't follow his orders exactly, he'd shoot them both and leave with her car.

From his point of concealment, he watched the car turn up the driveway from the road. The section of driveway leading to the garage curved out of sight behind a stand of ornamental pines sixty yards away.

The car swung into it, vanished behind the trees. There was a momentary squeal of brakes.

Jeff frowned, listening, Uncle George's .38 in his hand. He heard the purring throb of the engine, but the car obviously had stopped. It shouldn't make much difference if Tracy left it there; she still had to come to the house. But it wasn't the way Jeff had planned it, and he didn't like that.

He gauged the distance to the pines. He could reach them in a quick sprint and find out what she was doing. However, he didn't favor that idea either. If she had the car in motion again before he got there and caught sight of him in the open, he could have a real problem. Undecided, Jeff bagan to edge through the bushes toward the front of the garage.

He heard a sound then, a slight creaking, which he might have missed if his ears hadn't been straining for indications of what was delaying Tracy. He turned his head, and something stung the side of his neck. He swung around, startled, felt himself stumbling oddly as his gaze swept up along the side of the house.

A window screen in a second floor room above him was being quietly closed. Jeff jerked up the revolver. He was falling backward by then, and he fired two shots, wildly, spitefully, at the blurring blue of the sky before he was lying on the ground, the gun somehow no longer in his hand.

He had a stunned thought: that Brooke couldn't possibly have done it, that he had her tranquilizing gadget in his coat. And besides—

He didn't finish the second thought. Tracy was standing next to him, holding a gun of her own, when Brooke came out through the side door.

"Well!" Tracy said. "So now I know why you were giving me the high sign from the window." She glanced down at Jeff's face, back at Brooke. "Tranquilizer?"

"No," Brooke said reluctantly. "He spotted that while we were talking and took it."

"So it was a Last Resort, eh?"

"Yes."

Tracy grimaced. "Suspected it, by the way he looks." She shook her head. "Well, Brooke—curare. You know the rules. You may have quite a bit of explaining to do."

"I *can* explain it."

"Yes? Start with me!" Tracy invited. "A sort of rehearsal. Let's see how it will stand up."

"You know who that is? Was, I guess."

Tracy looked at Jeff again. "No. I should?"

"Jeff Clary."

Tracy blinked. "Clary? The escaped convict they're hunting for? You're sure?"

"I'm sure," Brooke said. "They've been broadcasting his picture and I recognized him as soon as he turned up in the house. Anyway, he admitted it. He's killed three people in the past twenty-four hours, and he had plans for you and me after you'd flown him across the border."

"Now, that doesn't start the explanation off too badly," Tracy conceded. "Still—"

Brooke said, "He had to go anyway."

"Probably. But not at your discretion. If you had to let him take your sleepy-bye kit, what about mine? You know where I keep it. The bag's upstairs in my closet at present."

"I thought of that," Brooke said, "but I didn't think I'd have time to hunt around for the bag. He had me gagged and tied to a chair, and he stayed right there in the room with me until you were almost driving in. Last Resort was quicker. I grabbed it."

"Um!" Tracy tapped her nose-tip reflectively. "Well, that really should do it! They can't give you too much of an argument." She smiled. "So the big bad convict ties you to a chair? Angelique the Eleven-Year-Old Escape Artist. Remember the howl you raised when they sent you off to the circus that summer?" She looked at the gun in her hand. "Might as well put this away, and we'll start tidying up."

"Hadn't you better use the gun first?" Brooke said.

"Huh?" Tracy looked thoughtful. "Yes!" she said then. "Good thinking, Brooke! They should prefer to let Clary be found if the coroner doesn't have reason to poke around too closely. We'll take away the reason."

She pointed the gun at a spot between Jeff's eyebrows.

There had been assorted activities in the house in the latter part of the afternoon and the early part of the evening, but around ten o'clock things were quiet again. The rain, after holding off to the south most of the day, had moved in finally, and there was a gentle, steady pattering against the closed windows in Tracy's room. For the past half hour, Brooke and Tracy had been playing slap solitaire at a small table. Neither was displaying her usual fierce concentration on the game.

Tracy lifted her head suddenly, glanced at Brooke. "I think the reporting committee's coming!"

Brooke listened. Footsteps were audible in the passage. "Well, it's a relief," she muttered. "They've been discussing it long enough." She put down her card pack and went to the door.

"Here we are, George!" she called. "Tracy's room."

She came back and looked on as the tuxedoed committee filed in. George Cameron, president of Ranfew College and scholarly authority on the Punic Wars, entered first; then Ricardo Achtel, who handled Baldwin Gems, Imports and Exports, among other things. Finally came Jason Cameron, best known in some circles as big-game hunter and mountaineer. Three big guns of the family. All gave her reassuring smiles, which struck Brooke as a bad sign. She drew a deep breath.

"What's the verdict?" she asked.

"Let's not look on it as a verdict, Brooke," said George Cameron. "Sit down; we'll have to talk about it." He glanced around, noted the absence of free chairs. "Mind if we use your bed, Tracy?"

"Not at all," Tracy told him.

George and Jason sat down on the bed. Ricardo Achtel leaned against the wall, hands shoved into his trousers pockets. "There was a special news report some ten minutes ago," George remarked. "I don't believe you caught it?"

Brooke shook her head.

George said, "They've found the unfortunate Rambow couple in their car. Each had been shot from behind almost at contact range—a deliberate execution. Clary deliberately ran. He demaged relict off the road, as he told you. A highway patrol happened to notice smashed bushes, investigated, and discovered the wreck and the bodies in a ravine."

"How far from where Clary was found?" Tracy asked.

"Less than four miles. We worked out his probable backtrail closely enough," George said. "And that should wind it up. The theory that Clary tried to kidnap another motorist, who was lucky or alert enough to shoot first, and may have sufficient reason for not wanting to identify himself, is regarded as substantiated. Either of the two bullets found in Clary's body should have caused almost instant death. Police will try to trace the gun. The usual thing."

There was a short pause. "All right, and now what about me?" Brooke asked. "I've flunked?"

"Not at all," George said. "On the whole, you did very well. You were dealing with a killer and stalled him off until you could create an opportunity to end the threat to yourself and Tracy. Naturally, we approve."

"Naturally," Tracy agreed dryly.

"However," said Jason Cameron, "there was a rather serious breach of secrecy."

"I've tried to explain that," Brooke told him. "I had to do something to keep Clary working to outfigure me. I couldn't think of a good enough set of lies on the spot. He didn't seem exactly stupid. So I told him the truth, or mostly the truth, which made it easy."

George scratched his jaw. "Yes, but there you are, Brooke! In doing it, you took a chance. Mind you, no one's blaming you. If there's any fault, it's in those responsible for your progress—which certainly must include myself. But as far as you knew, there was a possibility, however slight, that the police would trace Clary to the house and take him alive. We could have handled the resulting problem, but some harm might have been done. Further, in being frank with Clary, you made killing him almost a necessity—thus reducing your options, which is never desirable."

Jason nodded. "There's a definite streak of candor in you, Brooke. It's been noticed. Your immediate inclination is to tell the truth."

"Not," observed Ricardo Achtel, "that there's anything essentially wrong with that."

"No, of course not," George agreed. "However, one can also argue in favor of facile dissimulation. Those who don't seem born with the ability—I had a good deal of early difficulty in the area myself—must acquire it by practice. It's felt you fall short on that point, Brooke."

"In other words," Brooke said, "I didn't flunk out, but I didn't get upgraded tonight, either?"

"Not formally," George told her. "We believe you need more time. The matter will be brought up again at your next birthday."

"Seven months," said Brooke. She looked discouraged.

"They'll pass quickly enough for you," George assured her.

"In a sense, you see," Jason remarked, "circumstances did upgrade you today by presenting you with a difficult and serious problem, which you solved satisfactorily though in a less than optimum manner. It seems mainly a question of letting your experience catch up."

George nodded. "Exactly! So you'll continue your formal education at Ranfrew, but you'll also start going to drama school."

"Drama school?" Brooke said, surprised.

"Ours. The training you receive there won't precisely parallel that given other students, but you should find it interesting. Tracy went through the process a few years ago."

Brooke looked over at Tracy.

"Uh-huh, so I did," Tracy said slowly. She shook her head. "Poor Brooke!"

Leo R. Ellis
Small Town Justice

Sweet gum trees lined both sides of the two-lane state highway, except where they occasionally gave way to a growth of cypress when the road dipped into a marshland. The oiled surface was poorly maintained, and Eddie McCade was often forced to guide the old sedan around chuckholes. He made this maneuver with one hand on the wheel; there was no need to be alert, for he hadn't seen another car during the past ten miles.

Eddie stretched out in sheer youthful exuberance, his bare, tanned arms pushing his body away from the wheel. He bagan to whistle tunelessly, but stopped suddenly. He stared at the instrument panel, his lips still puckered. The heat indicator needle had swung over into the red zone and was resting against the pin.

The car coasted past a cottage on the right of the road and pulled up on the shoulder beside the highway. Eddie sat for a moment listening to the motor boil before he shrugged. "Doggone," he said, "sure looks like she ran dry on me."

The rear saat of the sedan was piled with fishing gear and camping equipment. Eddie rummaged through this until he dug out a plastic bucket, and with no effort at replacing the articles he had pulled down, he swung off up the road.

The cottage was almost doll-like in size and sat behind twin, regimented magnolia trees, each set in its precise position behind a white picket fence. Eddie's knock set up a din of dogs barking from behind the cottage, but no human response. He walked around the cottage and stopped when he saw two dogs trying to get at him from behind a chain link fence. "Okay," Eddie said, swinging the bucket at them, "you don't have to be so grouchy about it. I'll get the water somewhere else."

Back at the car, Eddie looked in the other direction. A hedge grew on the opposite side of the road, the vegetation so high and the growth so rank that it hid any sign of what lay behind. Eddie walked down the road and found an opening in the hedge, which was flanked by two square pillars of stone.

Eddie stood in what appeared to have been a gateway at one time and looked up into spacious grounds. The drive no longer existed as such, but was little more than an outline that curved gracefully up through the grounds. The outline ended before the wide verandah of a towering old home, built of the same stone of which the gate pillars were made. Even from a distance, the place appeared to have fallen into ruin. Only a thin trickle of smoke from a chimney proved the place wasn't completely deserted, or so it appeared.

Halfway up the grounds, an iron deer stood haunch-high in the wild growth that had once been a lawn. Eddie raised an imaginary rifle to his shoulder and sighted in on the deer.

"Bang," he said, and grinned when the lawn ornament refused to drop.

Honeysuckle had taken over the front verandah. Eddie continued around the side of the house on a gravel path and stopped when he reached the rear corner. The grounds behind were in as bad rapair as those in front. They, too, appeared deserted, until a tall, thin man came down through an orchard. He did not look up, but walked with his head bowed as he picked his way through thick growth of brier and berry vines. When he did see Eddie, he stopped. In the dead silence, the sound of some metal object striking on stone rang out loud and clear.

The man stood, his eyes wide and his mouth hanging open until he regained his composure. He hurried through the trees toward Eddie, holding his bared arms high to avoid scratching them on the vines. Both the arms, below the rolled up sleeves, and the skin behind the open collar had the unhealthy whiteness of a fish belly. His face was sweating and lanky strands of gray hair had plastered themselves over his damp forehead. "Get off my property," he said as he came out of the orchard.

Eddie held up the bucket. "My car ran out of water," he said. "I need some to get into town."

The man's mouth moved before he spoke. He pointed toward the road with a shaking finger. Suddenly he let his arm drop to his side. "There's a pump on the other side of the summer house," he muttered, and turned quickly to walk toward the house.

"Thanks," Eddie said, "I'll only need—" He stopped and shrugged as the back door slammed.

Eddie poured the bucket of water into the radiator. He stood and regarded it thoughtfully. He looked back toward the house, shrugged and tossed the bucket into the back seat. Eddie drove off, and less than a mile farther on a sign appeared.

STOP IN MILLVALE
The Friendly City
Pop. 4000

Eddie gave the sign a wave as he passed. "I could stand a little friendliness," he said with a wry grin. "The country people around here sure aren't passing it out."

At the first filling station he pulled on past the gas pumps and stopped before a garage building at the rear. He climbed out of the car as a surly young man in greasy coveralls came up. Eddie explained his trouble and the mechanic lifted the hood.

"It's your water pump," the mechanic said after an inspection. He glowered at Eddie. "I suppose you're in a big hurry, like everybody else that comes through here."

Eddie grinned. "Not especially," he said.

"Just don't try to rush me, that's all. It's noon, and I'm taking time off to eat before I even touch your car."

"Okay," Eddie said.

"There's no place you can hang around here."

"Okay," Eddie said again, "so I'll stroll on down and get something to eat."

After a sandwich, Eddie killed time by walking around the downtown section of Millvale. An hour and a half later, Eddie returned to the garage and waited until the mechanic lowered the hood. "You can fill it with water out front," the mechanic said. He held out his hand. "The bill is twenty-eight dollars and a half."

"That's a lot of money," Eddie said, frowning.

The mechanic moved forward. "You got the money, ain't you?"

"I've got it," Eddie said. "But that's not the point."

"It's the point as far as I'm concerned." The man clenched his right hand into a fist. "You going to give me trouble, bud?"

"I'm not going to give you trouble," Eddie said. "I guess it's my own fault. I should have found out what you were going to charge before you started."

"It wouldn't have made no difference. You couldn't go no place without water. Now pay up."

As Eddie puled out his billfold, a car drew alongside and stopped. Eddie paid, and as he turned, a short, compact little man climbed out. The man wore no coat, so the automatic in the shoulder holster was plainly visible. His small face had a pinched expression as he came up to regard Eddie from under sandy eyebrows. "That your car, boy?" he asked.

Eddie nodded.

The mechanic stepped forward.

"The guy gave me some guff about paying up, chief," he said.

"That so?" the small man said mildly.

"I thought the bill was a little steep, that was all," Eddie said. "Is something wrong?"

"Could be," the man said. "How about you coming down to the station with me?"

Eddie took a step back, and with the movement, the mechanic stooped quickly and picked up a tire iron. Eddie glared and looked back at the small man. "I suppose you're a policeman," he retorted.

"He's the chief of police," the mechanic growled.

"How about my car?" Eddie asked.

"We'll take care of it," the chief said, and walked back to his own car.

When Eddie had been downtown, he had seen the squat brick building with the bars on the windows. It stood on one corner of the square, and it was here the chief stopped. The room inside the door held a receiving desk, but the place was deserted and smelled musty.

The chief led Eddie into an office where the air was heavy with the smell of stale cigar smoke. The chief hooked his toe in a straight chair and kicked it toward a flat top desk. "Empty out your pockets, boy. Let's see what you've got."

Eddie took his valuables out and placed them on the desk. "That's all I have," he said.

The chief carried the billfold and car keys around the desk. He sat down in the swivel chair and leaned back. "Draw up a chair, boy," he said. "You can smoke if you want to."

"I don't smoke, thanks."

The chief chuckled. "I do," he said. He took a black, crooked stogie from his pocket and went through a ceremony of sniffing and drawing it between his lips. He scratched a kitchen match and applied the flame before he opened the billfold and took out a photograph. "You were in the army, eh?" he said after careful study. "When did you get out?"

"It tells you right there. It says I got out three weeks ago. It also tells you I'm twenty-one years old, and—"

"Don't get smart, boy."

Eddie stared at the desk. "I got out three weeks ago."

The chief nodded. "Where's your home?"

"I was born and raised in a little town in Oregon." Eddie looked up suddenly. "I don't mean to be smart," he said in a tight voice. "But I want to know—"

"Oregon's a long way from here," the chief broke in. "It's about two thousand miles, I'd judge offhand. What are you doing down here—are you on the bum?"

"No, sir, I'm paying my way." Eddie took a deep breath and compressed his lips. "I'd never been anywhere until I went into the service. I saved some money, and when I got my discharge, I decided to see some of the country before I went home and settled down."

"And so you ended up in Millvale, eh?"

"I didn't mean to end up here. I heard the fishing was good in this territory—" Eddie grasped the edge of the desk and leaned forward. "Don't I have the right to know why you brought me in here?"

The chief removed the stogie and studied it. The inspection completed, he put the stogie into his mouth and leaned back. "I reckon you do," he said slowly. "I'm holding you for the murder of Miss Lucinda Devlin, boy."

Eddie pushed himself halfway out of his chair. "You're kidding," he said, staring at the chief. "You must be kidding." Slowly he sank back. "I've only been here in town a couple of hours. I haven't been anywhere—I haven't even talked to anyone, except—"

"Miss Lucinda lived out on the highway," the chief said easily. "She lived in a little white house with a picket fence. Did you stop there, boy?"

Eddie bit down on his lower lip as he studied the desktop. "I stopped at a place to get water for my car," he said slowly. "There were a couple of boxer dogs there."

"That was Miss Lucinda's place."

"But there was nobody home."

"There was nobody home—nobody *alive* when you left. Is that what you mean, boy?"

Eddie raised up again. "No, that isn't what I said. Nobody answered the door when I knocked. I saw the dogs and left."

The chief brought his feet down with a crash. "Where did you hide her body, boy?" he demanded.

"I didn't have anything to do with a body."

"Did you have it in your car when you stopped at her brother's place?"

"I went to a place across the road, if that's what you mean," Eddie said. "I walked around in back—a man came down through an old orchard—"

"What did this man look like?"

Eddie's hand trembled as he stroked his chin. "He was tall," he said. "He had white hair—hanging down. He was sweating and he had his shirtsleeves rolled up."

The chief had the cold stogie clamped tight between his teeth. "What did this man say?"

"He told me where the pump was," Eddie said and then stopped. "At first this fellow acted as if he was going to order me off the place. Then he changed his mind and let me have the water." Eddie wet his lips and leaned forward. "If you haven't found any body, maybe the woman wasn't killed—maybe she's gone off somewhere and didn't tell anyone."

The chief took out a kitchen match, scratched it across the underside of his desk, and gave his whole attention to applying the flame to the charred end. "Nope," he said cheerfully, after he had tossed the match into the wastepaper basket, "we got too much evidence she was killed. After you talked to Miss Lucinda's brother, he got suspicious and went over to her place. He called me from there and I sent a man out to check."

"You can only hold me on suspicion," Eddie said. "I suppose I'll have to stay around, until this thing is cleared up."

"Yep." The chief climbed out of his chair and walked to a rack on the wall, where he took down a ring of keys." And to make sure you do stick around, I'm locking you up, boy."

The jail in Millvale was a large cage, separated into three cells by dividing bars. All the cells were unoccupied, and Eddie was placed in the center cell and left alone.

Eddie made only a brief inspection of the cell before he sank down on the iron cot and put his face into his hands. He was still in this position, half an hour later, when a bloated old man with a stubble beard shuffled down the corridor. The old man entered the cell beyond Eddie, and after locking the door, reached out and tossed the keys back toward the chief's office. The old man came over and looked through the bars.

Eddie looked up. "What are you staring at?" he inquired warily.

The old man grinned, exposing toothless gums. "I ain't never seen a real live murderer before," he said.

Eddie jumped up. "I'm no murderer," he said hotly. "I've never killed anyone. So go look at something else."

"That ain't what Mort Coop says."

Eddie had started across the cell. He whirled and came back. "Who's Mort Coop?" he demanded.

The old man continued to grin. "Mort Coop is the only detective the chief's got left," he said cheerfully. "Mort came in from Miss Lucinda's place. He said the kitchen had blood all over, and a butcher knife was gone from a place where she kept it over the sink. Mort says as soon as he finds her body, he's got you dead to rights."

Eddie strode across the cell and stared out through the barred window. "What are you in for?" he asked without turning.

The old man lay down on his own cot, face up, and stared at the ceiling. "Plain drunk, same as always," he said cheerfully. "It saves the town money to throw old Ben Zinhoff in jail. I sweep up the place, run errands, and feed the chief's hounds."

Eddie walked slowly to the dividing bars. "Hounds?" he said.

"Since the chief had to let most of the police force go, he got a couple of bloodhounds to fill in," Ben Zinhoff chuckled. "You don't have to pay a bloodhound wages."

Eddie paced the length of his cell and returned to the bars. "What's wrong with this town?" he asked. "You've got a sign out there on the road calling Millvale the friendly city, but I've never seen such a hostile bunch of people."

"I reckon it's cause the town's desperate," Ben said, staring at the ceiling. "When you're hungry, you don't go around grinning, and when a whole town's lost all hope, they're apt to want to put the blame on somebody."

"But why me?" Eddie demanded. "I didn't do anything to hurt them."

Ben closed his eyes. "Maybe you did, and maybe you didn't," he said. "But whoever murdered Miss Lucinda killed the last chance this town had."

"What do you mean?"

Ben continued to lie stretched out, his eyes closed. "The Devlin Cotton Mills was founded over a hundred years ago," he said. "Everybody in town has always worked there, or been dependent on the mills for a living. When the mills was running good, Millvale was prosperous, but when the mills was shut down, the town was broke." Ben opened his eyes and looked over. "I reckon you can see how being a Devlin is next to being God in this town."

"I suppose so. Are the mills shut down now?"

Ben nodded. "Been closed down tight for eight years now. I guess things started to go bad when the old colonel died thirty years ago and left the mills in charge of his son instead of his daughter, Miss Lucinda. Fran Lou didn't have the proper strength to be a Devlin."

"Fran Lou?" Eddie said thoughtfully. "Is he the fellow I saw out at that old, ramshackle house?"

"That's the Devlin mansion," Ben said with dignity. "The Devlins built that a long time ago, and every Devlin has lived there, except for Miss Lucinda. She moved out when Fran Lou married that city girl."

It took little prodding on Eddie's part to get the story of Millvale's decline. The town's economy had been wrapped up in the Devlin private affairs, and those affairs had been anything but promising. Under the old colonel the mills had prospered, but the old man, being a believer in male supremacy, had left the mills in charge of his only son, Fran Lou. The daughter, Miss Lucinda, was to share in the profits, but had no voice in running the company, his will dictated.

A succession of business reversals, caused by poor management, followed by a disastrous marriage that ended in scandal, and the Devlin mills were closed.

After the mills had been idle for six years, Miss Lucinda had wrangled control of the company from her brother. She had arranged a creditors' meeting, and had secured their consent to open the mills again. She was in the process of raising financial backing when she had been murdered.

Old Ben Zinhoff sat up on the edge of his cot. "Miss Lucinda should have been the man," he said. "She had a lot of the old colonel in her makeup. She was a real Devlin for sure."

Eddie ground a fist into the palm of his other hand. "What a rotten break for me," he said. "Why did I have to come through this town at a time like this?"

"Folks are mighty worked up about Miss Lucinda's murder," Ben said. "There ain't much chance of the mills' ever opening again now."

An hour later, a squat man came down the corridor and stopped before Ben Zinhoff's cell. "Get up, you old drunk," he growled as he unlocked the door. "Get on down to the restaurant and pick up some food for the prisoner."

"Yes, sir, Mr. Coop." The old man circled the man beside the cell door and scampered down the corridor.

Mort Coop came over and looked through the bars of Eddie's cell. His square face, framed by blue jowls, was set on a thick neck plunged deep into heavy shoulders. His eyeballs were set behind rolls of flesh and formed horizontal slits in an expressionless face. Finally he turned the key and swung the door open without speaking.

The chief sat in his swivel chair, a newly lighted stogie between his teeth. He gave no sign of greeting, but as soon as Eddie was seated, the man shoved a typewritten sheet of paper across the desk. "You might as well sign that," he said flatly. He placed a pen on top of the paper.

Eddie pulled back. "If it's a confession, I won't sign," he said. "I didn't kill anybody."

The chief looked up at Mort Coop and nodded. The detective walked over and opened the outside door. A man stepped into the room. He was tall, with gray hair showing beneath the hat brim, and the suit, although several years out of style, was neatly brushed and pressed.

The chief rose when the man entered. "Is this the young man who stopped at the mansion, Mr. Devlin?" he asked, pointing at Eddie with an accusing finger.

Fran Lou Devlin gave Eddie a passing glance. "That is the man," he said.

"Thank you, Mr. Devlin. I'm sorry we had to trouble you."

Fan Lou Devlin nodded curtly. "Quite all right," he said. "I trust I can expect quick justice for my sister's murder." He turned and left the room.

Mort Coop closed the door and walked to a steel file, where he took out a two and a half foot leather strap. He grasped the stubby wooden handle and stroked the oiled leather surface as he walked over and took the chair across the desk from Eddie.

The chief picked up the pen and placed it back on the paper.

Eddie shook his head. "Let's get this straight," he said. "I didn't kill anyone, and I'm not going to confess. I told you I stopped by Mr. Devlin's house, so his identification doesn't mean a thing. If you're going to charge me on suspicion of murder, I want to talk to a lawyer."

"Now let's not rush things," the chief said. He took Eddie's billfold from the desk drawer and leafed through the bills. "Three hundred and twenty-six dollars," he said thoughtfully. "That's about what Miss Lucinda might have at her place." He looked over at the detective. "I'd say Miss Lucinda would kick up quite a fuss before she'd turn over her money to a stranger, wouldn't you, Mort?"

The detective slammed the desk with the leather strap and grunted.

"You're not going to intimidate me," Eddie said in a tight voice. "I saved that money. I picked up some odd jobs on this trip. I don't spend much, I camp out and fix my own meals."

The chief put the billfold back into the drawer. He sighed. "You're making it tough on yourself, boy," he said.

"Why don't you try to find the real murderer?" Eddie demanded. "If this woman was stabbed, her killer must have smeared some blood on himself."

The chief blinked. "Who said she was stabbed?"

Eddie bit his lip. "Ben Zinhoff," he said in a small voice.

"Suppose there was blood," the chief said. "You had a couple of hours to clean up."

"You can't clean all the blood off," Eddie said. "Lab tests would prove my clothes never had blood on them."

"We ain't got no lab," Mort Coop said. "And this town ain't spending money sending your clothes out to no lab."

"How about fingerprints?" Eddie asked stubbornly. "You didn't even fingerprint me."

"We don't need to," Mort Coop said, his flat face impassive. "We got other ways to get at the truth." He slammed the strap down across the desk again.

The chief laid his stogie in the ashtray. He leaned back in his swivel chair and clasped his hands behind his head. "We want this to be all fair and legal," he said. "We don't want you to claim you didn't have your say—suppose you tell your story again."

Eddie told his story, and described meeting Fran Lou Devlin. "He was coming toward the house through an old orchard. He was in his shirtsleeves. At first he didn't see me, but when he did, his eyes bugged out."

"You sure he didn't have a coat on?" the chief asked.

"He did not," Eddie said firmly. "He was startled. He stared at me and dropped something. I heard it hit stones."

"Stones in an orchard?" the chief asked mildly.

"That's what it sounded like."

Mort slapped the strap across his leg. "You trying to throw blame on Fran Lou Devlin?" he asked.

"I'm trying to tell the truth."

The chief relit his stogie. He leaned back and closed his eyes.

Eddie hit the desk with his clenches fist. "Even if I did sign a confession, you couldn't get a conviction, no *corpus delicti*."

"You a lawyer, or something?" Mort Coop asked.

"No, but I know that if you can't produce that woman's body, no court will convict me of her murder."

The chief opened his eyes. "You're overlooking one thing, boy," he said. "Your case is liable not to reach any court."

Eddie wet his lips with the tip of his tongue as he stared at the chief. "What do you mean?" he asked.

"The people of this town are boiling mad about Miss Lucinda's murder," the chief said. "They were counting on her to get the mills running again, and they're going to want revenge."

Eddie glanced at the window and back again. "You mean a mob?" he said weakly.

"Call it civic justice."

"Court trials cost taxpayers money," Mort Coop muttered.

The chief nodded. "You're right as rain there, Mort. Folks are going to figure it's a shameful waste to spend money on a stranger like that. Especially when they can take care of the job themselves for free."

Eddie wet his lips again. He looked from one man to the other. "You're going to protect me, aren't you?"

The chief spread his hands. "We've whittled the police force down to two men," he said. "Now you couldn't expect two men to do much against an aroused town." He waved his hand. "We won't worry about that until after dark. Take him back to his cell, Mort."

Ben Zinhoff hadn't returned, and Eddie began pacing his cell as soon as he was alone. As he walked, he clasped and unclasped his hands, ran them over the nape of his neck, and muttered to himself. Every few minutes he would break his pacing to go to the window and peer out. It was dust now, and a shadowy gloom had settled down over Millvale.

Ben Zinhoff shuffled down the corridor, an enamel cup in one hand, a tin plate in the other, and the key ring hung over his arm. He unlocked Eddie's cell door and shoved the food in. "Save what you can't eat for the hounds. They don't get half enough." He relocked the door and entered his own cell. He locked the door and tossed the keys down the corridor and walked over to his cot.

Eddie began his pacing again. He paused when he saw Ben looking at the plate on the floor. "I'm not hungry," Eddie said. "I'm sorry you made that trip for nothing."

"That's all right. The hounds can use it." Ben looked up when a single overhead bulb went on in the corridor. "The chief and Mort Coop are leaving," he said. "They always turn on the light before they go."

Eddie hurried to the window and looked out. It was pitch dark outside. He turned and gazed at Ben as he leaned against the wall. "You mean they've left us all alone?" he asked. "There won't be anybody here tonight?" He watched Ben shake his head and turned back to the window again. A huge, yellow disk of a moon hung above the treetops.

"Why don't you drink some coffee?" Ben said.

Eddie rushed back across the cell. "Don't you understand? There's a mob coming after me tonight."

Ben sat down on the cot and stared at the floor. "Feeling is running high in town, all right," he said slowly. "Folks here are taking Miss Lucinda's murder real personal."

Eddie tried to shake the bars. "But they'd be killing an innocent man. I didn't murder that woman. Why doesn't anyone believe me? Why aren't the chief and Mort Coop out trying to find the real killer?"

Ben wagged his head from side to side. "I reckon they figure they've got him."

"I don't think they care whether I did it or not," Eddie said angrily. "They needed a suspect—they picked me up because I was a stranger in town. They can't find a body, and they know they can't get a conviction without one, so they're throwing me to the wolves. As long as somebody gets hanged for the crime, they're satisfied."

Ben looked up and nodded slowly. "They sure ain't found no body," he said.

Eddie turned and stared at the darkened window for a long moment before he spoke. "I've got a good idea where that body is," he said grimly. "Only they won't listen to me. Nobody in this town would listen to me." He walked to the window and leaned his forehead against the bricks. "Tell me something, Ben. Why do the people in this town hold Fran Lou up as such as idol? It was his fault the mills shut down. Why don't they blame him?"

Ben gazed at the floor, pinching his nose. "Mainly, I reckon. it's because he's a Devlin. When you're born and raised in Millvale, you don't believe a Devlin can do any wrong."

Eddie threw himself on his cot and lay face down, his arms wrapped around his head. He lay quiet, but when the sound of insects pinging against the light bulb was joined by Ben's gentle snoring, he raised up and looked into the other cell. The old man had turned away from him and was lying on his side.

Eddie got up and crossed to the window again. The moon had climbed high and had lost its yellow coloring. He turned from the window and walked back across the cell to the front. The keys were on the floor where Ben had tossed them. Eddie squatted down and reached through the space between the bars. His fingertips fell inches short of touching the key ring. He dropped flat on his stomach and pushed his arm through the bars to his shoulder. His fingers touched the key ring and worked it closer to his cell.

Eddie unlocked the cell door and tiptoed down the corridor. He passed the chief's office, where the stale cigar smell hung heavy in the darkness. He passed through the outer room and opened the front door by twisting the spring catch.

Not a store was lighted on Eddie's side of the square. On the other side, only the movie house and the drugstore were open. No pedestrians walked on the sidewalk near the jail as Eddie slipped around the corner and melted into the darkness.

A young attendant listlessly polished the gas pumps at the filling station where Eddie had left his car. The door of the garage in the rear had been pulled down—the building was dark and Eddie's car was nowhere around.

Beyond the filling station the sidewalks petered out. Eddie took to the highway, and once he was clear of the houses, he straightened up and covered the ground in long strides. Only two cars came toward him, and each time Eddie scurried into the weeds as soon as the head-lights appeared. He crouched beside the road until the automobiles had passed.

Eddie had reached the point across from the twin stone pillars that marked the entrance of the old mansion when a new sound made him jerk his head around and look back. From the direction of Millvale came the bell-clear bawl of bloodhounds set on a trail. Eddie dashed across the road, between the pillars, and along the drive.

Shrouded in moonlight, the crumbling mansion loomed sullen and aloof. A single rectangle of light glowing in the face of the building gave evidence that some life still existed inside.

The call of the bloodhounds became louder and sharper as they left the town and started down the open highway.

Eddie ran down the path alongside the mansion. He scarcely broke stride at the rear, and continued on to the spot where Fran Lou Devlin had emerged from the orchard that morning. There had been a flagstone path through the trees, but now it was so overgrown by brier and berry vines, the outline was barely visible. Eddie pushed through until he came to the spot where Fran Lou Devlin had stopped. He dropped to his hands and knees and searched in the darkness. A short time later he came to his feet, holding a spade with damp loam still clinging to the blade.

The path ended at the far edge of the orchard, but beyond, across a weed-grown space, a low wall gleamed white in the moonlight. Eddie stepped over the wall. He stood in an enclosure, where the knee-high wild grass hid all but the tallest tombstones of a small cemetery.

Eddie didn't pause to look back, even when the bloodhounds' cry took on a new, higher note of urgency—as though they knew they were nearing their quarry and were anxious to close in for the kill. Eddie had to make only a short search of the cemetery before he found the patch of trampled grass and newly turned earth. He plunged the spade into the ground and began to dig.

The grave was shallow, and when the spade touched the body, Eddie dropped to his knees and scooped at the loose dirt with his bare hands. He uncovered the head, and then the neck and shoulders of a thin, white-haired old woman.

The woman stared up at Eddie. The waxen skin glowed in the moonlight, with every line of the aristocratic face set in contemptuous disapproval. The features betrayed no last moment of terror in life—only disdain and scorn.

Eddie tore his eyes away from the face to look back. The bawling and baying of the bloodhounds had been joined by the shouts of men as they came around the back of the mansion. Eddie waited until the eye of an electric torch bobbed between the trees before he jumped to his feet and ran to the opposite wall.

Two bloodhounds, closely followed by a jumbled squad of men, erupted out of the orchard and charged across the weed-grown strip. They pulled up when they reached the low stone wall.

"Get those hounds back!" the chief yelled above the barking of the dogs. "I'll take it alone from here." As the protesting hounds were dragged away, the chief stepped over the wall. "You come with me, Mr. Devlin," he said. "The rest of you stay there."

Fran Lou Devlin, clad in a dressing gown, approached. "I don't know why you dragged me out here," he said, his voice filled with indignation. "This is the Devlin family cemetery. It is revered ground."

"We'll have to overlook that now," the chief said firmly. He half dragged Fran Lou over the wall and stood looking around before he guided the other man over to the newly opened grave. He snapped on the electric torch and tilted the beam down to shine into the hole. "Take a look at that, Fran Lou Devlin," he said.

The silence that followed was broken by Fran Lou Devlin's cry of anguish as he tore himself away from the chief and plunged away from the grave, only to trip over a sunken tombstone and fall to the ground. He huddled in a ball, his arms over his face. "Take her away," he cried. "She's accusing me. She's always accusing me."

The chief stood over the huddled figure. "She's accusing you of her murder," he said.

Fran Lou Devlin sobbed convulsively. "She thinks I'm not fit to be a Devlin—she considers me weak—she's calling me a failure. She hates me because I was born a man instead of her." Fran Lou Devlin crawled over and grasped the chief's knees. "I didn't kill her for her money," he said, his face upturned. "I went to her place to ask for a loan—I could take her refusal, but I couldn't stand her scorn any longer—I couldn't stand it any longer, don't you understand?"

The chief pulled Fran Lou Devlin to his feet and led him to the wall. "Take him down to the jail," he said to the now silent men.

The group moved slowly back through the orchard, the sobbing Fran Lou Devlin supported between two men. The chief stayed behind. He lit a stogie and turned. "You can come out now, boy," he said.

Eddie stepped over the wall and walked up to stand before the chief. He took out his handkerchief and dabbed at his forehead. "Did you know it was Fran Lou Devlin all along?" he finally asked in a small voice.

The chief shook his head. "Not when I picked you up," he said. "I was going to stick you for Miss Lucinda's murder until you told me about seeing Fran Lou in his shirtsleeves. Nobody had ever seen Fran Lou without a coat, so I figured something was wrong. Then I remembered the Devlin Family burying ground up here behind the orchard, and I knew where her body was hidden."

Eddie wiped a streak of blood from his arm. "Why didn't you come up here and dig it up?" he asked.

"I couldn't, boy. Four bodies buried in a plot constitutes a cemetery in this state, and you can't disturb a grave in a cemetery without a court order. Fran Lou could have blocked that. I couldn't charge a Devlin with murder without a confession, so I decided to let you uncover the real evidence for me."

Eddie stared at the chief. "You let me escape from jail?"

The chief relit his stogie and nodded. "I figured if I got you scared enough, and then had old Ben Zinhoff put the keys where you could get your hands on them, you'd take off."

Eddie shook his head slowly. "But how did you know I'd come up here?"

"I locked your car up," the chief said and gave a dry chuckle. "I knew you were suspicious of Fran Lou, so the logical thing for you to do was to try and find what he was up to this morning." The chief held out the billfold and car keys. "I reckon the town owes you something for your trouble, boy. If there's some little thing we could do—"

Eddie took the articles. He bounced the car keys in his hand. "There is one thing," he said slowly. "Have them take down that friendly city sign. The next fellow who accepts the invitation to stop could get killed by Millvale's hospitality."

Carroll Mayers
Man with a Hobby

Everybody knows it's smart to cultivate an avocation. Any spare-time activity which relaxes, rechannels the thoughts, and eases the daily pressures is bound to be beneficial. Aside from a brief spell of cigar band collecting, though, I had never taken up any special hobby in my callow years, and when I settled into the job of chief, and only, deputy to Sheriff Wexler of Surf City, I never had time for any. (I don't count a little discreet girl watching.)

Sam Hubbard did, however, and that's what this report is all about.

In strict truth, maybe Sam's activity didn't come under the "hobby" classification. It wasn't a spare-time diversion because time was what he was surfeited with, being a widower who had come down to Surf City on a modest annuity. And it kept him keyed up and expectant rather than relaxed. But because it involved collecting of a sort, and gave a point to his daily routine, "hobby" pegged it as well as anything.

The whole business started the day the sheriff recognized and collared a wanted bad check passer who had been lolling on the beach emulating my own covert practice of bikini appraising. Nine months of the year, Surf City is a quiet little seaside community of some three thousand citizens. The summer season, though, sees us triple that total, with tourists and vacationers jamming all available facilities. Undoubtedly, the influx includes some of society's less desirable characters, and the opportunity inherent in such a possibility, as evidenced by the sheriff's apprehension of the bad paper artist, abruptly triggered Sam Hubbard's imagination.

In short, Sam became what I can only term a criminal buff. He haunted our office, wheedling copies of flyers of wanted lawbreakers. He made regular stops at the post office, checking notices exhibited there, memorizing features and names. He collected the true detective magazines carrying similar material. The rest of his time was spent in the bus depot or on the boardwalk or beach, scrutinizing faces, checking physical resemblances.

The odds against his duplicating Wexler's fortuitous feat did not deter him. "You're only wasting your time," the sheriff would tell him, but Sam would shake his head and smile confidently. "Maybe so, sheriff, but you never can tell. I just might be lucky enough to spot some big-time crook who has slipped down here, somebody who is wanted real bad, with a big reward. I could sure use the money, all right."

All of which brings us to the day Sam Hubbard came bustling into the sheriff's office, bursting with importance. It was a hot August morning and Sam, a short, chunky individual with ample girth, was perspiring profusely. Personal discomfort, though, didn't concern him at the moment; he swiped indifferently at his beaded forehead, flashed me a broad grin.

"I've got something this time, Pete," he told me triumphantly. "I know I have."

I grasped his inference, of course, but I wasn't too happy about it. I was holding the fort alone, Sheriff Wexler being upstate at a four-day peace officers' convention. And several of Hubbard's previous "somethings" had proved somewhat less than fortunate. (A vacationing bank president, whom Sam had suspected of being a notorious numbers racketeer, and a demure little blonde secretary he had erroneously identified as the mistress of a crooked labor czar came immediately to mind.)

"Oh?" My rejoinder was deliberately cool.

He wasn't dissuaded by my lack of enthusiasm. "Yes!" he exclaimed. "Oh, I know I've goofed a couple of times, but I'm positive I've hit on something this time, Pete. Dead positive."

I stifled a sigh. "Somebody you've ... recognized?"

"Well, not exactly." Sam's admission was reluctant but he immediately played it down with a confident follow-up. "But he's a crook, all right. Real criminal type. Narrow forehead, weak mouth, bad eyes."

I let my sigh burgeon. "There's no real criminal type, Sam. We've already kicked that idea to death. You can't peg a man by his features."

He shook his head, ran a soggy handkerchief around his neckband. "I'm not so sure," he countered doggedly. "Anyway, it's more than that. You'll see when I tell you."

I shot a glance at the clock. Eleven forty. Another twenty minutes and I would have been out to lunch. The only trouble with that wistful realization was that Sam would have awaited my return, or hunted me up at Millie's Luncheonette.

I tried to get more comfortable in my chair. "All right, go ahead," I surrendered.

Sam perched on the edge of my desk, bent forward earnestly, blue eyes dancing with excitement. "I first noticed the guy yesterday," he said. "At the post office. You know how I go down there—"

"I know, Sam."

"Yes. Well, he was there. Getting a letter from General Delivery. As soon as I spotted him, I knew he was a wrong one ..."

He stopped, gaze both uncertain and challenging as he again broached his theory. I didn't belabor the point now; I just said, "And?"

"I followed him when he left," Sam said flatly.

For all my restraint, the revelation had a ludicrous aspect. I couldn't hide my wonderment. "You *followed* him?"

"That's right."

"In heaven's name, *why*, Sam?"

"I just told you," he said, his flushed cheeks reddening still more.

"The man's a bad one; I wanted to check on him." Same wiped his neck again. "After he'd read that letter, he went to the telegraph office, sent a wire. Then he walked back to Millie's, took a table at the front window, and sat there over an hour, ordering coffee as an excuse."

At that point in his narrative, Sam stopped again, eyeing me expectantly. Obviously, he considered his account both important and intelligent but he had lost me completely. After a moment, he confirmed the latter.

"You don't get it, do you, Pete?"

I blinked at him. "You might say that," I admitted.

Except that it wasn't his nature, his sudden smile was almost patronizing. "Where is Millie's?" he asked.

I blinked some more. "Eh?"

Sam's stubby forefinger tapped the desk for emphasis. "It's right across the street from the Fidelity Loan Company."

A glimmer of his inference washed over me. I considered the implication, slowly phrased my thoughts. "This character of yours, a heister, comes to Surf City, spots the Fidelity as a likely job. He'll need help, so he writes some associates." I paused, thinking it through. "When he gets word they're interested, he wires them to come ahead. Then he goes back to casing the site some more, checking traffic, the number of customers, slack periods." I gave him a searching look. "That about it, Sam?"

"That's *exactly* it."

I shook my head. "It won't wash," I told him. "Aside from that 'criminal type' bit which we won't go into again, you have no proof. Just because a man gets a letter, sends a telegram, and then spends an hour in a luncheonette opposite a loan company ..." I gave him an understanding smile. "I know there might be a nice hunk of reward money for nipping a crime in the bud and that you could use it. So could I. But you're letting your imagination run away with you."

He regarded me soberly. "You think that's all it is?"

"I do," I said.

Sam got off my desk. "In that case," he asked me, "how come that just ten minutes ago I tabbed the guy back at the scene? He hasn't got a group with him; just one other man. But the two of them are sitting in a parked car right outside the loan office. And they're both wearing jackets—in this heat—with bulges under their left arms."

"Mixed emotions" is a catchy phrase, and if ever I'd been in doubt as to the precise connotation, I wasn't now. Irritation at Sam's ploy spurted through me; he had shrewdly assessed my initial reaction, had tailored his account for maximum effect and credence. At the same time, full possibility registering, taut urgency gripped me. If the setup Sam had pictured was correct ...

"I figure they're waiting for the noon break, when the force will be smaller," Sam said.

I swore softly. Hubbard and his confounded "hobby" very well could be leading me down the garden path to a big fat zero. But I could no longer ignore the alternative.

"All right," I said shortly, surging to my feet. "We'll see it through."

Sheriff Wexler had taken upstate the car with the official insignia. The unmarked utility sedan into which I piled with Sam might have given me some slight advantage in reaching the scene unheralded, if indeed such an arrival was desirable.

As it was, my deputy's uniform not only broke the heist wide open, but instantly reduced it to the level of near-farce or downright humor.

Because Sam had been right, a holdup was the action. Even as I skidded the sedan around the corner downblock from our objective, I could see the operation already was under way. The sleek convertible parked in front of the building had its motor running, the curb door swung open. The driver hunched over the wheel, watching a second man pushing through the glass entrance doors of the Fidelity Loan Company.

"Stay here!" I shouted at Sam as I braked with a shriek of rubber. The driver of the convertible might not have heard my cry but he certainly caught the whine of tortured tires. His head jerked around, a took of dismay freezing his features (criminal type?) as he glimpsed my uniform. Then his head snapped back and he gunned the motor, zoomed away from the curb.

As I said, the panicky desertion had its comic touch, but I wasn't smiling then. I had my service revolver out, but only a direct score on one of the convertible's rear tires would have stopped the fleeing heister and I didn't want to risk a ricochet's hitting an innocent bystander. I let the car rocket away, sprinted for the loan company.

Again the action was frenetic and quickly decisive. Only two employees, a youngish fellow and an elderly woman, had remained on duty during the lunch break, and the second bandit already had cowed them with a stubby black automatic and was rounding the counter toward an open floor safe. At my lunging entrance, the heister whirled, recognized my status, and blasted a shot at me, whereupon the lady clerk promptly fainted.

The bandit's slug missed. Mine didn't. The gunman reeled back with lead in his thigh and collapsed. Before he could hunker around for a second crack at me, I had kicked the automatic out of his hand, slapped on the cuffs, and it was all over.

The wrapup, though, was equally hectic. As the echoes of the shots faded, the entire area swiftly congested. Pedestrians clotted the sidewalk, babbling, craning their necks. Some of the more venturesome surged into the building to stare, blurt questions. Disregarding my instructions to stay put, Sam Hubbard was one of the latter; the last I saw of him he had wormed his way inside, and was cradling the head of the good woman who had fainted.

By the time I had managed to quiet things down a bit, get an ambulance for the wounded bandit, alert the state police about his escaping associate, and untangle the traffic snarl out front, I had worked up a splitting headache. And my discomfort was destined to increase. Because two hours later, when I had returned to the office and was working on my fifth aspirin, I received a phone call from the loan company manager.

"You'd better get back over here," he told me bluntly. "We've just discovered there's twelve thousand dollars missing."

I'll pass over Sheriff Wexler's more caustic comments about my handling of the case when he returned and learned the details. We've picked up no trace of that twelve grand. Neither have we picked up Sam Hubbard.

Two hours gives you a mighty good head start if you act promptly. Long enough to clear out of town, out of the state, be well on your way to, say, the coast ... or Mexico ... or Canada. With simple living, twelve thousand should tide Sam over for the rest of his years, and wherever he is, I imagine he's getting plenty of satisfaction from realizing his "hobby" finally paid off, after he'd had a sudden stroke of inspiration and simply plucked the money from the open safe, unnoticed, when everybody was milling around ...

Myself, I'd just as soon forget the whole affair.

Beatrice S. Smith

Obligations

The funeral service for Rob Ramsey was held at the new, bright little Catholic church on Evergreen Road in the village of Northfield, where Rob had been born. Sheriff Wilhelmina Pride noted without surprise that at least two hundred local residents were in attendance. Most of them were friends of Rob's deceased parents, small-town people doing what was expected of them.

Wilhelmina looked with approval from one to the other of them during the unfamiliar ceremony. Joe and Ada Williams. Ed Schwartz. Flora Melhuse. Chet and Bertha Krueger. Good, decent people, they had even taken Rob's wife Cindy under their wing since the accident. Cindy had been a complete stranger until six months ago when Rob returned with her to Northfield from wherever it was he'd been for the past twenty years.

Wherever it was hadn't aged Rob much, Wilhelmina mused as she followed the congregation up and down from the kneeler in the back pew. Forty-one years old this coming May, Rob was still incredibly handsome—or had been. For an instant, the bloody mess that had been Rob Ramsey floated, unbidden, through Wilhelmina's mind. But she blanked it out immediately, concentrating instead on Cindy.

Cindy. Short for what? Wilhelmina wondered. Cinderella? She looked like somebody's stepchild—a small, thin waif, with long mouse-colored hair stringing around a pale, woebegone face. Who in the world would have dreamed that Rob Ramsey would finally pick such a wife? Cindy had probably appealed to his vanity, Wilhelmina decided. Rob had always needed adoration to give him confidence. Poor, stupid man. Well, it didn't matter now. Nothing mattered. Rob was dead. Dead! Wilhelmina still could hardly believe it.

The priest was standing up there in front of the altar, chanting the prayer for the dead, as the altar boy swung a censer filled with burning incense past the casket—*Rob's* casket. The smoke suddenly made Wilhelmina's eyes water. She dabbed at them, surreptitiously, hoping no one thought she was crying over Rob. Actually, she felt nothing at all.

"Sheriff," a voice hissed from behind her, as the Mass was nearing its end.

Wilhelmina turned. Ned Zander, her deputy, cupped his hand near Wilhelmina's ear and whispered, "We got the bear."

Wilhelmina got up quickly, effortlessly, in spite of her girth, and followed Ned outside.

"She was a big sow," Ned continued. "Had nearly two inches of pure fat over her rump."

"All bears get fat before denning," Wilhelmina said, squinting in the fall sunshine. "Who shot her?"

"Olaf Hanson. But he didn't shoot her. He set a trap over by the dump where it happened. He lives nearby, you know."

Wilhelmina stiffened. "Olaf set a *trap?* By whose authority?"

Ned hesitated. "Nobody's. I guess he thought he was doing folks a favor. And he was too, I'd say."

"I wouldn't!" Wilhelmina snapped. "Trapping bears is against the law in this state." She snorted. "It probably isn't even the same bear!"

"Yes, it is." Ned moistened his lips. "Old man Hanson found Rob's ring in the bear's stomach."

"Rob's ring?" Wilhelmina repeated, frowning.

"Yes. You know that black onyx one with the little diamond that he always wore."

Wilhelmina breathed an almost inaudible "Oh," and ducked her head for an instant, then abruptly headed for the police car.

Ned followed close behind. "I guess rings aren't so easy to digest as flesh and bones." He shivered. "I never saw such a mess as when you and I picked Rob up that night. Why, he—"

Wilhelmina whirled. "No need to go into that, Ned," she said sharply, then more calmly, "Where is it?"

"The bear? Old man Hanson butchered it. He likes bear meat, he says."

"I meant the ring." Wilhelmina's voice was impatient.

"Oh, the ring. I got it here. Old man Hanson said I should give it to you." Ned reached two fingers into his shirt pocket and plucked out a black onyx ring and handed it to Wilhelmina. "Look. It isn't bent or dented or anything. And the diamond is still there. Can you imagine that?"

Wilhelmina took the ring, looked at it briefly. A long examination wasn't necessary, for the ring was familiar. She herself had given it to Rob as a birthday present when he was eighteen. It had taken her months to pay back the money her father had reluctantly lent her. "From a secret pal" was all she had written on the birthday card. How young and foolish she'd been! It hardly seemed possible that she and that other girl were the same person.

"I don't think we ought to tell Cindy where the ring was, do you, sheriff?" Ned was saying. When Wilhelmina didn't respond immediately, he added, "We could just say we found it at the site of the accident or something like that, couldn't we?" He turned an anxious face toward Wilhelmina.

"I'm not sure what to do," she said. "I'll put it away until I decide. Right now I'm going out to see Olaf."

Ned cleared his throat. "Ah—sheriff—"

"Yes?" Wilhelmina turned.

"You—ah—aren't going to call the warden or anything, are you? I mean," he added quickly, "Olaf Hanson is an old man, practically senile. I don't think arresting him would do much good, do you?"

Wilhelmina sighed. "I guess not. But I'm certainly going to give him a good talking to. He had no business trapping that bear. Somehow he considers himself above the law. He—" She broke off. "Do you want a ride back to town, Ned?"

Ned bobbed his head. "If it isn't out of your way. The wife's driving mine to the cemetery."

"And you're not going?"

"I would, but I have to work." Ned glanced at Wilhelmina. "Aren't you going?"

"To the cemetery? No, not this time," Wilhelmina said quietly, her face expressionless. "Hop in." She gestured toward the big station wagon, then climbed into the seat behind the wheel.

They rode in silence for most of the way. Ned looked from time to time at Wilhelmina, whose profile was severe, with broad planes, a high-bridged nose, a strong, full jaw, and a thick head of hair, prematurely white and cut short. Ned was ten years younger than Wilhelmina and obviously uncomfortable in her presence, though he'd been working with her since she was elected eight years ago. He was so fidgety, in fact, that Wilhelmina felt an unfamiliar impulse to make small talk. But she wasn't naturally gregarious and could think of nothing to say.

A few minutes later she pulled up in front of the hardware store where Ned clerked in his off hours. "This all right?"

"Fine, sheriff, thanks." Ned raised his hand in a kind of salute as he hopped out of the car. "I'll be here if you want me for anything."

Wilhelmina nodded, waved, smiled absently. She sometimes wondered if she had made a mistake in appointing Ned her deputy. He was efficient enough, but unable to hide shock at the sight of violent death, too prone to overlook misdemeanors, too lenient in all of his dealings. The trouble was, people knew his weakness and often took advantage of him—as Olaf Hanson had, for instance. Or was the way Olaf behaved her own fault? Wilhelmina thought that perhaps it was.

Ten minutes later she turned into Olaf's front yard, scattering chickens and setting up a clatter of barking dogs.

"Easy, Duke, easy," she murmured to a collie that trotted beside her, growling, as she walked toward the house.

Olaf met her at the door. He was a big man in his late seventies, stooped, with a long bony face, sparse tobacco-stained teeth, and large knobby-jointed hands. "Howdy, Wilhelmina. I been expectin' you," he said, holding open the door.

The house smelled of stale coffee, improperly dried oak, and stale sweat. Wilhelmina ran a finger back and forth under her nostrils, angry for noticing, wishing such inconsequential things didn't bother her quite so much. Olaf was a decent man, she reminded herself, making do as best he could on a small pension. What did it matter how his house smelled? As old and arthritic as he was, he did well to keep a roof over his head without any help.

"How's your ma these days?" Olaf asked, as he lowered himself slowly into an ancient armchair.

Wilhelmina, still standing, shrugged. "About the same. Some days she knows me, some days she doesn't. But she's happy enough, I think."

"You was a good girl to come back home and take care of your ma, Wilhelmina. Your pa would of been proud of you." He snorted. "Most kids nowadays ship the old folks to the county home soon as they start slippin' a little." He took a plug of tobacco from a package and stuffed it into his mouth. "Guess I'm lucky I never had any kids." He looked up quickly. "Not that I woulda minded one like you."

Wilhelmina smiled. "I'm no kid, Olaf. I'll be forty-one in June."

The old man shifted his tobacco from one side of his mouth to the other. "That's a kid, as far as I'm concerned." Then brightly, "You want a cup of coffee? I got some from breakfast."

"No. No, thank you. I'm in a hurry today."

"You're always in a hurry," the old man grumbled. "Your pa never was. He always had time to chew the rag a little."

"I know." Wilhelmina sighed. Her father had been dead eight years and people still compared the differences between them. It annoyed Wilhelmina sometimes. Not often. She was well aware that it was mainly because she was Sheriff Herb Pride's daughter that she herself had been elected. The fact that she had been a policewoman in Chicago for ten years helped too, of course. But not as much as being her father's daughter. A folk hero, that's the way the townspeople had regarded Herb Pride, a paragon of wisdom and virtue, who not only was a good friend and fine lawman, but cooked and cleaned and took care of his daughter and invalid wife as well.

Olaf had been a close friend of her father. They had been born on adjoining farms, had gone to the same one-room school, hunted, fished, trapped together, belonged to the same Lutheran church, all those things. Was that why she had decided not to arrest Olaf for trapping the bear? Or was she becoming mushy like Ned? Wilhelmina scowled. It wasn't because she thought Olaf had done the right thing, that was certain.

"Here." The old man held out a cracked saucer. "You look hungry. Have a piece of candy."

Wilhelmina glanced at the small star-shaped chocolate candies wrapped in foil. "Ummm," she murmured appreciatively, picked one, unwrapped it, and placed the foil on the table.

"Still fond of them little chocolates, ain't you, Wilhelmina?"

Wilhelmina nodded, chewing, swallowing. "Yes. Dad used to buy them for me by the pound."

"I remember." The old man rubbed a bent finger over his right eyelid. "He was a good man, your pa, the best friend I ever had."

Silence for a moment, a silence too fragile for Wilhelmina to break; then she said, quietly, "Olaf, you had no business trapping that bear."

The old man shifted his tobacco once again. "That old sow was the one that killed Rob Ramsey. I found his ring. Didn't Ned tell you?"

"Yes, Ned told me," Wilhelmina replied. "But you didn't know that before you trapped her."

The old man grunted. "What's the difference? Ain't all bears supposed to be killers?"

"That's nonsense. You know it and so do I. Bears aren't any more vicious than other predators."

"Other critters don't kill people," the old man countered.

Wilhelmina frowned. "Neither would bears if people would quit feeding them and trying to make pets out of them."

"Yeah, you're right. Dang city folks don't know nothin'." Olaf wiped a dribble of tobacco juice from his lower lip. "But Rob Ramsey was born and raised here in bear country same as you and me. He shoulda knowed better than to sleep out there by the dump at night. Them bears been hangin' out in that exact same spot for years."

Wilhelmina took another chocolate. "Rob wasn't much of an outdoor type, even when he was young," she said, chewing slowly, reflectively.

"What was he doin' out there by the dump, then?"

"Taking pictures. Photography was his hobby. He was trying to get some action shots of the bears."

"Well, if'n it was action he wanted, he sure got it." Olaf shook his head. "He shoulda asked somebody first 'fore he started foolin' around out there."

"I warned him," Wilhelmina said quietly. "But he just slapped me on the back and laughed, as he always did."

The old man narrowed his eyes. "You was kinda sweet on Rob once, wasn't you, Wilhelmina?"

"Why—it was just a high school crush. Lots of girls were crazy about Rob Ramsey." Wilhelmina reached for another chocolate, her eyes blank.

The old man snorted. "Don't kid me. You was busted all to pieces when he took some other gal to the prom that time."

Wilhelmina blinked. "Who told you that?"

"Your pa. He used to come here and set and talk by the hour 'bout you." The old man took out a soiled handkerchief and blew his nose. After stuffing it back into his pocket, he said, "You gave Rob that black ring I found, didn't you?"

"Dad told you that, too?" Wilhelmina's face remained impassive, but it took some effort. She was surprised how much the small betrayal hurt. Yet, how could she blame her father? With a chronically ill wife, he likely had no one in whom to confide except Olaf. "That was a long time ago," she said softly.

The old man rubbed the stubble on his chin, shut one eye. "Only five, ten years. That ain't long."

"It was twenty-four years ago, Olaf. I was seventeen at the time." Wilhelmina smiled ruefully. "And a pretty dumb seventeen at that."

"Not dumb. No, you was never dumb, Wilhelmina." The old man leaned forward. "Neither your pa nor me could ever figure what you seen in that Rob Ramsey. Why, he wasn't worth your little finger, girl!" Olaf declared loudly.

Wilhelmina chuckled. "You and Dad weren't prejudiced, by any chance?"

"Nope." The old man leaned back and folded his arms across his chest. "You never forgot him, did you, Wilhelmina?"

"Dad? Of course not!"

"No. I mean Rob Ramsey. You never forgot him. And when he came back here to Northfield to live, you was awful happy at first, even if'n he did have a wife, weren't you, Willie?"

"Don't call me that," Wilhelmina said, her voice rising.

"That's what Rob called you, ain't it?" The old man smiled the sly, self-satisfied smile of superior knowledge.

"No—yes. I don't know. I've always hated it. It's a silly name."

"Especially for a girl," Olaf said. Then gently, "That was the trouble, wasn't it? Rob never thought of you as a girl. You was always 'Willie' to him. And when he come back after all them years, he acted the same, slappin' you on the back, treatin' you like you was a man. It 'bout tore your heart out, ain't that right, Wilhelmina?"

"Olaf, no, I—" Something seemed to have happened to her throat. The words wouldn't come out.

"It don't do no good to lie to me, girl. The only person Rob Ramsey had eyes for was that skinny little wife of his. And after all them years of waitin', you just couldn't take it no more, ain't that right?"

"No, Olaf, no—"

The old man broke in, "That's why he was murdered, ain't it?"

Wilhelmina stared at the old man, wide-eyed. Then she got hold of herself and said calmly, "What's the matter with you? Rob's death was accidental. He was camped out by the dump, waiting to take pictures of the bears, when one attacked him."

The old man shook his head. "Bears don't attack people less'n they have a mighty good reason. You and me know that, don't we, Wilhelmina?"

"What are you talking about?" Wilhelmina said, her voice sharp.

"I'm talkin' about these." The old man reached over and picked up several pieces of foil from the table and held them out flat in his palm for Wilhelmina to see. "I found a bunch of these inside the bear—besides the ring, I mean."

Her face colorless, Wilhelmina looked first at the candy wrappings, then at the old man.

"Yep," he continued. "When I seen these little bits of tinfoil, I knowed they come from them little chocolate candies you like."

Wilhelmina didn't answer. There was a dazed, unbelieving look in her eyes.

The old man continued: "Somebody musta give them candies to Rob before he bedded down that night, knowin' full well that this time of year before dennin', bears can't get enough to eat. They're huntin' to fill their bellies all the time. And they're lazy like the rest of us. They'll sniff out the nearest tidbit, 'specially if'n it's sweet, and tear apart whatever is 'tween them and it, no matter if it's human or not. Ain't that right, Wilhelmina?"

"No—" Wilhelmina choked. "That's crazy, Olaf!"

"No, it ain't crazy. It makes a lotta sense!" The old man spoke with passion. "After all you been through on account of that no-good Rob Ramsey, he deserved what he got!"

"Olaf—you—"

"It's no use talkin', Wilhelmina. I done it, just like I told you. And I ain't one bit sorry, neither." The old man reached out and patted Wilhelmina's arm. "Now run on home like a good girl, and tell your pa to come over. I want to talk to him."

Larry Niven

$16,940.00

When the phone rings late at night, there is a limit to who it can be. I had three guesses as I picked it up: a wrong number (all wrong numbers are the same person), Lois, or—I didn't bother to think his name. It isn't his, anyway.

"Hello?"

"Hello," he said. "You know who this is?"

"Kelsey." It's the name he tells me. "What is it, Kelsey? You're not due for another four months."

"I need an advance. Are you sitting down?"

"I'm in bed, you—" Reading a book, but I didn't tell him that. Better he should be off balance.

"Sorry. I just wanted you braced. I need sixteen thousand—"

"Bug off!" I slammed down the phone.

There was no point in picking up the book. He'd call again. Sometimes he waits a few minutes to make me nervous. This time the phone started ringing almost immediately, and I snatched it up in the same instant and held it to my ear without saying anything. It's a kind of bluffing game, one I always lose.

"Kelsey again, and I'm not kidding. I need sixteen thousand, nine hundred and forty dollars. I need it by the end of the week."

"You know perfectly well I can't do that. I can't make that much money disappear without somebody noticing: Lois, the bank, the Bureau of Internal Revenue. Dammit, Kelsey, we've worked this thing out before."

"The best laid plans of mice and men—"

"Go to hell." Something hit me then. "That's a funny number. As long as I can't pay anyway, why not make it seventeen thousand, or twenty? Why, uh, sixteen thousand, nine hundred and forty?"

"It just worked out that way." He sounded defensive.

I probed. "What way?"

"You aren't my only client."

"Client? I'm a blackmail victim! At least be honest with yourself, Kelsey."

"I am. Shall I tell you what you are?"

"No." Someone might be listening, which was the point he was trying to make. "You've got other clients, huh? Go to one of *them*."

"I did. It was a mistake." He hesitated, then went on. "Let's call him Horatio, okay? Horatio was a bank teller, long ago. He owns a hardware store now. I've known him about five years. I had to trace him myself, you understand. He embezzled some money while he was a teller."

"What did he do, die on you when the mortgage was due?" I put sarcastic sympathy in my voice.

"I wish he had. No, he waited for my usual call, which I make on April Fools' Day. Not my idea; his. I call him once a year, just like you. so I called him and told him he was due, and he said he couldn't afford it any more. He got kind of brave-panicky, you know how it goes—"

"Don't I just, damn you."

"—and he said he wouldn't pay me another red cent if he had to go to prison for it. I got him to agree to meet me at a bar and grill. I hated doing that, Carson. I thought he might try to kill me."

"Occupational hazard. I may return to this subject." I had threatened to kill Kelsey before this.

He sounded dispirited. "It won't help you. I'm careful, Carson. I took a gun, and it was a public place, and I got there first. Besides, there are my files. If I die the cops'll go through them."

I was going to need that information someday, maybe, but it wasn't fun to hear. "So you met him in this bar and grill. What then?"

"Well, he had the money with him. He put it right out on the table, and I grabbed it quick because someone might be watching. Someone was, too. I saw the flashbulb go off, and by the time my eyes had stopped watering, whoever it was had gone out the door. Ra—" He caught himself. "Horatio stopped me from getting out. He said, 'Do you know what the statute of limitations is for embezzlement?'

"I remembered then. It was seven years, and Horatio had me in a box. Blackmail. He figures I've taken him for sixteen thousand nine hundred dollars and no cents, plus forty bucks for the guy with the camera. He wants it back or he turns me in to the police, complete with photographs."

Kelsey had never heard me laugh before and mean it. "That's hilarious. the Biter Bit bit. If you turn in your files it'll only be more evidence against you. You'll just have to fight it out in court, Kelsey. Tell 'em it's a first offense."

"I've got a better idea. I'll get the money from you."

"Nope. If I make that much money disappear, too many people would start wondering why. If they find out, I'm dead. *Dead.* Now I want you to remember that word, Kelsey, because it's important."

"Files, Carson. I want you to remember that word, because it's important to you. If I die, somebody will go through my files and then call the cops."

Well, it hadn't worked. Poor hard-luck Kelsey. "Okay, Kelsey. I'll have the money. Where can we meet?"

"No need. Just get it to me the usual way."

"Now, don't be a damn fool. I probably can't get it until Saturday, which means I'll have to get it to you Sunday. There isn't any mail on Sunday."

He didn't answer for a while. Then, "Are you thinking of killing me?"

I kept it light. "I'm always thinking of killing you, Kelsey."

"Files."

"I *know*. Do you want the money or don't you?"

I listened to the scared silence on the other end. Dammit, I didn't want him scared. I was going to have to kill him, but I'd have to find out where the files were first, and for that I'd have to have him alone, somewhere far away, for several hours. He was going to be too wary for that. I could sense it.

"Listen, there's a third way," he said suddenly. "If you move the money, someone's likely to notice. If you kill me someone's *sure* to notice. But there's a third way."

"Let's hear it."

"Kill Horatio."

I yelped. 'Kelsey, what do you think I am, Murder, Incorporated? I made one mistake. *One*."

"You're not thinking, Carson. There's no connection between you and Horatio. None! Zilch! You can't even be suspected ..." He went on and on, but I was way ahead of him. If I could get the file Horatio had on Kelsey, I'd have Kelsey. No more payments. We'd have each other by the throat.

Poor hard-luck Horatio.

Talmage Powell
Bertillon's Odds

Dear Marshall:

Enjoyed the visit. Glad your trip coincided with my vacation. But you should have stayed over another day. Pete Gonzales pulled a hundred-forty-six-pound tarpon out of the Gulf where we spent that last day fishing. Anyway, your faith in the location, barely out of sight of the Coast Guard light on Panama Key, was justified.

The Langborn murder broke the day after I reported back to work. Knowing that your interest in police work has been more than academic since your days as a crime reporter (and as a comfort when you think of that hundred-forty-six-pounder), I'm going to tell you about the Langborn case. Because one detail in it is unique, and I don't use the word lightly. Nothing like it has ever turned up in the history of police work, and I doubt that it will ever happen again.

The Langborn of whom I speak was the crotchety old cuss, Carson Langborn. Just in case the name isn't familiar to you, he was a West Virginia coal mine operator who retired and came here about six years ago. A cantankerous citizen, he was forever pestering the city manager. Too many street lights were wasting electricity, or there was too much horn-blowing on our downtown streets. Nothing was done in City Hall without his vociferous opposition. His disposition was as gloomy as the damp burrows he caused to be made in the earth.

He was married six times, and even the best of his wives was unable to stay with him. The sixth, a Mary Scorbin, died of a sudden illness, making a dramatic escape from his tyranny.

All of his marriages were childless, although Mary Scorbin Langborn had a son by a previous marriage. His name was Gary. He was a good looking youth, dark, slender, rangy, with a suggestion of whiplike strength in his sinews.

Conditioned by twenty years of police work, my instincts didn't react favorably to Gary. There was a brooding in his face, a coldness in his eyes. He struck me as having more sneering contempt than conscience for the unimportant nonentities comprising the remainder of the human race.

I recognized the material groundlessness of my aversion to the twenty-year-old Gary, and I determined not to let it color my actions. As a police officer, it was my job to remain objective and impartial.

The old man and Gary were living alone on the Langborn estate prior to the murder. Gary discovered the body, called us, and was waiting quietly and unemotionally when we arrived.

A squad car, radioed out, was the first to reach the Langborn home. Following the two uniformed cruiser men were Marty Sims and myself in a black sedan assigned to the detective division. Close on our exhaust fumes were Rynold from the lab and Doc Jenkins, elected coroner just this year.

The house was an ugly, sterile, two story wooden structure reminiscent of a large Georgia or South Carolina farm. The dormer windows stared bleakly at us. I wouldn't have been surprised if Langborn had added lightning rods at the ends of the gable.

On the long front porch, leaning idly against a wooden post, stood Gary Scorbin. He took his cigarette from his lips and flicked it in the yard.

"The old man's in there."

Gary followed as Marty and I went inside. Langborn had seemingly transported his parlor from a much earlier West Virginia home. The furnishings were heavy and dark, out of keeping with our sunny clime.

"This way," Gary said in the manner of an impersonal guide.

Langborn had met his end in a room off the parlor. I suppose it was his study. There was a desk, leather couch and chairs, bookcase, a low chest—and a wall safe. I saw the safe before I saw Langborn. The safe had been ripped open.

"He kept three or four thousand in there," Gary said. "I warned him."

As I moved deeper in the room, I saw Langborn. The desk had obscured him. An old, dried-up hank of bones in his clothes, he lay as if he had pitched face forward. The side of his cheek touched the carpet. All the gray, brown-blotched skin of his face had collapsed against his skull. A single bullet had entered the back of his head. It remained in his brain.

The room remained very quiet as Rynold and Doc Jenkins came in. The two uniformed officers remained on guard, one at the door of the room, one on the porch.

Rynold marked the position of the cadaver (a very apt word, in its connotations, for this particular corpse) and started taking pictures. Doc chewed on his cigar and went to one knee beside the corpse.

As you know, there are few outward dramatics at such a scene. On the surface, it's a cut-and-dried job. Details are recorded, in brains and on paper. Each man knows his job and wastes few motions. The inner meaning of the scene depends on a man's individual reaction to death. There is no better reminder that you are mortal, and there is violence in the world.

"Been dead three, four hours is my preliminary estimate," Doc said. "No doubt the bullet killed him."

Marty had searched for the gun. "No murder weapon in here."

Rynold went over the empty safe for fingerprints. I motioned Gary Scorbin to the parlor. He obeyed quickly enough, but he was able to impart in his action a suggestion of insolence.

"Is everything in there just as you found it?"

"Yeah, I guess it is."

"You touch anything?"

He shrugged. "The old man. I half turned him, saw he was dead, let him fall back. Started to look in the safe, but didn't touch it. Thought you'd want to look for fingerprints."

"Any servants here?"

"Nope, just the old skinflint. Woman comes in three times a week to clean. Today wasn't one of her days."

"Better fill me in on your movements today."

Again he shrugged. I was to learn that he used the gesture habitually. He managed to make it irritating. "I got up. The old man hit the deck couple hours before, about eight. We squabbled, as usual. I told him to go to hell and went down the beach."

"Spend the whole day there?"

"The afternoon," he said.

"See anyone you know?"

That shrug. "Why should I? I didn't know he was going to get bumped off. I got no alibi, if that's what you mean. I guess people saw me here and there."

"I suggest you turn a couple of them up."

He looked at me levelly. He had heavy brows and thick, dark lashes a woman would have envied. "You want 'em, you turn 'em up. I don't have to prove anything, now do I?"

I endured the urge to give him the back of my hand across the petulant lips.

"What did you do all afternoon?"

"Drank beer. Watched some guys fish off the causeway. Swam at the public beach. Came home. Found the old twister and hollered for the law." His tone was flat, telling me I could like it or lump it. In either event I was going to have to swallow it.

"You and Mr. Langborn argue often?"

His shoulders rose and fell. "All the time."

"What about?"

"Money. Me getting a job."

"You don't work?"

"Why should I? He's got . . . he had plenty."

"You know," I said. "It's a wonder he didn't throw you out."

His laugh revealed complete lack of fear of me and total disregard for my opinion. "When you got right down to it, he was scared. I could see right through him. I was the only one who ever stood up to him. He'd disposed of everybody he'd ever had. I was all he had left."

Gary stretched and yawned, the back of his hand against his mouth. "You all finished?"

"For now, maybe. You see any strangers around, any suspicious characters?"

"Nope."

"No one leaving the house as you approached?"

"Nope."

"Any idea who might have done this?"

"Nope."

"Who knew about the safe, besides you and Mr. Langborn?"

"How should I know? People up and down the beach, I guess. You know word of a miser gets around."

"A miser doesn't usually broadcast the location of his strongbox," I said.

My meaning was clear, and he got it. "Look, pal, the secret wasn't so sacred with me."

In satisfied repose, his face was clean-cut, boyish. Those lashes gave it innocence. I'll admit I was frightened, in a strange, chilling way. More frightened by this boy than by a professional criminal.

Up and down the beach he'd gone, telling of the safe and its contents, hoping the fact would eventually fall on sufficiently greedy and unprincipled ears ...

I'm not easily shocked, but this shocked me, this invitatioin for some hoodlum or narcotics addict to rob and kill a hated and rich stepfather. It was as clever as it was cowardly and mean, and the boy was legally in the clear.

"You want me," he said, "I'll be at the Pelican Motel on the beach."

Rynold reported there were no fingerprints on the safe. It had been wiped clean. But we found the murder weapon a short while later, in a storm drain two dozen yards from the house, where the murderer had tossed it.

It was a .32 caliber revolver, one shot fired, loaded with jacketed slugs. Our later checkup showed the gun was unregistered, bought in a pawnshop or back booth of a dingy bar somewhere. Which made it untraceable.

Sims and I stayed close to Rynold as he went over the gun for fingerprints. As on the Langborn safe—none. Wiped clean.

Then Rynold, rating A-plus, carefully ejected the unfired bullets. On one of them we found a single print, put there when the gun had been loaded, perhaps days before the opportunity came to use it.

Rynold methodically ran a ballistics, and clinched it. The gun had killed Carson Langborn.

While I attempted a fingerprint identification, Sims and a small crew of men finecombed the Langborn neighborhood.

Our first findings were negative. I was unable to match the print with any on file here, in Tampa, Miami, or Tallahassee.

Sims was unable to find any evidence of strangers or suspicious characters in the neighborhood the day of the murder. His search extended to the bars and joints on the beach, to the questioning of every known hoodlum he laid hands on. He got nowhere. No thug was spending beyond his means. No hoodlum had boasted drunkenly in his cups. Stool pigeons were all as helpful as blank paper.

Meanwhile, the youth drank beer and swam at the Pelican's private strip of Gulf beach.

And I, as officer in charge of the investigation, was faced by the absolute paradox. For when I sent that print to Washington, it was readily identified.

It belonged to a man named Clement J. Smith.

He lived in Napa, Idaho.

During World War II he had worked at White Sands, New Mexico, where the FBI had fingerprinted him and given him top clearance.

He was a leading citizen in the community.

He had never heard of Carson Langborn. He had never been in West Virginia or in Florida.

He was beyond suspicion. Everything about him was known and could be proved. He'd been busy conducting his own affairs at the moment Langborn, a stranger among millions, was murdered.

In short, a fingerprint (which doesn't lie) had turned up in an utterly impossible time and place.

Surely, someone had made a mistake. I accused Rynold, and in our frustration, we almost argued. Then I doublechecked with Washington.

The possibility of mistake was eliminated. The final conference between Rynold, Sims, and myself lasted nearly two hours in my office. We dredged up every explanation our minds could devise.

Finally, Sims said haggardly, "We're losing sight on the case. I think we better back out of this hole and take a fresh start on solving Langborn's murder."

"How about the fingerprint?" Rynold persisted.

"Relegate it to the Fortian heap of facts science can't explain," Sims said.

"Science can explain any material fact with sufficient data," Rynold said. "If an explanation fails, it's because the data ..."

"Trouble with you microscope-lookers," Sims said, "is that you trot out your good guesses, then cover your ignorance with excuses."

I cut in: "You've given me an idea, Marty, and a good one, too."

"Yeah?"

"Well, both of you. You with your talk about getting on with the Langborn case, and Rynold with his talk of data."

Both of them gave me their attentiion.

"That boy killed his stepfather," I said. "Everything so far makes it more glaringly apparent. If it had been simple robbery and murder, we'd have heard some whisper, however faint, as thoroughly as we've covered this thing.

"We know what happened. He scattered the tale of the secret hoard in the old man's safe to give him the subtlest of alibis. He slipped unseen to the house, killed the old man, ripped the safe open—wearing gloves—and slipped back to the beach. Later, he returned, supposedly discovered Langborn, and called us. He probably destroyed the money in the safe. The amount was of no moment, compared to what he would inherit.

"And here we are, helpless. He's as cunning as any man we've ever faced. If he'd tried to set up an alibi for the exact time of the old man's death, all we'd have to do is crack it and we'd have him cold. As it is, he's dependent on nothing and no one but himself. No alibi witness for us to work on, no secrets about his relations between him and Langborn for us to turn up. He swims and enjoys his beer while we beat ourselves to a frazzle trying to find proof that'll stand up in court."

I started toward the door. "Come on, Marty. Let's see if we can't crack this young tiger."

"How about the fingerprint?" Rynold said, unable to get it off his mind.

"I hope," I said, "we can make it work for us."

The boy was rolling with the grace of a porpoise a quarter mile offshore when Marty and I reached the water's edge.

I cupped my hands and yelled Gary's name. He swam in and stood up in shallow water, his hide sleek and burnished.

He came out and walked to the spot where he'd spread a large beach towel on the sand. He picked up a smaller towel, dried his hands, and stooped to get cigarettes and matches.

"Have you made any arrangements about your stepfather, Gary?" I asked.

"Going to plant him tomorrow, if you release the body. I called the undertaker and told him to attend to it."

"Aren't you going to ask why we're here, if we've arrested someone?"

"I really don't care, flatfoot. Your arrests don't interest me."

"This one will."

"Yeah?"

"We're going to arrest you, Gary, and take you to headquarters and have a look at your fingerprints."

He looked from Marty to me. "If you're trying to scare me, forget it."

"I'd know better than to try and scare you, Gary. Anyway, you wiped the fingerprints off the gun."

"What's fingerprints got to do with it?"

"Well, somebody loaded the gun and then some time passed. And then he used the gun. He remembered to wipe it clean—but in the stress of the moment, he forgot that there might have been a print on one of the bullets."

Marty and I moved on him from different angles. He backed a step. He dropped his cigarette. "What kind of bluff ..."

"No bluff, Gary," I said. "Just a single fingerprint on a bullet. If you're innocent ..."

He kicked sand in my face, ducked past Marty, and ran down the beach. The bright sun shone on his fleeing figure, the pastel pink of the Pelican, and the pastel aqua of a convertible on the edge of the motel's parking lot. He was angling toward the convertible, a track man neither Marty nor I could come anywhere near matching.

Marty dropped to one knee, pulled his revolver, and fired over the boy's head.

The bullet gave Gary fresh speed.

Marty took careful aim. His second shot tore a piece of flesh from Gary's thigh. The boy pitched forward and went rolling.

Later, in a cell, Gary decided to trade a signed confession for a chance of escaping the chair. We still use the electric chair in our state, and the thought of it filled him with a particular horror. His story pretty well coincided with our conclusions.

I'm not at all sure we needed the confession. The fingerprint nailed it down for us. That's right. His print was a perfect match for the one Rynold discovered on the bullet.

And what of Clement J. Smith, a stranger nearly a continent away, an unknown among millions?

The explanation is simple. His print matched also.

You may recall that Bertillon himself, the great French anthropologist who laid the groundwork for the system, recognized the mathematical possibility of duplicate fingerprints. The odds against it are about two billion to one.

But the laws of chance are undeniable, and in a way, I suppose, what happened here was inevitable, somewhere, sometime.

So perhaps it isn't as unique as I'd like to think. I've no way of knowing how many millions upon millions of fingerprints have been taken throughout the world in all the long decades during which the science has been in use.

I only know that Clement Smith and Gary Scorbin possessed the first known two-billionth digits in common.

I'll give Pete Gonzales your compliments on the hundred-forty-six-pounder.

> Your friend,
> R. D. Singer—Captain
> Detective Division

P. S. Maybe the Langborn case will suggest a story to you. Not being a writer, I wouldn't know how to work it up. I imagine you'll think of the Clement J. Smith angle. He was lucky. But what if, tomorrow or two hundred years from now, another two-billionth print led to an accusation against a guy who wasn't so clearly innocent as Smith? Now wouldn't he be in a mess?

Don Tothe
The Zigzag Line

As he moved, noiselessly, along the narrow asphalt walkway, his eyes searched the pleasant surroundings of the quiet park. He thought about the girl he was looking for, pictured her in his mind, knew that she had to be found tonight, tonight in the next few hours.

He had started in downtown L.A. seven nights ago, had moved, relentlessly and systematically, westward through the city, pausing in a hundred dingy bars, wandering through the smoky lobbies of a dozen cheap hotels.

Now he had gone as far west as he could go without boarding a boat. The city and the land ended. The ocean took over.

The Chamber of Commerce of Santa Monica sign had welcomed him to this grassy park, shaded by towering palms and bordered along one edge by a jagged cliff that provided an aura of danger for the sightseers. It was called Inspiration Point Park.

The headache, more agonizing now than ever before, pounded at his temples without mercy. The pressure, steadily mounting for a week, since this latest search had begun, threatened to blow apart his skull.

His pace slackened. With his left hand he massaged the back of his neck. So tight, the muscles there so tense. His shoulders, too, were locked and aching from the tension that gripped his body.

His right hand remained in the pocket of his neatly tailored sport jacket, his fingers around the smooth wooden handle of the ice pick.

He stopped, his attention drawn to the sun just disappearing into the ocean, a gold coin slipping into a magic slot along the blue horizon.

"Beautiful," he murmured, "beautiful."

He stood perfectly still for several minutes, admiring the sight, his hands resting on the top board of the low fence that traced a wavy line ten feet back from the sheer dropoff. Two hundred feet directly below him ran the Coast Highway. Along the other side of the road stood a line of fancy swimming clubs interspersed with expensively rustic private beach houses. The sandy beach, continually attacked by the onslaught of the pounding, white-frothed waves, was almost deserted. Only a handful of brave swimmers, practically dots from where he stood, bobbed in the surf. Here and there a beach towel being shaken off fluttered in the air.

When the only thing left of the sun was an orange glow at the edge of the horizon, he turned away, saddened. His mind compared it to the sight of a woman dying. But then none of them had died as beautifully as the sun buried itself every day.

He was almost to the end of the park when he saw her. She sat alone on a bench, looking out toward the sea.

He stopped, shammed weariness by taking a deep breath. He adjusted the ice pick so it wouldn't stick him in the side as he settled on a bench twenty feet from where she waited.

Waited? He laughed to himself. Why was he always so positive they were waiting, waiting just for him?

He studied her face first. Her red hair was cut short, too short for his taste. But it was the right color. She appeared to be reasonably attractive. He guessed her to be close to thirty. Close enough, he thought, close enough for the plan.

As he watched her, she arched her back and stretched her arms over her head and yawned. Her shortsleeved red sweater tightened against her breasts. She crossed her legs after adjusting her skintight black Capris.

She hadn't looked directly at him but she was aware of his presence, his attention. Each one of her little maneuvers had been timed for his benefit. He was certain of all this. He'd seen enough of these easy pickups to recognize their tactics instantly.

She flicked open a lighter, torched a cigarette, and sensually inhaled. When she blew out the smoke it dispersed and quickly drifted away on the ocean breeze that raced up and over the cliff.

Finally, she did look at him. Their eyes met. A smile crossed her lips.

Without hesitating, he stood up. She continued to watch him as he walked toward her on the bench. He sat down next to her, took out a cigarette for himself.

"Nice view," he offered, without looking at her.

"Yes, isn't it?" He saw that she had difficulty forming her words.

"Mind if I sit here?"

"Mind?" She giggled. "I was beginning to wonder when you'd get around to it."

Her bourboned breath stung his nostrils. *Pretty well loaded. Good,* he thought, *that's good.*

Neither wedding band nor engagement ring graced the third finger of her left hand, or any other finger. Her skin was dark, suntanned. Obviously, no ring had been removed recently.

Unmarried. So far, so good. So far, perfect.

He matched her frankness. "I've never been called a slow worker before."

"You do all right, mister."

"Thanks."

He moved closer to her on the bench. She smiled, dreamily, drunkenly.

"Jo's the name," she told him, allowing the cigarette smoke to float out of her mouth as she spoke. "Jo, for Joanne. What's yours?"

"David." There was no need to lie to her—she had no more than two or three hours to live.

"Well, Davey old boy, how about a drink or two? Or three or four?"

"You seem to be a few ahead of me."

"Wanna try catching up?" She grabbed his arm and stood up. "We can take care of it in a hurry. Come on, handsome."

He allowed her to guide him away from the bench. When they had gone ten steps he pointed toward the curb. "There's my car."

She waved a careless hand. "Car? Who needs a car?" She giggled at the look of surprise on his face, and squeezed his arm. "My place is right over there."

She nodded toward what looked like a small white building surrounded by a parking lot. The driveway leading into it was no more than thirty yards from where the car stood.

When they reached the very edge of the park, he saw then that the parking lot was actually the top floor of a high-rise apartment house. What he had thought was a small building was simply the lobby entrance.

A sign told him the place was called The Surfwatcher. The Surfwatcher's south side hugged the face of the cliffs. Private verandahs on every floor, facing the Pacific, rose directly above the highway. He counted eight stories. The building was set on a plateau at least fifty feet higher than the road.

"You live alone?" The Surfwatcher seemed hardly a haven for single girls.

She nodded. "Surprised?"

"I was just wondering how you could—"

"Afford it? You don't read the papers much, do you?"

"No, I—should I know you?"

She laughed. "I'm no big star. But I have had my face on page one a few times. Kirk Bannister—does that ring a bell?"

"Sure. Plays that part—uh, yeah! Sheriff Pat Grant, on TV, doesn't he?"

"That's the one. The great Sheriff Pat Grant. Ha! If he ever pulled a real gun he'd shoot off his own kneecap."

David remembered now. "And you were married to him."

"Right, I was married to him. But he wasn't married to me. But that's a long, dull story. Anyway, his lawyer sees that I get fifteen hundred bucks a month to live on."

Divorced. The plan had called for a divorcee. *She lives alone.* His mind checked the items with cold detachment. *She has red hair. She's the right age. She's perfect. She's the one.*

They were in the elevator, going down. It ran along the north side of the building, and a picture window showed them the ocean and a string of sparkling lights along the higway, toward Malibu. She stopped the elevator one floor down. He stayed alert, automatically memorizing every step of the way.

The elevator opened into a hallway, dimly lighted. Along the left wall were two doors, 810 and 811. On the right side was 812. Down at the end of the hallway was a door marked STAIRS.

He checked the ice pick again—fingered the sharp tip as she unlocked the door to 812.

He followed her into an enormous living room, luxuriously furnished. The thick rug was spongy under his feet. She smiled at his silent appraisal of the apartment.

"It's livable," she sighed as she moved across the room, swinging her hips. She pulled on a drape cord. Floor to ceiling drapes, red and gold, parted to reveal a breathtaking view. She posed dramatically.

He couldn't help it—he sucked in his breath.

"What'll you have, David?" She walked toward a black and gold bar in the corner.

"Same as you," he answered, without looking away from the glass wall.

"Not fussy, huh? That's what I like, a man who's not fussy."

He opened the sliding door and stepped outside. The verandah was semicircular and completely private. He walked to the four foot high railing and looked down. Cars moved, silently, along the highway directly below him. He closed his eyes as a dizzy feeling overcame him. He stepped back, opened them again, and looked out toward the vast, foreboding darkness of the deep blue-black water stretching to meet the lighter blue of the early evening sky.

In a moment she was beside him, handing him his drink.

"Long way down," he told her.

"I know. You have to be cleared by a head shrinker before they let you move in here."

"Suicide?" He tried a sip of the bourbon. It set fires in his throat.

"Uh-huh. You know, I had to pay an extra five hundred to get the doc to sign me off. Plus I had to convince him I wasn't the jumping type."

He looked down to the pavement, and knew the plan would have to be altered. Just this one time. He'd never done it before. He had always followed the plan to a letter. But a man had to be adaptable, willing to take advantage of opportunities. He had to be adaptable to situations. And this was turning into an ideal situation.

The plan had called for an ice pick tonight. He hadn't used one before. But then, neither had he seen to it that any of them had fallen from a building. He was saving that sort of thing for the bridge in Frisco. But yes. Yes! He was certain now! The ice pick must wait.

She put her arms around him, pressed her lips suddenly, forcefully, against his. The thought of making love to her almost made him sick. It was wrong. One doesn't make love to—

She pushed him back, gently. "Hold on, honey, I'll climb into something more comfortable."

He took the plastic container from his pocket as she disappeared into the bedroom. He twisted off the lid and poured a small amount of white powder into her glass. It dissolved immediately, leaving no residue.

He watched the waves roll in, listened to the steady roar of the surf. He took a deep breath of the salt spray. The pain in his head was already beginning to subside.

Three hours had passed. Three hours of sitting, and waiting, and looking at her body, sprawled out on the couch. The ceramic ashtray on the coffee table was filled with his cigarette butts. Five minutes after finishing the drink she had passed out cold, on schedule. She hadn't moved a muscle since then.

He walked out to the railing, leaned over, and cocked his head to listen for the sound of voices above or below him. Only silence answered him. Silence and the rumbling of the ocean's restless pulse. Two cars, racing side by side, came into view at the south end of the highway. He watched them until they passed the building. The road was visible for miles along both directions. The mid-week traffic was light, very light now.

It was time. He took a deep breath. The longer he waited, the more likelihood of being surprised in her apartment. Of course, if someone came in now, all he would have to do is tell them the truth. He had picked her up in the park and she'd fallen asleep on him. Fine pickup!

He looked at her face. He squinted, blinked. Her features were changing, hardening, sharpening. Wrinkles appeared on the forehead. Her lips thinned. The makeup thickened and cracked. Her mouth drooped. She looked like an old woman desperately trying to appear young. He recognized her—it was the same every time. He sat down beside her. His head was pounding again!

"An easy pickup, Mother. Such an easy pickup. You always were, weren't you? Everybody on the block knew it. Everybody in school knew it. The pickup's kid, that's what they called me. All my friends. Even the teachers. Remember that history teacher, Mother? Sure you do—old Mr. Foster with the big, fat potbelly. He even tried to get me to fix *him* up with you, said he'd give me an A."

He stood up and went to the bar. He washed and dried the glass he had used. Then he wiped the faucet handles with his handkerchief. As he walked toward the apartment door, the girl on the couch smiled at something in her dream.

"Dreaming, Mother? Dreaming about getting picked up by some handsome young man? Like me! Like me, dear Mother?"

He fixed the chain on the door so nobody could surprise him until it was over. He dumped the cigarette butts into his coat pocket. As he did, his fingers touched the ice pick. He took it out and looked at it. He fought the temptation to use it, to use it just once. One little jab wouldn't—no, it could wait. He shoved the ice pick back into its place. He lifted the girl from the couch.

The phone rang.

He froze, stared at her face. Her eyes were still closed.

Another loud ring! Like a burglar alarm in a deserted dime store. He fought an insane urge to clamp his hands over his ears.

As he set her back down on the couch, the next ring blasted into his ears with painful percussion. He grabbed a satiny, giant-sized pillow from the end of the couch. *Don't panic!* his mind screamed.

Another ring. Her arm moved. She was waking up.

He lowered the pillow toward her face, stopped when it was inches away from her mouth. Instead, he forced it down on the white princess telephone, muffling the ring. He waited it out, watching her face as the phone rang four more times. Finally, the room was silent again, a deadly silence that made him fidgety. Her eyes were still closed.

He exhaled the breath he hadn't realized he was holding, moistened his lips with his tongue. He used his handkerchief to lift the receiver and set it aside on the table.

She seemed much heavier when he picked her up this time. He carried her onto the verandah. The air was decidedly cooler now. He lifted her, held her poised over the railing as he checked the highway. No cars in sight. He was lucky.

Her body suddenly trembled—a slight convulsion. She opened her eyes. She looked into his face, and opened her mouth to scream. She clutched at his arms.

He dropped her just in time. He did not stay to watch her journey, much as he wanted to. He turned, quickly hurried through the living room, replacing the telephone receiver as he went. He unhooked the chain on the door, looked out into the hallway. Nobody there.

Was that a thud? He looked back toward the verandah. Impossible. It had to be the slam of a door somewhere in the building. Or an extra heavy crash of the surf. Or could it be his own heartbeat?

He stepped from the room, carefully closing the door behind him. The elevator indicator read the second floor. No time to wait for it. He took the stairway entrance.

The parking lot and lobby were deserted when he reached the upper level. He walked, unhurriedly, fighting the urge to run, from the building, then covered the short distance to his car.

Groups of people were scattered around on the park grass, several couples strolled along the pathway, and kids ran around playing tag. None of them paid him any attention.

His headache had vanished by the time he sat in his car. He drove along Ocean Avenue, turned east on Wilshire. He stopped at the first pizza sign because it reminded him he had skipped dinner. He was famished.

He woke up, refreshed and rested, late in the morning in a Bakersfield motel room, a hundred miles from Santa Monica.

The L.A. papers were in the lobby when he checked out at noon. The late edition headlines told of a SUICIDE BY THE SEA. According to the papers, the Santa Monica police detectives hadn't even considered the possibility of homicide, especially since Joanne Bannister had tried to kill herself on four previous occasions, and her friends and relatives reported her to be extremely despondent since her divorce.

He was safe. Again.

The time came again the Reno. The periods between the headaches were definitely shortening. It had only been a week since the last one, since that beautiful view from the balcony of The Surfwatcher. Only a week but the pains were back again.

In his hotel room, he set his suitcase up on the bed, snapped open the latch, and raised the lid. He buried his hands among the socks and underwear, his fingers searching until they found the notebook. He took it out.

He sat down before the writing table and opened the plain black binder. He withdrew a folded map that was tucked into the front. He opened it out, spread it on the desk like a general laying out a plan of attack. A heavy red line zigzagged across the country. He traced its path with his eyes, recalling the events of his trip.

It began in Milwaukee, circled in red with a number one next to it. The line followed the western edge of Lake Michigan down to Chicago, circled with a two beside it. His gaze moved to Toledo, eastward to Cleveland, then on to New York, which carried two numbers, down to Miami Beach, back up to New York, then west to Salt Lake City, doubling back to St. Louis, and south to New Orleans. El Paso had an eleven below it. The blood-red line connected El Paso to L.A.

L.A. was numberless. He wrote a tidy twelve in the blue space off the adjacent Pacific. Then he drew a line from L.A. to Reno. There was no hesitation in his wrist when he jotted the number thirteen next to the town of quickie divorces. He wasn't superstitious, but he knew somebody was in for a stroke of bad luck. It was time to figure out what she was like.

The top page in his notebook was neatly laid out with a series of straight-lined columns. The headings across the top of the page were NUMBER, CITY, NAME, AGE, OCCUPATION, COLOR HAIR, MARITAL STATUS, LIVES WITH, METHOD. As neat as a CPA's ledger.

The top line read: 1, Milwaukee, Ellen Farley, 37, prostitute, blonde, single, alone, knife.

The second line told a different story: 2, Chicago, Pat Darr, 23, dental assistant, red, single, mother and father, strangled with stocking.

Now, he carefully filled in the data for number 12, remembering what he'd read in the papers: 12, Joanne Bannister, 29, Santa Monica, actress, red, divorced, alone, dropped from building.

The master plan—to insure that he would vary the ages, hair colors, occupations, types of girls, the means he used to kill them.

Only he, David Cronin, knew the common denominator of all the girls on the list. The single characteristic common to all twelve—they had all been easy pickups. And in most of the cases the local authorities had not even realized the girls had been picked up on the night they had been murdered.

He had been careful to move from city to city. There was no single set of authorities who could detect a pattern or even a connection between the twelve cases. Not like that strangler in Boston. He was bound to get caught.

But a man with a scheme that was foolproof! Perfect! He had committed not one, but a dozen perfect murders. He would never be caught. The next time around the country he would pick small towns. The cycle was endless.

He studied his chart, formed the image of the next girl. She would be a dark-haired girl this time. And she would be single and never married. And it would be the ice pick's turn.

He encountered no little difficulty fulfilling one of the plan's specifications. He was almost prepared to relax the "never married" requirement. So few of the women in Reno fit that category he almost decided to deviate, for the second time, from the plan.

But he found her. Of all places, in the cocktail room of his hotel, after looking everywhere else in the city.

She was young, possibly twenty-two or- three, hair so coal black that it looked unreal. She talked easily, but not loquaciously. She was friendly, but not forward. She was attractive, but not beautiful.

After two drinks he knew enough about her to decide she was qualified. She nestled up against him. They said no more until after the next drink.

"Would you like to go somewhere else?" He knew she was ready.

She smiled at him, and shrugged. "Why not?"

They left the hotel, arm in arm. He showed her to his car. He closed the door for her and switched the ice pick to his left pocket as he walked around behind the car.

It was past midnight by the time he found a motel with a flashing VACANCY sign. His head throbbed in rhythm with the blinking neon. She didn't say a word when he stopped in front of the manager's cabin. As he got out, she suggested, with surprising shyness, that she wait in the car while he registered. He agreed it was a good idea.

He used the name of Mr. and Mrs. Cecil Goodman. The manager, a short, bald man with bloodshot eyeballs, took the twenty and laid a key on the counter without taking his eyes from the love scene of a 1940's movie on the late, late show. It was better than David had hoped.

She turned off the light in the room as soon as he closed the door behind him. But enough moonlight filtered in so that he could see her shadowy form.

"Why did you do that?"

"It's nicer this way, don't you think?"

"Yes," he answered.

"You pick up girls like this all the time, don't you? I can tell."

"Does that matter?"

"It matters very much."

She was facing him. He could tell she was breathing heavily. Her handbag hung from her left arm. She reached into it. Reaching for a cigarette, he assumed. But she would never have time to smoke it. He knew how he was going to do it. He would walk up to her, put one arm around her, and then as he kissed her, he would—

"Don't come any closer." Her voice had changed. It wasn't the soft, girlish voice he had been listening to for the past two hours. It was the voice of an older woman.

He took a step toward her.

The moonlight reflected from something in her hand. It was neither a cigarette package nor a cigarette case. He stared at the gun with a deadly silencer attached to its barrel.

"I warned you, Father." Her words came fast. "I warned you about picking up girls all the time. I told you it would kill Mama if she ever found out. But you didn't believe me, did you?"

Her voice crackled with hatred, like that of an old woman. It became a familiar voice. It sounded just like—

"Just any cheap tramp who would give you the eye—"

It sounded like his—but it couldn't be—

"You knew it would break her heart."

It was—it *was* her—she was back again. How many times did he have to kill her? He took out the ice pick. He opened his mouth to speak, "Moth—"

The gun flashed. The force of the bullet knocked him down. She stood over his body, fired a second bullet into his head.

She shook her head, disbelievingly. "You keep coming back, don't you, Father? I keep killing you—but you keep coming back."

Pat Stadley

Something for the Club

We were sitting around down on the old Miller Pier waiting for the twins. Nobody was saying much, me least of all. I'd already opened my mouth and said I didn't want them in, but everybody howled me down and only Jess had looked at me and asked, "Why, Vince?"

I didn't really know why—just that maybe there was too much of them, if you know what I mean. Too many muscles, too much looks, and when they laughed it was like one smile, started the same moment and finished together. Maybe that was what was eating me, I thought—all that togetherness.

So I just sat there, my back up against a piling, staring down at the water where it slapped, black and oily, against the shoring and I kept wishing they wouldn't make it. Maybe the clerk would spot them lifting the gun, or they wouldn't get it out of the glass case or the fuzz would look them over and ask questions. Then everybody would see they were all mouth and didn't belong in a club like ours.

You see, we're something special—kinda like the inner circle of a big wheel. Outwards we're one of those "social clubs"; you know the kind, "to keep the boys off the streets," and we have "sponsors" and "outings" and "Friday dances" and all that jazz, but inside, well, we're like the prize in a box of Cracker Jack. We're what give it the kicks, man, and the name the rest of them whisper when they think we're not listening.

Tonight we were testing the twins. We'd been watching them ever since Manny said they wanted in. And when I say watching, I'm not just talkin'. There isn't anything escapes us—the talk, the act, the dress, the thinkin', the chicks they pick. Because we don't want any flash. We want 'em solid—hard solid.

We'd told them to meet us down at the end of Miller's Pier. It's an old condemned hunk of pilings, sticking way out in the water, and we always come here because it's like the end of nowhere—no lights, no people, no law—just us and the water underneath, swishing in soft and slow, or else, like tonight, pounding and shaking the pilings until they creaked, loose and uneasy.

We'd got here ahead of the twins and we'd opened the first case of beer and somebody had put on a stack of records and the music was beating, sweet and hot, and we just sat there, waitin'.

Dave spotted them first, walking down the pier towards us—their steps swinging together—the same height, the same charcoal jackets, the same black loafers, and I never been so restless in my life. It was just like I ached all over.

"They're sure big cats," Manny says. "Suppose we'll make them purr?"

"If we don't," I answer, "I got some special catnip." Everybody laughs.

We let 'em walk almost up to us and then Jess calls out, "Hold it!"

They stop and somebody reaches over and turns the music way down. When it gets real quiet, Jess rolls over and sits up. We always let him start the talkin' because he's a big name at school and he's got that smooth, slick cover. But underneath, he's squirrelly, and a mean cat when he's charged up.

Right now, he looks quiet and easy and his voice just slides out. "Somebody passed the word you two want in."

One of them gives a short nod.

Jess looks around at us and kinda grins. "It ain't easy. Ask Davey here—took him three times."

Somebody snickers and Jess's voice gets smoother. " 'Course Davey's gift *was* extra special." He stops a minute, like he's studying the twins. "You do know you're supposed to bring a gift, don't you?"

They shake their heads.

Jess acts real surprised. "You don't! Well, I'll clue you in. It's to show your appreciation. Nothing' big, jsut something for the club. Like Manny. He brought us a very nice hi fi; and Roberto over there lifted—pardon me—contributed a case of champagne; and Vince—" he turns and nods at me. "Well, Vince showed real imagination. He brought us a song and dance team—for an evening."

Everybody howls. But I watch the twins. They don't even smile, they just stand there watchin' first me and then Jess.

Finally, Dave pokes me. "What's with these two," he whispers. "They ain't for real."

But I don't answer. They're real enough, I think. To some people, the Devil ain't real.

I look back at Jess. He's still talkin', his words comin' out slow and careful like he's handpicking each one. "We got your gift all selected. We need somethin' to go hunting with—somethin' like that hand-tooled Weatherby rifle down in Dyman's gun shop."

We all look sharp at the twins and you can see this rocks them a little. But it don't show much of anywhere except in their eyes. I'll swear they slitted down like a cat's.

Jess moves his hand, stretching his fingers. "You understand, of course, there's no money involved. Just brains and slick fingers."

The twins take a quick look at each other and then they start to wheel away when Davey yells, "Hey, don't they get the treatment?"

And Jess kinda smiles and says, "Ah, yes, the treatment!"

We all sit up then and start poundin' on the pier and you can feel the drummin' movin' through the old wooden planks and right up your spine. And pretty soon Jess raises his hands and we quiet down. Then he crooks his finger at the twins and he points out a spot inside our circle and they walk forward and stand there.

"You know the rules for this?" Jess asks.

"We heard," one of them answers, short-like.

Jess turns his head and looks around our circle. "You first, Manny."

Manny snickers, "Which of you is the biggest stud?"

And it begins.

I take a beer and stretch out. It's gonna be the usual—love life, sex life, secret life. A question or a challenge to each of us, and they got to answer fast and straight.

I take a long swallow and I look at the twins, just standing there, their heads turning slow and their eyes watchin', cold and steady. And no matter what anybody asks, they give back good as they get and sometimes better.

Until it seems I'm burnin' all over and I can't hardly wait till it's my turn. When it comes, I stand up and everybody quiets down. They know I'm not askin' any question. I stand still a minute just lookin' at the twins and then I put my hand down and snap my fingers and Dave puts another beer in my palm. I tip the can up and I chug-a-lug it and then I say:

"You two are pretty close, aren't you? Same schedule, same teachers, same friends. You drive the same car, eat together, date together—scrub your teeth together?"

Everybody hoots on that one and the twins pivot towards me like I'd touched a hidden switch.

"That's nice." I take my time, drawing it out. "Nothing like brotherly love—except in this club. Here, it's everybody for everybody, but no more for one than the other—get it?"

Their heads move up and down, slow.

I drink the last of the beer and I'm feeling good now. "Okay. Just to prove that to all of us, suppose Kennie throws Dennie off the pier!"

For a minute it's so quiet, I can hear my own breathin' and then Jess snickers and Davey follows him and Manny and then they're all howlin' and banging on the wooden planks and I have to raise my arms to shut them off. But nobody says anything 'cause I'd made the challenge and only I could withdraw it. I hold up my arms until everyone settles down and I keep them up until we can hear the water rollin' in under us, sloshing up against the pilings.

Then one of the twins takes a half step towards me but the other one touches him and he stops. His words come out flat and mean sounding. "Okay. But suppose *you* pick Dennie. And if you're right, he goes in the water. But if you're wrong—*you* go in."

They had me there. And everybody knew it. 'Cause who in hell could separate these two? I look past them—out into the night. I'd dove off this pier before but it was daylight and you could see the water and there was no tide like tonight. Get thrown against these pilings by a wave and the barnacles would shred you like a cheese grater.

I look back at the twins and the same face, duplicated, watches me.

There just wasn't any real way of knowin' who was who, so I draw a breath and take the face to the left.

"You're Dennie," I say. And I'm lucky.

They wait a few seconds and then they move together towards the edge of the pier. The rest of us follow.

Dennie sits down and slips off his shoes and Kennie looks ove the side. "It's fifteen feet down," he says. "Tide's in and fast, moving against the pier." He stops, looks down at his brother. "Let's make it from the other side."

I wait until Dennie starts to stand up and I put my hand out. "Easy," I say, "I made the challenge. I make the rules. he goes over *this* side."

Kennie's face kinda flattens down. "The tide's runnin' this way. He'll get washed into the pilings."

I shrug. "So? You want in this club or don't you?"

He looks away from me and back out at the water. Dennie starts shedding his pants and pretty soon he's stripped down and he steps to the edge and stands there, just waitin'. Kennie puts a hand on him. "Dive shallow and swim hard to the right." Then he's quiet a moment, looking down at the water and suddenly he says, "Now!" and Dennie's over in a sweet, clean dive.

We all crowd to the edge staring out into the blackness and you can't see much except the top of the water, movin' big and restless out beyond you. And then Kennie gives a long, sharp whistle. And somewhere out in the water comes an answer.

Davey tugs at me. "How're we gonna get him up?" he asks.

And I see everyone is watchin' me and mainly the twin, only his eyes don't look right. But I figure nothin's gonna shake me on this one, so I look him straight in the face and I say, "He's such a big cat, let him swim to shore."

He just looks at me and then he gives another whistle that kinda upends a little like it asked a question. And then we hear the answer—a little fainter and ahead of us—and Kennie looks back at me and says, "Don't go away—we'll be back with your present."

And he starts walkin' towards the shore. Only he stays right at the edge of the pier and ever so often he gives another whistle and then he waits until he gets an answer. They keep going like that until we don't hear them any more and we know they've reached the shore.

And Manny says, "Ain't *that* somethin'. Did ya ever see anything neater?"

And everybody starts talkin' at once, but I go over and get myself a beer and I stretch out flat on the wooden floor, away from everyone. And I can hear the water boilin' in under me and it sounds like it was laughin' to itself and all of a sudden I wished I could get up and run like hell right down that pier.

Only Roberto turned the phonograph up real loud and someone passed around a bottle of bourbon and I took the biggest swallow I could and Jess looked over at me and started laughin'. I got up and walked to where he was sittin' and I handed the bottle to him.

"Go on, laugh!" I said. "But if we had a brain between all of us, we wouldn't be here when they get back."

He upends the bottle and he takes a fat swallow and then he grins that squirrelly grin and says, "Those cats sure got to you. Relax, man, maybe they won't even get back with the gun."

"They'll be back," I said. I went over and looked down at the water and it was higher and blacker than before and I thought, one big wave and this whole pile of lumber will go down right underneath it.

I wondered how it would be down in the water with the salt in your mouth and your eyes and the waves beating over you and pretty soon I'm shaking so hard I gotta sit down. And then it was like I knew—I took my shoes off and my jacket and I checked the zipper on my pants so it wouldn't hang up and I looked around at the other guys and I wanted to run to eaching one and holler, "Let's get the hell outta here!" But I knew it wouldn't do any good so I just sat there, real quiet because who can tell the world the end is coming?

I guess maybe I heard them first. It was like their walkin' was swayin' the pier even more and everybody quieted down and we just watched them coming, pulling somethin' big and heavy lookin' between them.

Davey edges towards me and grabs my shirt. "What they got with them, Vince?" he asks and I have to look at him 'cause his voice sounds thin and strange.

"Nothin'," I say. "Just a box. Probably chickened out on the gun and they're bringing a crate of liquor to soften us up."

Then Manny snickers, "Looks like a crate on wheels. Suppose they caught themselves a chorus girl?" And everybody laughs, but not easy, like usual.

The twins stop about twenty feet away and we can see what they're pulling really good. It's big and solid looking with a door in front, only you can't see inside.

Nobody says a word, waiting for Jess. He takes a step forward and jerks a thumb at the box. "I thought we sent you after a gun!"

One of them leans down and lifts something off the top of the crate and tosses it to Jess and he catches it and looks carefully at it and then he holds it up and we all crowd close and sure enough, it's the rifle. It's so black and shining everyone kinda puts their hands out and we pass it around and holding it is really somethin'. Then Jess takes it back and he opens the breech and he looks at the twins and says, "It's empty."

They shrug and one of them says, "You didn't ask for shells."

Jess waits a long minute and then he holds the gun out in front of him and he looks around at all of us and everybody nods their heads except me. But there ain't nothin' now I can say, so I just shut up and Jess turns back to the twins and says, "Okay. You're in."

They look at each other and they kinda move a bit like they're relaxing and then one of them smiles and says, "Which one?"

Jess looks surprised. "What d'ya mean—which one?"

And now the twin is really grinnin'. "Well, seeing that there's two of us and someone might object to our bringing just one gift—we brought two. Something more for the club—like you said, and especially for Vince." And he leans forward and grabs the handle of the crate's door and he gives it a quick tug and then he jumps back and then both of them turn and run like hell up the pier.

Only nobody is watching them too close. 'Cause the door was swinging open and somethin' comes out of the blackness of that cage like it's unfolding itself.

And Davey grabs me and hollers, his voice real high, "It's a cat!"

And it's a cat all right—only it's big and yellow and spotted and it moves towards us, sleek and fast, its head forward and its mouth open, snarling.

At first, it was like we were frozen and then everybody moves at once, pushing and shoving and yelling, with that cat weaving back and forth, till everyone is running like a big wave, first one side of the pier and then the other. And the pier begins shaking and twisting and I tried to get to the edge so I could dive clear but I began slipping and sliding and it was just like the water reached up and took all of us. Only just before I went down, I hear a whistle, sharp and clean, but I knew it wasn't for us.

Only Jess and I made it to shore. It was a week before they found all the others and the papers played it big on how the whole club had gone night fishing and the pier had collapsed and everything. Jess and I never told anybody different and neither did they.

Sure, we see them. They're the big names around here, now. They got their own club and they get the sharpest chicks and every time they pass us driving their convertible, that big, yellow, spotted, tame ocelot riding in the back seat turns and looks at us. And it really gets to you. Know what I mean?

Ernest Savage
The Park Plaza Thefts

I'd taken the call at the station and told Mrs. Martin to make a list of the missing items, and she was still working on it a half hour later when I got there. Over the phone she'd been fairly cool about the robbery, but at the door her elderly cheeks were damp with tears.

"They took everything," she said. "Things I've had all my life. My mother's—" She blubbered to a halt.

"Is that the list?" I said. A clipboard was cradled in her left arm and she handed it to me blindly. "I'm Sergeant Peckinpaugh. I talked to you over the phone. Why don't you make up a cup of coffee?" I figured it would help to give her a little chore, and it did. An aged beagle bitch limped along behind us to the kitchen.

She'd returned home from a two-week vacation five minutes before she phoned the station. One of the dining room windows was partly open, a chair usually in front of it pushed aside, and she'd noticed it right off. Then she'd noticed the silver service wasn't on the buffet and called us. The silver service was the first of about ten items listed on the clipboard. A coin collection, jewelry, some cash from a jar in the kitchen, six antique guns from her dead husband's collection in the den, two Dresden china figurines, and two silver candelabra were also listed. Pound for pound, a lot more valuable than a TV set, for instance. They were worth almost three thousand dollars, Mrs. Martin guessed, and you could get it all into a good-sized pillowcase. It reminded me of a list of missing items I'd seen last week from a house about five blocks from Mrs. Martin's in the same solid upper-middle-class neighborhood.

The beagle was sitting on a throw rug in the open doorway between the kitchen and utility room, watching Mrs. Martin fix the coffee. I noticed its water dish was empty, and got up and filled it at the sink and put it back. The dog wagged its tail in gratitude and drank copiously.

"Oh, I forgot!" Mrs. Martin said. "Poor Trudy, she must have been dying of thirst."

Trudy nearly emptied the dish while Mrs. Martin told me for the third time that she knew—she absolutely knew—she'd locked that dining room window and all the other windows in the house, and her son Harold double-checked everything before she left.

Trudy finished drinking and waddled to the doggy-door set in the bottom panel of the utility room door leading to the back yard. She stood there for a moment with her nose against the top-hinged plastic flap of the door and then, with an old-bones effort, jumped through. A minute later, the job done, she returned and curled up on her pad on the floor. I excused myself to Mrs. Martin and went over and opened the utility room door, went outside, and closed it again, first twisting the inside

knob to the lock position. Then I sat down on the back stoop, reached
my right arm through the doggy-door, and very easily twisted the knob
to unlock, got up and opened the door, and came back in. Mrs. Martin
had been watching this procedure with her fingers splayed against an
open mouth.

"Why, I never—" she breathed. "So that's how they got in! But the
dining room window—?"

"That's known as a red herring, Mrs. Martin," I said. "May I use your
phone?"

Lieutenant Stanley Wells was thumbing through a brochure on the
delights of Hawaii when I got back to the station at five thirty. For the
seven years I've been on the Clausen police force he's been searching
the literature and maps of the world for the ideal place to retire. But it's a
game, a *divertissement*, as we used to say in Madame Gautier's French
class. He was born here and he'll die here, and he knows it because his
wife has told him so. And he'll never retire; it's not in him. It's just that
he wishes Clausen had stayed the same size it was twenty years ago. He
misses its lost innocence.

"Tomorrow," he said, setting the brochure aside, "get a haircut."

"Is it the first of the month already, *mon général?*"

"Do it!" he said. "What's this hot scoop on the Martin case that
Escalera was talking about a while ago?" He lit a cigar ritualistically,
rolling it in his mouth.

"It's not just the Martin case, boss, but all five of the Park Plaza
thefts—my two and Escalera's three." I held up a finger. "Number one,
they all had doggy-doors, and number two, they all got hit while on
vacation. Number three, they all lost the same kind of stuff—smallish,
light, and valuable—and number four, in all cases a window or door was
left open to look like the point of entry."

"Why fake a point of entry?"

"To draw attention from the real point of entry—the doggy-door."

"Which means what, Sherlock?"

"It means that people with doggy-doors who go on vacation this
summer are gonna get burgled. And now for the wonderfulest point of
all, leftenant, point number five—in each case the doggy-door was
bought from the same store."

"You're positive?" It was beginning to interest him.

"Yessir. The thought crossed my mind halfway through the afternoon's work and I checked with Escalera, and then with each of the
victims."

"All right, Peck, what store?"

"Graham's Plaza Pet Shop."

"To which you are about to repair, I presume." He glanced at his
watch. It was an hour past my quitting time, but since he never quits it's

difficult for him to remember such irksome details.
"First thing tomorrow," I said.

The next morning I beat Graham to his shop in the Plaza by a half
hour and sat outside on the curb, musing over things past. It was a
bright clear morning, the smog five or six hours away from the first-
stage alert level it would no doubt attain today, as it had yesterday.
Approximately where I sat had been second base of the Little League
ball park where I'd made my first bad fielder's choice and socked my
first homer. At that time it had been surrounded by lush green groves, a
mix of the orange and avocado trees that were the twin symbols of
Clausen Valley.

But this monstrous Plaza Shopping Center had obliterated all of that.
Now there were thousands of houses in satellite suburbs where the dark
green trees used to be, full—as Wells said every day—of dangerous
strangers.

I belched—I'd had a pickle for breakfast. I live alone in the old family
bungalow, a poor orphan boy.

Four stores down from Graham's, a barber pole began to turn and I
got up and went down and told the man a little off the sides and back.
"Just a trim," I said, "and I want a receipt."

Graham was indignant about it—in fact, furious. He said that if I
thought that he had enough energy left after a long tough day with the
dogs, cats, birds, fish, monkeys, and whatnot in his store to go about
robbing people, then I didn't know the first damn thing about the pet
shop business. "With all these animals," he said, waving his arms at the
walls, "I'm on all fours myself at the end of the day!"

"I didn't mean you personally, Mr. Graham," I said. "How about
your help?"

He laughed bitterly. "What help? The last good man I had," he said,
"the *only* good man I ever had, quit two months ago—just like that! He
just didn't show up one morning after three years on the job—have you
ever tried to hire somebody in today's labor market?"

"What's this guy's name?" I said, and he took me into his little office
and handed me the ex-employee's personnel card. I said, "As long as
we're here, tell me the name of everybody who's ever bought a doggy-
door from you."

He pointed to a file cabinet and said, "Help yourself," and went back
out into the tangy air of his shop to feed his barking, meowing,
splashing, chittering stock in trade.

An hour later I had a list of fifty-four people who'd bought doggy-
doors from him since he'd opened three and a half years ago. A bunch, I
thought, and thanked him carefully on the way out.

Graham's ex-employee, Daniel Richards, was nowhere to be found.

The address I had on him was Space 14 in an old mobile-home park near a freeway interchange on the east edge of town. He'd lived there until two months before in an ancient two-bedroom trailer with a retired uncle named Edward Richards, to whom I talked.

"He just up and left," Richards said. He was drinking a can of beer in the dinky little patio alongside his trailer. "He didn't take no more with him than the clothes on his back."

"In a car?"

"Well, this VW van he drives. What's he done, sergeant?"

I sat down in the shade of the patched awning over the patio and refused an offer of beer. It was turning hot. "Nothing that I know of," I said, "but he might be able to give me some information I'm looking for. Was he alone when he left?"

"He was always alone. He's what you call a loner."

I looked at my notes—Daniel'd be twenty-four in August. "No girlfriends, Mr. Richards?"

"Well, he had this one girl, I guess, although I never seen her. She used to phone him now and again last spring, and I'd kid him about it the way you do." He finished his beer and crushed the can abstractedly in a powerful old hand. "But it'd embarrass him so much I quit doing it. He's a shy boy, sergeant, not your typical hotshot troublemaker. And a good boy, too. He was saving up to go to veterinarian school next fall up at Davis."

"Oh? Where'd he keep his money, Mr. Richards? Here?"

"No, down at the Clausen Savings and Loan. He put every second paycheck in there, regular as clockwork."

"Did he take his passbook with him?"

"As far as I know he did."

"How much had he saved? Enough for school?"

"Well, I don't know—" He ran a hand over a tan freckled scalp. "He always figured he had another year to work, but I guess he changed his mind."

"Maybe he came into some money or something. Or got some lined up for himself."

"Maybe he did, but I doubt it. He'd have told me." His sharp blue eyes squinted at mine. "You think something happened to him, sergeant?"

"I don't know, Mr. Richards. What do you think?"

He shook his head. "I'll admit I'm worried. I haven't let myself really think about it until now. I don't know—"

"What's the girl's name?"

"I don't know. All I know about her is her voice—real sexy voice over the phone, real low, pleasing to a man's ear."

"How about friends, Mr. Richards?"

"Well, he really didn't have none that I know of. He went over to the coast now and again for surfing, and last winter he went to one of those karate schools for a couple weeks, but like I say, Danny's a loner."

"Parents?"

"My brother got killed in the service. His mother's somewhere in Canada, last anyone heard."

"When did this girl call last, Mr. Richards?"

"Just before Danny took off."

"Do you think there's a connection?"

"Damned if I know."

In the trailer he found a snapshot of Danny leaning against the back of his van, a surfboard sticking out the open rear window, the license plate on the engine hatch clearly legible. It would save a little time, that plate. Danny was a short slender man with more hair on his head than I fancy and a ten-inch-wide guardsman mustache that surprised me with its bravura touch. I pointed at it.

"Maybe he was only shy on the outside," I said. "That's quite a growth."

"Nope. It was a silly damn thing and he knew it. He kept it out of mulishness."

"Well, it might make him easier to find," I said. "How about filing a missing persons report on him, Mr. Richards?"

He said he didn't want to. He said if Danny was dead it wouldn't do any good and if he was alive it was none of his damn business where he went. I gave him my card and he promised to call me if he thought of anything else.

On the way downtown to the station, I passed the *Press-Sentinel* building and, heeding a baby impulse, pulled in. It was crowding noon and I snagged my old school friend, Ed Munsey, who was circulation manager now, and made him buy me lunch in the employees' cafeteria.

"What I want to know," I said at our little table in the noisy room, "is what happens when a subscriber cuts off his paper for vacation?"

"We stop delivery and resume it when ordered. It's pretty complicated, Peck."

"Yeah, I know, wise guy, but what I'm asking is what happens here in the plant. Who handles it?"

"Jean Romero, one of my most delectable assistants. In fact, my only delectable assistant. She's that girl over there in the barely adequate red dress and the dark flowing hair."

She was a dish and I let loose the expected low whistle. Ed grinned.

"Watch it, shamus," he said. "She's a karate buff, and she'll break your groping arm with the edge of her hand." He paused. "How come your brows went up just then, Peckinpaugh?"

"Did they? Who else knows when somebody goes on vacation?"

"The concerned district manager and the concerned delivery person—we have to say 'person' now because we're using girl delivery boys. What's up, Peck? You've got that awful cop look in your eyes."

"What else does Miss Romero do? Is it Miss?"

"Ms., you barbarian. Well, let's see, she handles most of the field problems with the district managers, delivers the complaints at night, and—let's see—"

"You mean if one of the kids misses a delivery and the customer complains, she brings the paper out?"

"Right. What's up, Peck?"

"Ed, can you get me the current list of people who've ordered their papers stopped for vacation? I mean without Ms. Romero knowing, and I mean *particularly* without Ms. Romero knowing?"

"Well, sure, but you're spoiling my lunch, Peckinpaugh. Am I to infer that she's into some kind of a bad gig?"

"It could be, but mum's the word, Munsey. This is police business now."

"You want the rest of my sandwich, copper?"

"No, but I'll want that list by this afternoon. Does Romero have a boyfriend?"

"Thousands of them."

"What's this karate bit?"

"Hell, I don't know, but she's good at it. She really racked up one of the pressmen a couple weeks ago. She goes to this school over on Market Street. Level with me, what's going on?"

"Later," I said. "Get that list over to the station this afternoon, right?"

Lieutenant Wells said, "I thought I told you to get a haircut, Peckinpaugh."

I was prepared. "You did, and I did," I said, and laid the barber's receipt on his desk.

He looked at it and then at me. "You mean you *paid* for that? You got trimmed, sergeant."

"Exactly, boss, exactly."

Escalera came in then with a report on his morning's work. He'd been checking pawn and antique shops within a reasonable range of Clausen, looking for the Martin loot, and had found nothing. "It's all in L.A. by now," he said morosely. "You could sell your grandmother's bones down there if you knew where to take them."

He was sweaty hot and miffed with himself for having missed the doggy-door connection in the thefts. He hadn't even noticed them, he said, and that always rankles a good cop.

We talked over the situation for a few minutes and then Wells summarized in his usual blunt way. "Romero tells Richards when the next mark is scheduled to go on vacation, right? Richards, probably in L.A. somewhere, comes over, hits the place, goes back and fences the stuff there. Then they split the take." His eyes swept us.

"We could get L.A. to find him on a don't-alarm basis," Escalera said, going along, "and keep him under surveillance."

"Sure, and we could write Washington too," Wells said, "but we don't have the time. I'm getting pressure on this thing. I need something now." Escalera grinned sardonically, and Wells went on, "Okay, Luis, your people have to riot in the streets to get a little attention, Park Plaza people just pick up their phones. Don't let's go into that again."

"Our day will come," Luis said, and you never knew with him whether it was banter or grim promise. About a quarter of Clausen's eighty thousand people (present count, and growing) are Chicano—including Ms. Romero, I thought.

Outside the window behind Wells' head, visible through the orange interstices of the steel frame of the future police building across the street, a pale ivory cloud of smoke was ballooning slowly over the silhouette of the hills ten miles away. Another brush fire underway in the baked brown range to the east. Rainfall this season was half normal, and everything was tinder dry, including tempers.

"What do you think, Peck?" Wells said.

"I think we need some hard facts," I said. "Number one, we're not even sure Richards and Romero know each other—I mean, that karate hookup is pretty skinny; and number two, what makes us think he's in L.A., if it is Richards; and number three, how do we know he's even alive?"

"I wish to hell you'd quit numbering things," Wells said irritably.

"The process of an orderly mind, boss."

"*Uno, dos, tres*," Luis said. "*Y quatro, que es numero quatro*, Peck?"

Tim Bashaw knocked on the frame of Wells' office door just then and came in with an envelope for me. It was the list from the *Press* and I spread it out on Wells' desk next to the list of the doggy-door owners I'd compiled that morning. Two names appeared on both lists and we all looked at each other. "Grebs and Ellison," I said. "Grebs cutting off tomorrow and Ellison Monday."

"Well, the least we can do is call them," Wells said, "and tell them to lock their doggy-doors."

"Hah!" Luis snorted. "Have you ever looked at one, lieutenant? You can push them in with your nose, if you want—locked or unlocked."

"All right, we'll tell them to board the damn things up."

"No," I said. "I've got an idea."

"Don't mention stakeout," Wells snapped.

"No stakeout, boss, just me. That's *numero quatro*, Luis. Whoever he is, I wait for him in the Grebs house starting tomorrow night, the first night they're gone. That's probably when he'll hit."

"What if he doesn't?"

"Then I hang in there."

"Jeesh!" Luis said.

Wells leaned back in his chair and sighed wearily. Behind his head, the ivory cloud of smoke was twice as big now. Both Luis and I were watching it. "Well, it's all right with me," Wells said finally, "if it's all right with Grebs. But I'll want permission in writing from Grebs."

"A deal," I said.

Luis grinned at me. He was starting a three-week vacation tomorrow. *"Buena suerte,"* he said in that ambiguous way of his.

The brand new (and almost offensively rich-looking) Clausen Savings and Loan building was on North Main about halfway from the station to the Grebses' house and I stopped there on my way out. Bonny Johnson's mother, Martha, had worked there for twenty-five years and practically ran the place. She was behind the counter studying the big new Burroughs machine when I walked in.

"Jeffrey Peckinpaugh!" she said in a ringing voice. "When are you going to make an honest woman out of my daughter?" Bonny Johnson was my girl, as we old fashioned types say.

"When they repeal the equal rights amendment, Ma," I said. I laid the snapshot of Danny Richards on the counter between us. "Official police business today, Madame Johnson. Do you recognize this cat?"

"Certainly—the mustache. That's Daniel Richards. What's happened to him, Jeffrey? He hasn't been in for a couple of months."

"His account's still open, then?" It surprised me—most people take their money with them. Unless—

"I believe so. Has anything happened to him?"

"What's his balance, Martha?"

"I'm not supposed to tell you that without a—"

"Don't tell me. Just write it down on a piece of paper and I'll read it over your shoulder."

"All men are criminals," she said. She got a ledger sheet from a file, stuck it in the Burroughs, and pushed buttons. The ultimate answer, which she wrote down and held so that I had to read it over her shoulder—she was being very literal about it—was an eyeopener: $6,176.98. She crumpled the paper and turned toward me, her lovely fifty-year-old blue eyes pools of innocence.

"Martha darling," I said, "how tough would it be for someone other than Richards to come in here and close out his account?"

"If I handled it, impossible. I know him by sight."

"What if one of your transient little helpers handled it?"

"Well, whoever tried it would have to have the passbook, of course, and a proper signature, but—"

"Martha, can you tag his sheet so that only you can cash him out?"

She looked dubious. "Well, I suppose I could, but—"

"Do it, Ma."

Now she looked alarmed. "Is someone apt to try it, Jeffrey?"

"You never know," I said, and patted her hand with real affection. "But don't worry about it."

Mrs. Grebs had promised over the phone that her husband would be home at four-thirty and he was—dog-tired and mean-eyed. I'd typed up a statement of permission for the project and he read it over three or four times and made me tell him the full story of the doggy-door caper before, finally, he signed it.

"You don't really know a hell of a lot about this case, do you, sergeant?" he said sourly. "It appears to me you're fishing—in my pond."

"We don't know anything for sure, Mr. Grebs, that's true. But we think our theory is solid and I'm willing to bet a lot of my own time we're right."

"So in effect I turn my house over to you for two weeks, right?" His dog, a middle-sized poodle named Fritzi, was growling at me softly from next to her master's chair.

"Hopefully just one night," I said. "Tomorrow night."

"Why don't I just nail a board over the damn door and be done with it?" Heat was building between us.

"We'd like a chance to catch this man in the act, Mr. Grebs. He's raised quite a lot of hell in your neighborhood."

He turned to his wife who'd been standing in the kitchen door. "What do you think, Helen?"

"Well," she said, "you've had this 'Support Your Local Police' bumper sticker on the car for three years, Gerald. Now's your chance." Her voice was unloving.

He sighed. "Okay, we'll go along, Peckinpaugh. But see that nothing goes wrong, or it'll be your ass."

"Pray for me," I said coldly. "And now let me look around."

It was a big split-level house full of the small portable expensive things our thief preferred, some of them three or four generations old, Grebs said, handed down on his wife's side. A dream hit for any thief. Back downstairs I had Mrs. Grebs sign the authorization and took a front-door key from my reluctant host before he could change his mind. I had the feeling they should take separate vacations, but didn't express it.

At the front door we both paused and looked at the smoke clouds building up east of town, like pale dry thunderheads.

"Jesus," Grebs said, awed. "I wonder what started it."

"A match, probably. Most of them are pure arson, Mr. Grebs."

"Maybe I'll just stay away," he said tonelessly.

On the way back downtown, I stopped off at Richards' place. It was five forty. An idea had crossed my mind and it was such that I'd have to work it up fast or forget it. He was on his patio, beer in hand, looking at the smoke clouds, and I asked him if I could borrow his phone for a minute and him for an hour or so, and he was quick to say sure. Not much happened in his life, I imagine.

Inside the trailer I phoned Bonny and told her to call the *Press-Sentinel* immediately and complain about a missed delivery, and that I'd be there in about twenty minutes with an explanation and a guest for a drink.

Richards changed his shirt and ran an electric shaver over his chin, and at six fifteen I was introducing him to Bonny in her apartment and watching him brighten up, as men always do when they meet her.

"What's up, " I said in answer to her question, "is this—Mr. Richards here heard a voice on the phone about two months ago and I want him to tell me if it's the same voice we'll hear from the girl who'll deliver your paper."

"Girl?"

"Yes, girl, as soon you will plainly see. Mr. Richards will stand right here against the wall, out of her sight, and you, my beauty, will engage the subject in enough chitchat for Mr. Richards to make a sound decision."

"The subject," Bonny said, "said delivery would be made about now, so maybe we'd better get ready." She smiled at Richards. "I'll fix you a drink," she told him as he melted away before her eyes, "and you don't need to stand, as our leader says, you can sit right there in that chair and be comfortable."

"Of course," I said.

Her apartment was the third back from the street in a two story unit of sixteen. As I was watching out her living room window, a car pulled up at the curb and in a moment Ms. Romero came trotting up the walk. "Ready!" I said, and Richards took his seat.

Bonny talked to her for a half minute, but Richards was nodding his head from Romero's first words. When Bonny closed the door, he said, "No doubt about it, that's the girl!"

I beckoned him over to the window to see if maybe he'd recognize her, but he was too slow. She was in her car and moving by the time he focused in, but he said, "Hey! I think I've seen that car." It was a fading green Porsche, about five years old. "There's one like that at the park—just like that, same color."

"Whose?"

"I don't know. It belongs to somebody in one of the little rental units out back, I think. I see it now and again coming in or going out. A girl drives it."

"How long's she been there?"

"I don't know, but I've been seeing the car for four or five months."

Bonny was still standing by the door, the paper in her hand, and a wry twist to her lips.

"Some dish," I said, "what?"

"Some dish," she agreed. "But I've never seen a colder eye in my life. Peck, there's something wrong with that girl."

"Maybe she hates beautiful blondes," I said. "Beautiful brunettes frequently do."

I was awakened in the morning by the acrid smell of smoke and got up coughing. The air outside my bedroom window was a marbled blue-brown, the houses across the street ghostly behind its scrim. The wind had shifted during the night, blowing fire smoke in from the east. It was the worst I'd ever seen.

I got to the station at nine and checked into Wells' office. Hawkins and Jones, two of the night-side men, were with him. There'd been a stabbing death at a Chicano wedding party at one A.M. and none of the forty guests had seen a thing. It would be a long and maddening case. Only Escalera could penetrate the macho maze of the Chicano community, and he was gone. Wells had been at it since two o'clock and when Hawkins and Jones finally dragged themselves away, he glared at me like a hurt bull. The air was full of brushfire smoke and bad vibes.

"I got the Grebses' statement," I said cautiously.

He didn't even glance at it. "You got nothing, Peckinpaugh! That gives you permission to fall asleep in a guy's house, that's all. Find Richards! That's what you've got to do. Put out an APB on him, or get that uncle of his to file an MPR, but find him! Put his picture on the wire, pull out all the stops, but find him. No more trick stuff, Peckinpaugh—find the man!"

"Yessir," I said.

In the communications room, I dawdled. I didn't want Richards found, I wanted him to walk into my arms tonight at Grebs' place. I wanted to feed him to Wells like meat. There wasn't enough to hold him on if we did find him, I told myself, and wasted three minutes listening to a technical analysis of the fire coming over the radio. By noon, this confident voice promised, heat would rise from the sun-baked desert to the east, drawing in cool moist air from the coast and clearing the Clausen Valley of smoke. Hallelujah!

I went out to my desk and phoned Richards and talked him into filing a missing persons report on his nephew. I told him the alternative was an APB, which he liked even less. I told him not to hurry getting here. The MPR would take me partway off the hook with Wells and still keep my option open for tonight. I was beginning to want a collar on this thief more than I wanted a good gun-control law.

After Richards came and went, I spent the rest of the day looking busy and when Wells left at four P.M., I did too.

I let myself in Grebs' front door at seven thirty, while there was still enough light left to set myself up and make my plans. The doggy-door was in the lower panel of the Hollwood door leading from the kitchen to the patio and pool area beyond. He would come in that way and probably go to the dining room first to arrange his phony entrance and then begin his tour of the house.

I could take him at any point after he came in, but decided he should have at least one item of Grebs' property in his bag before I made my move. It would make a stronger case of it.

I would sit, I decided, on the lower step of the stairway leading to the bedroom level. From there I could see the kitchen door, most of the dining room, and part of the living room. I memorized the location of the light switches I might need, and checked the entire house again.

From the master bedroom I could see the wall of smoke, richly hued in the rays of the setting sun, roiling high over the charred silhouette of the hills to the east.

He came at ten thirty, silent as a cat. I saw him before I heard him, his black shape deepening the dark of the kitchen door as it slowly opened. Instinctively my hand touched the bump of my gun in its shoulder holster, and I crouched lower on the stairs, blood sounding in my ears.

He stood for a moment in the kitchen, then moved swiftly to the dining room and opened a window. It was Richards; in the dim wash of outside light I saw that brave mustache sticking out from both sides of his face. It would be a piece of cake, I thought.

I heard buffet drawers whisper open and shut, the sound of rummaging, a thump as something went into the big black bag he carried. He was in business now, time to make my move. I got up and crept into the living room and stood in the arch between it and the dining room, my left hand reaching for a wall switch, gun in my right.

He was bent over an open drawer in the buffet. My fingers scrabbled against the wall, missing the switch. He heard, turned, and leaped like a leopard. I said, "Police, hold it!" and went over backwards from a blow on the chest, gun flying. I rolled and came up on my feet and felt a fierce jolt of pain in my right shoulder as I was spun and slammed down again in a classic karate throw. He was a tiger. His shoe glanced off the side of my head as I rolled away and came up. It hurt. I grabbed him and drew him in like a bear and got a knee in the groin. I bent down and lurched away and took the edge of his hand on my neck and the hard front of his upthrusting thigh on the side of my face. I was over on my back again, my head hitting something that rang bells—

My watch said ten forty-one. I hurt in many places. Bonny, who taught phys. ed. at Clausen Central High, had said I needed exercise. I was going soft. I said, look, there's no fat on this magnificent body and she said it didn't matter about the fat, I needed regular heavy exercise to get my heart rate up to one twenty-two per minute for two minutes a day, every day. I said I lead a life of violence. She said you'd get murdered in a fight.

I rolled and pushed to a sitting position and had trouble remembering where I was and why. My name was—something Peck—Jeff—Peck—I got up and grabbed a chair to keep from going down again. What was this place? That's a door over there, open, and a slab of dim light. I went to it like a swimmer in a dream. Outside the air was cool. I closed Mr. What's-his-name's door. My car was where? Around some corner, up some street. That way—

I got out of bed at six thirty and knew right off it was my own bed. And I knew my name—all of it. Jeffrey Peckinpaugh, custodian of multiple pains. I groaned out loud at the incredible thing in the bathroom mirror—there wasn't a mark on it. It should have been lumpy with bruises, a study in dark colors, an object of horror. I felt it with stiff hands, found only a lump on the back of the head under the thick hair that Wells, in his envy, hated. Wells? Ah—Wells!

I was at my desk at seven forty-five. The clock on the wall told me so. There was a new pile of case folders on the desk with the name Escalera on the outside of each and for a moment I didn't know who or what an Escalera was. I opened the top folder. A rape case.

Wells appeared in front of my desk, looking strong. I'd heard coming in that he'd solved his Chicano killing last night, had the perpetrator downstairs in a holding cell, and had a signed confession.

"So nothing happened last night," he stated bluntly. "Right? You got stood up like I knew you would."

"Er."

"Now is it okay with you if we warn the doggy-door people? I mean, I wanna clear it with you first, naturally."

"Ah—"

"And now maybe we can get out an APB on Richards instead of this feeble little missing-persons thing you've got going."

"Why sure, chief."

"Lieutenant, not chief."

"Sure, boss."

"Not boss, lieutenant."

"Certainly, lieutenant."

"And now, Peckinpaugh, I want you to go see Richards' uncle and I want you to sweat him. You got that? He knows more than he's telling you, whether he knows he does or not, and I want him squeezed dry. You got that, sergeant?"

"Yessir!" I stood up, activating seven distinct sources of pain, and said, "Oooomph," through my teeth, but he'd turned and stomped into his office.

Richards was on his pocket-size patio looking east at the rim of the charred hills. He wore a lightweight robe, and his little line of hair was unbrushed. "They got it out, by God," he said, and reminded me that a bad fire had come and gone. The sky above the hills was a clear morning blue. "You're early, sergeant. Had breakfast?"

"What?" I was still a half beat off the rhythm of the world. "Oh. No."

"Join me."

I followed him into his trailer and he pointed me toward the tiny kitchen. "Coffee's done," he said. "Have a grapefruit if you want—good for the blood. There are doughnuts in the bag there. Have at it. Me, I got to shave before I eat—old habit."

He disappeared down a narrow hall and I picked up a grapefruit from a wicker basket of them on the counter and looked for a knife.

And stopped abruptly. The grapefruit was small and soft and warm in my hand, and I squeezed it gently once or twice and then dropped it like a hot rock and felt sweat pop out all over my aching body. It was a *breast*, that grapefruit, a human female breast! Last night for a fleeting instant I'd held a female breast in my hand and I knew then where it was and why, and the whole thing came together with a rush of blood in my ears that nearly knocked me down. "Romero!" I whispered, and then hollered at Richards that I'd be back and went pounding out of the place.

The Grebses' living room was a mess, but it didn't surprise me and I didn't stare at it long. The first thing I looked for and found was my gun, the barrel protruding from under a chair, and not far from it a ten-inch fake mustache that didn't surprise me either.

Nothing in the disarrayed room, thank God, had been broken, and within five minutes not even Mrs. Grebs could have told that a hundred and twenty-pound girl had beat up a two hundred ten-pound man in her living room; but she could have told in a trice that one of her valuable antique chased silver pouring vases was missing from her buffet in the dining room. A thousand bucks' worth, Grebs had told me in passing, and sweat flowed freely on my brow again. I was an accessory to that theft, and of the worst kind—dumb. I locked up and left the place fast.

I was back at Richards' at nine thirty, still not entirely in gear, still sensing little time lapses and memory blanks, but clear on one point—I was in trouble. Richards was watering petunias on his patio. He saw me returning and put down his watering can with a frown. "Where in hell'd you go, man?"

"It's a long story," I said. I stared at him, not wanting to tell it, while his eyes tracked a car passing behind my back.

"There it goes," he said.

"What goes?"

"That little green Porsche."

I turned quickly enough to see its tail disappear around a bend and then took the last baby step back to being all there again, mad now, and not scared. "I want to use your phone," I said snappily, "and while I'm doing that you go find out what space Romero's in. It's even money," I added, "that she killed Danny, so put your heart in it."

I called Ed Munsey at the *Press-Sentinel* and found out she'd be on duty until around twelve thirty. The Saturday edition of the paper is delivered in the morning and the deadline for complaints is eleven o'clock. It usually took her an hour and a half to deliver them, he said, and then she was off until Monday noon.

She was in Space 179, Richards learned, and had been since February, just about the time Danny took his two karate lessons. It was one of the twenty-four foot rental units at the far end of the big sprawling park. We got in my car and Richards guided me back to where it was, and we pulled under her parking canopy like we owned the place. I told Richards to stand watch and picked her door open in twenty seconds.

What struck me instantly was the absolute absence of the female touch. No aroma, no smell of powder, no touch of color, no frill, no flower, no nothing. It was a cell—sterile, cold, and superneat. To my far left was a double built-in bed, trimly made. A tiny john cubicle next to the bed faced a hanging closet across a narrow aisle. In front of me was the kitchen wall, and to my right a gimbal-rigged table slung before an upholstered bench that would fold out into another bed. Not a hair out of place.

At random, I opened a drawer in the kitchen counter and looked down at a Polaroid portrait of Danny Richards, so big and clear it startled me. I pushed it aside with my pick. Beneath was his Clausen Savings and Loan passbook. I lifted it out by the edges and opened it on the counter with the pick again. Inside the book was a folded *Press-Sentinel* letterhead. I opened it carefully by the corners. It was covered with practice signatures of Daniel H. Richards, some nearly perfect duplications of his signature in the book. Any time now, she'd make herself up as Danny and go for the money—

It was terrific circumstantial evidence that she'd killed him, but I couldn't touch it, not without a warrant. Any other way it would be inadmissible as evidence. I nearly cried putting it back the way I'd found it, in a carefully squared-away stack.

I found her black bag on a hook in the hanging closet and, in the bottom of the bag, Mrs. Grebs' silver pouring vase. I couldn't touch that either, for the same reason. If I took it now—as I almost desperately wanted to do—she could raise the question of where it had gone, admitting she'd stolen it from Grebs, and when the truth eventually emerged she could claim that all the evidence in the place had been discovered through illegal entry, and was therefore inadmissible. The worst she would face then would be a robbery charge, greatly to be preferred to first-degree murder.

Richards stuck his head in the door just then to say I had a radio call and I went out to the car, locking the trailer behind me.

"Peckinpaugh," I said into the mike.

"Where are you?" It was Wells, still sounding strong.

"At the trailer park with Mr. Richards. I was about to call you. I need a search—"

"Can Richards hear this?"

Richards was leaning in the window. "Yes—"

"Well—" Wells' voice changed to softer "—I think we've found his nephew. Dead."

Richards' eyes flinched. "Where?" I said. I gestured Richards to open the door and sit down.

"In a little arroyo off Davis Canyon."

"In the burn area?"

"Yeah, about an hour ago. A helicopter was making a low pass over the canyon and spotted this van. The pilot radioed the sheriff and he sent a man out. The van is Richards' and so's the body in it probably. I want you to go there now and if Richards can handle it, take him along."

Richards nodded affirmatively, his jaw clamped tight. "He can handle it," I said. "We're on our way—but listen, boss, I want a search warrant on Romero and I want it fast."

"What for?"

"I think she's got some of the Park Plaza loot at her place."

"What makes you think so?"

"Damn it, boss, I'm sure!" My brow was wet again.

"How sure? You know how Bailey is on warrants—no guesswork."

"I'm a hundred percent sure."

There was a two-beat pause before he said, "You're not telling me the whole story, are you?"

"Can I tell you later, boss?"

"Is it solid?"

"Yessir."

"Okay, get going. It'll be on your desk when you get back. What's her address?"

I told him and then we moved out.

We had to walk the last two hundred yards into where Danny's van was. The final tag-end of visible road had ended a quarter mile behind us, but if you drove a car farther in than we'd gone it was only because you didn't want to drive it out again.

The burnoff had been complete. There wasn't a living thing left in sight. A few charred stumps of cottonwood, some still smoking in the quiet hot air, were all that remained of a trail of them that had run prettily up the narrow canyon floor. It hadn't been burned in living memory.

The air stank with the smell of charred wood and baked rock. Old man Richards was stumping along beside me, his chin up, his eyes narrowed against the hot acrid air.

The van was in a small draw off to the right of the canyon floor, slammed through the rocks as far as it could be made to go—hidden before the fire, in a small stand of trees. The smell of burned rubber dominated the air immediately around the hulk.

Two sheriff's deputies, the M.E., and a lab man with a camera were there. The deputies were standing well behind the van, waiting; the M.E. was leaning through the open side door and the photographer was alongside him, camera up.

"It's Danny's all right," Richards said, and went to where the M.E.

was bending over his work.

One of the deputies looked at me and said, "What gets me is how he got it in here—and why."

She, I amended silently. And why? Because there was a better-than-even chance it would never be found. I shrugged. "Who knows?"

"Is he your man?"

"I'd bet on it."

Richards came back and took a deep breath. He looked wobbly and I caught his arm. "It's Danny's boots," he said. "The rest—" He didn't finish. He pulled away from my grip and walked down the canyon a way and stood there.

The M.E. came out, pulling off soot-smeared rubber gloves, his glasses steamy. He took them off and wiped his forehead. "What I can tell you for sure right now," he said, "is that the fire didn't kill him. I think he's got a broken neck." He lit a cigarette and threw the burning match to the ground and watched it go out.

"How long dead?" I said. "You just broke the law, doc."

"At the moment, Peck, your guess is as good as mine. Sue me."

"Two months, maybe?"

"Could be."

I looked at my watch and was startled. It was eleven twenty. Ms. Romero could be through with her work in an hour or less and I wanted to be there when she got home. I went to the van and looked briefly in the side door. He was on his back behind the blackened driver's seat, head to the rear. His western-style boots, oddly almost intact, had two bright silver stars embossed in the tan leather of the pointed toes, a sad epitaph for a young man who would have made a good vet someday if he hadn't thought he'd like to learn the martial arts.

"There's no way," I said to the M.E., "he could have come in here alone, is there?"

"Not with a broken neck, he couldn't."

"Well," Richards said, "I guess I'd better try to find his ma now. It seems only right the woman who brought him into the world should know he's dead." He'd gotten out of the car at his place and closed the door. "She did it, didn't she, sergeant, that Romero woman?"

I nodded. I was itchy. I wasn't sure I'd beaten her back. I had the warrant in my pocket. It was twelve fifteen.

"Can you prove it?"

"I think so." He saw the uncertainty in my eyes. The case against her was circumstantial at every point, and on the stand she'd use her good looks and guile and maybe beat the rap. "We'll get her," I said. "I promise."

Her parking space was empty—I'd beaten her home. I drifted on past, parked a hundred feet away, came back, and let myself in. There wasn't a soul in sight. The neighbors were all inside their aluminum cells watching the ball game, swamp coolers thrumming away like distant freeway traffic.

She hadn't been back; nothing had changed since I'd left. I walked down the narrow aisle between the john and the hanging closet and sat on her bed. I took off my jacket, unholstered my gun, wiped sweat from around my eyes, and waited in the warm motionless air.

It wasn't long. I heard the Porsche turn in and stop, the door open and close, her heels clack across the concrete slab, the tick of her key touching the lock, and then a long spell of silence.

I leaned forward, ears cocked, heart slamming around. It was too long now. She'd rigged something I hadn't seen over the seal of the door, a hair, a thread, something I hadn't seen when I came in the first time, something no longer there. I took a deep breath and sensed danger as I've seldom sensed it before.

Behind my back, the small window illuminating the bed area was curtained and closed. She couldn't see me through it if she tried, but she'd know that if I was in the trailer at all I'd be where I was. Then the key ticked again in the lock and the door opened wide, light flooding the kitchen area.

She came in low to the floor. I saw her gun first, spitting fire, the bullet smashing through the john door at a slant. I hollered, "Hold it! Police!" as she came further in, her gun spitting again—this shot going through the hanging closet to my right. My gun, fired an instant after hers, hit high on her left shoulder. She rolled away and I hollered again, but she was in it to the end. She came up firing, two quick shots as my second bullet entered her chest six inches below her chin, blowing her against the gimbal-rigged table, her legs twitching for a moment on the trailer floor.

Outside, I heard someone scream.

By two thirty all the official personnel had gone, along with the body, and the crowd outside had dispersed in the boiling heat of mid-afternoon. Only Wells and I remained, seated on the dining bench. He shoved a cigar in his mouth and looked at me a long time.

"How do you feel?" he said finally.

"Beat," I said. "'Spent' is the classier word."

"But still a little sassy, huh?"

"I don't mean to be, chief."

"It just comes out that way, doesn't it?" He lit the cigar and threw the match out the door. "Now," he said, "I want you to tell me all about this affair and I want you to leave nothing out. You got that?"

"I'll be glad to," I said truthfully, and started at the beginning and ended up with the way the shots had gone.

When I'd finished, he looked solemn. A false face, I thought, for the week's work had gone well for him—two murders solved and the Park Plaza thefts at an end.

"She probably figured," he said, "that you were the guy in the Grebses' house last night and if she killed you here she could plead self-defense, or claim she thought you were a rapist."

I nodded. "She had that kind of a mind. Cunning as an alley cat. A psychopath."

He blew smoke at me. "It looks as though more things went right than went wrong, despite your best efforts to the contrary. One of these days you'll learn to respect procedure and then you'll be a good cop."

"Yessir," I said.

"So what I suggest is this—take the Grebses' piece back out to their house and put it where it belongs. And don't mention it in your report. Then keep your fingers crossed."

"Yessir," I said.

"And on your way back—"

"Yessir?"

"Get a haircut, goddamn it!"

"Yessir!"

He left and I got up and went over and got my jacket from the bed and the black bag from the hanging closet. I closed the place up and was walking back toward my car when I noticed the bullet holes in the bag, an entry hold and an exit hole—low down where the bulge of the vase was.

I stopped in mid-step and gulped hot air for a moment and then moved on. Maybe it went through the space where the handle is, I told myself, but I couldn't bring myself to open the bag and look.

It was in the hands of the gods, anyway, like everything else.

Gary Brandner
Waiting for the Coroner

I lay on my back in my bed with the covers pulled up to the pale blue monogram on my eggshell silk pajamas. From the very center of the monogram the hilt of an Oriental dagger pointed toward the ceiling. I was dead as a trout.

It was almost time for Nurse Bundy to waddle in with my morning medicine. I knew she wouldn't be late. It always gave her pleasure to jerk me out of a restful sleep so she could pour some horrid concoction down my feverish throat. Well, this morning there would be a surprise for Nurse Bundy and for everyone else in the house.

Right on schedule she pushed through the door, a bulging tub of suet with fat arms and legs and a mean little face. I thought how fitting it would be if she had a coronary when she saw the knife in me and fell writhing to the floor. It was too much to hope for.

She came over to the bed and set the morning's concoction down on the night table. As she started to take up the glass that had held last night's potion she caught sight of the knife. The color drained out of her grapefruit cheeks. She drew in air through her tiny mouth and let out quite a commendable scream. She dropped the glass, spun around, and thundered out of the room like a rhino in full retreat.

I stayed where I was—I had little choice—and waited for Bundy to bring the others. Soon I heard voices in the hall outside my door.

Son-in-law Paul's nasal tenor: "Calm down, Miss Bundy, I can't make any sense out of what you're saying."

Nurse Bundy's blubbery soprano: "It's Mr. Ogilvie—on the bed. He's—he's—"

Daughter Wendy's vacuous contralto: "Do you mean something's happened to Daddy?"

Dear Wendy, flesh of my flesh, with a typical flash of insight.

"Well, we'd better go in and see." A note of hope from the sterling son-in-law.

Into my room they trooped—dark-browed Paul, whose good looks were tempered by his habitual pout, graceful Wendy in her new Dior negligee, and the blimp.

Wendy and Paul approached my bed while Nurse Bundy remained prudently in the background. The handsome couple gazed down at me.

"What is it, Paul?" My beloved daughter had used up her quota of insights for the day.

"Your father's been stabbed." My observant son-in-law. He knew a man with a knife in his chest when he saw one.

"Who could have done such a thing?"

No one volunteered an answer. The rhino started to cry into a wad of Kleenex.

"Miss Bundy, stop that sniveling."

Stout fellow, Paul. No time for sentimental nonsense just because the patriarch has been done to death.

"I'm sorry, sir, it's just—well, his face looks so awful."

Well, excuse *me*, Nurse Bundy. I should have used my dying moments to arrange my features into some more pleasing expression. A gentle smile, say, with a twinkle of benevolence in one fishy eye.

"Could we at least close his eyes, Paul?"

Wendy was not without aesthetic sense.

"I don't think we should touch him until the police get here."

"The police?"

I don't know who else my daughter expected to summon. The plumber?

"I'll go downstairs and call them," Paul offered.

"I'll go with you," Wendy volunteered quickly.

"*I* don't have to stay up here, do I? With *him*?"

"No, Miss Bundy, you can come down with us and wait for the police."

They left me alone with evident relief. It didn't matter. I wasn't going anywhere.

In about half an hour footsteps approached in the hall. The door opened and the members of my household filed in with a rumpled man whose grey eyes flicked over everything in a professional manner.

"This is where we found him, inspector."

Inspector. It had a nice ring. Better than "sergeant," or "officer." I approved of the baggy tweed suit he wore and, especially, the magnificent sandy mustache.

"Mm-hmmm," he said. "Aah."

A thoughtful man. He leaned over me and peered at the knife in my chest.

"Do any of you recognize the weapon?"

Wendy spoke up, a bright student.

"It was one of a pair of Oriental daggers. The other is still there on the wall plaque."

"Aah. Hmmm."

A reflective man. I figured him for a pipe smoker.

"Do you mind if I light my pipe?"

I knew it.

"No, go right ahead." Tolerant Wendy.

While the inspector set fire to a bowl of strong tobacco, there was a series of throat-clearing coughs at the door. "Nobody answered the bell downstairs so I came on up."

My friend and partner, bless his skinny frame, had never let closed doors keep him out.

"Who are you?" asked the inspector.

"My name is Oscar Hanratty."

"He's my father's partner," Wendy supplied.

"Who are *you*?"

"I'm Inspector Grubb."

"Inspector? Is something wrong?" Oscar followed their gaze over to me on the bed. "Good Lord! Is he—is he—?"

"He's dead."

No cloying euphemisms for Inspector Grubb.

"But who? Why—?"

"All in good time. First I think we can narrow down the *when*. We know Mr. Ogilvie died some time after he took his evening medicine and before seven this morning when the nurse here came in to wake him. It *was* last night's medicine in the empty glass there, was it not?"

"Yes, sir. I gave it to him at eight o'clock. I was about to take the glass away this morning when I saw that—that thing sticking in his chest."

The look on her face, I recalled, had almost made it worthwhile.

Paul leaned over me, studying the wound. "What does the *E* stand for?"

"What are you talking about?" my daughter asked.

"The *E* in the monogram *AEO*. I didn't know the old man had a middle name."

"It was Ervin. Arnold Ervin Ogilvie. Daddy didn't like it so he never used it."

I wished they would get on with it. I had no way of knowing how long I would be allowed to stay, and it would be nice to see my murder solved before I had to leave.

"Damned shame," Oscar said. "Well, if no one minds I'll be pushing along. I only stopped by to get Arnold's signature on some papers. Obviously he won't he signing anything now, poor devil. Couldn't somebody close his eyes?"

Good old Oscar. I was touched by his grief.

"Just one minute, Mr. Hanratty."

I was liking the inspector better and better.

"Yes?"

"You said you had some papers to be signed."

"That's right. Nothing important, really. Nothing I can't take care of at the office. I just thought that since I was coming this way I'd bring them along."

Oscar never did know when to shut up.

"Where are they?"

"Where are what?"

"The papers. I see you're carrying no briefcase or folder of any kind. The papers are in your pocket perhaps?"

"Uh—er—oh, yes, that's right. In my pocket."

"May I see them, please?"

Oscar went through a bad pantomime of patting his pockets. "Well, now, that was stupid of me. I—uh—*thought* I had them right here. I must have left them in the car. Or back at the office."

Oscar never could lie for sour owl droppings, not even when he was telling me how our investments were in trouble when he siphoned off the profits. In another couple of days I would have had the proof to nail him.

"There aren't any papers, are there, Mr. Hanratty?" The inspector fixed him with the unblinking eye of the law.

"I—I don't know what you mean."

"I think you do, sir. Your real reason for coming here this morning was to establish the idea that you expected to find Mr. Ogilvie alive. In fact, you knew full well he was dead. You knew because sometime last night you slipped into the house the way you did just now, came up here to his room, took the dagger from the wall, and plunged it into his chest."

I knew that with a mustache like his, Inspector Grubb was going to be all right.

"I want a lawyer." They were Oscar's first intelligent words since he walked in.

Wendy touched the inspector's tweedy sleeve in admiration. Even Paul left off his inventory of my belongings to give him a grudging nod.

"Only doing my job, ma'am."

For a moment I feared he was going to start being modest a bit too soon.

Nurse Bundy gathered her flab and started toward the bed. "I might as well get things cleaned up in here. I'll start with these bottles and the dirty glass."

"Not so fast, nurse."

I would have applauded had it not been for advanced rigor mortis.

"Sir?"

"I'd like all of you to take a close look at the dagger protruding from the late Mr. Ogilvie."

They obeyed, and for one last time I was surrounded by beloved friends and family.

"Do any of you see anything odd?"

They all looked at the knife, then at each other, then at the inspector. Four pairs of eyes empty of all intelligence.

The inspector spoke to my son-in-law. "It was you, sir, who called my attention to it."

"To what?" Paul's eyes shifted guiltily.

"The monogram on Mr. Ogilvie's pajamas. A stab wound in that location should have bled profusely, thoroughly obscuring a pale blue monogram on white silk."

The color, as I noted, was eggshell, but it was no time for nitpicking.

"What does it mean, inspector?"

Leave it to Wendy to ask the incisive question.

"It means that when Oscar Hanratty plunged the dagger into your father's chest, he was already dead."

For a moment the room was so still you could have heard my heart beat, had I not been dead.

Nurse Bundy was the first to speak. "I really should clear away these things."

"I can understand your impatience," said the inspector in clipped tones. "Because in that glass, unless I miss my guess, we will find traces of a deadly fast-acting poison."

Foul-tasting stuff, too, I could have told him.

Wendy and Paul turned to stare at the tub of lard in white.

"Nurse Bundy—you ?"

"But why?"

Bundy's pinched little mouth twisted into a sneer. "He deserved it, the old miser. For more than a year I've taken care of him, and not even a mention do I get in his will. Yes, I found the will. I also found the tin box he kept hidden away filled with cash."

Paul's ears seemed to swivel forward.

"Box of cash? Wendy, do you know anything about a box of cash?"

"No. What box of cash, Nurse Bundy?"

I posthumously urged the old lard bucket to keep her mouth shut for once.

"Find it yourself," she told them.

Nobody, as they say, can be all bad.

The inspector took charge then. "I think we can all go downstairs now and I'll take your statements while we wait for the coroner."

Luckily, it was time for me to leave. Waiting for the coroner did not sound like much fun. My last regret was that I could not recover the power of speech long enough to thank them all for the most entertaining morning of my life.

Maybe I ought to rephrase that.

Henry Slesar
Ruby Martinson's Poisoned Pen

For years, I lived in mortal terror of G-men because of my cousin Ruby Martinson. The three most horrifying letters in my alphabet were F.B.I. and I couldn't see a picture of J. Edgar Hoover without wondering if it saw me. And the worst part was, the whole trauma was the result of the wildest crime that Ruby Martinson, World's Greatest Unsuccessful Criminal, ever perpetrated.

By this time, of course, I was getting used to Ruby's inability to make Crime pay. Even though Ruby was an accountant, he never seemed to get out of the red in all the capers we pulled together. Fortunately, he was making good money (sixty-five dollars a week) for his age (twenty-three) so I never worried about his finances. But I was five years younger, a great deal poorer, and in contrast to Ruby's iron nerves, mine were made of chicken fat.

On the evening that it started, I was poorer than usual. I had just been fired from my fourth job in the garment district, merely because I had pushed a hand truck into an open manhole on 33rd and Seventh Avenue, sending half a dozen Max Teitelbaum originals into the sewer system of New York. So when I met Ruby at Hector's Cafeteria on Broadway, I was forced to ask him for coffee-and-cruller money. Ruby, who was normally pretty tightfisted, handed me the coins without a murmur.

"You okay, Ruby?" I asked, genuinely concerned.

He looked up at me, and his small freckled face had never appeared so tragic before.

"I'm okay," he said bitterly. "I'll be even better when Dorothy gets that letter tomorrow."

"You wrote Dorothy a letter? What for?"

My astonishment was real. Dorothy, Ruby's fiancee, lived on 76th Street, and Ruby saw here every night that wasn't devoted to his Fiendish Activities. Not that she knew about his secret life; I was Ruby's only confidante in crime.

"I wrote her a letter, all right," he said, with a mocking laugh. "She'll never forget it. She'll be sorry for the rest of her life."

It was obvious that the bumpy road to love was bumpier than usual.

"You know what I told her?" Ruby said. "I told her what I really think of her. And I told her what she could do with that four-eyed freak she's so crazy about."

I looked at him queerly, since Ruby wears the biggest eyeglasses I ever saw in my life. I mean, they were so big that an optometrist could have hung them up as a sign.

"She doesn't know I saw her," Ruby continued with a snarl. "I was in the delicatessen across the street from her house, the Savoy. You remember the place."

I did, of course. We had robbed it once, and lost money on the deal.

"I was just standing there, when I see this taxi pull up in front of her place, and Dorothy gets out with this four-eyed tall guy. I mean, they were friendly. Real friendly!"

I liked Dorothy, so I rushed to her defense. "Gee, Ruby, he was probably some guy from where she works, probably gave her a lift—"

"Yeah?" Ruby said cynically. "So how come he kissed her good-bye? I mean a real passionate kiss?"

That stopped me, and I joined Ruby in a morose sip of coffee and an angry bite of cruller.

"So today," Ruby said, "I wrote her this letter and told her off good. Women are all alike, pal, don't trust any of 'em. They'll two-time you the minute you turn your back. I shouldn't have just written her a letter. I should have gone up there and leaned on her a little."

"Gosh, Ruby, you wouldn't really hurt her?"

Ruby didn't answer. He picked up his coffee cup and downed the brown stuff like it was a hooker of rye. It's a good thing alcohol made Ruby sick, or he would have gotten potted that night. I watched him and felt an emphatic melancholy; the idea that Ruby and Dorothy might part seemed as shattering to me as if my own parents were breaking up. Big tears welled up in my eyes, and I think I would have blubbered right in the middle of the cafeteria, except that a sudden thought intruded. "Hey!" I cried. "Maybe Dorothy has a brother!"

"Naw," Ruby said. "She's got a lot of relatives out in the middle west, but nobody like that. Besides, that wasn't any sisterly kiss, let me tell you."

I stood up, and made a feeble excuse about washing my hands. I tried not to show my excitement because I had decided to call Dorothy and see if there were some reasonable explanation for her behavior. I knew vaguely that the way of the peacemaker is hard, but I didn't know how hard it was going to become.

In the rear of Hector's, I put one of Ruby's coins into the telephone and dialed Dorothy's home number.

When she answered, I didn't know how to approach the subject delicately, so I just blurted it out.

"Hey," I said. "Who was that guy last night?"

"What guy?" She sounded surprised.

I forced a laugh. "I was across the street yesterday, and I saw you getting out of the taxi. You better not let Ruby know about that, hah-hah."

"I don't know what you're talking about; I came home by subway. Are you with Ruby? Is he playing a joke on me?"

I didn't know whether she was covering up or not. So I laughed again, in a kind of cracked debonair manner, and that made her sore.

"Look, will you stop acting so silly? If Ruby's there, tell him to be sure and get here at seven thirty. My cousin Ruth has to leave at nine, so we have to have dinner early."

"Your cousin Ruth?"

"Ruby knows about it. Ruth came in last night to go see her husband off. He's going into the army. Would you please ask Ruby to come to the phone?"

"He's not here!" I said wildly. "I mean, I don't know where he is," I stuttered. "Dorothy, does this cousin of yours look like you, even a little?"

"She does, as a matter of fact. Why?"

"Nothing," I said miserably. "If I see Ruby, I'll tell him to call you." And I hung up.

I went back to the table, and told Ruby what I had done. When I got to the part about Dorothy's cousin, his eyes glazed and he realized the truth.

"Her cousin!" he said, slapping his high forehead. "I thought Dorothy looked different. Something about the hairstyle—"

"Boy, that's a relief, huh?" I said. "But you better call her back."

Ruby still looked stunned. I had to jog his elbow to get him to say something. When he did, the words gagged him.

"The letter!"

"What?"

"The letter I sent Dorothy! If she gets it, it's the end!"

"Gee," I said calmly, "why not just call her and tell her not to read it?"

"Are you nuts? Did you ever try and tell a girl not to do something? She'll be so curious she'll have to read it. I've got to get that letter back!"

"Maybe if you called the post office," I said timidly. His glare told me what he thought of the suggestion, so I tried another. "Well, tell her the truth, then. Tell her how jealous you got when you saw her cousin—"

"You don't understand. It was a real nasty letter. I said things she could never forgive. I even said she was fat."

I smiled pleasantly. "She is getting a little plump, isn't she?"

Ruby groaned and looked worse off than he had before. He slumped into his chair and hid his face in his hands. I didn't know what else to do, so I went and got some cheese danish from the pastry counter. By the time I got back, Ruby looked entirely different. I had forgotten how swiftly his ingenious Criminal Brain worked.

"There's only one thing to do," he said. "We got to steal it back."

"We?" I said, soprano. "Steal it?"

"It's the only way. You've got to waylay the postman that comes to Dorothy's apartment house."

"I've got to? But Ruby—"

"You're the only one who can do it. The mail comes at ten, and I'll be at work then. I'd take tomorrow off, but we're doing a job for our biggest client."

"Ruby, you're talking crazy. You can't rob a postman. I mean, that's a federal offense, it's like killing somebody."

"You're not stealing money, just a lousy letter. Now listen carefully how it's gonna work—"

I put my hands over my ears. "I'm not listening! I don't want to listen! I did a lot of nutty things for you, Ruby, but you're not getting no F.B.I. on my neck!"

"You won't have any trouble," Ruby said contemptuously. "I've seen the guy who delivers the mail there. He's about four feet high and built like a sparrow. When you shove that gun in his face, he'll fold up."

"Gun?" I said, spraying the landscape with the cheese crumbs in my mouth. "Ruby, I'm not sticking up any postman with a gun!"

"What else you gonna use, a bow and arrow? It'll be a fake, of course, we'll pick one up at Woolworth's. All you have to do is wait around the hallway until he shows up. When he's about to put the letter in Dorothy's mailbox, you jump out and grab it." He studied me reflectively. "Better wear a mask," he said. "Nobody could forget a face like yours."

I stood up and folded my arms. I had been browbeaten, coaxed, and cajoled into plenty of capers with Ruby Martinson, but this time I was going to be firm.

"I won't do it," I said, with manly simplicity.

Then I waited for Ruby's barrage. It didn't come. He just put his thumbnail between his teeth, looked dejected, and turned his head away.

"Oh, heck," I said. "All right, Ruby."

I had nothing but nightmares in my dream life during those years with Ruby Martinson, and that night was no different. James Cagney was after me with a machine-gun, and wouldn't even let me surrender. I went down in a hail of G-man bullets, and woke up clutching my stomach. My mother heard my groans and suggested castor oil. I said no, but from the fishy taste of my orange juice, I suspected that she had her way.

I showed up at Dorothy's apartment house a little before nine. In the hallway, I scouted the best hiding place; it was easy enough to find. Behind the staircase was a dark, damp corner used for the storage of baby carriages, discarded tricycles, and a large piece of nude sculpture. It was embarrassing to be around the thing, so I sat on the seat of the tricycle and tried not to see it. While I waited, I checked the artillery that Woolworth had provided: it was a small, menacing pistol that went clickety-chuck when you pressed the trigger, and emitted a small hard piece of sickening candy. I hoped I would remember not to fire the darned thing; I might actually hurt the guy.

It was a long wait. For an hour, I sat there with nothing to do but eat the revolting candy and try not to stare at the naked stone lady. After awhile, I got so bored and reckless that I not only stared at the statue, but started firing little hard pieces of candy at it.

Then I heard the shuffling footsteps and the out of key whistle. The postman was here.

I peeked out to size up the opposition, and felt just a bit better. Ruby had been correct, if not precise. The postman was a little guy not much over five feet, and so frail that I didn't see how he carried that heavy mailpouch on hs pack. He had already sorted out the building mail, and now he was opening the bank of boxes against the wall.

I fixed my eyes on Dorothy's mailbox, and tied my handkerchief around my face. Then I took out the gun, put my finger on the trigger, and got ready to pounce. I really amazed myself that day; I wasn't even nervous.

Then it was time to act. He had an envelope in his hand and was about to drop it in the box; once he locked it, it would be irretrievable. I jumped out, waved the gun, and shouted:

"Stick' em up!"

To tell you the truth, I didn't shout anything. I just jumped out and opened my mouth. Not a sound came out. I wasn't nervous, but my mouth was. We looked at each other stupidly for a moment, and I wondered if I would have to write it out for him. Can you imagine borrowing a guy's pencil and writing "Stick'em up?"

We were at an impasse. He didn't know what I wanted, and I didn't know how to tell him. Then I fixed everything by snatching the letter out of his hand.

He knew what I was up to then, all right. He yelled and called me something that I never saw in print, and then he picked up that big mail pouch of his like it was a pillow, and whopped me right in the head. I mean, that bag must have weighed a hundred pounds and he just slung it at me! I staggered against the wall and he raised the thing again. It must have felt heavier this time, because he wasn't so fast anymore. I had time to duck underneath his arm and make it to the front door of the apartment house.

I didn't even look back to see if I was followed. I just tore the handkerchief from my face and ran. If there's one thing I could do, it was run. I ran so hard that my shirttails came right out of my trousers. I didn't stop until I reached 68th Street.

But I had the letter! Panting but triumphant, I stopped in the doorway of a hardware store and looked at the envelope.

It was neatly typed, and in the upper left hand corner were the words: FRESH AIR FUND.

I opened the letter, praying that Ruby had used a secondhand envelope. But the worst was immediately evident. The letter had been run off on a duplicating machine, and its opening line was:

"YOU CAN SEND A BOY TO CAMP THIS SUMMER!"

Right then, I fervently wished the boy could be me. In my haste, I had snatched the first letter the postman had destined for the mailbox. Ruby's letter was still in the pouch; by now it was nestling snugly in the mailbox where it belonged. And that night, Dorothy would open it blissfully, and all would be over.

My first thought was to go down to the docks and see what ships were leaving. Then I decided it wasn't fair to Ruby to tell him anything but the truth; his fertile-brain might still hatch another scheme for the letter's recovery. I phoned him at his office, and he called me exactly what the mailman had called me. Then he said to meet him at Hector's Cafeteria at noon.

I showed up, expecting to be tongue-lashed. Instead I found Ruby looking crafty. The Great Mind had arrived at another solution.

"It's all fixed," he said cheerfully. "It took some figuring out, but I did it."

"That's great," I said. "I knew you could do it!"

"It came to me in a flash. What would stop somebody from opening their own letter?"

I concentrated, and tired to match Ruby's uncanny powers, but I got no place.

He laughed. "Would you open a letter that might kill you?"

"Kill me? How could a letter do that?"

"If it was contaminated! Don't you see?"

I wasn't even sure what contaminated meant.

"I called Dorothy at the office," Ruby said, chuckling happily. "I told her she'd get a letter from me in the mail today, but she wasn't to open it under any circumstances."

"Wasn't she curious why?"

"Sure she was. But I told her the letter wasn't anything important, just a poem I wrote for her."

It was like hearing that Dillinger did needlework.

"You write poems?" I said.

Ruby scowled. "So what? Anyway, I told her that I was over at a chemical laboratory, visiting a friend of mine yesterday, and I had the poem in my pocket. I sat down at one of the counters and started to read it, when all of a sudden I accidentally knocked this beaker over. some white liquid got spilled on the letter, but it dried fast so I didn't think anything of it, and put the poem in the mail."

"What a screwy story," I said.

"Let me finish," Ruby snapped. "Anyway, after I mailed the poem, I got to talking to one of the guys in the laboratory, and mentioned about spilling the beaker. He got real excited, because he said the beaker contained a virulent-type disease germ. If you just touch the stuff, you curl up and die."

"Wow!" I said. "Are you sure it didn't get on you, Ruby?"

He punched my arm. "This is what I told Dorothy, you dope, it didn't really happen."

"Oh."

"Anyway, I told Dorothy the letter should be burned before she opens it, to make sure she doesn't get infected. She got real upset, of course, and said maybe she ought to leave work and go to the apartment. She's got this cleaning woman who brings up the mail every day, and who knows? But I told her not to worry, that I'd go up there and burn the letter for her. so that's your agenda for the afternoon, pal."

"Me? Aw, gosh, Ruby, I don't want to go back there."

"Don't give me any arguments. Nothing can go wrong this time. All you got to do is let yourself into Dorothy's apartment—the key's under the mat—and get hold of that letter and burn it. Even you can handle that."

"All right," I said reluctantly. "I guess that won't be so hard."

Ruby looked at his watch. "Call me at the office and let me know how things went. And I'll meet you here at six. Check?"

"Check," I said.

This time, the trip to 76th Street wasn't nearly so depressing. It was a simple enough assignment; all I had to do was burn a letter. I liked fires.

I walked up the street to the apartment house, whistling nonchalantly. To this day, I can't explain the cockeyed confidence which made me believe that a white handkerchief was an impenetrable disguise. Even if I had suspected that the two burly types lingering in the doorway of Dorothy's building were officers of the law, I think I would have merely gulped hard and kept on going, secure in the belief that I was unrecognizable. Only let me tell you what I was wearing. A pink sports shirt with a picture of a hula dancer on the back. A leather belt with a nickel-plated buckle the size of a cantaloupe. A pair of bleached denim pants, and orange shoes. Orange. They had been tan to begin with, but my shoe polish went rancid or something, and they turned orange.

It never occurred to me that the postman would take any action, and describe my outfit to the Law. After all, what was one Fresh Air Fund letter, more or less? But when I went up the elevator to Dorothy's apartment, the two big guys went with me. When I found the key under the mat, they stood at the end of the hallway and acted indifferent. When I entered the apartment, and found Ruby's letter on the coffee table, I was smugly certain my troubles were over.

Just to make doubly certain that I had the right letter this time (and because I was so curious) I opened the envelope and took a look at the contents.

The letter wasn't very long, but neither is a stick of dynamite.

Dear Dorothy, it said, *I saw you with that ugly four-eyed boyfriend of yours, and you can have him. Please send me back my ring on account of our engagement is off. If you can get it off your finger, which I doubt, since you've been getting pretty fat lately. You look lousy.* And it was signed, *Yours sincerely, Ruby Martinson.*

I chuckled to myself, and was about to leave when I saw them standing in the doorway.

"You live here, son?" one of them said. He had a nose like a piece of modeling clay.

"Who, me?" I said. "No, my friend lives here. She wanted me to get something for her. A letter."

"A letter, huh?" the second one grunted, looking at his buddy sideways. "You got quite a thing about letters, don't you kid?"

"What's that?" I said, starting to shake.

The first one took out a wallet the size of a club. For a minute, I thought he was going to sock me with it, but he was only flashing his identification.

"I'm Lieutenant Jakes," he said. "This is Lieutenant Cochran."

"Hello there," I said. I started to grin. That's my worst symptom when I'm nervous. I grin so hard my jaw hurts. "I didn't do anything," I said. "I was just doing my friend a favor. You could call and ask her."

"We just might do that," Jakes said. "Only there's something else we wanted to talk to you about. Were you in the building this morning?"

"Me?" I said, grinning and shaking.

"Mr. Finchley, the postman who works this building, he got attacked this morning. Somebody snatched a letter from him. You know anything about that?"

"Me?" I said.

"Is that all you can say?" Cochran growled. "Did you take that letter? The postman described you and that outfit you got on to a T, so no use acting coy."

I was about to say "Me!" again, but I figured he must have meant Me. My legs went rubbery and my eyes blurred. I held up Ruby's letter and tried to croak out an explanation.

"Wait a minute," I said, "wait, I had a reason, a very good reason!"

"You know what the penalty for mail theft is?" both of them asked, seemed like both of them.

"I know, I know," I squealed. "But I had to do it. So help me! I was looking for this letter—this letter's poisoned—"

That stopped them. They stepped back from the envelope I was waving in my hand, as if it were a hand grenade.

"What are you giving us?" Jakes said gruffly. "What do you mean, poisoned?"

"It is, it is!" I shrieked. "That's why I was trying to get it from the postman, so he shouldn't get infected. My friend sent it to his girlfriend from some chemical laboratory. A test tube got spilled on it—it's full of deadly germs—"

They looked at each other, and I could see they were uncertain about what to do next. That made three of us.

Then Cochran twisted his mouth sourly. "Oh, yeah?" he said. "Then how come you're touching it, kid?"

"I was going to burn it!" I shouted wildly. "I'm immune to this kind of thing, I've had shots!"

"It's a nutty story," Jakes muttered. "But who knows? Maybe we better check on it."

"Please," I stammered, "call Dorothy. The girl who lives here. She'll tell you it's true. She'll prove it."

"We'll do better than that. We'll take you and that letter into our lab. Then we'll get this thing straightened out."

"No!" I yelled. "You can't do that! I have to burn it—"

"Come on," Jakes said.

He jerked his thumb at me, and failing to think of anything else to say, I preceded them out. It was at times like these that I wished (a) to have Ruby's power of invention, or (b) to have never met Ruby at all.

I thought there would be a prowl car in the street, but there wasn't. Instead, they prodded me into a nondescript gray Buick. I was put in the back with my diseased letter, and Cochran sat beside me, well away from me and it. The officer named Jakes drove, but I don't think he was happy having me behind him. I felt like Typhoid Mary.

I thought this lab would be in a precinct house, but it wasn't; it was located in a quiet brownstone house on East 48th Street. As they led me into the place, I kept pleading with them to call Dorothy. I didn't mention anything about Ruby Martinson; some crazy sense of honor kept me from dragging his name into the mess. I guess I figured that once he was in the hands of the Law, his whole Criminal Career might be exposed.

The fellow in the lab was named Fusco. He listened to their story with interest, looked queerly at me with Ruby's letter in my hot little hand, and then beckoned us into an inner office.

Fusco was one of these kindly white-haired types; he didn't look like a cop or an F.B.I. man at all. He listened calmly to my own version of what had happened, and asked if I knew what kind of virulent germ Ruby had spilled on the letter. I said I didn't know, but that I thought Ruby had said that its victims turned blue. He then examined my face, my throat, my pulse, and took my temperature.

"Well," he said, "if you've caught anything, there's no sign of it. But maybe we'd better see the letter."

I held it behind my back. "We have to burn it," I said. "I was told to burn it."

Fusco smiled gently. "I'd like to take a look at it under the microscope."

"No!" I yelled. "You can't do that! I mean, you might catch it yourself—"

He took a pair of forceps out of a drawer, and held them toward me. With a sinking feeling, I let him take the letter.

When Fusco disappeared into a back room, I looked at my captors and wondered what my mother would say when she learned that I was going to jail. I began thinking about prison life. I hoped she wouldn't mail me a lot of cakes and cookies and stuff like that. I mean, I wouldn't want the other prisoners to think I was a sissy.

Five minutes later, Fusco reappeared. There was no letter in his hand, and he was looking grave. I shut my eyes and waited for the worst.

Then I heard him say:

"The young man was right. There were deadly disease germs on that letter, but fortunately, he didn't become infected. You really can't blame him for trying to steal it—he was only protecting the mailman."

"You see?" I said ecstatically. "You see?"

Jake grunted. "What do we do, give him a medal?"

"Gee, you don't have to do that," I said.

"I've burned the letter as instructed," Fusco said, looking at me with a funny kind of twinkle. "So you can forget the whole thing."

"What kind of germs were they, doc?" Cochran asked.

"One of the deadliest," Fusco smiled. "I'm not sure of the exact name, but I think it's something like *zelus excessus*. But everything's fine now."

"Then I can go?" I said eagerly. "Will you let me go?"

Jakes rubbed his jaw, and then looked at his buddy.

"I guess so. If the doctor says it's okay."

I made the door so fast that I think I broke Nurmi's record. But something stopped me before I turned the knob. I looked back at the doctor, and said:

"Say, you sure I didn't get infected? I've got an awful weak constitution. I mean, I can catch anything."

"You're absolutely fine," the doctor said.

But I wasn't so fine by the time I met Ruby Martinson at Hector's Cafeteria that night. I was seeing spots before my eyes, my head was feverish, and my tongue felt two inches thick.

"Ruby," I said, trembling. "Ruby I'm feeling sick. Why didn't you tell me it was the truth?"

"Don't be stupid," he said.

"Ruby, you heard about what the doctor said. I think I'm coming down with this *zelus excessus*. Do I look blue to you?"

He laughed happily. "You dope! Don't you see what happened? This Fusco must be an all right guy; he read the letter and figured out what had happened. So he just played along with the gag, and pretended that there were deadly germs on the letters."

"He did?"

"Of course! You know what *zelus excessus* means in Latin? Too much jealousy!"

Ruby was feeling so good that he bought me a slab of lemon meringue pie. But I was too sick to enjoy it.

Stephen Wasylyk
The Desperate Theft

As Hoke Beckett finished his second cup of coffee and reached for his luncheon check, he heard his name. He looked up to see Maxine beckoning.

"Call for you, Hoke," she said, handing him the phone at the restaurant's reservations desk. "Larry Gitlow at the radio station."

Beckett held the phone to his ear. "I'm listening, Larry."

"Since I'm sure you never listen to our talk program, you'd better come over here," said Gitlow. "I have a tape any detective lieutenant would be interested in. If the man was serious, you have only a few hours to keep him from committing a crime."

"What kind of crime?"

"Hearing is believing," said Gitlow. "Come over and listen to the tape."

Beckett swung into the local FM station's parking lot twenty minutes later and pulled up before the low red brick building.

The phone-in talk show was Gitlow's latest innovation in his constant battle to keep the small station competitive with the larger ones covering Meridian County, and he had an erudite college type named Si Youngblood taking the calls and handling the discussions and gripes.

Youngblood was good. He had an instinctive sense of when to be sympathetic and when to be insulting, and the midday program had become very popular.

Beckett found Gitlow behind his desk—a rack-shouldered young man with long sideburns, bright eyes, a halo of curly dark hair, and a long nose—his shirtsleeves were rolled up and his collar was open.

"You know we tape all calls, Hoke, and broadcast with a six-second delay so we can delete language that's out of line. We didn't cut this one because we had no reason. Youngblood took the call at twelve forty-five. I made a copy from our master. Listen."

He punched a button on a small cassette tape player on his desk.

Youngblood's voice was clear.

"Si Youngblood here. What's on your mind today?"

The other man's voice was a bit thick and muffled, as if he had neglected to speak directly into the mouthpiece. There was a hollow sound in the background.

"You've been talking about doing things you want to do, right, Youngblood?"

Youngblood: "More or less, friend. All of us have things we'd like to do and intend to do, but for one reason or the other we put them off. Maybe we lack the nerve, the proper incentive, or the money. Be that as it may, we've been saying that we all ought to just sit down one day and say, hey, I'm going to do it."

Voice: "Yeah, well, I think you're right. If you're going to do something, do it. None of us is getting any younger, and the next thing you know, bang, you wake up dead and you never did it at all."

Youngblood: "That's one way to look at it. What little thing do you intend to do?"

Voice: "Steal the horses."

(Pause)

Youngblood: "I don't think I heard you right, friend."

Voice: "I'm going to steal the horses. I've always wanted them, so I'm going to do it."

Youngblood: "What horses are those, friend?"

Voice: "They're beautiful. I guess they're just about the most beautiful horses I've ever seen."

Youngblood: "When do you intend to do this, friend?"

Voice: "Tonight. Listen, Youngblood, I've got to go."

Youngblood: "Wait, you can't ..."

A click and a pause and then Youngblood's voice: "Well, people, I never did expect to hear from a horse rustler ..."

Gitlow turned off the player and looked at Beckett. "Well?"

Beckett shook his head. "I have no idea of what he was talking about. I don't suppose you have any way to tell where the call came from?"

"Only that it was local, but that covers a lot of real estate."

"So it could be the immediate vicinity."

Gitlow smiled. "I know what you're driving at. I wondered where a man could find horses to steal in this community and then it came to me. The Meridian Horse Show. It opened today. We've been carrying the announcements all week."

Beckett nodded. "If the man wants beautiful horses, he'll find them there. I suppose I'll have to look into it." He held out his hand. "I'll need that tape."

Gitlow handed him the cassette. "I must tell you, Hoke, Youngblood draws a lot of far-out calls. My opinion is we turned up another flake."

"Maybe," said Beckett. "But he's made the threat and I can't just walk away from it."

Beckett drove back to the Municipal Building slowly. Steal the horses, the man said. But how? You couldn't just pick up a horse and run with it. Nor could you simply leap astride and gallop off down the highway with police cars in pursuit. You *could* load a horse into a van, which would conceal it, and then tow it away. But, Beckett thought, the man had plainly said *horses*. How could anyone steal more than one horse at a horse show? If it was to *be* at the show?

Perhaps the man wasn't talking about real horses.

Beckett grinned. There were sawhorses. But sawhorses were neither beautiful nor valuable enough to steal.

He parked behind the Municipal Building, entered the back door, and made his way down the corridor to the marble-floored lobby at the front of the building.

Just inside the door was a small newsstand. Arms folded, a stocky middle-aged man in a plaid shirt and red baseball cap leaned against the counter.

He straightened when he saw Beckett approach. "Anything I can do for you, Hoke?"

"A copy of the Meridian *Weekly*, Manny."

Beckett flipped to the entertainment section and found the ad for the horse show, listing the schedule of events in one column, the other attractions alongside, then closed the paper and reached into his pocket for a coin.

Manny was leaning against the magazine rack behind him, his arms folded, staring blankly ahead.

Beckett frowned. That wasn't like Manny.

"Hey," he said. "Stop worrying. Just because Commissioner Powers entered that resolution to eliminate the newsstand because he thinks it's undignified in the lobby of the Municipal Building doesn't mean it'll pass."

Manny shrugged. "I guess it don't matter, Hoke. Anything else I can get for you?"

"A couple of packs of spearmint gum and your usual smile."

He paid Manny and started up the stairs. The news dealer lived straight and worked hard, which should have guaranteed something of a good life, but Manny had always been dogged by luck that might have made another man wake up screaming during the night. Maybe Manny did that, but behind the newsstand during the day he was one of the most pleasant people Beckett had ever known.

He bypassed his office and went into the one marked CAPTAIN TOLLEY. Tolley was tall and bald, his angular face as smooth as when he had been a patrolman twenty-five years before.

Beckett placed the gum on his desk. "For your granddaughter."

Tolley smiled. "She already has a six months' supply, thanks to you."

Beckett held up the tape cassette Gitlow had given him. "Let's go down to the lab. I'd like you to hear this and I want Nicholson, the mad scientist, to wave his magic wand over it."

"Is it important?"

"Well, it isn't the latest release by the Lavender Long Johns."

They took the elevator to the basement and walked down the dingy corridor.

"How does Nicholson stand it down here?" asked Tolley.

Beckett grinned. "He likes it. He would like it even better if the maintenance people let the cobwebs alone."

Nicholson was young, tall, and thin, with thick spectacles and long hair. Beckett had always had the feeling he'd cut his teeth on a test tube because his father headed the chemistry department at the university. Beckett handed him the cassette. "Play this."

Nicholson stared at him. "How did you know I had a player?"

"Because the mice came to me and complained that you listen to classical music all day. We have political mice. They prefer patriotic music."

Nicholson shook his head, pulled a small player from his desk drawer, and slid the cassette into place.

When it was finished, Tolley asked, "He's going to steal *horses*?"

"That's what he said."

"The horse show?"

"It seems likely." Beckett showed him the ad in the paper. "It mentions a pair of matched bays."

"How could anyone steal a pair of horses at a horse show?"

"I don't know but we'd better beef up security there tonight." Beckett motioned to Nicholson. "Take that tape and see what more it will tell you."

"Anything in particular you want to know?"

"The man's name and address would be nice, but I'll settle for whatever you get."

"I'll have to take it into the city police sound lab."

"Go," said Beckett. "And call me as soon as you have anything worthwhile."

Beckett and Tolley walked back toward the elevator and Tolley pressed the button. "Spocker will handle it. I can't get excited about someone threatening to steal some horses. It sounds too weird to be true, but even if it is I need you more for a budget committee meeting. You have a way of convincing those commissioners."

"If you remember, the last time I threatened to bust one of them in the nose," said Beckett.

Tolley grinned. "Exactly what I mean, and we *did* get the money for Nicholson's lab, didn't we?"

They came out of the meeting at six and made their way through the deserted halls to the third floor detective headquarters.

A round-faced, heavyset detective, massaging a foot propped on his open desk drawer, a plastic cup of coffee in his other hand, was talking to Rozinski and Keller, the two detectives who manned the second shift. Limping slightly, he followed Beckett and Tolley into Beckett's office.

"What happened to your foot, Spocker?" asked Tolley.

"One of those damned horses stepped on my toe," said Spocker. "I think he broke it."

"You should have gone to the hospital," said Tolley.

"I wanted to report to you first. I talked to everybody about the phone call and I think they're still laughing. They all said such a thing was impossible. No stranger could come in there and steal a horse—

there's no way they could get away with it. So I told them it didn't have to be a stranger, it could be someone who worked there. They still laughed. The guy in charge said it had to be some kind of joke. So where do we go from here?"

"I'll tell you where we go," said Tolley. "We go home after I tell the dispatcher to have the place patrolled all night."

Spocker limped to the door after him. "I'm going to the hospital."

"How could you let such a dumb thing happen?" asked Beckett.

"It wasn't my fault. The horse hates cops."

"How did you arrive at that conclusion?"

"His name. It's Voleur, which means thief in French." Spocker sighed. "I tell you, Hoke, they come at us from all directions."

Beckett waved him out.

He glanced at his watch. Nicholson hadn't called yet but that wasn't unusual. The lab man forgot time when he became involved.

Beckett decided to wait. He had nowhere to go and nothing to do other than have dinner and return to his empty apartment. Ever since his wife died, he found himself spending more and more time in the office, and he told himself more than once he should put a stop to it. But waiting for Nicholson's call was legitimate and not an excuse.

It was almost seven when Nicholson came through the door, a portable tape player in one hand and several reels of tape in the other.

"I'm glad you're here," he said. "It's easier to demonstrate than explain." He placed the recorder and the reels on the desk. "I borrowed this because of the higher fidelity. We took the original tape and separated the sounds as well as we could with filters." He held up the reels. "Listen to these."

Behind the distorted speaking voice of the caller, the first one consisted of a dull hollow roar, punctuated by heavy regular thuds and clicks, some rapid, some slow, all beginning softly, rising in volume, then fading. At the high end of the register Beckett could hear voices.

"That was the background noise," said Nicholson. "We eliminated the announcer's segments, spliced the remaining bits together, and duplicated them several times to get a pattern. What does it sound like to you?"

"A big room with a lot of people walking by," said Beckett.

Nicholson nodded. "That's what we thought. A bus terminal or the lobby of a building or a department store. One thing is certain—the man called from a public phone. Either he didn't close the door or it was one of those clamshell types."

He replaced the reel with another. "Now this one."

The sounds were higher-pitched now, the background voices occasionally intelligible. Beckett leaned forward.

"After lunch—"

"So I said to her—"

A woman's voice, very clear: *"I hope he lets us out early."*
Individual voices. Snatches of conversations that didn't fit together.
Beckett shrugged, "Makes no sense to me. The call came in at twelve
forty-five."

Nicholson extracted a roll of paper from his coat pocket. "Here's
something we *can* use. This is the man's voiceprint. If you ever locate a
suspect, we can get a positive identification."

Beckett glanced at the jagged lines. If he ever located a suspect. If
anything happened tonight that would cause him to go looking for one.
He came from behind the desk wearily, telling himself he really hadn't
expected Nicholson to perform a miracle. "Let's lock it up in the lab and
go home. All we can do now is wait."

Neither the old Charlie Chan film on the late show nor the uneasy
feeling was enough to keep Beckett from falling asleep in his easy chair.
The film had ended and the empty television screen was flickering when
the shrill ring of the phone brought him up through several layers of
sleep. He reached for the receiver and winced as he flexed his cramped
muscles.

Tolley's voice was grim. "The man stole the horses just as he said, but
they weren't real horses at all. They were a couple of valuable pieces out
of the art collection at the Carew mansion."

"I should have thought of that," said Beckett.

"So should I," said Tolley. "And we both should have given the
whole thing a lot more attention, because he killed Mrs. Carew to get
them. Meet me there fast."

Beckett parked alongside the police cruiser in front of the turreted
stone mansion that stood on the highest point in Meridian County. It
had been built by Foxworth Carew, who had made money when men
were allowed to keep it and had passed it on to Mrs. Billingham Carew,
his granddaughter, who had reigned as the queen of Meridian County
society.

As he closed his door, Tolley's car pulled in beside his, and farther
down the long driveway an ambulance and another car were drawing
up. They ran up the broad steps and were met at the door by a
uniformed patrolman who led them into an enormous entrance hall,
through a large room, and down a long carpeted hall to a room at the
end of the house. As he walked, Beckett felt a sense of intrusion,
thinking wryly that the cost of the grand piano alone would have paid
the rent on his apartment for two years.

The patrolman stopped and motioned them into the room. A
luxurious red rug covered the floor. One wall was lined with books that
framed a huge stone fireplace, before which deep soft leather furniture
was grouped. Placed diagonally in one corner was a large walnut desk
that gave the person sitting at it a magnificent view of the rolling

countryside through french doors. The wall opposite the desk was covered by paintings, each individually lighted, and a row of museum-like glass cases occupied the center of the room.

The top of one of the cases lay broken on the floor. A few feet from it was the body of a grey-haired woman dressed in a full-length pink satin robe. Beyond her outstretched hand was a revolver.

The other patrolman was standing awkwardly before a couple seated on the sofa. The man was bald, his face thin, his nose aquiline. The woman was easily twenty years his junior. Both were in dressing gowns. Standing alongside the fireplace were an elderly couple and a young woman.

Tolley indicated the body on the floor. "Mrs. Carew?"

The patrolman nodded. "They told me she often had trouble sleeping and would come down here to read for a while. She would generally fall asleep in one of the chairs. Either she was asleep when the guy broke in through that door over there or she walked in on him after he was already here. Her son, Mr. Carew, heard a shot and came running down. He found her and called us."

Beckett pointed at the empty case. "The horses?"

The patrolman nodded. "A couple of bronze statues. Mr. Carew says they're worth a fortune."

Beckett walked to the open french door. One pane of glass had been broken so that a hand thrust inside could unlatch the lock. He stepped through onto a small patio edged with shrubbery. The night was cool and clear, the distant lights from the valley pinpricks of brightness.

They're beautiful. I've always wanted them, the man had said.

Whatever they were, he had wanted them bad enough to kill for them. That bit of madness hadn't come across in the phone call.

The horses, Mrs. Carew's son explained, were a pair of bronze sculptures about a foot long and ten inches high. His father had acquired them on a trip to China fifty or sixty years earlier. Perhaps nineteen hundred years ago the horses had been so prized among the rich and powerful of the Eastern Han Dynasty that they were usually interred with their owners. They were considered priceless.

Beckett and Tolley had nothing to work with. There were no prints on either the broken glass or the gun, which had belonged to Mrs. Carew. It was one of several in the house, and Mrs. Carew had been quite capable of handling any of them.

At breakfast at Maxine's, Tolley said, "The big question is how the man knew about the horses. Any fool would know that there would be plenty worth stealing in that house, which incidentally has no security whatsoever—I'm surprised someone hasn't taken a truck up there and emptied the place long ago. But he went there specifically for the horses."

"He had to have seen them sometime," said Beckett. "They caught his eye and he fell in love with them."

Tolley grimaced. "Do you know what that means? Hundreds of people who have been in that house have to be checked out—friends of the Carews, servants, tradespeople, maintenance men."

"We can cut that down a little. Eliminate the friends. They're not the type to listen to Youngblood's talk show, much less call him up. It's possible, of course, but not likely. Also, I don't think we have to go back too far." Beckett grinned. "Time has a way of dulling desire. The man saw those horses fairly recently. Let's send Spocker out there to make a list of people who might have been in that room within the last year. I'll stay with the one thing we have, the tapes that Nicholson made."

Nicholson gave Beckett a pair of earphones. He closed his eyes and concentrated on the sounds. After what might have been the fifteenth or twentieth time he ran the tape, he heard a word buried deep in the background—a ghost of a word, slurred and faint. By itself it meant nothing, but placed within the context of the other words it made sense. He removed the earphones and turned to Nicholson. "I'm going out and call you on the phone. Record it. You have twenty minutes to get set up."

At twelve forty-five, Beckett dialed, requested Nicholson's extension, and asked, "Are you recording?"

"Yes," said Nicholson.

"I'm going to hold the phone out to give you a minute or two of background. Then I want you to compare it to that on the Youngblood call."

When he brought the phone back to his ear, he asked, "Enough?"

Nicholson's voice held an edge of excitement. "I think you may have it. Where are you?"

"None of your business," said Beckett. He hung up and looked around. The lobby of the Municipal Building was crowded with people flowing toward the various accesses to the interior. Beckett joined the stream mounting the staircase and went down the hall to Tolley's office.

Tolley set aside a sheaf of papers. "Any luck with the tapes?"

Beckett nodded. "The call came from the lobby here."

Tolley's eyes narrowed. "Are you sure?"

"Sure enough. I caught the word 'jury' on the tape. There's only one likely place where that word is part of an ordinary conversation because a great part of our lunchtime crowd is made up of jurors from the courtrooms on the second floor. Someone also said, 'I hope he lets us out early,' which is something the presiding judge has been known to do when a jury pool is no longer required for the day."

Tolley scrubbed at his chin. "It's possible—but a great many people pass through that lobby every day."

"Wait. It struck me as odd that the call came from a public phone.

Where are people when they listen to Youngblood? At home, at work, in cars. At home or at work, they have easy access to a phone. That would seem to leave only a driver who would have to stop at a public phone. But chances are it would be alongside a curb somewhere. The call would be more likely to be made by someone already here, someone in this building who listens to the radio and has easy access to the public phones in the lobby. The only people in that lobby all day long are the guard at the information desk and Manny at the newsstand. The gurad doesn't have a radio. Manny does. He keeps it under the counter, turned low. I've heard it."

Tolley came around the corner of his desk, moving fast. "Let's go talk to him."

"He isn't there," said Beckett. "That retired friend of his, Wilson, is taking care of the stand."

"Then we talk to Wilson," Tolley said.

Wilson was slight and bony, his eyes a young blue in his old face.

"Manny's on vacation," he said. "He came to me yesterday and said he wasn't feeling well and had to take a rest. He asked me to handle the stand. It was short notice, but it isn't as if I have anything else to do."

"Where did he go?" asked Beckett.

"He didn't say. You know Manny, he keeps a lot to himself. He said something about it was time the dice rolled his way, so I figure he went to Las Vegas. We talked a lot about going there."

Beckett and Tolley walked back to Tolley's office.

"I'll have the Las Vegas police check," said Tolley. "If he's there, they can pick him up for questioning. Wherever he is, I have an idea he sold those horses to finance the trip."

"Maybe," said Beckett thoughtfully.

The Las Vegas police couldn't find him, nor did any of the airline flights leaving that morning have a record on him. By evening, Beckett drove to the small apartment building where Manny and Wilson lived in separate apartments. The superintendent let him into Manny's apartment.

Manny lived in two small, poorly furnished rooms. Incongruous against one faded wall was a white plastic etagere, its shelves loaded with small china figurines, none of them expensive, some so badly rendered they were almost grotesque. Beckett went through the bedroom closet and found one out-of-style suit, a limp sportcoat, and several pairs of slacks. On the floor was a battered suitcase.

He found a prescription bottle when he examined the bathroom. Empty, it was standing on the sink, and Beckett recognized the trade name typed on the label as a pain killer. The prescription had been issued by the Meridian County hospital.

Beckett drove there.

They told him Manny was on the sixth floor.

The middle-aged nurse at the station on six flicked her eyes over his I.D. without interest. "You can't see him without the permission of his doctor."

Beckett pushed the phone toward her. "Then get the doctor."

She spun out the numbers and handed him the phone. "Dr. Scoleri."

Beckett introduced himself and explained his mission. A deep voice at the other end of the wire said, "I can't permit you to upset him. He's scheduled for major surgery in the morning."

"What major surgery?"

"He has a brain tumor. Tests we made today confirmed our diagnosis."

"What are his chances?"

There was a pause. "Perhaps fifty-fifty, but even if he survives there's a strong possibility he will lose his sight."

Beckett felt a little sick. Manny's luck, he thought.

"Listen to me," he said. "A woman is dead and it appears he killed her. I don't like to force the issue but I must talk to him or we may never know how it happened."

There was another pause. "Let me speak to the nurse."

The nurse listened, said, "Yes doctor," and hung up.

"You may talk to him for five minutes," she said.

She led Beckett down the hall and pushed open a door.

Manny was lying on the bed, his eyes closed.

"Hello, Manny," said Beckett.

Manny opened his eyes and smiled. "It didn't take you long, Hoke."

"I'd just like to know why you did it."

Manny sighed. "A man can't go through life without a touch of beauty, Hoke."

Beckett said nothing.

"You know what my life has been, Hoke. One thing after another so that I never had an extra dollar. It seemed that the older I got, the less I had. I always wanted so many things—a nice home, car, clothes. But I could never afford any of them and I tried to live with that. I did the best I could with what I had."

He paused. "Did you see my collection?"

Beckett thought of the figurines. "Very nice."

Manny's voice was low. "I always thought so, but when this tumor thing turned up I saw it for what it was. Junk. I got a little mad, Hoke. God, I thought, to live a whole life and have nothing to show for it except junk. Why couldn't I have just one thing that was beautiful and valuable and that no one else had?

"I saw the horses last summer. The Municipal Building was closed because it was a holiday and a man I knew wanted me to help him reset some flagstones at the Carew house. The doors were open and I stepped inside and looked around." His voice became a whisper. "They were the most beautiful things I'd ever seen, Hoke, and I couldn't forget them. And then yesterday Youngblood was talking about doing things you'd like to do and I thought, why not?"

"Where are the horses now?" asked Beckett.

Manny gestured toward the closet.

Beckett opened the door and found a small heavy canvas bag. He placed it on the table by the foot of Manny's bed and zipped it open, pulled out two bronze horses, and stood them alongside the bag. Even in the dim light of the hospital room, their magnificent artistry was evident. Each with a foreleg lifted, heads held high, backs arched, and tails plumed, they stood proudly, covered with the patina of age—the crowning achievement of an unknown Chinese artist nineteen hundred years before.

Manny's voice was husky. "Aren't they beautiful, Hoke?" He waved a hand. "Take them back where they belong, but tell Mrs. Carew I'm not sorry I stole them."

Beckett stared at him. "Mrs. Carew is dead. She was shot last night. We thought that you ..."

Manny sat up slowly, horror in his eyes. "Me!" He shook his head. "Not me, Hoke! I couldn't do anything like that! When I broke into the room, I thought all I had to do was lift off the top of the case, take the horses, and run, but I couldn't get the damned top loose. I was working at it and sweating when I heard someone coming. I hid behind a desk in the corner. Mrs. Carew came in. She didn't notice the broken window. She took a book and sat down in one of those big chairs. When she stopped turning pages, I realized she'd fallen asleep, and I started to sneak out, but I thought I'd try once more. And the top of the case came loose this time. I stood it up against the leg of the case, took the horses, and started out. My foot hit the glass top, knocked it over, and it broke. I heard her say, 'Who's there?' but by that time I was through the door." He passed a trembling hand across his upper lip. "I didn't kill her, Hoke!"

The nurse returned. "You'll have to leave."

Beckett cleared his throat. "Manny, I'm going to send Nicholson and Tolley over with a tape recorder. You tell them what you told me, but don't worry about a thing. Whoever killed Mrs. Carew is sitting around feeling very nervous. I'll see to it that whoever it is sweats a good deal more before I break the news. In the meantime, I can't think of a better place for these horses than here with you."

On the steps of the hospital, Beckett paused and looked up at the Carew mansion, a small pattern of lights in the darkness. Someone there had seen an opportunity, taken it, and killed Mrs. Carew.

As Spocker had said, they came at you from all directions.

Ann F. Woodward

The Girl from Ishikawa

In the pale light of early dawn the palace was dim and quiet. The Lady Aoi passed slowly over the smooth boards of the passageway on her way back to her own room after a night spent trying to ease the empress's pains of age. Her own pains were lessened by the exercise of massaging and manipulating the limbs of her old friend. As she came into the main hall, she was surprised to see that the doors were open. The soft, glowing aspect of the courtyard arrested her steps. Fine rain beaded every leaf and diffused the light, making the outlines of walls and trees and sand go soft as those of a painting done with quick washes of a wet brush.

Struck by this eerie beauty and spent from the long night, she sank to the floor, well in the shadows along the back wall, and bemoaned this love of beauty of hers that kept her tied to the world each time she tried to leave it and retire to a temple for the good of her soul. In her robes of brown and grey she might have been a denser shadow except for the occasional flick of a fan held automatically before her face, even in such solitude.

There was movement outside the door, just beyond her line of vision, but so discreet it was some while before she noticed it. A sudden shift of ox hoof and creak of axle stilled her fan. Against the luminous light of the doorway, colored silk flashed and retreated, then swirled into view on the boards of the veranda, and resolved into a woman's figure, closely follwed by two others.

In the next moment Aoi understood. It was the prince, and he was bringing the girl after all. Rumors about her had been the chief interest at court for months now, ever since his return from exile.

The girl stood for a moment, as if still bent from sitting in the carriage, then she straightened and turned to face the courtyard, dropping her fan with a clatter, raising her head from its graceful droop, and looking swiftly and carefully at her new surroundings. There was a gasp from the serving woman, who ducked after the fan and in her haste knocked it off the edge and into the sand.

The prince moved to the girl's side and held the long edge of her sleeve to hide her face. At once she turned, her posture softened, and she swayed toward his protective arm. He led her off into the shadows of the long corridor of the west wing, the girl gliding along with a palace walk, her hair trailing the floor behind her, a black river against the lustrous silks she wore. Aoi knew she had not been seen and, after the men had closed the doors and left, she rose and passed again into the shadows.

* * *

The news was out by the time her morning meal was brought. A young serving girl knocked and slid back the door.

"By your leave, my lady, just a little something."

She set the small table with its short legs on the mat with a bump and Aoi feared for the soup.

"They're busy in the west wing this morning and some of us have to go and help," the servant explained. "They have a new lady over there."

Aoi's silencing glance passed over her head and the girl prattled on. "The prince himself is there, sitting beside her curtains, sending for all sorts of special food and ordering more screens be put up on the garden side. As if we hadn't been doing that room over for the last month! He won't let any of us see her, but I heard her speak to him and her voice—"

This time the glance stopped her and she bowed and moved to the door. Just before closing it, she leaned inside. "The princess has a headache and asks if you will come to her."

The servant's last bow did not quite hide her smile.

The rainy season ended, and during the brief spell of fine warmth and sunshine before the heat of July began, the morning glories in Aoi's courtyard opened and displayed their intense blue along one whole wall, where they climbed and ran in rapid growth. Aoi gave herself up to the wonder of the blossoms at their beginning, spending long hours in writing practice until the poems, old ones and new ones, lay scattered all around her.

> Blue you are and tender,
> But how strongly you grip the wall!
> My heart too is held by this blue.
> It opens to the morning,
> This cup of blue.
> How will it ever hold the dew
> That comes with evening?

Her mind ran along familiar tracks into the past and she begrudged any time spent away from her own room. But she was often called to the princess, whose headaches required Aoi's soothing fingers.

"My lady, why don't you go to the mountains for a while? It is cool there and life is simple," Aoi said to her.

"No. I am quite comfortable here." The princess sat cold and still, her face smooth except for a small line between the eyes drawn by the headache. She was practicing calligraphy, seated before her writing box. It was a special box, sent to her by the prince during his exile.

In a year of unrest, when he had seemed to threaten his father's reign, he had retreated to a rough coastal area. There he lived with a small company in attendance for three years while his wife fretted with worry in the capital. At first there had been frequent messengers with letters and poems about rain and tears. Gradually the messengers had become less numerous on the road from the sea village beside the rocky river where he was waiting out his father's displeasure. The princess had kept her smooth face, but a stillness had come into her figure so that when she saw her Aoi had felt that even the folds of her robe lay just so, under tight control.

There had come a day in winter when the princess sat with Aoi and her other ladies about the charcoal brazier. The cold was such that they were wearing layer after layer of robes, not caring about the set of them but pulling them close and warming their hands inside their sleeves. Only the princess sat sewing as usual, making a warm vest for her husband, while the rest talked in apathetic gloom.

Footsteps in the hall brought them all upright, and before they could adjust their curtain fully a maid opened the door to announce a messenger from the prince.

He came striding in with a stirring of cold air about him, and they could see through the cracks in the curtains that stood between them and him that he had come straight to the princess without stopping to change his clothes or warm himself. Behind him was another man bearing a large straw-wrapped box.

"I have the honor to bring you good news from my lord the prince. He bids me inform you that his honored father has written that he has discovered that indeed my lord had nothing to do with the incident that so displeased him, and that he is requested to return to the capital. My lord asks me to say to you that he will be with you before the violets bloom." His face remained stiff as he made this reference to an old poem.

The princess sat quietly amid her ladies' exclamations. Aoi observed that her hands dropped their sewing and sought the warmth of her sleeves. A rising flush was checked before it reached her cheeks. Even her blood obeys her will, Aoi thought.

The princess murmured some words of concern for the messengers' comfort, but the man turned to his companion and motioned to him to unwrap the box. When it was set before her in its covering of brocade, the princess untied the cords with steady fingers and the cloth fell away to reveal a writing box of fine-grained dark wood, the top decorated with a design of sea grass etched in gold. Inside, every use imaginable had been made of sea shells.

A pair of dark razor-clam shells, cleverly hinged, held sticks of black ink, and a fat whorl had been partially sealed to make a water dropper; for mixing, there was an elongated curve of pale tan set into the inkstone, and a pointed twist protected the tip of a slender brush. All were rimmed and reinforced with gold in a way so novel and imaginative that the ladies' voices were hushed at this exquisite work of some unknown craftsman of the shore. This time the blush would not obey the princess and she lowered her head to hide it.

Once away from the princess's presence, the ladies' comments were as sharp as they had been for the last several months.

"So he's coming home, is he? Too bad for that one there by the shore!"

"Yes, I wonder how many messengers he'll keep busy going the other way, once he's back."

"She's never said a word, has she? But a writing box—even one so fine as that—won't make her forget all those months of waiting for letters."

"Surely someone is keeping him company there! Though how he could find anyone to interest him in that wild place—"

"Our lady is so beautiful he'll never think of that other one once he's back."

Now the princess sat before the writing box and twirled the sharp tapered shell between her fingers, not writing, the tiny line set between her brows. Aoi persuaded her to lie down and submit to a gentle massage.

The princess was protected by her ladies from the gossip and stories about the Ishikawa girl. She accepted calmly all the prince's excuses for his absences and no one dared criticize him in her presence. Yet incidents concerning the girl completely absorbed the court.

Her ladies were all women of beauty and taste, carefully chosen by the prince himself to help her in her adjustment to the royal life style. Soon these same ladies were seen in the palace halls wearing robes of a novel dyed pattern learned from their mistress. The secret was enticed away from them and the fashion spread.

Notes from her were left casually lying about by their recipients so that callers might admire her handwriting and her skill at poetry. Though the prince kept her carefully hidden behind the thickest curtains, many visitors were received in her rooms and word of her beauty was spread even by those who had only glimpsed her sleeve. At night there were so many courtiers in that part of the palace that it almost amounted to a parade of finely dressed gentlemen looking for a chance to slip a note beneath her curtains or to spy the hem of her robe under her blinds.

Aoi kept aloof from all this. Gossip and speculation were not what kept her in this palace when her spirit yearned for the peace of a mountain temple. She saw to the tending of her morning glories, sat with the empress playing the koto through the long warm nights when the moon was full, or chose the finest paper on which to write a poem for the princess celebrating the pleasures of high summer.

A note from the girl herself destroyed this detachment. It was brought by a pretty little serving girl wearing a thin robe dyed in the new way. The paper was light green, folded into a narrow strip, and tied with a few long stems of fresh grass. The handwriting showed originality and an almost masculine strength.

> The sea-bird has left the shore
> And sails among the clouds.
> How bright the stars!
> But one has not yet shown itself.
> I have heard of your many skills and I long to meet you.

Aoi went the next day in the early morning. Chiding herself for her pleasure in the day and in the light smooth flow of silk along her skin as she passed through patches of sun on the gallery floor, she arrived at the girl's apartment and was taken at once to her curtains. Speaking in a low voice, the girl ordered refreshments and another cushion brought for her guest, then dismissed the serving women and at once threw up the gauzy cloth that hung between them and set the curtain frame aside. "It is best that there be nothing between us from the beginning," she said. "From what I have heard of you, I am sure we will become friends."

Then, as on that first morning when Aoi had observed her unseen from the shadows, her posture changed from soft meekness to a straight-gazing directness. She smiled and invited Aoi to move her cushion closer.

For an agreeable hour they spoke of superficial things. Finally the girl said, "I must admit, lady, that I have a special request to make of you."

Aoi was not surprised. Her knowledge of medicines and cures was well known and she often found that conversations took this particular turn. But what followed was not what she expected.

"I have some learning in Chinese but my scrolls were all left behind when I cam here. I wonder if it is true, as they say, that you too read Chinese?"

The spiteful comment that Aoi gave herself airs with her Chinese letters had followed her all her life, though her reading in that language was done in secret. She was not one to drop poems about that looked as if they had been done by a man, though her education had taken a masculine turn when her father, finding himself with no sons, had allowed her to persuade him to teach her. It was because of this skill and a collection of scrolls of many sorts that she had learned of herbs and proper massage for the relief of pain.

How in the world had a girl from that wild region of the coast come to have Chinese learning? She asked the question, in spite of herself.

"After my father's death, my mother continued to resent the injustice done him when he was exiled. She refused to return to the capital, though her family urged her to do it for my sake. She determined to give me a complete education and bring me here when I was old enough to marry. She was very strict with me and kept me well hidden from the villagers and the priests of the temple, which stood across the river from our house. But my father's disgrace and death had been almost more than she could bear and she became fond of wine in the evenings. For years she left her bed very late in the mornings and she never knew that I often ran across the stones of the river at dawn to meet an old priest who taught me secretly."

"How could he dare to do it?"

"He was a very learned man, and you know how they are there in the country so far from civilization. The local boys came reluctantly to their lessons and the novices had no aptitude. I liked to copy the Chinese letters and when he found that I learned them quickly he could not help himself. So he taught me to read the poems of Po Chu-i and eventually the sutras.

"A few years ago, the maid became alarmed because I was growing up and said she would tell my mother if I went any more." She was quiet for a while. "The prince is not with me so often now, and I have little to do. I would so like to study again if *you* would teach me."

Like the priest, Aoi could not help herself. After that day she went regularly to visit, concealing a scroll in the fullness of her clothing. The girl had a quick memory and a speculative mind. At times when Aoi arrived she was greeted with a repressed enthusiasm that was almost feverish, and she soon found that she had forged a new link with the world, stronger than any of the others.

As the summer progressed the heat and humidity increased. Tempers became rough as people faced days of windless heat after sleepless nights. In the city there were frequent incidents of violence involving the militant monks of the surrounding mountains, who came down to protest recent cuts in their land allotments. They were dressed in straw sandals and ragged brown robes, wild in appearance and well armed. The men of the government became alarmed after some were attacked as they passed through the city in their elaborate carriages.

In the palace, the women persistently reported seeing a fox spirit about at night, a white wraith that drifted through the halls and sent them screaming. Only Aoi slept alone. The rest sought company for safety, lest the spirit enter their bodies in a moment of unwariness.

They wore themselves out with watchfulness. The empress chided them for their hysteria. The princess stilled their high-pitched speculations with a cold look, but she herself was so pale and exhausted she avoided company as much as possible. Violent storms wracked the night, bringing only brief refreshment.

The trouble with the priests became so insistent that a special council was held. It was decided to send to the east for help, and the strongest lord of the warlike eastern clans sent troops, with his son to command them.

They entered the city's broad central avenue late in the afternoon and the carriages of the nobles lined the way, along with the townsmen on foot. The prince gave a banquet in the evening to welcome the lord's son and his officers. The palace was alight well into the night as they sat drinking.

Suddenly lightning flashed and the wind sent curtains and blinds standing out into the room. The storm struck almost before the men could heave themselves to their feet or the servants rescue the furnishings and lanterns. There was one fire, hastily doused with a wet curtain, and the rest of the lights were extinguished, leaving the prince and his guests stumbling about in confusion, orienting themselves by the lightning flashes, struggling along with the servants to close the rain doors against the wind.

In the end, the prince and his courtiers retreated before the practical vigor of the warriors from the east, who, though they were as drunk as the rest, soon had the doors secure.

But that was no sooner accomplished when several women ran in, crying that a tree had fallen through the roof in the west wing. The eastern men surged off after them to help. The damage was in the Ishikawa girl's apartment. Aoi arrived in the doorway just behind the eastern lord's son. He stood facing the girl. The lightning was almost continuous. Quickly she raised her sleeve to hide her face, but before lowering her head to slip past him and join Aoi her gaze met his. The lord's son stood wiping the rain from his face, and with it all his drunkenness.

The next day the soldiers began their forays into the mountains to chastise the monks. They went in small groups, each with a commander, and returned after a night or two to rest before going out again. The heat and the storms continued. Workmen began to repair the girl's rooms and the prince, hardly able to take her into his own quarters near his wife, asked his mother to look after her. He himself was busy night and day directing the campaign against the monasteries, keeping himself accessible to the commanders, carousing into the night with those who had just returned. But the empress became ill with a fever and the princess lay mysteriously spent and listless, hardly eating at all. The fox spirit continued to frighten the women. Aoi had never known such a time of confusion and unrest. Caring for both the empress and the princess, she was often up through the night.

After one of these nights, it was barely dawn when she left the empress asleep at last and Aoi decided to go into the garden to enjoy its coolness before returning to her room for a few minutes' rest before the day began. She found a large level stone by the lake's edge and sat in the stillness, letting her worries float off and away in momentary abandonment to beauty.

As she turned to go, she raised her eyes to the palace behind her.

They sat together facing the dawn, the girl and the son of the eastern lord. She wore only a loose robe of apricot beaten silk which was open to the waist, he a white loincloth. As Aoi watched, he turned to the girl, leaned forward to grasp her shoulders briefly, stood to tie on his clothes, and left. The girl lowered the blinds, her figure melting into the shadows of the room.

Aoi felt a stirring in her breast that was the beginning of tears. As she walked the long corridors back to her room, she found herself battling to subdue memories aroused by the emotion she had sensed between those two as they watched the dawn. Ah, these pains of love that she thought she had left behind! Her feelings for her husband and her desolation at his early death sprang strong and fresh within her, sweeping away the calm that had become her weapon against them. She stopped to steady her breathing and clear her eyesight, standing hunched and grey in the dim hall.

A brushing on the floorboards behind her brought her erect and she turned to see who it was at this early hour. The princess advanced slowly toward her, holding one hand against the wall as if to guide her steps. Aoi bowed low and breathed a greeting, looking sideways at the pale-robed shadow, so curiously stiff and silent, but the princess passed her without speaking, her sleeve falling over Aoi's head and dropping away as she went. She seemed not to know Aoi was there and kept on her way until she reached her own doorway, where she vanished into the gloom. Aoi noticed only that the princess had come from the direction of the empress's quarters before she bowed to the grief of awakened longings and fled to her own privacy.

There days later, the eastern men left at first light to begin the long march back to their province. Soon afterward the cries of women came from two parts of the palace—the halls filled with maids and hastily dressed ladies-in-waiting. Urgent requests for Aoi were passed from the princess's women and those of the empress too. Aoi went first to the princess, who was nearer.

She found her writhing on her bed, speaking in a rapid babble no one could understand. Her ladies said she had awakened them just after dawn with her ravings. It was the fox spirit, they said, who had entered her and was speaking with the voice of one dead. Aoi sent a maid to her room for her box of medicines and powders.

Meantime, from the empress's wing, it was reported that a maid had been found dead in the bed of the Ishikawa girl. The girl herself was gone.

The prince arrived, pulling his clothes together. He knelt to look at his wife, who could not be quieted, and shouting for his men, left to investigate the death in the other wing. Priests and a medium were sent for to begin spells to identify and placate the spirit inhabiting the princess's body. Aoi mixed a powder to be given her when she could be calmed enough to drink it. Then she set out for the empress's wing, holding her arms tightly to her waist to still the shivering inside.

The prince was with his mother. Aoi could hear his angry questions and her weeping replies. The dead girl lay on her back on fine sleeping mats. She was a plain serving maid, dressed in a delicate sleeping robe that had belonged to her mistress. She appeared unmarked, but examination revealed a small, almost bloodless hole in her breast. Something had pierced her heart. The Ishikawa girl was gone without a trace—no letter, no disturbance of the room, no missing articles gave a clue as to how or why she was gone. Her women reported that they had seen her retire and that they had heard nothing alarming during the night from their adjoining room. There was no evidence of a weapon.

Aoi looked carefully at the wound, then went to the empress to calm her and to entreat her son to let her rest. As she sat dampening the empress's temples a fresh breeze from the garden ruffled the hangings and lifted the blinds. Rain splashed the leaves outside and coolness rose from the ground.

After it was all over—after the prince admitted to himself that the girl from Ishikawa had gone east with the soldiers, after the evil spirit was exorcised from his wife and she returned to herself, after the long summer of disturbances had been compacted into tales and memories—Aoi often found the prince seeking her out. They spoke of the girl as of one who had died, but the question remained in his eyes for her to read. *Why? Why* had she left? Any woman in the empire would have given half her life to be in her place. What could she have wanted that she did not have?

The question was never asked and so it could not be answered. But Aoi told him a story:

"My lord, you know that I saw her often. We had a special bond. She told me something once that I thought strange.

"As you know, she went in a carriage with the other ladies to see the troops arrive. It was the first time she had left the palace since she came, but she said she saw nothing on the way but the ground. The dust, the litter, the stone of the road drew her eyes and she looked from them to her elegantly clad feet that knew only the polished floors of the palace and she tried to lower her foot to the ground, with a longing to get herself dirty and feel the roughness underfoot. But the other ladies noticed her movement and so she withdrew her foot and remained still.

"When the men came into the city, hot and dusty, their horses sweating, riding in an aura of mixed, sensual sounds and smells, she said she felt that for the first time in her life she was experiencing something real."

Aoi paused, studying the prince's face. "It must seem strange that I should tell you this small thing that has no meaning. But I am just an old woman and I have thought of it often since she left. It wasn't that she wanted *more* than she had here perhaps—just something different."

The prince's face showed no enlightenment. Aoi seemed to change the subject.

"Those people in the eastern provinces! They say they are hardly safe from month to month, there is so much unrest on the frontier—the men are always ready to ride out and even the women must carry the short sword. Can it be true, do you think?"

The prince motioned impatiently and rose to go. Aoi's speech trailed off into numerous graceful syllables of honorifics as she bade him goodbye.

The death of the serving girl was never solved. Aoi made sure it would not be. She sent a trusted man to the coast to find the craftsman of seashells and gold. When he reutrned he bore a replica of the slim pointed shell that had protected the princess's writing brush. Aoi found it easy to put the new one in the special writing box.

After that hot summer, the fox spirit was not seen again in the nighttime halls. Aoi was grateful for the terror of ghosts that had sent the others running with glazed eyes. It seemed that only she had seen that pale wraith as a human figure.

Though it sails round and whole in the sky
The moon is torn to bits
On the wind-ripped lake.
I too show a smooth round face.

The poem seemed to float from the brush onto the paper as Aoi sat thinking. She did not know if it was for the princess or the girl, or perhaps for herself. But she tore it up at once.

Brian Garfield
The Gun Law

Deke Allen was arrested Friday afternoon on his way home from his uncle's house in Yorktown Heights.

He'd had a call that morning from his father. Mostly just to ask how Deke was doing, how was business, how's that girl what's-her-name, the one you live with, pretty little thing. So forth. But during the call his father mentioned that Uncle Bill was having a problem with rats in his basement. Deke's father said, "If you happen to be heading up that way you can drop by and pick up my shotgun. Take it on up to Bill's and see if you can take care of those rats for him."

Uncle Bill didn't like to put down poison because he had a houseful of dogs. He adopted stray dogs; it was his avocation. The place—a four-acre farmstead near the Croton Reservoir—was fenced in to contain the cacophony of orphaned dogs. Deke liked Bill and had nothing better to do that Friday. His next job wasn't scheduled to start till Monday. So he went by his father's house in Ossining and picked up the pump-action sixteen-gauge and a boxful of shells for it, and drove out along Baptist Church Road to his uncle's dog farm.

Deke Allen tended to carry just about anything a human being might need in his Microbus. It was his factory, craft shop, tool warehouse, and repair center. Deke, in his anachronistic two-bit way, was a building contractor. He specialized in restorations of old houses, preferably pre-Revolutionary houses; there were plenty of them in the Putnam county area and he had a good deal of work, especially from young New York City couples who'd made themselves a little money and moved to the country and bought "handyman special" antique houses for low prices, hoping to meet the challenge. Most of them learned that it was harder work than they'd thought; most of them had city jobs to which they had to commute and they simply didn't have enough time to repair their old houses. So when an old cellar sprang a leak or an old beam needed shoring up or an old wall crumbled with dry rot, Deke Allen would arrive in his Microbus with his assortment of tools. Most of them were handmade tools and some of them actually dated back to colonial times. He was especially proud of a set of old wooden planes. He'd had to make new blades for them, of course, but the wooden housings were the originals—ironhard and beautifully smooth and straight. And he carried buckets filled with old squarehead nails and other bits and pieces of hardware he'd retrieved from condemned buildings and sheriff's auctions and the Ossining city dump.

He kept all his toolboxes and hardware in the Microbus; he'd built the compartments in. He even had a little pull-down desk in the back where he could do his paperwork—measurements, billings, random calculations, the occasional poem he wrote. He kept an ice cooler in the back for soft drinks and beer and the yogurt he habitually consumed for lunch. Deke was a health food nut. The only thing he never carried in the truck was marijuana; he knew better than that. Show a state cop a psychedelically painted Microbus driven by a young-looking twenty-five year old with scraggly blond hair down to his shoulder blades and a wispy yellow beard and mustache and a brass ring in his left ear—show a state cop all that and you were showing him a natural reefer repository. So the grass never went into the Microbus. And he was always careful to carry only unopened beer cans in the ice cooler. It was legal so long as it was unopened. Deke got rousted about once every three weeks by a state cop on some highway or other. It was an inconvenience, that was all. You had to put up with it or get a haircut and change your lifestyle. Deke wasn't tired of his lifestyle yet, not by a long shot. He liked living in the tent with Shirley all summer long. Winters they'd spring the rent for an apartment. This was March; they were almost ready to move out of the furnished room and a half; but they were still living indoors and that was why his father had been able to reach him on the boarding house phone.

This particular Friday he went on up to Uncle Bill's dog farm and went inside with the shotgun. They took a lantern into the dank basement and they sat down until the light attracted the rats. They'd put earplugs in; it was the only way to stand the nosie in the confined space. When Uncle Bill judged that all the rats were in sight, Deke handed him the shotgun and Bill did the shooting. Deke didn't like guns, didn't know how to shoot them, and didn't want anything to do with them. He was lucky he'd been 4-F or he'd probably have dodged the draft or deserted to Canada. It was one moral decision that hadn't been forced upon him, however, and he was just as happy he hadn't had to face it. He was half deaf, it seemed, the result of too much teenage exposure to hard rock music at too many decibels. Deafness qualified you for a 4-F draft status. It also made life fairly miserable sometimes; he wasn't altogether deaf, not by a wide margin, but there were sounds above a certain register that he couldn't hear at all and he generally had to listen carefully to hear things that normal people could hear without paying any attention. Conversation, for example. If he looked at TV—which wasn't often, since he and Shirley didn't own one—he had to sit close to the set and turn the sound up to a level that was uncomfortably loud for must other people in the room.

But he could hear it all right when Shirley whispered in his ear that she loved him.

When Bill got finished shooting the rats he handed the gun back to Deke and went down across the basement floor with a burlap sack to pick up the corpses so they wouldn't make maggots and houseflies or stink up the house. They left the basement—it was then about two in the afternoon—and had a couple of sodas out of Deke's ice cooler. They talked some, mostly about the dogs that kept jumping up and trying to lick Deke's beard. Finally Deke slid the shotgun carelessly across onto the passenger seat, got in, and drove out of the yard. Behind him Uncle Bill carefully closed the six foot high gate to keep the dogs in.

A few miles down the road a state cop pulled Deke over because one of the bolts had fallen out of the rear license plate and the plate was hanging askew by one bolt, its corner scraping the pavement and throwing the occasional spark. Deke (because of his hearing problem) hadn't heard the noise it had been making. The cop had to use the siren and the flashers and get right up on top of the Microbus before Deke knew he was there. Deke hadn't been speeding or anything. He figured it for another tiresome marijuana shakedown. He was glad he didn't have beer on his breath; they'd had sodas back at Bill's, not beers.

He pulled over against the trees and got out, reaching for his wallet. The cop was walking forward; behind him the lights on top of the cruiser were still flashing, hurting Deke's eyes, so Deke looked away and waited for the cop to come up.

"Your license plate's hanging crooked," the cop said. "A lot of sparks. Could hit the gas tank. You want to fix it."

Deke was relieved. "Say, thanks." He opened up the back of the Microbus and the cop saw the tools and hardware in there. Deke got out a screwdriver and found himself a nut and bolt in one of the compartmentalized toolboxes. He fixed the license plate back in place. Meanwhile, the cop was hanging around. One of those beefy guys with a Texas Ranger hat and his belly hanging out over his Sam Browne belt. He wasn't searching the truck exactly—he was jut hanging around—but when Deke went to get back in, the cop saw the shotgun on the passenger seat.

The cop's face turned cold. "All right. Get out slow."

Deke stood to one side and the cop slowly removed the shotgun from the seat. He worked the pump-action and a loaded cartridge flipped out of the breech. The cop stooped down to pick it up. "Loaded and chambered. Ready to fire. What bank you fixin' to rob, boy?"

After that it was inevitable. The cop handcuffed Deke and locked him in the cruiser's back seat cage and drove him into the Croton barracks. There he was handed over to two other police types. They ran him on into Ossining and he was booked.

"Booked? For what?"

"Possession," the sergeant said.

Deke still didn't think much of it. He was a hippie type. They harassed hippie types on principle, these cops. They'd throw him in the tank overnight and tomorrow he'd have to hitch a ride back to pick up his truck.

Only it didn't work out that way.

Stanley Dern figured himself a pretty good country lawyer. He'd known Harv Allen for several years, not well but as a lawyer knows a casual client: he'd drawn Harv's will for him, done a few minor legal chores for him from time to time. When Harv called him about his son, Stanley Dern at first tried to put him off. "I'm not really a criminal lawyer, Harv."

"Nor is my son a criminal," Harv replied. He had an old fashioned New England way of talking; the family—and Harv—was from New Hampshire.

"Well, I'll be glad to go down there and talk with him. Have they set bail?"

"Twenty-five thousand dollars."

Stanley Dern whistled through his teeth. "What's he charged with?"

"I can't remember the exact words. Possession of a deadly weapon, in substance."

"I'll see what I can do."

Stanley Dern had practiced in Ossining for thirty of his fifty-four years; he knew everybody in the district attorney's office and he knew most of the cops in town. Criminal court activity in Ossining had always been more intense than in other cities of comparable size because Ossining was the home of Sing Sing, the old New York State penitentiary.

Stanley Dern went to the Criminal Part Clerk and found out that the prosecution had been assigned to a young assistant D.A. named Dan Ellenburgh. Stanley didn't know this one; Ellenburgh was new.

He was also large, as Stanley found out when he entered the office. Ellenburgh was half bald, small eyed, and at least a hundred pounds overweight—a shame in such a young man, Stanley thought.

"Now, it's a Sullivan Law violation," Ellenburgh said after he'd pulled out Deke Allen's file and looked into it to remind himself which case they were talking about. "Possession of a deadly weapon. He had it on the car seat right beside him. Armed and charged. Ready to fire."

"Now, come on, Mr. Ellenburgh. That's a ten year rap. The kid could get ten years."

"That's right," Ellenburgh said blandly. "Of course you'll probably cop a plea and he"ll end up serving one-to-three and he'll be out in nine or ten months on good behavior."

"Nine or ten months out of the kid's life just because he helped his uncle shoot some rats?"

Ellenburgh put on a pair of granny glasses—Ben Franklins. They made him look ludicrous; they were far too small for the fleshy massiveness of his face. "Do you think we should just let any hippie kid ride around with a loaded gun on his car seat, counselor? What do you suppose we have gun laws for?"

"Mr. Ellenburgh, this young man isn't a dangerous felon. He's never been convicted of anything worse than a traffic violation. He runs his own business in this community. He's well regarded by the people he's worked for. He may not cut his hair the way you might prefer but he's certainly not a menace. The facts in the case are clear enough, it seems to me."

"The facts in the case—it seems to me—are that the man was caught redhanded with a loaded gun on his car seat. That's in clear violation of the law. It's a felony law, counselor, and a loaded cocked shotgun is nothing if not dangerous. Therefore I've got to disagree with you. I'd classify this case as a dangerous felony."

"Come off it," Stanley Dern said.

"You think I'm playing some sort of game with you, counselor? Well, you come to court and see whether I am." And Ellenburgh got up and turned his back rudely, replacing the file in his steel cabinet, indicating plainly that the interview was ended.

Stanley Dern went down to the jail to see Deke Allen. He asked Deke if he wanted him to be Deke's lawyer. Deke said, "I'd love it, Mr. Dern, but all I've got is about forty dollars to my name right now. If you'll put me on the cuff I can pay you off in installments. Assuming it doesn't cost too much."

Stanley Dern didn't have any remote idea whether it would cost forty dollars or forty thousand to defend Deke Allen in this case. He said, "Never mind the fee, Deke. Whatever it is, I'll bill you no more than you can afford to pay. This idiot prosecutor's got me mad and when they get Stanley Dern mad they'd better hunker down and watch out."

Then Stanley Dern arranged with a bondsman to put up Deke's bail; it cost Deke's father $2,500 but there was no question of his not paying it—Deke's father was a retired baker of no particular importance in the community and certainly no wealth, but he was a decent man and he loved his son even if he didn't understand his son's so-called lifestyle.

And finally Stanley Dern went into the law library at the firm where he worked and began to read up on the gun law.

The law stated quite clearly that it was illegal to carry a loaded weapon on one's person or in one's car escept on one's own premises— home or place of business. For the benefit of hunters a loophole had been built into the law whereby you could carry a "nonconcealable weapon"—that is, a shotgun or rifle—on your person or in your car so long as it was unloaded and broken down in such a way as to be not easily assembled and fired. The wording of the loophole was quite strict and specific. There was no way to get around it: the weapon, in order to escape the provisions of the gun law, had to be unloaded and dismantled. Clearly Deke Allen's case didn't meet those criteria. Technically he was guilty. Or so it appeared.

Stanley's instinct was to wait and see which judge's docket the trial would be set for. A reasonable and sympathetic judge would either throw the case out or, at the worst, administer a slap on the wrist to Deke.

But Stanley's heart fell when he saw the court calendar for that May seventeenth. State of New York vs. Allen 5/17 CC Pt. III. Criminal Court Part Three. That was Judge Elizabeth Berlin. Of them all she was the most hardnosed, the least tolerant of youthful offenders, the judge most inclined to mete out the harshest possible sentence.

Of course he could shoot for a jury trial, he supposed, but there wasn't much point in that, a jury could only determine the facts of a case, not the law that pertained to it, and the facts of the case were such that in terms of a jury Deke couldn't help being held guilty as hell. And while a jury could recommend a lenient sentence it couldn't require one. It would still rest in the hands of Elizabeth "Lucrezia Borgia" Berlin.

The years' minimum, Stanley thought dismally. Not to mention the permanent loss of citizenship rights: a felon, once convicted, could never again vote or hold public office or hold any number of jobs. Because he'd done his father and uncle a harmless favor and been ignorant of the fine print of the state gun law, Deke Allen could have the rest of his life ruined.

It wasn't good enough.

Stanley went back to his law books. There had to be an answer.

Court day.

Stanley and Deke waited silently in the courtroom while Judge Berlin dispensed several cases ahead of them. She was formidable in her grey suit, a white-haired woman with a humorous but ungiving face. Stanley had practiced before her for many years; he knew her quite well. She was not a nasty person, merely a sternly tough one: she was honest and, in terms of her own standards, fair—in that she dealt equally harshly with all guilty parties and equally sympathetically with innocent ones. (That is to say, those whose guilt was not proved. Trials do not establish innocence. They only establish whether or not the prosecution has proved its case.) She had, much to her credit, a fine shrewd sense of humor and she was not reluctant to laugh at herself when the situation called for it. It was her saving grace; trials in Part Three often were highly entertaining because of the witty repartee between Ms. Berlin on the bench and the lawyers on the arena floor.

Two hours dragged by. Then a possession-of-narcotice case was continued to some future date and bailiff rose to intone: "State versus Allen."

The arresting cop testified as to the circumstances of the arrest and the condition of the shotgun in the car at the time. Stanley cross-examined the cop with little hope of accomplishing anything useful. The cop stuck to his story: yes, the shotgun was handy, right there on the seat. Yes, it was assembled. Not only assembled but charged, loaded, and cocked. All you had to do was pull the trigger. The safety catch wasn't even on.

When the prosecution rested its case, Ellenburgh was sweating; the fat man glared at Deke and Stanley before he went back to the D.A.'s table and sat down, wiping his face with a handkerchief. Then Stanley called his witnesses. He called Harv Allen to the stand. Harv testified how he'd given the shotgun to Deke and why; he also testified that Deke detested guns and never used them, not even for target practice. Then Deke's Uncle Bill got on the stand and told the story of the rat hunt—how he, not Deke, had shot the rats and how he'd handed the gun back to Deke afterward, not thinking to put the safety catch on or empty the gun. "It's my fault maybe more'n his," Uncle Bill said earnestly. "I know a little about guns, at least. The boy doesn't know a thing about them."

Then Stanley called a few character witnesses—people who knew Deke, people he'd worked for. They testified how he'd done good honest work for them, never stolen, worked like a beaver out of that cluttered old Microbus of his, always been amiable and cheerful—a little hard of hearing, maybe, but certainly not a criminal type.

All through the trial—it lasted about five hours, not counting the break for lunch—Deke's live-in girlfriend Shirley sat right behind the rail and surreptitiously held hands with Deke. Judge Berlin saw that, of course, but she made no objection to it and Stanley was slightly encouraged by her evident sympathy for the boy. Just the same, he realized that the facts in the case were clear, that there'd been a violation of the felony law and that he was going to have to pull something very clever indeed if he was to save Deke from misery.

Ellenburgh made his closing argument—very brief, it didn't need much elucidation. Then Stanley stood up and addressed the bench.

"Your Honor, I don't think anybody's disputing the facts in this case. We seem to be caught up on a legal issue rather than a factual one. My client makes no secret of the fact that he had the gun on his truck seat as the officer testified. That its presence was not intended for felonious purpose is, in the eyes of the law, immaterial. We seem to be faced with a mandatory situation here, wherein the accused—even though our sympathies may go out to him wholeheartedly—appears to be uncompromisingly guilty in the eyes of the law. Even a suspended sentence in this case would brand my client a felon for the rest of his life and deprive him of vital constitutional rights, as you know."

Judge Berlin watched him suspiciously: apparently Stanley was only confirming the prosecution's case. She said, "Are you defending the young man or simply throwing him on the mercy of the court, Mr. Dern?"

"I'd like to defend him, Your Honor. I'd like to point out to the Court the provision of the state's anti-gun-possession statute which specifically exempts from prosecution the honest citizen who, for purposes of self protection or otherwise, elects to keep a gun—loaded or otherwise —on the premises of his own home or place of business."

"Mr. Dern, I'm fully aware of that provision. I don't see how it applies in this case."

"Your Honor," Stanley said quietly, "my client maintains, with perfectly good reason, that his Microbus is in fact his place of business."

There was a loud objection from Prosecutor Ellenburgh but Judge Berlin had begun to laugh and Stanley knew by the tone of her laughter that he'd won.

Deke Allen told me, some time later, after he'd had time to reflect on the experience, "I guess Justice is blind. But the rest of us sure as hell have to keep our eyes open, don't we?"

John H. Dirckx
A Bully's Downfall

PART I

Mr. Alfred Pinksett rested his elbow on the window ledge and his chin in the hollow of his hand as, puffing serenely at his pipe, he regarded his nominal domain with a lordly and contented eye. This domain, which figured in the rental agent's circulars as Sea Mist Terrace, comprised a sprawling tract of coastland a mile or two from Bexhill, adorned here and there with a villa of the sort rather absurdly designated as "semi-detached." Fresh from the builder's trowel and still untenanted, the villas lay scattered amid broad expanses of gravel and mud, varied by an occasional heap of broken bricks or a tangle of splintered timbers and rusting iron. The only verdure in the landscape was contributed by several exuberant patches of weeds and some stunted evergreens of the hardier sort able to survive winter's cold and to subsist on a rocky soil liberally dosed with sea salt.

The vantage from which Mr. Pinksett so complacently surveyed the Terrace was the sitting room of an old but very comfortable house. In return for managing the properties, Pinksett and his wife had the house rent free and a modest wage besides. The position seemed a very pleasant sinecure indeed.

As he sat at his ease, perhaps Alfred Pinksett let his thoughts stray to a former day, in which his life had not been so tranquil nor his conscience so untroubled. Perhaps he lingered, a little reluctantly, over a chapter of his past that shed a distinctly unflattering light on his character, and of which even his wife knew nothing.

Whatever his thoughts may have been on that summer morning, it is certain that he had no inkling of the events that a cruel and ironic fate was even then preparing for him, nor did he dream that a part of the past was moving inexorably back into the present in the person of a heavy, brutish-looking workman who was at that moment trundling a barrow along the path that led down from the cliffs to the house.

Leaving his barrow at the garden gate, the workman made his way to the porch and executed a heavy-handed flourish on the knocker, augmenting it immediately with a penetrating and rather unpleasant whistle.

"Name of Crownower?" he inquired in a barely civil tone of Mrs. Pinksett, who opened the door. "About a leaking roof?"

"My, how quickly you've come!" twittered Mrs. Pinksett. "It was only yesterday that I told Mr. Crownower about it. It's Rose Arbor Villa, the one with the two gables, over there."

"I can see the arbor all right, missus, but not the roses," remarked the workman, in a surly attempt at wit. "What about this leak?"

"It's in the bedroom at the back, to the left of the hall. The plasterers only finished a week ago Wednesday, and now they have their work to do over again, for the rainwater came down the wall in a perfect flood during the squall we had Sunday night."

Had the roofer been content to go about his clear-cut duties at that moment instead of indulging a penchant for disputation, his whole future would have been very favorably affected. But he did not fetch his barrow and go to work. He merely scowled in the general direction of Rose Arbor Villa and shook his head with heavy skepticism.

"That there is a brand-new roof missus," he said. "I expect your rainwater came in around one of them gable windows."

"Why, no, that can't be so; the ceiling is wet through and ready to fall down like a great slab of dough, if it hasn't done already."

"Must be an open place under the eaves, then," affirmed the roofer, still reluctant to believe that the problem lay in his line. "Look you, missus, I'll just trot down there and take a look, if you'll hand me the key. The barrow may as well stay where it is for the moment; it may not be wanted, and that is a devilish steep path."

Just as Mrs. Pinksett stepped into a snug little wainscoted room off the hall, which by reason of its diminutive but businesslike desk and a rack of keys on the wall was designated "the office," her husband emerged from the sitting room and peered inquisitively through the front door. No sooner did he see the man who waited on the porch than his jaw dropped open and his face turned a sickly shade of grey. Without stopping to speak to his wife, he quickly slipped out through the door and banged it shut behind him.

At this, the roofer looked up with a start, and then he too changed color, though in his case the resultant hue was more like that of an old penny. "Tom Snedden!" he exclaimed with a savage leer. "So there is a just God in heaven after all!"

"Tom Snedden is dead," replied the other. "I am Alfred Pinksett now, *Mr.* Pinksett to the likes of you, and I'll thank you to take yourself off from here this instant."

"What a ranting whelp it is!" exclaimed the roofer, who showed no inclination to depart. On the contrary, he leaned his broad back against the railing of the porch and inserted his thumbs into the armholes of his vest. "How long is it, Tom, since you run away and left me and Phil Dewmassy to stand the racket alone? Four years me and Phil spent in Dartmoor, and eleven I've been in Hastings—that's fifteen all told, Tom, and you don't look a day older than you did that night in Maidstone."

"What's past is past, Jack," said Pinksett. "For God's sake say nothing—"

At that moment the front door opened and Mrs. Pinksett, somewhat surprised to find her husband on the porch engaged in animated conversation with the roofer, handed out the key of Rose Arbor Villa.

"That's all right, Bett," said Pinksett, taking the key from her and fairly pushing her back into the house. "I'll attend to this gentleman."

He drew the door shut and struck resolutely along the path that led to the villa with the leaking roof, with the other following closely. When they had gone some ten paces, Pinksett stopped and turned to confront his companion. "Look here, Jack Eadleigh," he said in a tone meant to carry no farther than the other man's ears, "the police nabbed you fair and square in that job at Maidstone. What would have been the good of me coming back to give myself up? It isn't as if I got away with any of the swag—you and Phil Dewmassy had it all between you, and as like as not you never meant to give me an honest share anyway. And id wasn't me decided to break a stick over the old man's head. 'Get in at night,' said I thirty times if I said it once. It was your own doing if you got four years instead of six months."

The dull coppery flush, which had faded momentarily from Eadleigh's coarse features, now returned, accompanied by a feral scowl. "You was always a sneak, Tom" he growled, "and you're a sneak yet. Afraid to take your own part in a dust-up, and now afraid to look the world in the face under your own name. Perhaps I ought to stop back another time and tell your missus what a rotter she's got linked up with."

"If you did that, Jack, it would be the last thing you ever did on this earth," countered Pinksett. "I may have been a sneak once, yes, and a coward, too, for I didn't have the strength of character to keep clear of scum like you and Phil Dewmassy. But that's all past now. I've begun with a clean slate and a new name, and I haven't spoken a hard word nor done a mean thing since Maidstone. My wife is a far better woman than I deserve, but she loves me, and I will do what I must to keep her. Take care how you bluster and threaten; I may not be the milksop that I was."

But Eadleigh seemed unimpressed and only gave a scornful laugh. "You don't frighten me, Tom Snedden," he said, "no more'n a rabbit in a trap. For it's a trap you're in, though you may not know it. Do you think I can't go round to the police any time I like, and tell them who and what you are?

"That's all talk," snapped Pinksett, "and you can stow it. The time has run out on that job at Maidstone, and all the others too. The police don't want me any more; they can't do nothing to me now, and no more can you."

During this exchange, the two men had gradually moved along the pth in the direction of Rose Arbor Villa, which still lay a great way below them. They had just reached a point where the path traversed a picturesque but treacherous rockslide when Pinksett delivered his last defiant speech. Eadleigh, overcome by rage and exasperation, turned on the man upon whom, in his twisted view, lay the blame for all his earthly woes, and raised his fist.

Pinksett had spoken more truthfully than his assailant dreamed when he affirmed that he was no longer the coward of former days, and he faced up the bully with a pluck that a much larger man might not have displayed. Somewhere he must have acquired the rudiments of boxing, for he threw one arm before his face by way of a guard, and, taking up a widely based stance, was drawing back his right arm preparatory to landing a punch on Jack Eadleigh's pugnacious chin when fate intervened once again in the relations of the two men.

Eadleigh, somewhat disturbed by the warlike posture of his adversary, hastened to buttress up his own position by throwing back one leg, a proceeding that unfortunately had anything but the desired consequence, for instead of planting that leg on solid ground he stepped backwards off the path into thin air, and, without uttering so much as a grunt, plummeted out of sight.

For a long moment, Alfred Pinksett stood staring in awe at the empty space that had just now been occupied by the very real and substantial Eadleigh. Then, dropping to his hands and knees and craning his neck over the edge of the path, he saw, some twenty feet below, the crumpled and inert figure of his erstwhile opponent. With considerable difficulty, he scrambled down the steep face of the cliff, dislodging torrents of broken rock at every step, until he stood at last over the motionless form.

He had no need of professional advice to be assured that Eadleigh was dead. The big man had fallen head first upon a broad flat boulder and must have died instantly, for already his right eye seemed glazed over with a film. The left one was swollen shut and buried in the midst of a huge purple tumescence that spread from the left side of the brow to the chin.

Pinksett's first care, after ascertaining that Eadleigh was beyond help, was to learn whether in incident had been observed. Instead of trying to regain the upper path, he crawled on all fours to another that lay lower down, and then doubled back at a trot in the direction of the house. There were two or three vessels on the quiet slate-grey water, but all of them appeared near the horizon, and unless one of them contained ain inquisitive party equipped with a mariner's glass, the chances seemed remote that the accident had been noticed in that quarter.

To landward, all seemed equally secure, but just be make doubly sure, after casting an anxious glance at the windows of the house, Pinksett climbed the path to the top of the cliffs, where he had an uninterrupted view of the land for half a mile round. To his satisfaction, there wasn't a soul in sight, and only the roofer's lorry in the road to show that he had come that way.

Pinksett now descended the path again, but instead of approaching the house he tood up the shafts of the barrow that stood at the garden gate and wheeled it as rapidly as he dared along the path to Rose Arbor Villa. The barrow was uncommonly heavy, and encumbered with a long solid ladder, so that Pinksett had a great deal of difficulty keeping it from racing off down the path, or worse, throwing him over the side. When he came to the place where Eadleigh had gone over, he kept close to the face of the cliff and passed the spot without mishap.

The lower path, which led up from the beach, intersected the upper path at a point not far from the first of the villas, and here he came to a halt and carefully moored the barrow against a thick woody shrub growing wild out of a cleft in the rock. Almost without being conscious that he was thinking, he had matured a plan for the disposal of Jack Eadleigh's body and, what was more important, for preserving the secret of his own identity.

Alfred Pinksett was at bottom a perfectly honorable man. In his younger days a certain lack of fortitude had combined with dire pecuniary straits to lead him into occasional criminal enterprises of a petty nature, but through it all he had preserved a fundamental integrity that, even now, recoiled from the notion of deceiving the authorities, not to mention his wife. But he had also that instinct of self-preservation which in military heroes is called strategy and in criminals low cunning, and it was that which prompted him to adopt the measures that he now took.

Of course Eadleigh's death had been accidental; the most biased observer would have admitted that, for Pinksett had never swung the first punch, much less landed it. But there had been no observers, biased or otherwise, and if the police questioned Bett she would be bound to say that she had last seen Eadleigh walking off along the path in company with her husband. The police would be certain to inquire into the relations of the two men and might even turn up that malevolent drunkard Dewmassy, who would lose no time in identifying Pinksett as Tom Snedden, the retired cracksman.

It was not a prison term he feared–for in truth the statutory limit had long since run out on the last of his peccadillos–but just the unwelcome disclosure of his past life coming to the ears of hiw wife. How would the dearest and purest woman take the news that her husband of six years was nothing but a common criminal, had in fact married her under a false name, which rendered their marriage contract a cheat and a lie?

Without pausing to consider the answer to that question, Alfred Pinksett set about concealing the circumstances of Eadleigh's death, aided and inspired by that instinct of low cunning to which we have alluded. He had observed that the iron wheels of the barrow left a very conspicuous track in the patches of soft sandy loam that occurred intermittently in the course of the path. To wheel the barrow along the lower path to a spot below that where the body lay might easily draw the attention of the police to that spot. And as Pinksett had decided to sue the barrow as a means of transporting the body to the place where he proposed to set the stage for a counterfeit accident, he now found it necessary to bring the body across twenty yards of extremely rough ground.

After an uneasy glance in the direction of the house, he climbed to where the body lay, more ghastly than ever now that a sticky purple patch of blood had run over the lethal boulder. He seized it by the collar and succeeded in dragging it to the barrow and tumbling it in on top of the rolls of lead and chest of tools that lay within.

Once more lifting the handles of the barrow, he pressed on down the path toward Rose Arbor Villa, noting with grim satisfaction that the weight of the dead man, instead of making the handling of the barrow more difficult than before, served as a sort of ballast.

When he arrived at the villa, he redoubled his caution, for he was now in plain sight of anyone walking along the cliffs, or of his wife if she should chance to look this way from the house. Moving with great urgency, he pushed the heavy barrow over a stone-paved court and into a barren garden where the villa effectively screened him from observation, except from the sea where the water was as clear of craft as before.

Pinksett now set about the most difficult and dangerous part of his scheme. Eadleigh had been sent off to repair the roof of Rose Arbor Villa; subsequently he had died in an accidental fall. Was it not merely a break of fate that his fall had been from the path instead of the roof of the villa? What was this undertaking upon which Pinksett had embarked but simply an effort to amend this curious quirk?

He hauled the ladder erect and placed it against the roof of a shallow verandah that faced the garden and the sea. Conspicuous among the miscellaneous tackle stowed in the barrow was a coil of stout rope. Having deposited the lifeless Eadleigh unceremoniously on the ground, Pinksett proceeded to uncoil the rope and to take two turns of it round the dead man's torso just under the arms, making the end secure with a bowline. Then, ascending several rungs of the ladder, he carried the line over the topmost rung and began laboriously hauling the heavy corpse aloft.

He was obliged to stop many times for breath, and at length to mount the ladder again and struggle his grisly burden over the coping of the roof, but at last the thing was done.

After undoing the rope and casting it free, he thought of the key to the villa which lay in his pocket. With what appeared to him to be sheer inspiration, he drew out the key and thrust it into one of Eadleigh's trouser pockets. Then, crouching low and being careful to maintain his foothold on the gently sloping roof, he tugged and strained the great motionless carcass of Jack Eadleigh nearer and nearer to the edge until it began slipping away by its own weight. And for the second time in an hour Alfred Pinksett, the former Tom Snedden, watched in horrified fascination as his old nemesis plunged away into space.

Despite a sudden feeling in his nether limbs, as though they had turned to rubber, he made his way back down the ladder. Having restored the rope to the barrow and cast a sharp eye over the scene to make certain that no detail had escaped him, he set off along the path with clammy skin and pounding heart, intent upon applying for succor to a certain square bottle he kept in the pantry.

Meanwhile, at the foot of the sharp declivity just below Rose Arbor Villa, the remains of Jack Eadleigh, more battered than ever, lay stark and still among a litter of smashed bottles and carpenter's scraps.

PART II
Narrated by Christopher Jervis, M.D.

"We find," announced the foreman of the coroner's jury, "that the deceased, Roderick Cowgill, met with his death accidentally and by misadventure.

"Yes," said the coroner, noting down the decision. "That is the only reasonable conclusion from the facts that have been presented in the course of this inquest."

As the finding of accidental death became for all time the official explanation of the demise of the unfortunate Cowgill, several of those assembled in the grand ballroom of the Hampton Hotel gave visible and audible signs of relief.

Before adjourning the inquest, the coroner relaxed slightly and addressed one of those persons in the following terms: "Mr. Eckwelm, I need not tell you that I share in the relief that you and your family must feel at this decision. I only hope that you are properly aware of the immense debt of gratitude you owe to Dr. John Thorndyke, whose presence here and whose admirably lucid presentation of the facts surrounding Rory Cowgill's death have spared you the ignominy of a trial upon the capital charge of murder, and perhaps even the death sentence.

"And," he continued, turning now to a pale-faced little man with a scholarly roundness of shoulder who sat fidgeting in a corner, "I also hope that this demonstration of the fallibility of circumstantial evidence will prove a valuable lesson the the official police, who have in this case displayed much more zeal than discretion."

The coroner abruptly shut his manuscript book and adjourned the session, whereupon most of the persons in the great echoing room crowded around young Joe Eckwelm to congratulate him on the outcome of the inquest. One or two stepped up to Thorndyke and expressed their gratitude in awed whispers. As we prepared to leave, the representative of the police to whom the coroner had directed his rather plainspoken remarks stepped forward and saluted us hesitantly.

"That was a fine piece of reasoning, Dr. Thorndyke," said he, without a trace of rancor or sarcasm, "and no man can be more grateful than I that you broke down our case against Joe Eckwelm so completely. Mr. Boynes spoke the truth when he said it was a lesson to us to watch our step in a murder case–that is, in a case that looks like murder but may not be.

"And now, would you believe it, sir, while this inquest was in session a message was handed to me, to the effect that another man has been found dead, at the bottom of a cliff. There appears to be no question of foul play, but I am wondering whether you would consider coming with me and my men to the scene and showing us just how a scientific investigator goes about gathering evidence."

Thorndyke nodded genially as, turning to me, he asked, "We've no pressing engagements until Friday, have we, Jervis? I don't see why we couldn't go along with Inspector Middlerand and lend him a hand."

The inspector–who looked as unlike a police detective as it is possible to conceive–evinced great pleasure at Thorndyke's rejoinder. Having collected a constable from the police station, we proceeded in an ambulance of sorts, which had evidently begun life as a char-a-banc, to a barren-looking stretch of coast two or three miles outside the town.

Here were met by another uniformed constable, who was lounging against a lorry near the edge of the cliff but snapped smartly to at our approach and reported to Middlerand: "A roofer, inspector–this here's his lorry. He fell off the roof of one of them new cottages down there and sent smack on over a rockslide. Must be a drop of forty feet in all. Cracked his head open, sir. It's not going to be easy getting him up from down there."

"How near is the body to the water?" asked the inspector.

"No more than a hundred yards, but you'd never get a boat in under them rocks. If I may make a suggestion, inspector, there's a long coil of rope in this fellow's barrow, down beside the house. There are enough of us here, if every man lends a hand–"

"See here, Southward," said the inspector, in a tone of mild reproof, "these gentlemen are not a couple of navvies come to recover dead bodies out of gravel pits. This is Dr. Thorndyke, the medicolegal expert who came down from London for the inquest of Rory Cowgill, and this is his assistant, Dr. Jervis."

"That's all right, inspector," laughed my colleague. "Jervis and I will cheerfully take our turn at the ropes, but just now perhaps we ought to get as close as practicable and survey the scene."

"Very right, doctor," agreed Middlerand. "Who was it found the body, Southworth?"

"A lady, by the name of Pinksett," replied the constable. We had started down a rather steep path cut in the face of the cliff and were now passing a handsome old house of weatherbeaten brick that seemed perched on the rim of an overhanging rock ledge. "The lady lives here, sir. She and her husband look after all them cottages along to the west. They're all brand new and still empty. I've taken her statement already, and we may as well go straight down and see the body.

"Lead the way, Southward. Has he been identified?"

"Yes, sir." He produced a greasy imitation-leather wallet. "His name is John Francis Eadleigh, and he is employed by a firm of builders in Hastings. I've spoken to the manager and he said this chap had no family and precious few friends, for he was an ill-natured brute, and worse when he was drinking, which I gather was pretty often–"

"Yes, yes, Southworth," interrupted the inspector. "And these people–what d'you call'em? Pinksett?–are in charge of the properties? They must know this fellow, eh?"

"Not exactly, sir. The lady sent word the other day to the contractor who built these cottages that one of them had a leaky roof– that one there, with the two dormer windows like eyes and that trellis thing stuck on by the chimney. Then this Eadleigh come along this morning and asked for the key so he could go down and mend the leak. She gave it to him, but it was her husband who took him down and showed him the house."

"And how did they come to find him dead?"

"They went looking for him. As you can see, they have a clear view of the cottage from their place, and they saw never a sign of him on the roof, nor heard the first tap of his hammer. About two o'clock when they went down to investigate, they found his cart in the garden and his ladder leaning against the roof, but no Mr. Eadleigh. Fallen asleep over his lunch pail, they thought, but when Mr. Pinksett went up to the door he found it shut fast and when his wife happened to look over the porch railing she saw the poor chap down below on a heap of rock."

We had been descending all the while, but now the path, after intersecting another that seemed to run up from the beach, became almost level and led us straight to the scene of the accident. The little cottage stood at the edge of a half acre plot of rock-strewn mud. Just beyond it the land fell away abruptly almost to the water's edge, and it was obvious that a fall from that side of the roof would be likely to propel a man straight on down to the foot of the cliff.

As we passed round the side of the cottage, two mute witnesses of the tragedy came into view–a ladder propped against the porch roof and a two-wheeled handcart drawn up in a little court paved with flagstones.

"You can see him better from the porch, sir," said Constable Southworth. "And that edge is as crumbly as peat. I had to go half a mile round before I could climb down to him without breaking my own neck."

We crowded onto the porch and tood turns standing two abreast and peering over the railing down the dizzying drop, at the bottom of which lay the unfortunate John Francis Eadleigh. A hideous wound of the head was visible even at that distance, and it was obvious from the flailed attitude of the limbs that Eadleigh had died instantly.

"The first order of business," said Thorndyke, "is to examine the body *in situ*. Let us see the rope, constable—yes, this will serve nicely, I think." He took the coil of rope from Constable Southworth and, with speed and dexterity, fashioned a large loop in one end. Then, taking two turns of the rope around the stout cornerpost of the porch roof, he proceeded to place the loop around his middle and draw it up tight below his arms.

"Why, you're not going down there on that rope?" exclaimed Inspector Middlerand. "It may do very well for hauling up a dead man, but for sending down a live one—"

"I am sure it will do admirably," said my colleague, handing the coil of rope with serene confidence to the inspector. "Pay out the line slowly and steadily, and when I am down you may draw it up and send Jervis after me."

As soon as we had taken up the slack, he mounted the porch rail, lowered himself over the side, and disappeared gradually from our view as we let out the rope.

I then made the descent without any worse mishap than the loss of my hat, which Thorndyke had already retrieved before I reached the bottom. The spot where the body lay was a bleak and forlorn hollow, hedged all about with fallen rock.

Having restored my hat and assisted me to disengage myself from the rope, Thorndyke resumed his inspection of the body. The lethal wound had quite crushed the victim's face, no doubt shattering the underlying bone. It was obvious that the neck was broken. With meticulous care, Thorndyke changed the attitude of the body in order to examine the wound more fully, then turned his attention to the limbs and, finally, the clothing.

He seemed to find something interesting about the boot tops, and as he proceeded from them to the waistband and thence to the collar, his interest steadily grew. Inserting his finger within the collar, he withdrew a small mass of green vegetable matter, which he examined critically with his lens, then sniffed, and finally held up for my inspection.

"Fool's parsley," I announced after a careful survey of the withered sprigs.

"You will recall," Thorndyke commented, "that it is also know as the lesser hemlock–a rather nasty poison. It is occasionally responsible for outbreaks of sickness among cattle and horses, though it is seldom lethal."

"Well, this chap was certainly not poisoned with it," said I. "This is an even clearer case of accidental death than that Cowgill business."

"Look around you, Jervis," said my companion. There was something so grave and sinister in his tone that it fairly made my flesh creep. "Do you see any fool's parsley, or for that matter any other vegetation worthy of the name, along the path the body must have taken in falling from that roof?"

"No, Thorndyke, I'm hanged if I do."

"There are quantities of crushed weeds inside the deceased's boot tops, said my companion, "and also inside his waistband and collar. His hip pocket, which, as you see, is provided with a flap, is empty, but the button is stained green and has a few scraps of vegetable matter caught under it. All this looks as though the body had ploughed head first through a patch of weeds, whereas nothing of the sort can have happened."

"Perhaps he'd taken another fall earlier in the day?" I suggested.

"That is possible, but hardly a likely explanation for these findings. No man would endure a sensation of all this herbage inside his collar for a quarter of a minute before plucking it out."

The police officers, who have been peering over the porch railing now began to signify their curiosity and impatience by calling down a variety of irrelevant questions. At length, to their great satisfaction, I raised the upper part of the body while Thorndyke worked the rope sling down over the shoulders and under the stiffened arms.

"Stand by to haul away," I heard Middlerand sing out with a jaunty nautical air.

"Just a minute!" shouted Thorndyke. "We haven't finished here yet." In its new position the corpse had presented some previously unobserved feature to Thorndyke's alert eye, for he produced his lens once again and stooped over the rumpled shirt front, where it protruded above the chalk-smeared vest. "What do you make of this, Jervis?" said he, pointing to a yellowish-brown stain on the rather dingy linen.

I bent close to examine it through the lens. "A smear of roofing tar," I hazarded dubiously at last.

"Use your nose again," he suggested.

"Why, it's tobacco!" I cried. "Or rather, some product of tobacco. I don't suppose he was chewing it?"

"There is no tobacco in any form on his person," replied Thorndyke. "That stain is, nevertheless, exactly what you have called it–a product of tobacco. I shall leave it to you to think of a way in which it might have come there while we are getting the unfortunate gentleman aloft."

Puzzle though I might over this enigma, I had arrived at no conclusion by the time the body of John Eadleigh lay upon the porch and Thorndyke and I had been hauled up again.

While the constables coiled up the rope and returned it to the handcart, Thorndyke reviewed his findings with Inspector Middlerand, who seemed most impressed, and spent considerable time peering through my colleague's Coddington lens at the aberrant scraps of vegetation, the tobacco stain, and particularly at various aspects of his own left hand.

"This is surely very queer," he said at last. "How do you suggest that we proceed, Dr. Thorndyke?"

"I should recommend getting the body to a mortuary as soon as possible," replied Thorndyke. "But first may I suggest a look inside the house? This key is evidently not the property of the deceased." He held up a steel latchkey attached by a ring to an immense slab of hardwood on which the words "Rose Arbor Villa" had been burned with an iron.

"And just as evidently this house is not our property," observed Middlerand. "If you really think we ought to look inside, we must have a warrant."

"I fancy that, as the place is clearly unoccupied, the Pinksetts would make no difficulties about a search. Unless you positively forbid it, I propose to step inside and have a look around while your men are placing the body on that barrow."

Without giving Middlerand the opportunity either to object or to assent to his proposal, Thorndyke whipped open the front door of the cottage and stepped inside. I followed him round from one empty and echoing room to another and observed nothing more sinister than a smell of fresh paint and a pot of whiting that had been overlooked in the kitchen. Thorndyke apparently saw nothing of note either, for he never once brought out the inevitable lens. "It seems doubtful that the deceased ever set foot in the house at all," he remarked to Middlerand as we came out.

The body now lay in awkward repose atop the tools and roofing materials in the handcart and the constables were taking down the ladder when Thorndyke stopped them with a word. To my surprise and their unmitigated horror, he mounted upon the porch roof and crawled coolly along to the point where Eadleigh had apparently gone over the side. "For God's sake, Thorndyke," I cried, "stay clear of the edge!" I felt not a little relieved when my colleague rejoined me.

Still he would not permit the ladder to be taken down, for now he appeared to have found something on one of its lowermost rungs to examine through his lens. "Just look at this, will you, gentlemen?" he said. "No, you don't want the lens." And indeed there was no need of a magnifying glass to see the article in question, for it was a scrap of cloth a good two inches long which had evidently caught on a splinter of wood and been torn away from some article of clothing.

"That's made a wreck of a good pair of britches, that has," was Constable Salton's comment.

"Agreed," said Thorndyke. "And that pair of britches is not far to seek." He stepped to the handcart and raised one of the legs of the corpse to show, in the back of the trousers just above the ankle, a tear corresponding exactly to the scrap of cloth on the ladder. "It is a little hard to understand how this cloth could have been torn away from the back of his trousers in the ordinary course of events," he said, "for no one but a madman goes up and down a ladder with his back to the rungs."

"He might have got onto the ladder backwards once in a while in coming off a steep roof," suggested Constable Southworth. "If he had the ladder the other way, this rung might have caught the back of his trousers before he had turned himself around."

"That is an excellent suggestion," said Thorndyke, "except for one small matter. The ladder has a pronounced taper at the top, and it seems very doubtful that a man who earned his living by climbing ladders would make the mistake of erecting one upside down. Still, as the deceased is reputed to have been a drinker, you may be perfectly right."

Now began the melancholy–and arduous–climb up the steep path with the heavily laden handcart. The constables had hung the ladder on the hooks provided for it, and this made the task of pushing the cart a little less difficult for it gave another man a means of contributing his shoulder at the steep places, but even so it was a difficult climb.

We were nearing the point where the path became steeper, and Thorndyke and I were walking several paces behind the others in case of a sudden backsliding when my companion stopped abruptly and looked back along the path. "Have you observed how the wheels of the cart leave a track in the sandy places?" he asked.

"Yes," said I. "I noticed the wheel marks as we were going down, and now I see that it must have been this very cart that made them, for the two tracks are perfectly identical. Here is the mark of a chipped tread that the wheel has just made, and there is the identical mark on the other side going down."

"Right you are, Jervis. But I fancy that the tracks are identical even to a further extent than that." He stooped down and measured the depth of on of the tracks in a particularly loamy spot with the steel millimeter rule he always carried in his vest pocket. Then he repeated the proceeding with the immediately adjacent impression, and finally with two on the other side of the path. "That is perfectly conclusive, I think. The wheels have sunk to the same depth in coming up the path as in going down."

I glanced up sharply, and in the brief instant that our eyes met, the sinister import of his discovery dawned fully upon me. Meanwhile the handcart had come to a stand, and Inspector Middlerand, dabbing at his brow with a handkerchief, left his place between the shafts and came down the path to us.

"You must be a magician, Dr. Thorndyke, if you can make anything out of that jumble of footmarks," he said.

"I am more interested in the marks made by the handcart," said my colleague. "Jervis and I have just ascertained that the tracks made in the soft places by the cart going down the path are equal in depth to the tracks we are making bringing it up."

"Why, how can you tell the difference between the two tracks?" asked Middlerand.

"We could distinguish the one track from the other quite easily by comparing the marks of the two wheels, which are slightly different owing to some damage to the treads. But the great question is not which track is which, but how they can be of equal depth if the cart is now laden with a burden that must double the weight that rested on the wheels when it went down the path."

"I see what you mean!" cried Middlerand. "But what can he have taken down there is his cart, and what has become of it?"

"I rather imagine it was Mr. Eadleigh himself that went down in the cart," observed Thorndyke. "There is abundant evidence to suggest that he was killed, or at least struck unconscious, in some other place, and his body transported to the roof of the cottage and deliberately thrown off to conceal the true circumstances of his death."

"Doctor, it looks like we've got a murder case after all!"

"It does look that way," agreed Thorndyke, "but let us not be hasty. We have reason to suspect that a deception has been practiced, but not necessarily that Eadleigh was the victim of a murderous assault."

"Here, Southworth," called the inspector, "was there anyone else about when you first came down?"

"No, sir, just Mr. and Mrs. Pinksett."

"Did they say they saw this chap take his cart down there?"

"I don't recollect that they did. Mr. Pinksett walked down to the cottage with him to show him the leaking place in the roof, but he left his cart at the top of the path until he had looked over the damage."

"And so they never actually saw him come back along the path and wheel his cart down there?"

"They didn't say so, but of course he must have done.

During a rest period, not long after the path leading up from the beach had intersected our course, Thorndyke dropped to his knees

again and applied his rule to another set of marks in a patch of soft
sandy earth. "That's it!" he announced triumphantly, rising to his
feet and dusting off the knees of his trousers. "The tracks made by the
cart in passing over this stretch of the path are very much shallower
than those we have just made in pushing it up. If, as seems likely, the
body was taken down to Rose Arbor Villa on the cart, it must have
been put on near the spot where the patch from the beach joins this
one."

"Let's get this job finished, I say, panted Inspector Middlerand,
"and when the body is at the top of the cliff, we can come down again
and have a look along that side path."

We all agreed to this proposal, and presently had the satisfaction
of feeling the iron wheels run easily over the level pavement at the
head of the path. We loaded the body into the ambulance and, leaving Constable Southworth in charge, hastened back to the beach path
and started along it with our eyes peeled.

Almost at once we became aware of a rather pronounced disturbance
in the surface of the gound alongside the path. There were long linear
furrows in the gravelly soil, and the weeds, more lush here in the
shade of a ridge rock, had been bruised and uprooted as by a heavy
object dragged over them. The story told by these traces was only too
plain, and when we had followed the trail through a patch of fool's
parsley to the foot of a rockslide, where it abruptly ended, none of us
doubted that we had reached the point where Eadleigh had actually
met his death. But if confirmation of the fact were needed, it was
there in plenty. A rather conspicuous mound of gravel and freshly
turned earth, upon being cleared away, was found to conceal a wide
and irregular splash of blood that had soaked into a slab of chalk at
the foot of the slide.

"This is the upper path directly above us, affirmed Thorndyke,
pointing to a spot halfway up the rockslide where the path had been
rudely buttressed from below with stout timers driven into the face of
the cliff. "The obvious conclusion from what we have observed is that
Eadleigh either fell or was thrown off the path at that spot and that
his body was moved from here to the cart to Rose Arbor Villa, hauled
up the ladder to the roof, and thrown off into the pit where we found
it."

"Why go to all the trouble of taking the body to the roof?" asked
Middlerand. "If it had been thrown over the porch railing it would
have come down in almost the same place."

"No doubt, but the scrap of cloth on the ladder, and some traces
that I found upon the roof, point the other way. I think a visit to the
Pinksetts is indicated."

We ascended the path again and filed rather solemnly onto the
porch of the Pinksetts' house. Inspector Middlerand's knock was answered by a pretty little blonde woman, who was evidently quite

overwhelmed to find such a throng of people on her doorstep. When the inspector had introduced himself and us, we entered and passed into a sort of sitting room with windows along two sides commanding a splendid view of the sea.

"Now then, Mrs. Pinksett," began the inspector in a businesslike tone, "Constable Southworth, who took your statement earlier, tells me that you did not see this man Eadleigh pushing his handcart down to the place where it was found. Is that correct?"

"Why, yes, inspector, it is. My husband walked along the path with him to show him the damaged walls in Rose Arbor Villa, but he left his barrow there at the garden gate, for he thought it might not be wanted and the path is very steep. He must have come up later and taken it down, for when we went to look for him we found it in the little paved court next to the villa."

"You say your husband walked down with him? Where might Mr. Pinksett be at this moment?"

"My husband is in bed, inspector. This has upset him terribly and he has gone in to have a rest. I am sure, though, that if you wish it he will get up and speak to you."

Upon Middlerand's signifying that that was exactly what he did wish, the little lady disappeared through a darkened doorway, and after a delay of many minutes returned with her husband in tow.

Pinksett had evidently taken the time to adjust his clothing and brush his hair, and to have a strong dose of the sort of nerve tonic that is customarily sold by the pint.

"We have been talking to your wife about this fellow's handcart," said the inspector. "Did you see him wheel it along the path to Rose Arbor Villa?"

Pinksett had taken down from the mantelpiece an ancient cherry-wood pipe with a long cracked stem, and this he proceeded to fill and light with great deliberation before answering. "I did," said he at length, amid clouds of blue smoke. "I stood there at the garden gate and watched him all the way down. I thought of going to help him, for it was all he could do to keep hold of the cart at the steep places, but he was a big'un, and he got it down all right."

"Then you actually saw him wheel the cart into the garden next to the villa?" pursued Middlerand.

For a while Pinksett puffed at his pipe in dogged silence, laying his finger mechanically over the fuming carck in the stem each time he drew in a mouthful of smoke. In spite of its dilapidated condition it must have been his favorite pipe, for both his index fingers were deeply stained with smoke and tobacco tar. "That's what I said," he replied at last.

"Now, see here, Mr. Pinksett," said the inspector, "that can't very well be true. The deceased never lived long enough to push his cart that far—now, did he?"

My attention was drawn away from Pinksett's haggard but impassive face by his wife's anguished cry. "Oh, Alf!" she sobbed, covering her mouth with her apron, "they know, *they know!*"

"Know what, my dear?" asked Pinksett in unfeigned surprise, and his voice grew tremulous as his wife crossed the room and put out her hands to him.

"They know, Alf, about that man and how he fell backwards off the path just when he was going to hit you!"

Pinksett let his pipe drop to the hearth, where it broke in pieces, and sat limply in his chair staring at the woman who knelt before him. "Bett!" he exclaimed, "how did you know about that?"

"I saw it happen, Alf–from the kitchen window. Even–even when you pushed him off the roof of the villa."

"You saw that?" said Pinksett, half choked with emotion. "And you said nothing? Why?"

"Oh, Alf, don't you know why? I saw it was an accident, but it might seem different to other people–to the police–" she stopped short, suddenly conscious that this heart-rending domestic drama had a large and disconcerting official audience.

"Better make a clean breast of it, sir," recommended Middlerand in a stodgy matter-of-fact tone. "If it was an accident, as the lady says, you've nothing to fear. But just don't you go trying to put one over on the police. You left a trail of clues a yard wide, such as a one-eyed goose could have followed, and we know pretty much the whole story already. I should advise you to come along with us to the station and make a full statement, when we shall decide whether any criminal charges are in order."

It is perhaps needless to add that the local magistrate, having reviewed the evidence and questioned Pinksett and his wife at some length, dismissed them from his court with a benevolent but solemn warning against future attempts to hoodwonk so astute a criminal investigator as Inspector Middlerand.

Lawrence Treat
A Matter of Arson

After the fire one windowless room of the house still stood, slippery underneath, smelling of burnt wood and drenched with a wet, watery, oily black slush. Inside the ruin, a few articles of smoke-damaged furniture remained for the taking.

Kids stared at the mess. A few scavengers rummaged through the meager pickings and took whatever pleased them. A raw thinnish man with a long nose hovered over a bureau. Bending down, he studied the hardware, ran his hand over the black smudge, and found the brasswork underneath. Careless of the way the bureau smeared his clothes, he lugged it across the floor, slid it to the ground, and hauled it to a blue station wagon with the sign, CLARK RAMSDELL, PLUMBING CONTRACTOR.

Later in the day, the fire marshal sifted the ruins and, in the course of determining the probable cause as arson, found the body of a woman charred beyond recognition. She was curled up in the fetal position and clutching some green glass that had melted into a shapeless mass.

The marshall called Chief Dan Moorhead of Morgan County, who arrived within the next twenty minutes. He assumed that the body was that of Livia London who had owned and occupied the house. Subsequently the medical examiner decided that death was probably due to smoke inhalation. By evening, Dan had questioned Livia's husband and her houseman, both of whom had seen her on the previous day.

At nine P.M. Dan walked into the Right Side Bar & Grill in Le Page County, just across the state line, and headed for his usual booth to the right of the door. Chief Willy Wahrton of Le Page County was hunched over the table and cradling his glass of beer in one hand. He seemed to be made of pure granite, hacked out of a quarry, and fashioned with broad, slashing strokes. Dan, sitting down opposite him, had a softer face and outweighed Willy by ten or fifteen pounds.

Dan said nothing until he'd taken a long gulp of ice-cold beer. Then he made a face.

"Lousy," he said. "And a lousy day."

Willy nodded sympathetically. Since this wasn't his case he could afford to be philosophical about it. "These arson cases are tough to prove."

"Arson, hell!" Dan said. "This is homicide. Murder in the first degree."

"Who says?"

Dan patted his ample belly. "Me. My gut." When Willy tried to shrug off the statement, Dan said, "You didn't know her. Livia London. She used to have a yacht and houses in Cannes and Miami and New York."

"And after a terrible accident she retired to Tiffin," Willy added. "Population three hundred. I know all about her. She lost half of her face. After the accident she stayed in Tiffin and never left it."

"Ever see her?" Dan asked.

"No. Did you?"

"No, and neither did anybody else, except Cholly Hupp, who lived there and was her houseman, chauffeur, general factotum, and maybe a couple of other things."

"What's he like?"

"Round. Round face and round body. He'd bounce nicely and come up laughing, which is what he does mostly. He probably laughs in his sleep too. The question is, is he laughing off a homicide or is he always that way?"

"Where was he when the fire started?"

"He claims he spent the night with Seraphina Brickell at the Good Samaritan Motel, and he did. I guess you know her track record. A hundred dollars a night, recommended customers only. I spoke to her and Cholly, and ther stories check in every detail, but how do I know he didn't duck out of the motel for an hour or so and do a torch job? She says she slept all night. He says he slept until two A.M., when he heard the fire whistle and went to Tiffin, along with the rest of the volunteer fire department."

"Why would Cholly go in for arson?"

"I don't know. Maybe the strain of his job. The ambience."

"Amby–what?"

Dan spread his hand on the table. "The surroundings," he said. "Everything about the place. It was like living with a ghost, and maybe it got to him. For instance, the way he hardly ever saw her. She spoke to him through doors or through an intercom, and if he had to come into a room, he was instructed to knock first. If she was there, she usually told him to wait a minute so she'd have time to disappear."

"Didn't he ever see her?" Willy asked.

"Once in a while, at night and at a distance, but even then she always wore a veil." Dan pulled his hand back as if he felt ashamed of its good solid strength. "There were no mirrors in the house," he said. "None at all, except the one that Cholly had at his end of the house. That's the part that's still standing. It's damaged and most of the roof caved in, but the walls are still upright. It's the last section the fire hit."

"The radio said you'd questioned her husband," Willy said.

"Yeah, Tony London, a hundred and twenty pounds of him, stretched out over seventy-four inches. I figure he works on strings, like a puppet."

"What does he do?"

"Collects fifteen grand from her in two annual installments. He visits her twice a year, and each time he spends the night. He has to wait until dark before she lets him in, and once he's inside he finds her sitting in a dark room with all the shades down, wearing that veil. They talk about money and drink champagne. She must have had a bottle of it in her arms when the smoke got her."

"Then she was probably drunk by the time the fire started. What does London say?"

"That he left early. Here's the sequence, Willy, the way Hupp and London tell it. In the afternoon, Cholly iced a few magnums of champagne and put them in a cooler, and left them in front of her door, then beat it to see Seraphina. I have witnesses to his departure and to London's arrival, which was around seven. He claims she was drunk already and they had an argument and she kicked him out, and after that he was nowhere near the vicinity."

"What was the argument about?"

"Money. He said she wanted to cut his allowance and he told her he didn't need her money, he had a job offer and expected to take it. He says he told her he was tired of being dependent on her."

"Do you believe him?" Willy asked.

"Not all of it, but I think they did have an argument and that he left a few hours before the fire. He had a magnum of PiperHeidsieck with him. He parked on a side road in the state forest and drank the full bottle, and woke up this morning with a hangover. His car was spotted twice during the course of the night, but there's nothing to say he didn't drive back and set the fire between those two times when he was seen. Willy, these are kooks, all of them, but you've got to feel sorry for Livia and that face of hers, and I'm going to hang somebody for it. But who?"

"The first day's always the toughest," Willy said. "Go home and sleep on it. The cases you don't solve in the first hour or so come slow. You got to squeeze the juice out of them, drop by drop, like an old lemon."

"I wish I could drop the whole business in your lap. Why do I always get the tough ones, while you take it easy in Le Page? Half the time I earn my salary and yours too."

"Sure," Willy said "Makes you a damn saint, so don't talk about it. Saints are modest."

"This beer," Dan said, scowling, "is lousy, and gets lousier with every sip."

"You bet," Willy said, and finished his own beer with gusto.

The following morning an insurance adjuster showed up at Dan's office and introduced himself.

"I'm Oliver Wenzel," he said. "I'd like to go through the ruins and

I'd appreciate it if one of your men could come along with me to verify anything I find."

"Glad to help out," Dan said, "but I think you can save yourself some time by starting with the fire marshal. He has all the information about the house and the fire."

"I'm not too interested in the house," Wenzel said, "but we carried a quarter of a million dollars' worth of insurance on her jewelry, and I'm hoping to recover enough of it to reduce our losses."

"I wish you luck," Dan said, "but I understand it was a pretty hot fire. What does that do to jewelry?"

"You never know," Wenzel said, "which is why I have to be thorough about my search. Only, first, I want to make sure the stuff was in the house at the time of the fire, and particularly a necklace of hers that was insured for one-fifty. I have a picture of it here, courtesy of the people she bought it from."

Dan gave the photograph a casual glance. "Let me have a copy," he said. "And I'll send Robinson along with you. You can rely on him."

Robinson, however, did a lot more than stand around and watch an insurance man sift the ruins in the hope of finding the remains of some jewelry. He asked questions, and on the basis of the answers he reported to Dan.

"Chief," he said, "the kids around here, they tell me Ransdell, that's the plumber, maybe you know him—"

"Sure. What about him?"

"He was hanging around the ruins yesterday morning and carted off some stuff. He did it while the place was still smoking."

"I'll get hold of him," Dan said.

Ramsdell looked nervous when he came into Dan's office. His long nose seemed to sniff trouble. He sat down gingerly on the edge of a chair and answered questions in a low voice that at times was almost inaudible.

"I hear you took some things from the London house," Dan said.

Ramsdell nodded, and when Dan asked him what, he mumbled, "Stuff. Nothing much."

"What?"

"An old bureau. Brass hardware on it."

"What made you go to the ruin?"

"Nothing. I just wanted to see."

Ramsdell clasped his hands, unclasped them. "Fires—you never know. You find things, Fittings."

"And bureaus?" Ramsdell didn't answer and Dan said, "What was in the bureau?"

"Clothes. Belonged to Hupp. I told him to come over and get them, so he did. Expensive shirts, but just junk now. They're scorched, no good. Wouldn't fit me anyhow."

"You tried them on?"

"No. They tore in two when you picked them up. Two drawerfuls, ruined."

"Two drawers?" Dan said. "A two-drawer bureau?"

"Three. Nice hardware. The top drawer's stuck, got to dry out some, but I got the lock out. Good lock."

"How could you get the lock out without opening the drawer?"

"It opened a couple of inches. There's nothing inside it, though. It's empty. I could see that much."

Dan told himself he'd reached a dead end on the bureau.

"You did the plumbing for Mrs. London, didn't you?"

Ramsdell nodded and looked away.

Sensing something, Dan said, "When was the last time you were there?" Ramsdell muttered something unintelligible. "When?" Dan repeated.

"Well, you see—"

"When?"

"The night before."

"You mean the night of the fire?"

Ramsdell studied the floor, then nodded.

"When did you arrive," Dan asked, "and exactly when did you leave? You have a time sheet and people know your truck, I can get the answers right down to the minute, but you'll be a lot better off if you tell me. And whom and what you saw.

At the end of Ramsdell's story he said, "You won't tell the papers, will you? Or the radio? It would ruin me, and I'm having trouble right now. You won't tell, will you?"

Dan didn't tell the papers. Instead, he told Willy that night, while they were sitting in their booth at the Right Side Bar & Grill.

"I had a talk with Ramsdell," Dan said. "That man can't even talk in sentences."

"What did he have to say?" Willy asked.

"It seems he has a little racket," Dan said. "If you call him for something simple that ought to take ten or fifteen minutes he claims a few other things have to be done. He charges by the hour and kites up his charges by two or three hours. He usually goes down to the cellar and pretends he's on the job for as long as he's there, which is what he did at the London place."

"What does he do down in the cellar? Take a snooze?"

"Sometimes. And sometimes he just listens, which is what he did at the London place. He was there from about five o'clock to eight, and he says he heard Cholly leave and Tony London come and go.

"Sounds like you got a nice break."

"Well," Dan said, "you know the way voices will sometimes go up or down a pipe, they'll be audible from one part of a room and in another part of the room the people might as well be talking in Azerbaijan."

"What's that? A new language?

"It's a Soviet republic and province in Iran. Take your choice."

"I'll say here," Willy said. "So what happened? Seems that Ramsdell can tell you anything he wants to, he can make things up and hold out on whatever suits him. What did he say?"

"That London came in and made some remark about her starting in to drink too early in the day. A champagne cork popped and then he didn't hear anything for about ten minutes."

"Because they were in another part of the room?"

"Who knows? But by and by he heard her tell London she was short of money and the only way she could work things out was for him to come live with her. He said, 'With that face?' They started yelling at each other, and after about fifteen or twenty minutes London left. Whem Ramsdell thought the coast was clear, he climbed back upstairs and sneaked out without seeing anybody. That's his whole story."

"What time did he leave?"

"Around eight," Dan said. "I checked with his wife, and he got home around eight thirty. With the state the body was in, the M.E. can't guess at the time of death. Even his smoke-inhalation diagnosis is guesswork—all he's really sure of is that she wasn't shot and no bones were broken. I'm going on the theory that she was alive at eight when Ramsdell left, and that she died in the fire, which was going full blast at two A.M. There's no telling when it started, but the odds are it was around midnight."

"Well now, you got yourself a nice little puzzle," Willy said. "If Ransdell is giving it to you straight, then London or Cholly is lying. But if Cholly and London are telling the truth, Ramsdell's the one. He had the opportunity."

"They all did. Each one of them could have set the fire that killed. But something else has turned up. It seems Livia had some valuable jewelry. The insurance agent is trying to check it out. He found most of her stuff in the ruins—some of the gold's melted and the gem stones ain't what they used to be—but a necklace worth a hundred and fifty grand is missing. Want to see a picture of if?"

He handed Willy the copy that Wenzel had given him, and Willy studied it as if he was an expert jeweler and lapidary. Turning it sideways, squinting at it, and rubbing his fingers along the glossy surface.

"Diamonds?" he said. Dan nodded and Willy said, "It would look pretty nice on Katie, except she doesn't go in for jewelry."

"The idea of Livin, who couldn't stand to look at herself, walking around the house and wearing that thing—it's spooky, isn't it?"

"Do you think she was wearing it that night?" Willy asked. If she was, then London or Ramsdell or Cholly could have taken it and then gone and set the fire to hide the larceny."

"So far," Dan said, "that's pretty much my theory. If we're right, about all I can do is wait for the necklace to show up, and try to trace it back to whichever one of the three sold it, or tried to."

"That might take a year or more."

"Might," Dan admitted. "In the meantime, I'm putting a tail on all three of them, twenty-four hours a day." He took a slip of paper from his pocket and handed it to Willy. "In case any of them drive over to Le Page, here are the license numbers and descriptions of their cars. Ramsdell lives in Le Page, so you could start spotting him in the morning when he starts out and see where he goes."

"I'll do that," Willy said. "Get yourself a good night's sleep, and I'll put the watch on Ramsdell."

At three A.M. Willy's bedside phone rang. He reached out and dragged the receiver to his ear.

"Wharton," he growled.

"Robinson here. That kid of mine–the one who wants to be a detective and is always helping me–he decided to go on night duty and watch the Ramsdell house. A little while ago he sees somebody drive by and douse his lights, then park off the road and start for the house. He sees whoever it is go in the back door, and then he calls me."

"That kid of yours," Willy said. "He's okay."

"I checked the car. It's Hupp's, and it looks like he's in Ramsdell's house right now. What do I do?"

"Stay put," Willy said. "I'll be right over."

Katie, waking up, said, "William. What's happening?"

"One of Dan's cases came across the line and plunked itself in my lap. Why can't people stay in Morgan where they belong?"

"William," she said vaguely, and was asleep before she could say his name again.

Robinson, a drowsy man with a drooping mustache, was just one more shadow among the many that seemed to camouflage his car. He shrank back when Willy's headlights picked him up. Willy braked, parked behind Robinson's car, and switched the headlights off.

"Where's that kid of yours?" Willy asked.

"I sent him home. I don't want him around if there's any trouble." He pointed at the house. "Hupp's still in there, you can see his flashlight every once in a while. He was nosing around downstairs, but he's in the cellar now. Look–there's his light in the cellar window."

"Chances are the bedrooms are upstairs," Willy said. "If he goes up, there could be a confrontation and we'd have to go in and take him. Otherwise let's wait till he comes out. Where's his car?"

"On the other side of that signpost. Any idea what he's after?"

"I'd say a necklace, except who looks for a necklace in a cellar?" Robinson didn't answer.

Staring into the darkness, Willy said, "If he comes out the back door and heads over to the left, we could lose him. You'd better go and wait at his car. If he shows up there it'll mean I missed him and it's up to you to nab him."

Robinson turned and walked off noiselessly. One moment he was standing next to Willy, the next he'd melted into the shadows. Like a zombie, Willy told himself, and wished he had a few more zombies like Robinson.

When Hupp left the house, his roly-poly figure was outlined against the whiteness of the driveway. He came forward confidently and just before he reached the road Willy snapped on his flashlight and caught him squarely in the beam.

"Police," Willy said. "Put your hands up and walk forward, slowly."

"Why not?" Cholly said.

He seemed relaxed as Willy frisked him and found no weapon.

"What were you doing in there?" Willy asked.

Cholly laughed.

"Look," Willy said. "We saw you go in, we saw you making a search–that's breaking and entering with criminal intent."

"I didn't break in," Cholly said. "The door wasn't locked."

"It doesn't have to be. It was closed. That makes it a breaking."

Cholly laughed again.

"Criminal trespass," Willy said.

"That's a misdemeanor," Cholly said.

"Okay, so it's a misdemeanor. But breaking and entering at night with criminal intent, that's a felony, and it's five years. What were you after?"

Cholly laughed. Whereupon Willy made the formal arrest and locked him up in the county jail for the night.

"You couldn't really call it a laugh," Willy said to Dan at the Right Side that evening.

"Loud?" Dan said.

"No. Kind of a –well, sort of a–"

"So what was he after?" Dan asked. "What did he expect to find?"

"It has to be the necklace," Willy said, "but I couldn't break him down. When he gets through laughing, maybe I can get it out of him, but he's a tough nut to crack. What I need is a break of some kind."

Judging by his grin the following evening when he arrived at the Right Side Bar & Grill he had had it.

"Dan," he said happily, "you know what? Katie burnt the beans."

"So?"

"First time it ever happened. Here she is, the best cook in Le Page—wins prizes at the county fair–and she comes a cropper over a pot of beans."

"Are you trying to kid me?" Dan said.

Willy shook his head, but he kept on grinning. "It was worse than that. She burned the whole dinner. We had to go out and eat."

"Well?" Dan said, scowling. "Stop clowing around. What are you trying to tell me?"

"What was the word you used the other day? Ambience? I'm giving you the ambience. So think of her there in the kitchen, making dinner on her new stove. Have you seen any of these new stoves lately?"

"I'd appreciate it," Dan said, "if you'd get to the point."

"The point," Willy said, "is the way they make these new stoves. You can set them automatically, you can start them high and program them to turn to low all by themselves. They've got automatic features and timers and you can dial them to do whatever you want them to do. They grill, and barbecue, and spit, and roast, and they vent themselves, and you can't even see where the heat comes from. You can even cook on them if you push the right buttons."

"So what about it?"

"All those buttons," Willy said, "they scare her. They look like the cockpit of a plane. So there she is, making one of those bean casseroles of hers, and the phone rings. And you know who it was? The hospital!"

"Where the hell does that come in?"

"Dan, one of the things I teach my men is never to scare people. Never say, like they did to Katie, this is the hospital and your sister has had an accident. It scares people. You want to avoid that kind of a shock. Suppose Katie had a heart condition?"

"If you're finished with the lecture, maybe you'll tell me what happened."

"I just did. They told Katie her sister had had an accident and was in the hospital, and Katie beat it over there."

"How is her sister?"

"She twisted her ankle, and they thought it was a break, but it turned out just to be a bad sprain, so Katie took her home from the hospital. That was when she remembered the beans."

"What about them? She turned off the stove before she left, didn't she?"

"She thought she did, but in her excitement she must have pushed the wrong button. Maybe a few of them. They've got directions printed all over the stove and an instruction book to tell you all about it, but Katie was in a hurry and didn't have time to sit down and read about what a wonderful stove she had."

"So your dinner got burnt? What about it?"

"Burnt?" Willy said. "You should have seen the place. It's lucky the house didn't burn down. There was all this smoke–smoke from the beans, smoke from the bacon, smoke from a bunch of other junk including a wooden bowl that got charred up. There was black smoke all over the kitchen walls. Katie spent the rest of the day cleaning. The walls in back of the stove, the counter, a drawer that was left open. Half the stuff in that drawer was coated with heavy black gook."

"What are you getting at?" Dan demanded.

"You don't know Katie. Nothing floors her. Here are her best kitchen things smeared up so she can't use them, and what do you think she does? She puts them in the dishwasher, turns it on, and presto! Her stuff if like new."

"I better get another beer," Dan said. "Are you finished yet?"

"No. Because when she goes to put the things back in the drawer that used to be lined with clean white paper, she sees it's smudged except where stuff was lying–it looks like a photographic negative. Where anything was in the drawer, it's still white–you can see the shape of a spoon or a fork on the blackened paper. Get it? The outline of every object is on it–a little hard to make out, but it's there."

"The fire!" Dan said. "Is that what you're leading up to?"

"Yeah. I thought of the bureau Randall took from Cholly's room after the fire. The top drawer was stuck, remember? It was just a hunch, Dan, but I went to the Ramsdell house. He was out working, but Mrs. Ramsdell's a nice woman–you ask her for something and she's glad to oblige.

"So you asked her to show you the bureau Ramsdell took from the fire. And?"

"It had three drawers, remember, and the top drawer that wouldn't open before? Only now it was dried out and slid out real easy–and there on the paper lining was the outline of the things that had been in it at the time of the fire. And the outline of the necklace couldn't have been clearer. Dan, that necklace was in Cholly's bureau drawer before the fire. Which means he stole it. And later on when he was at the fire, when he went inside the house as a member of the volunteer fire department, the first thing he did was look for that necklace."

"Which was in his room," Dan said, "where the fire never really got going. So he just grabbed the necklace and slammed the drawer shut without thinking of outlines on paper or anything else.

"And when Ramsdell called him and told him he could come and get his shirts," Dan continued, "Cholly saw that drawers two and three had the outlines of their contents, and knew that drawer number one must have the outline of the necklace. That's why he broke into the Ramsdell house. He wanted that paper drawerliner."

"Which I now have," Willy said, "and which I showed to Cholly."

"And?"

"And he stopped laughing., Willy said contentedly.

Dan leaned back. "If Cholly had set that fire, he'd have taken the necklace first, so that lets him out. Larceny, yes, but he's clean on the arson job. What about Ramsdell?"

"A cheap little chiseler," Willy said. "I can't see him setting the fire. What for? If Cholly stole the necklace, then Ramsdell didn't, so he's have no reason to burn down the house."

"Which leaves London," Dan said. "He's Livia's heir and he has the motive. He probably collects insurance on the house and on the necklace, Or at the very least, as her husband he gets his legal share of everything she owned." He sat up straight. "Give me a good night's sleep and I'll break him down. Give me two or three hours tomorrow morning and he'll be confessing the whole business.

But Dan was wrong. It took him a full five.

Miel Tanburn

Faithful Viewer

Clara Push was delighted. She often talked to her friends in television but it was an unexpected pleasure when they began talking
back. First it was poor, confused young Victoria Revelstroke in *Livable
Marriage*.

"Don't you see you're just trying to punish your mother?" Clara
counseled the actress. "You should give the baby up for adoption."

Surprised, the girl peered out from Clara's twenty-one inch color
screen. "You might have a point, lady," she said.

"It's good advice," Clara assured her.

"I'll take it.," Victoria decided. When she turned back to her
mother, Victoria's smile was so selfless and and brave that Clara
Push applauded right there in her own living room. The girl was quite
an actress. But had she really spoken out that way to Clara Push? It
certainly seemed so. And when similar instances followed, it became
obvious to Clara that her friends in television were indeed bringing
their problems directly to her. But with the problem faced by Aroma
Coquille of *Forever Summer*, Clara's involvement entered a new di-
mension.

Aroma looked out from the TV screen and said, "I'm in a fix. Can we
talk for a sec?"

"By all means," Clara said, pulling her chair closer.

"Not here," the actress said, "Too many ears." And Aroma Coquille
climbed out of the television set. Clara thought the actress exposed
too much thigh, but perhaps there was no graceful way to make an
exit from a picture tube.

"Nice place," Aroma Coquille said, smoothing her dress and looking around the living room. "Lived here long?"

"Forty-two years," Clara answered proudly.

The actress laughed. "You must have a great real estate agent,"
she said. "For L.A. that's a record."

Clara could overlook Aroma Coquille's flippancy. She understood
that Hollywood people often developed a protective veneer to mask
their sensitive natures.

"The word's out that you're worth listening to," the actress said.

"I try to be helpful." Clara looked expectantly at her visitor. "You
said you have a problem?"

"I've seen some scripts," Aroma Coquille said. "*Summer's* going to
clobber me in a car wreck and put me in the hospital."

"Summer?" Clara asked.

"*Forever Summer*– that soap you were watching. They're dropping
my character–but first I have to linger for a month in intensive care.
Meanwhile, though, I've got a chance in a musical–except rehearsals

start next week. So timing's the problem."

"I see," Clara said.

"Yeah. Say, what's in this Miss Lonelyhearts routine for you?" Aroma Coquille asked. "Is there a catch?"

"Goodness, no," Clara answered. "I was Henry's nurse for many, many years. Helping people in difficulty is my profession. Isn't that what you call type-casting?" Clara smiled at the aptness of the phrase. "Henry was my husband, Dr. Push," she added in explanation. "General practice. He passed to his reward last year."

"The curtain drops but you stay in character, huh?"

Clara's eyes misted in memory for a moment, but then she brightened. "At first I was terribly depressed, but thank heaven for television. It's my constant companion, and it's brought me so many interesting new friends. I'm sure that without them I would have been beside myself after Henry's passing. But you don't want to hear about me. Is there some way I can help you, my dear?"

The actress shrugged. "Like I said, I've got a chance for a song and dance part that would give the old career a helluva boost. But I can't just walk out on the soap. What I need is a kosher way to exit in a hurry. Any suggestions?"

Clara pushed her lips in thought. "The character you play in the serial is rather—detestable. Isn't she?"

"You said it." Aroma Coquille laughed. "In your day Gretchen would have been called a witch. Today we spell it a bit differently. Why?"

"Since she's going to perish anyway—in an automobile accident, you said?—wouldn't it suit the purpose equally well if Gretchen were sent to her reward more directly?"

"How do you mean?"

"Wait here a moment, dear," Clara said. "I believe I do have a solution for you.

She returned to the living room shortly with a pleased look on her face. "These were Henry's medicines. They're just the thing."

"What are they?"

"Sleeping pills," Clara said. "Administer all twenty of them to Gretchen before she retires tonight. It should solve your problem."

Aroma Coquille glanced toward the bedroom. "You keep a drugstore back there?"

"I brought Henry's office supplies home with me, of course," Clara said.

The actress looked at the vial. "I take twenty of these tonight?"

"You'll find it quite sufficient," Clara said.

Before climbing back into the TV set the actress told Clara, "People in show business stick together, 'hon. Remember that. If you ever need a favor—"

"Nonsense," Clara interrupted. "I'm just flattered you've let me help."

"That's sweet," Aroma said. "But the offer's good. Keep it in mind."

The next afternoon Clara watched what appeared to be a hurriedly rewritten script of Forever Summer. The actors let it be known that the difficult Gretchen, who was to have departed that day on a motor trip, had died of an overdose instead. And a short item in the next morning's newspaper stated that Aroma Coquille, the dramatic actress and former model, had been signed as co-star in a musical comedy that was about to enter rehearsals. Clara nodded happily at the news article, pleased to have been able to help another of her friends in television.

It was several days later that the cosmetics salesgirl broke into tears on Clara's davenport. She was a slim, attractive young thing with an alabaster complexion and fluffy red hair, rather like cotton candy.

"Please forgive me," the girl sobbed, foraging in her purse for a handkerchief, "but I've got terrible problems. I want to die."

"Don't you worry," Clara comforted, putting an arm around her. "Just have yourself a good cry."

Clara wasn't surprised. Even at the front door the girl, who said her name was Lynda DuBarry, had seemed forlorn. After a moment's chat on the front porch, Clara had invited her inside where she began a sales talk for her line of cosmetics. Clara thought that Lynda DuBarry, despite her tears, was pretty as a picture. She placed a box of facial tissues in the girl's lap and said, "Tell nurse all about it now."

As her sobbing subsided, Lynda DuBarry told Clara her story. She'd come to Hollywood eight months earlier as Miss Hinton County, hoping for a career in the movies. She'd knocked on a thousand doors, worn out her wardrobe, gone through her savings, and was no closer to appearing on the silver screen than she'd been a year earlier when her name had been Francine Gurnsey and she'd sold popcorn back home at the Bijou on Friday nights.

"I finally had to take this awful job," she told Clara, "because I'm so far behind in my rent. And that's not all. They repossessed my car and my stereo, and I think I'm pregnant. I wish I was dead!"

Clara said encouragingly, "Lift your spirits, dear. I've helped many girls in show business."

"The important thing is to get rid of the old character," Clara explained. "Don't you see? That's crucial. It worked for Aroma Coquille and it will work for Lynda DuBarry. When you're bogged down in a bad role, you must change the script. Wait here a moment."

Clara left the room and when she came back she gave Lynda DuBarry a bottle of pills. "Take these before retiring tonight," she said.

"What are they?"

"The answer to your problems, dear. The end of your role as the un-happy door-to-door salesgirl. "They're sleeping pills.""

Lynda examined the pill bottle. "Downers? There's enough here to kill a horse!" She looked at Clara and asked, "Where's a glass of water?"

"Not here," Clara said, her eyes twinkling. "The proper place to take these is on the set, in your bedroom. Then tomorrow a new chapter will begin—in the drama of Lynda DuBarry!"

The girl threw the pill bottle in her purse and quicly gathered up her notebook and sample case. "I'm getting out of here before you change your mind," she said. "I don't know what your game is, lady—but thanks!"

"You're entirely welcome," Clara beamed, and as the girl hurried out the door she called after her, "Break a leg!"

That had been Wednesday. It was Friday when the police sergeant called. He was a tall, weary-looking man who entered the living room after showing Clara his identification.

Clara looked him over critically. "I would think," she suggested, "that some sartorial quirk would help the viewer identify with your character more readily. A fedora hat, say, or a rumpled raincoat."

"Or an unrumpled one even," the sergeant said, "especially if it was raining. Do you know a Francine Gurnsey?"

"That's an unappealing name," Clara said. "It sounds bovine."

"Yeah. Well, the landlord didn't think she was very appealing when he found her body. This Gurnsey O.D.'d Wednesday night. No note. But your name was the last one in her order book—"

"If you'll forgive me sergeant," Clara interrupted, "that's an unin-spired reading. You'll never get a series that way. Let me make a sug-gestion." She brought a hand to her throat and exclaimed. "Lynda DuBarry dead? Why that's impossible! The girl had everything to live for!"

"—and it was your late husband's name on the pill bottle," the sergeant said. "You being a registered nurse and all, I thought I better talk to you."

Clara whirled, pointing her finger at an imaginary third person in the room. "And only *you*," she said, "had the motive and the opportunity— and it was *your* thumbprint on the murder weapon! Try it something like that, sergeant."

"Yeah, well, I'm sure murder's stretching it," the sergeant said. "But in case there's a problem here I better give you your rights."

Clara frowned at him. "You're not trying at all. I'm tempted to change channels on you."

"You don't have to say anything," the sergeant told her flatly. "You have the right to remain silent. You have the right to have an attorney present—"

"Very well, then," Clara said. "You may leave, sergeant. I can't help you if you won't cooperate."

"Why don't you get your coat, Mrs. Push, and we'll go downtown? Okay?"

"I can't possibly," Clara said. "My friends are expecting me for the afternoon."

"I wasn't actually asking," the sergeant said. "It's more like you have to."

Clara looked at her watch. "In fact, I'm already late joining them," she said anxiously. "I'm sorry, sergeant, but you've come at a very bad time. You'll have to leave." She opened her front door.

"See, we're practically outside already," he said. "That's easy. Where would your coat be? In that back room there?"

Oh, the bother! Clara hurriedly followed him to the bedroom and while he opened her closet door she found what she needed among her late husband's medical supplies. She wasn't exceptionally strong but Dr. Push's scalpel was exceptionally sharp. And the sergeant's carotid artery offered exceptionally little resistance.

"Goodness," Clara said. The man had made quite a mess. Well, she'd have to clean up later. What if one of her friends had already missed her?

Clara Push quickly turned on her television set. But just as it warmed up, her doorbell rang again. Bother! This time a uniformed policeman stood on the porch. "Any trouble in there? Sarge?"

"I'm busy, officer," Clara said, trying to close the door. "You'll have to return later."

He looked at her. "Yeah? You wait right here, lady." He forced his way inside, took in the living room at a glance, and ran into the hallway.

Clara raised her arm to stop him and saw that her hand was red—quite red. And dripping. "Dear me," she said.

At the same moment she heard an exclamation from the officer in the bedroom. Moving quickly, Clara Push discovered that her assumption about Aroma Coquille had been accurate. A picture tube doesn't allow one to enter it gracefully.

The officer stormed into the empty living room with his revolver drawn. For a fraction of a second he imagined he saw something crazy out of the corner of his eyes—a small bloody hand reaching out from the television set and turning it off. But his attention was on the front door, not on the television set, and he ran outside in pursuit of Clara Push. He had no luck, though, and in a few minutes he called downtown from the radio in his car and had them put out an APB.

But Clara Push was never located by the police. In fact, she was never seen in Los Angeles again, except by faithful viewers who occasionally see someone of her description now and again on a late movie–in a bit part, usually playing a nurse or some other kindly person.

Kevin O'Donnell

Alternate

It was lucky for her that he was a science fiction writer because he could suspend disbelief more easily than the average man on the street. A woman in trouble needs someone to have immediate faith in her, no matter how incredible her situation might seem. He was perfect: he'd been writing about that sort of thing for over ten years; he more than half-believed every one of his own stories. Since the art of the genre lies in basing plausible stories on improbable premises, the science fiction writer learns early that he can't afford to blink at impossibilities. He has to be willing to take each farfetched idea seriously, at least until it breaks down through internal inconsistencies. This is not to say that SF writers are broadminded; it's just that they don't close their minds as quickly as other people. The minds of writers who puff joints to fire their imaginations and who gulp Scotch to loosen their tongues close even more slowly.

When the woman came into his cluttered study and announced that she was not who he thought, but an exile from an alternate time track that closely paralleled his, he didn't lean back in his ancient wooden swivel chair and laugh.

"Sit down," he said, gesturing to the overstuffed chair in the corner, the one he'd hauled back from the Salvation Army. From behind the screen of the flaming match, he watched her movements, trying to pinpoint the source of the nebulous difference he had already perceived. "This is...somewhat unusual," he said, painfully conscious of his own banality. "I mean–oh, never mind. You say you're from an alternate time track. Is it very similar to ours?"

She shrugged. "How should I know?" Something in the way her long blonde hair bounced caught his eye. He studied it for a moment before realizing that she parted it on the left. His wife parted hers on the right. "I just got here, George." A well-known frown of fleeting worry brought her plucked eyebrows closer together. "Your name *is* George, isn't it?"

"Yes. And yours is Ellen, right?"

"Right." She leaned back in the chair, twisting until the broken spring was out from underneath her. Her nose wrinkled at the odor of stale dope. "You told me–I mean, George on my–in my–oh, nuts. *My* George stopped using that horrible stuff when I asked him to. Doesn't your Ellen mind?"

He shifted uncomfortably. "Well, yeah, she does, a little. But she pretty much keeps it to herself now, since I explained that without it I couldn't write." He shook his head sadly. "She understands that science fiction is pure imagination, and that without it I can't sell my stuff. SF pays the rent here, so..."

"Oh, are you still writing *that*?" She put a condescending emphasis on "that," just like his Ellen often did. "*My* George hasn't written it in years...he's doing much better financially, too, now that he's given it up." One pale hand on her pearl necklace, she turned her head slowly, scanning the walls, looking for other points of difference. The way she ignored the shabbiness of the room–and of George–seemed a little self-conscious. Apparently she found her surroundings distasteful but was making an effort to be tolerant. By then he had noticed her hands. His wife wore her wedding band at all times; this woman had only an emerald ring on the middle finger of her right hand. Evidently, the two Ellens had different tastes in jewelry. His didn't like pearls.

"Do you wear wedding rings on your world?" he asked, prompted by the thought that she was material for a story.

Flickering to his hands, her ice-blue eyes rested on the simple platinum ring. "Yes, we do," she replied. "Why?"

"Well," he said, feeling awkward, "you're not wearing yours."

"I don't have one."

"Didn't I–I mean, didn't your George give you one?"

"How could he? Did you give your Ellen one?"

"Of course," he retorted, slightly offended. He tried to look dignified. "I may have been broke in those days, but I was able to scratch up enough bread to get her a ring."

She looked puzzled. "But...wait a minute, are you married to–her?"

"Sure." An uncomfortable silence fell on the room. He had time to notice that the storm was passing and that the corners of the study were becoming visible again. "Are we–I mean, are George and you married?"

"No." She held her chin high, but he could see a sparkle of moisture in her eyes.

"We aren't. He...he says she won't give him a divorce."

"She?"

"Barbie." Scorn was in her voice, and on her curled lips.

"Oh." He remembered Barbie, dimly. A few weeks of passion in his sophomore year, passion that had cooled with the suddenness of nightfall in the tropics. So that's how close he'd come.

"But you and he–"

"I'm his mistress," she said with proud defensiveness. "And if–"her chin trembled"–if I can get back, I'll be his wife, eventually."

"Get back?" Somehow, the thought hadn't occurred to him, but of course she'd want to get back. She was a stranger here, even though she had a...a parallel, a double, who'd probably lived most of the same life, thought most of the same thoughts. He watched her rise from the chair with the graceful flowing motion that his Ellen had. Turning her back on him, she went to the window and looked up at a small patch of blue. As he studied the curves of her waist and her hips, another piece fell into place; another explanation of his feeling of not-rightness came to him. The clothes she was wearing–his Ellen didn't have any of them. This Ellen wore a royal blue sweater; his Ellen had one in the same style, but navy blue. This one had white corduroy slacks; his had beige. Of course, of course. He slapped his forehead, and felt more at ease. The difference, slight as it was, had been bothering him. "*Can* you get back?"

"Yes," she said softly, almost as though she were talking to the window. "Yes, if I get to the right place, at the right time."

"Do you know where the right place is?"

"Oh, yes." She turned to face him. The strengthening sunlight silhouetted her, casting her face into shadow. "George used to do a lot of research on things like that–back in his SF days, you know."

"Yes." His gesture told her to go on.

"He found several places where people from–from my world have disappeared, and other places where strangers have arrived. He's made charts and graphs and things, and he thinks...you see, it's his theory that in certain places, when conditions are right, a...a sort of gateway opens up. But the gateway goes only in one direction, wo you have to be at the right one."

He shook his head. "Sorry, I'm confused."

Her glance said that was understandable, considering his condition. "There's a gateway here in New Haven–it opens onto the Green, from the Green in my world–but you can only travel from there to here, not from here to there, and it's only open during the worst kind of thunderstorm."

"Well, how did you happen to go through it?"

"It was her." Sudden fury contorted her features, and threw a scarlet flush into her cheeks. "Barbie!" she spat. "She knows what's going on; she knows he wants a divorce so he can marry me. She invited me to lunch downtown. I didn't suspect, so I went. The next thing I knew, she had a gun. She held it in her purse so nobody else would see it, and marched me to the center of the Green. There was thunder, and lightning, and pouring rain, and...and nobody to witness it. The place was right, she had to wait for a minute or two, till the sun got to its highest point–George says that does something to the magnetic field, I'm not sure what–and the next thing I knew, I was on *your* Green, in *your* thunderstorm." She sank into the chair again, leaned her head against its wing, and pleaded, "Please help me get back."

"Sure." Buoyed by the feeling of omnipotence that swells one when a friend in trouble comes for help, he nodded three times before thinking to ask, "How?"

For the first time, she looked uncertain. "If you're anything like my George, you're not going to be happy about this, but I have to get to the Yucatan Peninsula. That's where the gate to my world is."

"Oof!" She was right; he didn't like it. Even though his Ellen worked, and he wrote full time, money was a problem. What with his dentist bills, he didn't have more than a couple of hundred dollars in the bank. Ellen had emptied the joint account the day before because her boss had insisted that her clothes weren't elegant enough for his jewelry store. "The Yucatan, huh?"

"I'm afraid so." Docilely, she bowed her head, like a petitioner waiting for the king's judgment. Then her head snapped up sharply and her hand flashed out. "Look," she said with surprised glee, "My ring! I'll give it to you–it cost George four hundred dollars on our world, and that was a few years ago. You give me as much money as you can spare, but not more than say, five hundred, and it'll all even out. Okay?"

Her perfume–another difference noted by the mechanical portion of his brain that was keeping a tally–eddied around him. Dizzied by its power, he hesitated. "Well...I can only give you about a hundred and fifty dollars. Why don't you just sell the ring? That way..." He trailed off as he saw the fire in her eyes.

"George," she said firmly, "I want to get to the Yucatan as quickly as possible. I want to get moving now."

"Well, you couldn't do that in any case. I don't have any cash here. It's all in the bank. It really wouldn't take that much longer to get the ring sold." He watched her set her jaw. His Ellen often used the same expression. For a moment he marveled at how close the two worlds were. "Besides," he urged, "a couple hundred could make all the difference."

"Please, George." She sighed heavily. "George, selling the ring will take time, which means that I'll probably run into your Ellen after we sell it. And that's something my George warned me about. He said that never, under any circumstances, must a person meet...well, her double. He said it can cause madness, or worse. Please, George, take the ring, give me what money you can, even if it's only a little, and let me get going." There was desperation in her eyes, and it softened him.

"All right," he said at last, opening a drawer and rooting around for his bankbook. "I'll go across the street to the bank and get the money. But what are you going to do once you get it? That's not enough for a plane ticket."

"True," she admitted, "but I'm going to take a bus to New York and find a pawnshop there. I can sell my necklace–" she tapped it lightly "–and go right out to Idlewild where I can get a plane."

"Idlewild?" He felt his forehead crease at the word. "You mean Kennedy?"

"Do you call it Kennedy here?" she asked innocently. "Why?"

His mouth opened to answer, but his eyes glimpsed the clock on the wall: two forty-five. The bank would close in fifteen minutes. "Never mind," he said as he moved to the door. "It's an awfully long story. I'll be right back."

He returned in ten minutes, his wallet bulging with one hundred and seventy dollars in tens. "Here," he said as he handed it over to her, "that's all I had in my account. Luckily, Ellen–my Ellen– gets paid today. You sure you can't stay to meet here? She'd be tickled pink."

"No," she answered regretfully as she rose, "I don't dare. It's too much of a danger to our sanity. I've already checked the buses. There's one in twenty minutes, so I called a cab. Thank you, George, thank you very much." Impulsively, she leaned over and kissed him in the mouth. "You're almost as sweet as my own George, you know?" A beeping horn stopped her from giving him another. "That's my cab." After one last, wistful, grateful glance, she started walking toward the front door. As she went through the dining room she picked up a raincoat George had never seen before. Her rolled umbrella rested against the wall.

"Uh," he said as he followed, "look, I'm going to sell the ring, and if I get more than–"

"Keep it, okay?" She was out the door and clattering down the stairs.

"Well, thanks, but if you need more, write, huh? Let me know, and I'll send you...I'll send you what I can."

"Thank you, George." She stopped at the bottom of the staircase and threw him one more kiss. "Take care of yourself, now."

It was seven P.M. and Ellen wasn't home yet. He called the store for the fourth time; for the fourth time, he got no answer. A sick feeling was growing in the pit of his stomach. She often hitchhiked home to save the bus fare, and she laughed at his fears. But dammit, there *were* crazy people in the world, and–

He caught the phone halfway through its first ring. It was Ida Jenkins, the wife of Ellen's boss. "Hi, George," she began, "I just thought I'd find out how Ellen's feeling. Is she better?"

"Feeling?" he repeated numbly. "Did something happen to her?"

"Why, yes," came the thin, metallic voice. "She got sick at work. Were you so buried in your study that you didn't notice her come home early?"

"Uh–"His eyes darted frantically around the kitchen; his ears strained for any hints of sound in the apartment. "I don't think"

"Look, I've got to hand up. Tom's supposed to call me from New York to tell me about the new items he bought. Tell Ellen she doesn't have to come in tomorrow, or Friday, either, if she's still not feeling well. Ask her to give me a call tomorrow night."

"Uh–"

"There is one other thing George. She was feeling so ill that she didn't notice this, but remind her, when she's better, that she has one of our display rings. A big green one, looks like an emerald. She'll know what I mean. "G'night, now." Before he could say anything, Ida had dropped the receiver onto its hook.

A postcard came in the next day's mail. He recognized the handwriting, but his stomach hurt so much he could barely read it. "George," it said, "I'm sorry, but I needed *your* money, too. Even with Tom, a new start can be expensive, and, as you said, a couple hundred could make all the difference. You'd better explain it all to Ida. And, George, you really should stop writing SF. It can give people too many wild ideas.